**Challenged Love
(Consequential Love Series #2)
by
Elaine M. DeGroot**

ALL RIGHTS RESERVED

No part of this book may be reproduced or transmitted in any form or by any means, electronic or mechanical, including photocopying, recording, or by any information storage and retrieval system, without permission in writing from the author, except in the case of brief quotations embodied in reviews.

Publisher's Note:

This is a work of fiction. All names, characters, places, and events are the work of the author's imagination.

Any resemblance to real persons, places, or events is coincidental.

Solstice Publishing - http://www.solsticeempire.com/

Copyright 2022 – Elaine M. DeGroot

Challenged Love, Consequential Love Series #2 is dedicated to my 99-year-old Aunt Ev Spielman. She always asks me about my writing. As soon as she finished reading *Resolute Love*, she called to tell me how much she loved it.

You are my super fan, Aunt Ev. I love you.

CHAPTER ONE

The weekend from hell ended with no one dead and no physical injuries sustained, so they considered their first meeting with Leigh's parents a success. Garrett bonded well with her dad, Frank, but her mom, Lois, never warmed up to him. Correction, she had been darn right cold and hostile toward him. Neither of them remembered her ever using his first name.

The drive from the cabin to town proceeded with limited conversation. The familiar sounds of country music filled the car. They each contemplated what happened over the weekend.

"I'm glad the roads are clear of all the snow. Riding the snowmobiles cross-country didn't give us any indication of the road conditions." No response. Leigh continued in hopes of drawing him into a conversation. "We have time for breakfast before your appointment."

"Hmm…uh-huh." Garrett stared out the passenger window lost in thought. The snow-covered scenery didn't register with him.

"Garrett, you're so quiet; a penny for your thoughts."

A sigh escaped as he faced her.

"Plenty of things are on my mind. Guess the highlights are my bewilderment at the intense hatred your mom harbors against me; my concern over leaving you alone; and my curiosity about my new job and boss." His voice trailed away as he shifted to the right. Focused out the side window, he mumbled, "Lots of things on my mind."

She cleared her throat. "Please don't let my mom mess with your head. For some reason, she wants me back with David, so she'll continue pushing her agenda. I hope she'll drop her efforts after we're married, but I honestly have no idea what we should expect."

"You're not helping." He rapped his knuckles against the cold window and rested his head against it.

She took her eyes off the road and glanced at him. Instead of sitting tall, he slumped in the seat, an uncharacteristic posture for him.

His cell phone rang, so he punched the screen to answer the call. "Hi, this is Garrett."

"Joe Henderson here. Something came up, and we need you sooner than expected for the assignment. Can you report for work tomorrow and leave that night?" His new boss asked an unexpected question.

"Yes, sir, my fiancée and I are headed your direction later today." Garrett held back a sigh of frustration.

"Outstanding! You'll have time for a review of the information on your assignment and…wait a minute, did you say fiancée?"

"Yes, our engagement happened recently. She's joining me in Brainerd."

"Congratulations! Bring her with you on Tuesday, so she can meet everyone. See you then." A click ended the call.

"Perfect." He stared at his cell phone in disbelief.

"What's up?" The sarcasm of his tone worried her.

"That was my new boss calling. He needs me on the assignment right away, so we're going into the office tomorrow morning."

"What? A whole week early? But we planned on looking at houses all week."

Garrett glanced at her. "Sorry, he said something came up."

"I'll just look by myself since there's no choice. With you on the case, your assignment will be over in no time."

"While I appreciate your confidence in my abilities,

please don't assume my presence will speed the investigation to a conclusion. At this rate, I'll be gone for a year, and your parents get exactly what they wanted." He rubbed his forehead. "We have so much to do and no time for accomplishing anything together. Maybe you shouldn't come with me. You'll be alone in a new location. The wedding planning and house hunting shouldn't be dumped on your shoulders."

They were pulling into town, so Leigh headed toward the diner. After turning off the car, she faced him.

"Garrett, I love you." The look her words generated in his eyes thrilled her. She leaned into his arms, and her lips brushed against his. "We can handle you beginning your assignment early. I don't mind looking at houses on my own, and I'll find the best one for us. Wedding plans will be simple enough since we want a small one. With all that going on, I'll stay too busy to miss you."

He smiled at her, warmed by her words. "I love you, too. I'll call the realtor I've been working with and schedule an appointment for late Tuesday. Hopefully, we can meet with him before I leave. Once this assignment's over, I promise my focus will be on you, our wedding, and your career. Come on, let's grab some breakfast." He landed a kiss on her nose and exited the car. He hurried around it and opened her door. "This way, I'm buying." He led her into the diner; they selected an available booth and ordered their breakfasts.

"We should check on marriage license requirements. Fortunately, Brainerd is the county seat, so I expect all the paperwork can be completed there." Garrett's fingers drummed against the table.

"This is why smartphones are so handy." Leigh dug her phone out of her purse. "Hmm…the state lists two different prices for the marriage license."

"What's the difference? Does a guarantee come with one?"

His smile and a single raised eyebrow put the dragons in her stomach on high alert.

"Would you stop being so sexy?" She thought her heart skipped a beat at his devastating smile.

"I don't think I can."

"Not too modest this morning, are you?"

A deep chuckle answered her.

Garrett sipped his coffee and tried reading the screen upside down. As she read the fine print, she pulled the phone closer, so he sat back in his seat. He gave her his undivided attention. "Well?"

"We can save seventy-five dollars by taking a twelve-hour class from a minister."

"Sounds doable. Is the subject of the class described?" He tried reading her screen again.

"A partial listing includes a premarital inventory and the teaching of communications and conflict management skills. The inventory thing isn't attached or described."

"Conflict management?" Garrett leaned toward her, and his deep voice rumbled in her ear. "I'll need those skills whenever I deal with your mother."

"Hmm...yeah, the skills will come in handy." Distracted, she continued reading the information displayed on her phone. When what he said sunk in, she swatted his arm. "You're terrible! I would think the purpose of the training is to strengthen relations between the couple and not with in-laws."

"Only speaking the truth, darlin'. You must admit we had quite a weekend with your parents and experienced plenty of conflict." He sat back and drained his coffee. He caught the waitress's eye and signaled for a refill. "Your mother doesn't share your appreciation of my...er ..." he searched for the proper wording for his observation, "...worthiness as a husband for you."

Leigh snorted in response. "I'm the one who

determined your worthiness when I said yes to your proposal. My mother's exhibiting poor judgment regarding you and your attributes." Her eyes blazed with heat as she looked at him. "You're not only worthy, but you complete me in every way imaginable."

"In every way?" He reclined in the booth, and his smile brought color across her cheeks.

The waitress delivered their food, and they fell silent as they ate.

A sudden thought struck. Setting her fork on her plate, she leaned across the table.

"We never discussed buying a house, or what we want in a home. What size we want, in terms of square feet, or what location, in town or in the country? If we meet with your realtor tomorrow, shouldn't we discuss this beforehand? Plus, how are we paying for a house? Should we apply for a joint loan in both our names? How much money do I need to add for a down payment? The questions go on and on!" As she rattled off her thoughts, she wondered what important items she missed.

"I'm already approved for a home loan. The realtor has been looking for homes with acreage out in the country. How does country life sound to you?" He dropped his eyes, sipped his coffee, and directed his attention back to the food in front of him.

"I love the idea of country living, but won't acreage be expensive?"

"Yup, land's not cheap."

"Couldn't the addition of my funds with yours increase the limit for the loan?"

"Probably, but I doubt we'll need your money," he answered in between bites.

"Garrett." Leigh waved her fork at him as she cast him a serious look.

"Yes?" He continued munching his toast as he met her gaze.

"Why shouldn't we as a couple be approved?"

"Not necessary."

"Why not?" She reached for her coffee and took a long drink.

"Well, I'm sure two million dollars will be sufficient for our purposes."

He waited for her reaction to the dollar amount, and she didn't disappoint him. Coffee spewed all over her plate.

"How much?" Her voice cracked. She wiped off her chin, lips, and plate as she stared at him.

"Two million dollars." He sat back and smiled at her.

"Are you a secret millionaire or something?"

A hearty laugh answered her.

"Not really. Remember I told you my parents died when I was twenty?" At her nod, he continued. "I invested the money from their life insurance, the car accident settlement, and the sale of their property. Over the years the funds grew into a sizable nest egg and provided the basis for the loan amount." He looked pleased with himself. "Also, I stored their furniture and some household items, so furnishing a house right away is taken care of. Buying new furniture after we settle in is fine. A few pieces hold precious memories for me, so they stay."

"I put furniture in storage, too. Establishing a household will be easier and less expensive than I thought. What all do you own?"

"An entire household of furniture. We can review my inventory in conjunction with your furniture and decide what else we'll need, dependent on the house we buy."

"So, you think everything will be fine."

He nodded in response. "We'll figure out the details together."

She checked her watch. "If we don't leave now, you'll be late for your doctor's appointment."

He signaled for the check, and they were on their way in ten minutes.

When Leigh entered the hospital parking lot, a flashback of their encounter with Jonas Klein struck. Here Garrett saved her life and killed Klein. A strange twist of fate brought them together after Klein's vengeful attempt at killing Garrett. His hatred for Garrett resulted from the collapse of the man's criminal enterprise during one last Air Force case. Distracted by the vivid memory, she almost clipped a parked car; Garrett's quick grab of the steering wheel prevented a collision.

"What's the matter?"

"I'm sorry. I misjudged how far the car stuck out." She tried an outright lie but failed to fool him.

"Your breathing sped up after we turned into the parking lot. You remembered Klein and what happened here, didn't you?" He fixed his eyes on her.

"This isn't fair; I can't hide anything from you." She let out a frustrated breath, glanced at him, and recognized his concern for her. "Yes, all of a sudden, memories hit me. I remembered his hands on me, the smell of him, and the intensity of my fear for you." Tears welled in her eyes, and her body shook.

"Believe it or not, your reaction is normal. I should have realized a reaction might happen and driven us here. Why don't you park over there?"

He pointed out an open spot, so Leigh pulled in and parked. He walked around the car, opened her door, and drew her into his arms.

"In time, the memories will fade. You made my nightmares from the past disappear and replaced them with your love. Let me do the same for you." He held her close.

The low tone of his voice filled her head with thoughts of all they'd experienced together. She treasured his strength, melted into his body, and raised her face for a kiss.

His head lowered, and he brushed his lips against hers in a gentle caress. "Let's head inside out of the cold."

He wrapped an arm around her, and they walked into the hospital side by side.

Check-in for his appointment was with the same receptionist who assisted him the first time they visited the ER. Leigh's eyes narrowed and a frown replaced her smile as the woman flirted with Garrett. Again! He didn't respond, but she had enough of women flirting with her man. She removed her mittens and caressed his arm with her left hand ensuring the woman couldn't miss the sight of her ring. When she made eye contact with the receptionist, her eyes flared a warning.

"Sweetheart," Leigh purred at him, "we should let Marcy complete her duties and tell the doctor you're here. We can sit by the windows and discuss our wedding plans."

"Sure thing, darlin'." Garrett played his role as doting fiancé to perfection, masking his surprise with a heart-stopping smile and sparkling eyes.

Leigh couldn't decide if they reflected love or lust. Regardless, she planned on reaping the benefits later.

With an arm around each other's waist, they approached a row of empty chairs.

"Effective extraction technique," he said.

"Sorry, I couldn't handle her flirting with you."

She plopped into a chair and sent another glare toward the receptionist. Garrett shook his head and laughed as he eased into the chair beside her. Before he asked about her concerns, a nurse called his name. He gave Leigh a swift kiss and joined the nurse.

With her cell phone in hand, she dialed the inn.

"You've reached the Aspen Inn. This is Edna. How may I help you?"

Edna was the owner of the inn where they had gotten engaged. She had treated them like family during their stay.

"Hi, it's Leigh! We're back in town and will pick up Garrett's Jeep. We should be there within the hour. He's with the doctor now for his follow-up appointment. As soon as he's done, we'll head your direction."

"I'll put the coffee on! The reporters stopped lurking around the inn yesterday, so you shouldn't be bothered when you come by." Edna referred to the multitude of reporters who had camped out around the inn after Klein's death. Somehow, reporters learned where they were staying and staked out the inn for days in hopes of obtaining an interview or pictures. Garrett and Leigh stayed inside for a day and snuck out on snowmobiles the following morning.

"I'm glad they gave up the hunt; without reporters camping outside, a stop at the inn will be easier for us."

"Their departure was a blessing. They distracted my customers. See you soon."

Leigh relaxed as best the plastic chair allowed. The receptionist stared at her, so she smiled back. *Hah! You can stare all you want, girl, he's all mine.* The cramped chair was so uncomfortable, she shifted position every few minutes. When she spotted Garrett returning from his appointment, she sighed her relief. She met him in the center of the waiting room. "All checked out?"

"Yup, I am A-OK. Are you ready to go?" He circled her waist with both arms and pulled her close, so their chests pressed together.

She nodded as she pulled on her coat.

"I spoke with Edna. The reporters are gone, so no evasion required when we reach the inn. While we're there, why don't we ask her if we can hold our wedding at the Aspen Inn? The size should limit the number of people we can invite."

"Smart idea. Let's do it."

Garrett knew a small wedding didn't meet Lois's expectations, but what the heck. This was their wedding, not hers. Leigh deserved the wedding of her dreams. Besides, they planned on paying all the wedding expenses, so her parents shouldn't expect a say in the details. Should they? After witnessing his future mother-in-law in action, he'd shoulder the responsibility for ruining Lois's plans rather than subject Leigh to her mom's wrath. From this point forward, his goal in life centered on ensuring her happiness and safety. If that meant handling increased hostility from Lois, so be it.

CHAPTER TWO

As they approached the Aspen Inn, Garrett scanned the area with a practiced eye searching for reporters. With none in sight, he motioned Leigh toward the shed where his Jeep would be found. Once parked, they hurried out of the car and entered through the back door. Edna met them there.

"Welcome back!" She hugged Leigh and then Garrett. "Come in! The kitchen is warmer, so we'll sit in there."

"Edna, it's good being here again." Leigh pulled off her coat, hat, and mittens. "We're sorry if the reporters caused you problems."

"Nothing I couldn't handle. We offered more events for the guests in the evening as entertainment and shuttled them around town during the day. My driver made more tips over the weekend than he did last month, so he never complained!"

"What a relief; we worried they would negatively impact your business." Garrett held a chair for Leigh at the family-sized oak table before sitting on one himself. "We want to discuss something with you."

"Wait until I pour your coffee."

Once she set out mugs of steaming coffee and a plate of cookies, Edna joined them.

"Now, what's your question?"

Their eyes met. Garrett nodded at Leigh, grabbed a snickerdoodle, and sat back.

"We'd like to hold our wedding here." She sat with one hand in her lap with her fingers crossed.

"Here at the inn?" Edna's eyes widened with a hint of tears forming. "Of course you can. We're limited on how many guests you can invite. Will the limitation be a problem for you?"

"No!" Leigh and Garrett responded at the same time. They broke into laughter.

"Your size constraint is a plus because we prefer a small wedding," Leigh explained, once she controlled her laughter.

"Why do I believe you failed to mention additional factors surrounding your wedding plans?" Edna sipped her coffee while watching the two of them. Amusement glittered in her eyes.

"Our preference for a smaller wedding and being married as soon as possible doesn't match what Leigh's mom prefers. She wants a huge, fancy wedding event, and her parents suggested we wait a year. A conflict of sorts. I start a BCA assignment tomorrow—"

"The BCA?" Edna interrupted.

"The Minnesota Bureau of Criminal Apprehension." At her nod, he continued. "The assignment will keep me away for an unknown length of time. So, the wedding is delayed, but no longer than this spring if my assignment ends in time." He snatched another cookie.

"Let me check our reservations, and we can discuss what's available." Edna left them alone in the kitchen as she retrieved her book.

"This is exciting," Leigh said. "We just started our wedding plans!"

"I prefer us doing the planning rather than your mom. I'm sure she'll be pissed if we don't let her participate with some of the plans."

"Yeah, she won't be thrilled being left out."

He gave an elegant shrug of his broad shoulders. "She'll blame me for our decision, not you. Since she already hates me—" He stopped speaking when Edna re-entered the room.

"Ah, let's see now...I have dates in March and April open. You'll stay in the honeymoon suite after the wedding?" They nodded. "Here are the available dates."

She handed them a list. They considered the possibilities.

"If we pick a date, we can move forward with other plans," Garrett suggested in between munching another snickerdoodle. "Which dates would you recommend, Edna?"

"The later April date should guarantee warmer weather. If the trees are in bloom, the garden will be a lovely setting for outdoor wedding pictures."

"Late April sounds wonderful. Do you often hold weddings here?" Leigh asked as she made note of the dates.

"We've hosted a few, so I can assist you with contacts for the cake, flowers, a photographer, and music. If you're interested, I'll give you their contact information. You finalize decisions, and I coordinate with them ensuring everything runs smoothly on your wedding day."

"You're simplifying our planning, thank you." Leigh wrapped her appreciation and relief in a hug for Edna. "How many guests can we invite?"

"The max number is forty."

"Forty sounds adequate. The two of us and my three guests are only five leaving thirty-five guests for you, Leigh." Garrett refilled coffee mugs after he took another cookie. "Do they bake snickerdoodle wedding cakes? I love these!"

The women stared at him in amazement. Edna broke the silence with a hearty chuckle. "I'll pack some for your trip, and I'll entrust my recipe with you. I fear I'm aiding in your snickerdoodle addiction."

He planted a kiss on her cheek and happily munched his cookie.

"I'm not aware of any laws against snickerdoodles, so don't worry."

Leigh rolled her eyes. "You're pleased way too easy, Garrett. Promise me you'll never change!"

He smiled at her as he grabbed yet another

snickerdoodle.

She continued. "I prefer a more traditional flavor for the wedding cake, but maybe snickerdoodle can be incorporated in a groom's cake. What do you think, Edna?"

"The flavor may be a challenge, but the baker I use thrives on challenges." Edna made a note of the groom's request for a snickerdoodle cake. "Here's my card with my email; contact me with any questions or concerns. This checklist is my way of documenting the details. If you provide me your emails, I'll send you an electronic copy. Will you reserve any of the other rooms?"

"With only four other rooms, why don't we? Chief Martin and Candace will need a room. My friend, Matt, and your friend, Deb, will need rooms. I'm sure you'll want her nearby. That leaves us with one room for another guest or a family member."

Relishing how he remembered her best friend, Leigh thought, *he is such a keeper*. She voiced her approval. "What a wonderful idea. Mom and Dad will stay at the cabin. Alex and Tina, my brother and his wife, can stay with them as well as my grandparents."

The mention of grandparents caught Garrett's attention. In all their discussions, they never covered her extended family. He grew up without any, so the thought of gaining grandparents through marriage thrilled him, especially if they were her father's parents. The thought of contending with an older version of Lois at their wedding concerned him. He made a mental note to discuss her extended family later.

"How many days shall I reserve the rooms?" Edna took notes.

"The guest rooms for a day before the wedding, and, what...one day after? But we want the honeymoon suite from the day before the wedding until the following Saturday." Leigh counted off days on her fingers. "Would a week and two days be too much time away from your job?"

"Let's reserve those dates, and I'll run them by my boss tomorrow. If we need fewer days, we'll call you," Garrett decided.

"Works for me. So, rooms are done. Mark one item off the checklist." Edna stacked all her papers neatly together and stood. "I'll print out the contact information and the snickerdoodle recipe."

She winked at him as she left the kitchen.

"Wow! I didn't imagine this being so effortless. Reserving dates makes our wedding more real." Leigh reached for his hand and squeezed it.

"You sure you don't mind working the rest of the planning on your own? I feel lousy for not being able to help you." He held her hand and rubbed his thumb across the back of it.

"I'll work on initial contacts and leave the final decisions for when you're available if possible. Oh, we can't forget invitations. Printers! We'll need a printer for them. I should make a list!" Determination glinted in her eyes.

"Slow down, Leigh." The deep warm brown of his eyes took her breath away. "We'll start a list tonight. Can't we decide what things your mom helps with and those we deal with on our own?"

"Of course we can." Her blue eyes sparkled as she gazed at him. For the first time today, a sense of relaxation came over her, and her anxiety lessened. "Do we have a room reservation for tonight?"

Her thoughts ran over the many things she planned to do with him before he left for his undercover assignment. Because this was their last night together for an unknown length of time, her mission narrowed to ensure they made the most of being in each other's company.

"Dang it! Knew I forgot something! This'll only be a minute, and I'll set us up." He stood, drew his cell phone out of his jacket, and left the room.

Mesmerized, she stared as he walked away, admiring the view of his legs and butt framed in tight blue jeans. His body was rugged, toned, and all hers. During their short time together, she learned every delectable inch of his body. Her cheeks heated at the thoughts and memories rolling in her head like a movie—X-rated at a minimum.

"Leigh, are you okay? You look flushed. Is sitting in the kitchen too warm for you?" Edna returned with paperwork in her hands. When she followed Leigh's gaze and spotted Garrett standing in the back entry, she smiled. "The sooner you two are married the better."

The blush intensified at being caught ogling her fiancé.

"If we could marry today, we would. But fate won't allow us." She sighed.

"You'll be married in April; only two months from now. The day will be here before you're ready." Edna gave her a sympathetic look before handing Leigh a stack of papers. "Here is the contact information, the dates we discussed, and room rates. Tell your friends the cost of the rooms and how they can confirm their reservations. Now, I have snickerdoodles to pack for Garrett." At the far counter, she pulled out a tin and a cookie jar. She spun around and pointed at the papers. "Oh, the snickerdoodle recipe is in there, too. In Garrett's opinion, the recipe is probably the most critical piece in the entire stack, so be sure you don't lose it."

"He'd be devastated if we lost it." Leigh tried looking serious but broke into a smile.

They looked at each other and laughed. They were still laughing when Garrett returned.

"What's so funny?" He glanced from Leigh to Edna and back at Leigh. They didn't stop laughing. "What are you laughing at?"

Leigh controlled her laughter and made eye contact

with him. "We were discussing the safeguarding of the snickerdoodle recipe."

She started laughing again. Edna fared better while busying herself with packaging his cookies, although her shoulders shook now and then.

"Hey! The recipe is key information, and I should take it into my custody for protection purposes. After all, I'm a trained professional and armed." He mocked himself for their enjoyment and wore a stern expression on his face.

As a result, Leigh lost total control, and her laughter exploded across the kitchen.

Garrett leaned over her. "Laughing at me because you think I'm funny? I'll show you funny." He tickled her, so the volume and intensity of her laughter increased.

"Garrett! No! No, stop! I'm gonna pee in my pants! Please, stop! Please!" The last words barely made their way out of her mouth.

Edna rescued her by announcing, "Garrett! Here are your cookies."

The tickling attack ended with his acceptance of the cookie tin. "Thank you."

Edna smiled and nodded at him.

"Make him promise he'll share his precious cookies, Edna," Leigh gasped out, still out of breath from laughing.

Garrett looked over his shoulder at her, showing a sexy half-smile and warm brown eyes. "Rest assured, I'll share."

She'd bet her share of the snickerdoodles his promise held pleasures for her beyond cookies. The timbre of his voice reverberated through her body. His slight accent sounded magical and sent the dragons into attack mode in her stomach. Whenever he focused on her with those eyes, she ached for his love and longed for his touch. She decided they wouldn't reach their hotel fast enough. The sooner they left, the sooner they'd arrive.

"We should get going," he said.

Leigh hugged Edna. "Thank you for everything. I'll be in touch regarding the details."

"This is one wedding I'll take pleasure in working on." Edna gave Garrett a big hug. "Drive safe."

CHAPTER THREE

Garrett walked Leigh to her car. "Follow me, okay? The hotel's in Baxter. Flash your lights if you need to stop for anything."

"Why don't we program each other's cell numbers in our phones?" Leigh waved her phone at him and smiled.

A deep blush covered his cheeks as he mumbled, "Since we've always been together, the thought of calling you never dawned on me."

"You're cute when you blush." Leigh couldn't stop herself from laughing. "I love you so much." She threw her arms around his neck and kissed him.

He ended the kiss by drawing back. "We should leave. The sooner we reach the hotel, the sooner we're in a room…a room with a bed." His eyes darkened.

She looked at him and wished they were in their hotel room, utilizing the bed in all sorts of creative ways.

"No way can we reach the hotel fast enough for me. At least we don't need a stop for lunch, between breakfast and the coffee and cookies Edna gave us, I'm full. Don't stand around doing nothing, tell me your number, I'll call you, and we can depart." She tossed the paperwork into her car, punched in his number, and called him.

As he headed for the shed where his Jeep sat, his phone rang. "Yes, Leigh."

"Move your delectable tush, Garrett. We have places to go and things to do." She honked her car horn for extra emphasis.

"You got it, darlin'." He ended the call with a smile.

After he sent a quick email to his realtor about an appointment, the Jeep rumbled to life. Clear of the shed, he hopped out to close the doors. He rested a hand on the Jeep's roof and contemplated how different his life became over the course of a few days. His contemplation ended when a car horn honked at him, again. With a slight shake of his head, he settled in the driver's seat. The Jeep kicked up snow as he drove out the back entrance.

A half hour down the road, his cell phone rang. The caller ID displayed his realtor's name.

"Nick, hi. You read my email already."

"What time were you thinking?"

"As late as possible. I report for work first thing in the morning, and I'm not sure how long I'll be in the office."

"Tell you what, I'll set you up for two in the afternoon, but whenever you come by will be fine. I have other things to do until you arrive."

"I appreciate your consideration on this. Ah, there's been one change since we last spoke." He didn't anticipate any issues, but he wanted Nick aware of his changed circumstances.

"Nothing bad, I hope. What's up?" Nick used his serious business voice instead of the chipper buddy sounding voice.

"Nothing bad. I got engaged recently. My fiancée is coming with me, so she'll be looking at houses and will have a say in everything. In fact, I won't be available for a while, and she'll be your contact while I'm gone." Garrett realized the huge benefit of Leigh's being with him because of his schedule change. Now the house search could continue while he worked on the undercover assignment. "She's a photographer, so we'll need a place with space for a studio. Eventually, we may look for a storefront where she can display and sell her photographs."

"Wow! That's a significant change for you. Congrats on the engagement. I don't foresee any problem working with your fiancée. Will she have a power of attorney to sign for you?"

"Power of attorney? How do we get one?"

"We have a Notary and the necessary forms in our office. If you arrive early enough today, stop by, and complete the paperwork. I'll inform the receptionist what you need. The process is simple. Anything else?"

"Nope, nothing else. Thanks, Nick. See you tomorrow."

"Right. Oh, one other thing."

"Yes?"

"What's your fiancée's name?"

"Leigh. Leigh Ramsey."

"Alright. You're on my calendar for tomorrow at two."

"Thanks again, bye." Within seconds of ending the call, Garrett's phone rang again.

"Hi, this is Garrett."

"Hey! I miss you." Leigh sounded excited.

"And I miss you, too." His voice was warm and full of love. "I just spoke with the realtor. I told him I'm engaged, how we need a place with room for your studio, and mentioned we may search for a storefront in the future."

"What'd he say?"

"Working with you isn't a problem, and he asked if we had a power of attorney authorizing you to sign paperwork for me."

"How do we obtain one?"

"Nick, our realtor by the way, said his office can complete the required paperwork. If we get to town early enough, we can stop by. No telling what tomorrow holds for us, so I think we should stop at his office after we check into the hotel. What do you think?"

"I agree, although stopping delays my plans for you."

"Plans for me?"

"Yes, I thought of some fun activities for us once we're in our room. All I need is you naked in bed as soon as possible." Her voice turned low and sultry.

"These plans of yours sound interesting."

"First, I'll kiss you senseless and, because I'm very talented, your shirt comes off for additional kisses and some erotic caresses. Second, I'll remove your jeans and shorts, so you're properly naked. Of course plenty of kissing, touching, and stroking will happen by this point. Next, I'll—"

"Leigh! I can't drive and listen to this; you already gave me a hard-on. I'm hanging up now."

But he didn't disconnect right away as he figured she had more to say. He shifted around in the seat and swore under his breath. The Jeep became uncomfortable and too warm after his body reacted to her enticing words.

"I was reaching the most tantalizing part."

"How 'bout you finish your plans and surprise me later. Meanwhile, I'll conjure up plans of my own."

The tone of his voice combined with his words sent the dragons in searing circles and elicited a response from her body. "I expect extraordinary foreplay and sex tonight, Garrett Dane."

"And I expect equal surprises from you, Leigh Ramsey. Bye now."

He disconnected the call and chuckled. Her acceptance of his challenge was a given and would manifest in extra attention and creativity on her part. His mind wandered and settled on Leigh, her silken hair, her lush body, and her wanton responses whenever he touched her. Oh, yeah, tonight will be magical.

With the call ended, she concentrated on her driving. She contemplated the man she planned to marry, the man she first met a short nine days ago. She pictured his rugged, lean body, and his eyes darkened to a warm brown as making love filled his mind. Without much effort, she imagined him hard and inside her. He possessed her body as no other had. Since their first time together, he learned ways to excite her and increase her need for him. Her desire for him held no limit. Tonight, she'd be the predator, and he'd be her willing prey.

Less than an hour after hanging up with Garrett, Leigh's phone rang. The ringtone for her father chimed away.

"Hi, Dad."

"Leigh, it's Mom."

As soon as her mom's voice sounded out of the car speakers, her defenses went up. "Oh, hi. Did you and Dad leave for home?"

"Not yet. I was disappointed you didn't say goodbye." A note of dismay sounded.

"You were still sleeping, and we departed early because of Garrett's medical appointment."

"That's what your father said, but he could have woken me."

"This wasn't the best of visits for us. You were extremely rude toward Garrett. In all honesty, I asked Dad not to wake you." Leigh drew in a deep breath. "I'll see you soon enough to discuss our wedding plans." She hoped her mom would accept this as a peace offering.

"I appreciate being included. Where are you now?"

Her mom sounded happier. Did the small offering bring a semblance of peace?

"On our way to Brainerd, but our hotel's in Baxter. Garrett's boss called this morning. They need him at work tomorrow. So, we'll meet with our realtor tomorrow afternoon, and I'll search for a house while he's working."

"You'll be so busy; don't exhaust yourself, dear. What hotel in Baxter?"

"I didn't ask him. Once we're settled, I'll call home."

"Just don't forget to let us know where you're staying."

"I should pay attention to my driving. Tell Dad hi

for me."

"I will. Drive carefully."

***

Her mom disconnected the call and yelled to her husband, "Frank! They're on the road. Her fiancé starts work tomorrow, so Leigh will be on her own as soon as they arrive."

"She can handle being on her own. She did fine by herself in Chicago, a busier and bigger place than Brainerd," Frank replied.

"Yes, but she'll be away from him for a while."

"I didn't hear what you said," Frank shouted as he headed for their bags in the bedroom.

"Oh, nothing, Frank, I'm merely thinking out loud." A cold calculating look came over her face as she turned away from her husband. "Time to work on plans of my own."

CHAPTER FOUR

After four hours of driving, Garrett and Leigh stopped in front of their hotel. Leigh parked behind his vehicle. The sight of Garrett approaching mesmerized her. All she saw was his broad shoulders, his fluid long strides, his confident demeanor, and his wind-tousled hair. She imagined his eyes behind the sunglasses darted everywhere and assessed everything. In a feeble attempt at breaking his hold on her from simply walking toward her, she reached for her hat and mittens. Shoot, maybe she'd be the prey tonight.

"Will you come in with me?" He pulled open her door and held out his hand. She took the offered hand and walked with him into the hotel.

"Good afternoon. Welcome to the Country Inn and Suites. Checking in?" the clerk at the desk greeted them.

"Yes. Reservation for Garrett Dane."

Upon entering, Leigh gravitated toward a display of tourism brochures. Garrett glanced at her. Awareness of his eyes on her radiated through her, so she smiled at him. Warm brown eyes and a lop-sided smile beckoned her to his side. She hurried beside him intent on reaching their room in record time.

The efficient and pleasant desk clerk completed their check-in within minutes. With key cards in hand, they walked out and moved their vehicles near the closest door for their room location.

"I'll carry the bags if you open the doors," Garrett offered as he emptied her car trunk.

"Okay." She went ahead and located their second-floor room.

After dropping the bags on the first bed, he turned toward Leigh as she pulled one arm out of her coat sleeve.

"Keep your coat on."

"But we're in our room with two comfortable looking beds waiting for our full enjoyment. Aren't we…" Her voice trailed off as he eased her back into her coat.

"Getting a power of attorney completed before we enjoy ourselves on either of those beds? Yes, we are." He hustled her out of the room.

"Oh, I forgot we needed one of those; good thing you remembered."

"It's what I do, Leigh." He made sure the door closed and locked behind them. "While we're there, we can pick up a recent book of listings."

They crossed the snow-covered parking lot and climbed inside Garrett's Jeep, grateful for the residual warmth.

Within minutes they reached the realtor's office. A short time later they walked out with the notarized power of attorney and a book of listings in their possession.

"Now can we return to our room?" Leigh plopped into the passenger seat of the Jeep. She looked at Garrett as she pulled off her hat. "Please?"

He laughed. "Yes, unless you prefer having dinner first?" He put the Jeep in gear and headed for their hotel.

"I'm only snacking on one thing—you!" She leaned over and nibbled on his ear.

"Hotel it is."

As he drove, his right hand caressed her thigh higher and higher. Leigh settled back and enjoyed the pressure of his hand as he neared the junction of her thighs. She spread her legs, a silent encouragement for his continued exploration. Her eyes closed as she relaxed further into the seat.

"We're here."

"Already? What are you waiting for? Let's head up to our room!" She exited the Jeep before he removed his seat belt.

"Why didn't you wait for me?" He voiced his

complaint when he caught up to her in the stairwell.

"You're too slow. Hurry up, there are things we should be doing!" She raced up the steps but stopped on the landing to catch her breath.

"Who are you calling slow?" He passed her on the stairs and entered the hallway before she reached the second floor. He stood in the doorway of their room with a wide grin on his face when she exited the stairwell.

"Show off," Leigh mumbled as she trudged down the hall. When she reached the doorway, he ducked down and threw her over his shoulder. Once the door closed, he carried her to the bed nearest the window.

She soon found herself bouncing on the bed.

He assisted her out of her coat and flung it along with his jacket on the other bed. "What should we do first? Review the house listings or my furniture list?"

"I thought we agreed on demonstrating our plans we came up with during our drive here."

"You did? Well, I shouldn't disappoint the woman I love, should I?"

"No, you absolutely shouldn't."

"What if I delay her a little?"

"Delay me? I don't think so." She grabbed hold of the front of his shirt and dragged him down on the bed with her.

"Our time together is running out, faster than either one of us wants." He kissed her forehead and each cheek before finding her lips. "We need to discuss lots of things and decide on house hunting particulars before tomorrow, and the morning will arrive earlier than we expect." He pressed kisses down her neck.

"Don't you want to make love with me?" Lowering her lashes and her voice, she added, "Shouldn't we be making love together now?"

"Of course I want to make love with you, but shouldn't we address some items from our to-do list first?"

"Such as?"

"Review the house listings, so we figure out what to tell Nick tomorrow. Check out my furniture list, so you know what's available for our home." To avoid the disappointment in her eyes, he focused on her fingers as they toyed with the buttons on his flannel shirt. He grasped her hands and grazed them with a kiss. "After supper we'll make love as long and as often as we can, I promise."

"Why are you always so practical? Fine, let's start with the house listings, so we can compare our preferences. Bring your snickerdoodles over here. If I can't coerce you into bed, I'm eating your cookies." She settled pillows against the headboard behind her and arranged others for him to lean against.

They sat together on the bed and paged through the house listings. They took their time, laughed at some pictures and descriptions, and remarked on costs. As they reviewed the magazine, Leigh captured notes on various properties and began a list of their likes, dislikes, and must-have features. By the time they reached the last page, her notes summarized their preferred style of home and an acceptable price range.

"Here's the inventory of my furniture in storage." Garrett showed her a printout with pictures of the items. "Some pieces might be considered antiques. If you don't want most of my furniture, I'll understand. Although, I can't let go of my dad's desk, his chair, and a few other pieces." His fingers caressed the pictures as he spoke of them.

"The furniture is lovely. I doubt we find any reason for not keeping all these pieces." She paged through the list, touched an occasional picture, and made quiet comments on others.

Her delight in the furniture made him smile. He hoped for Leigh's acceptance of his parent's furniture because the pieces linked him to his past and many happy memories. When he arranged the sale of the family farm, the thought of selling the furniture weighed heavy on his soul, so all the pieces sat in storage over the years. Each piece represented his only remaining physical connection with his parents.

"What do you say we leave for supper before we discuss the wedding plans?" Leigh hopped off the bed and stretched.

"The wedding plans?" Garrett's voice cracked. He looked forward to the actual wedding but lacked confidence in his aptitude for planning one.

Unable to decide if his face showed fear or disinterest on his part, she dropped the lid on the cookie tin before responding.

"Yes, the wedding plans. Since I'll be working on the details while you're unavailable, I need your ideas and preferences."

"Oh." He looked at her with a hopeless expression.

Intrigued, she probed further. "What's bothering you?"

"I've never attended a wedding, so my input may not be of any benefit."

"How did you reach the age of twenty-eight and never attend a wedding? Were you such an outcast you didn't make any friends?" She laughed at the insulted expression on his face. "I'm kidding! I endured enough of them for both of us. I'll be gentle with you and lead you through the wedding details." Her smile widened as she spoke.

Although grateful for her playfulness and light approach, his lack of wedding experience still bothered him. He shook his head.

"You can joke all you want, but I'm at a loss here. I doubt I'll be of any assistance."

The concerned and flustered tone of his voice told her he was being truthful.

"We have a wedding to plan. We, not just me. We'll work through the planning together. You can do this." She crossed the room and wrapped her arms around him.

"If you say so." He shook off his unease, and his voice reflected added confidence.

"I do say so. I'm starved; let's grab some supper."

"You're right. We can discuss basic wedding—" The ringing of Leigh's phone interrupted him.

She glanced at the screen and smiled.

"Deb, hi!"

"You didn't call, and I got concerned. Then I remembered the lack of cell service at the cabin, so I hoped I might catch you in an area with decent reception."

Her friend chattered along, so Leigh made a talking signal at Garrett. He nodded and stretched out on a bed.

"So how did your folks react when you shared your news?"

"What news?"

"Duh, the news of your career transition from financial investments to photography."

"Oh, they accepted the change for now, reluctantly, I might add. They knew I didn't really care for my work at the investment firm." Leigh paused and drew in a deep breath. "Deb, I need to ask you a question."

"What?"

"Are you free the last weekend in April?"

"Nothing's on my calendar. What's up?"

"I need you as my maid of honor. Will you do it?" Leigh winced and held the phone away from her ear.

Garrett didn't miss the sound of her friend's squeals of delight. The positive reaction of Leigh's best friend gave him hope.

"How did this happen? When did this happen? Who's the guy? I wasn't aware of you dating anyone."

"Slow down, Deb. Take a breath."

"Tell me everything. What's his name?"

"His name's Garrett Dane, and we met when he sort of fell into my life nine days ago."

"Only nine days ago? This must be some story. How can you be so sure after such a short time?"

"He's the one. Love at first sight can happen. We're having the wedding at this fantastic inn we stayed at for a few days. We reserved all five of their rooms, and I hope you'll stay there with us."

"Of course I'll stay with you guys and be your maid of honor. When can I meet him?"

"I'm not sure. He's been hired by the BCA, and he'll be out of touch awhile on an assignment. Maybe when he returns but for sure at the wedding." They laughed. Leigh realized how desperately she needed this talk with her friend. "I'll email you the information for the inn, and we'll discuss the wedding later."

"If I can help you with any of your planning, call me."

"Thanks! I appreciate your offer. To have someone, other than Mom, to discuss wedding plans with means a lot. And you're gonna love this news! The BCA office he's assigned to is in Brainerd, so we won't be far from you! Surprising how life works, isn't it?"

"Surprising is an understatement. This will be the closest we've ever been since college!"

"We're staying in Baxter for the time being and looking at houses right away."

"This is so unexpected and so thrilling! Did your folks meet him yet?"

Leigh cringed and glanced over at Garrett. Closed eyes and the gentle rise and fall of his chest indicated he'd fallen asleep. He appeared so cute curled up on the bed. A deep sigh preceded her response. "Yes, we met them at the cabin for the weekend. Garrett and my dad bonded over pool and beer, so Dad likes him."

"What did your mom think of him?"

"She disliked him from the moment I told her of our engagement and never called him by his name. I'm convinced her feelings for David are behind her negative reaction."

"Your ex-boyfriend?"

"Yes. I can't describe the worst parts with Mom; they were too hateful. I felt awful for Garrett. The cruelty she directed toward him amazed me, and she said some horrid things. My visit with her was challenging and not pleasant, either."

"No!"

"She made the entire time agonizing for us." Leigh's brittle voice echoed in the room. She wiped a tear from an eye and glanced at Garrett, relieved he still slept. "He deserves so much better than what he went through this past weekend."

"She'll come around, and if she doesn't…well, it's your life. I can tell you're in love; your emotions fill your voice." Deb's words hit home, and Leigh loved her friend for her support.

"Thanks. You're exactly who I needed right now. I'll call you back another day. We were headed out for supper when you called. There are things we need to discuss before he leaves on his first assignment tomorrow. So many I'm afraid we'll run out of time for a little pillow talk if you catch my drift."

"I understand and suggest discussing the things quickly without getting bogged down in the details. Call back soon. I expect to learn *all* the details about your engagement. Bye for now!"

Deb's call eased her concerns over her mom's attitude toward Garrett. She couldn't hold back a sigh when she gazed at him, so handsome and so perfect.

Her fingers ran through his hair. Although he found the length bothersome, she thought the shagginess was sexy. She adored the color—a combination of blonde and light brown. The exact word for the color evaded her. His eyes had mesmerized her from the first moment she lost herself in their depths. The unique hazel irises, colored blue and brown, served as a barometer for his moods. Icy blue warned of anger and danger. Warm brown indicated a peaked sensual nature and playfulness.

She kissed his cheek and whispered in his ear, "Garrett, I finished my call. We can leave for supper."

He stirred, his eyes focused on her face, and he smiled.

"Sorry, I didn't plan on falling asleep. I don't usually nap."

"No apology necessary; I spent the time admiring you up close and personal, committing you to my memory." Her lips caressed his. "Let's go; I'm starving. Cookies only last so long." She smiled at him as she grabbed her coat.

He pulled on a stocking cap and zipped up his jacket.

"A restaurant is nearby. Are you okay with walking?" he asked as he closed the door behind them.

"Sure. We can both enjoy a drink or two or three."

"Hmm, are you planning on a drunken evening?"

They had almost reached the stairway.

"No, but I may become tipsy." She grinned at him, turned, and raced down the stairs.

"That must have been some phone call," he muttered as he took off after her.

"Hah! I won!" She danced about in celebration by the exit door.

"You didn't tell me we were racing. I demand a rematch later." He caught her by the waist and escorted her outside. "So, you had an enjoyable talk with your friend?"

"Yes. I didn't realize how much I needed a conversation with her. She's available for our wedding, and she's thrilled. She's looking forward to meeting you."

Leigh held his hand as they walked in the winter night.

"She shares all your secrets, right?"

"Yes," Leigh answered with a wariness reflected in her eyes.

"I can't wait until she visits."

"She's my best friend. There's no way she'll divulge any secrets you don't need to know about."

"I can be very persuasive, and my interrogation skills are highly effective. "

He hugged her close.

"You may not use those skills on my friends. Interrogation of a friend is unacceptable and…and not fair!" Frustrated, she squirmed against him.

"Haven't you heard? All's fair in love and war."

He chuckled as he released her.

When they reached the restaurant, they sat in the bar area. Garrett ordered a beer, and Leigh opted for a gin martini.

"You drink gin?" Garrett took a long drink of his beer.

"On occasion I do." Leigh grinned at him. "Do you?"

"I drink a Gin Buck now and then." He noted she looked at him with a question in her eyes. "A Gin Buck is gin and ginger ale with lime run around the rim of the glass and dropped in."

"It sounds delicious, I'll try one sometime." Leigh sipped her martini and snagged an olive to eat. "So, about the wedding." She stared at him.

"Right, the wedding. What's first on your list?" He drank long, set his beer aside, and gave her his full attention.

She pulled out the paper and pen taken from their room. "Since I didn't start a list, we'll begin one tonight."

"You may need a notebook, so you can track

everything."

"Maybe an app exists for wedding planning." She grabbed her phone.

Garrett laughed and covered her hand holding the phone with his larger one. "Why don't we do our planning the old-fashioned way on paper?"

The warmth of his fingers on her hand distracted her. She set the phone down and let him hold her hand. She marveled at the thrill generated by his thumb rubbing over the top of her hand. When she noticed his eyes reflected a dark brown, the dragons launched in her stomach. Her concentration disintegrated while she lost herself in the depths of his eyes.

"Sure, we can start a list tonight and transcribe it into a notebook tomorrow; plus, Edna's sending us her checklist. Without you around and distracting me, I can organize the information during the evenings." The thought of him being gone left her with an overwhelming emptiness. Now she realized how his presence and love had become essential for her existence. She would wait forever for his return.

"If you want, you can delay the house hunting and visit Deb for a few days while I'm working. Don't you think shops for wedding stuff are available wherever she lives?"

"She lives in the Fargo-Moorhead area, so there should be plenty of shops there for wedding stuff. Do you really think we can just lump it all together? Okay. Let me put that as number one on our list." She exaggerated writing on the paper. "Wedding stuff. Look at that! Everything's covered with one entry." She glared at him.

"Leigh, I'm sorry, but I don't know anything about wedding…ah…stuff."

Unsure of whether he was distressed or terrified, she didn't hold back any longer and broke out laughing.

He looked confused at first and soon smiled at her.

"Hah! I thought you were mad at me."

"Mad at you? Never. Enough goofing around; let's be serious." He nodded as he sipped his beer. "First thing, attire. Do you prefer wearing a suit or a tux?"

"I'm ready either way. The guys at the Aspen Inn gave me their contacts for a tux rental and a tailor."

"Sweet, so we're partially done with you. I always thought a vintage wedding dress would be nice."

"Vintage? Sounds interesting; can you show me what you mean?"

"Sure." She entered a search on her phone. "I found a store in St Paul that specializes in those kinds of dresses, but this site is mind boggling! The prices are reasonable, and the shipping time is only a few weeks. Oh, what about this one?" She handed over her phone, and he studied the picture.

"The reality of marriage sinks in by looking at these. This one is striking. Are there others?"

She nodded, so he browsed through a variety of dresses.

"Shopping for a wedding dress may turn out to be quite the challenge," Garrett mused. "The task reminds me of chopping down a live Christmas tree. Although you find a perfect one, you can't stop yourself from checking out all the other trees. By the time you come to the last of them, you forgot which one you picked out in the first place."

"Hmm, I'll try not letting a situation like that happen during my search. I found a couple of bridal shops around here and quite a few in the Fargo area. If I can't find one here, I'll visit Deb and shop up there. Let's view some tuxedos now." In minutes, she scrolled through pictures of tuxes and suits fit for a wedding. "Here's the tux for you. Imagine how dashing you'll be wearing one of these."

She handed him her phone with a black cutaway tuxedo displayed.

He studied the picture with keen interest. Before

returning her phone, he looked at some other styles.

"I could pull that one off," he agreed.

"Alright. I'm adding cutaway tuxedo to our list, so one down and a gazillion to go." She sipped her martini and ate another olive. "Should we have music?"

"No music, at least not for dancing."

She cocked her head as she stared at him.

"Don't you dance?"

He drained his beer before answering and signaled for another round.

"Oh, I dance, but I don't care for the idea of having to dance with your mother. Sorry."

"I understand." She downed her martini and offered him the last olive, which he accepted with a smile. She grabbed her list and made a note. "No dancing at reception."

She flashed him a smile, and he responded with a kiss.

"Thank you." His breath warmed her cheek.

"You're welcome. Shouldn't we order soon?"

"Probably a smart idea." He motioned to the bartender. "Hey, partner, could we get a couple of menus?"

After they ordered their meals, Leigh picked up her list again. "What flavor for the cake? I mean the wedding cake, not your snickerdoodle groom's cake."

"How about the same as the cake at our engagement party? It was moist with good flavor, especially the frosting. Almond, right?"

"Yes, it was almond. You have hidden talents. The decorations can't be snowflakes in April though."

"Well, our date falls in the spring, and what says spring more than flowers? So, we consider tulips, crocus, daffodils, and hyacinths."

She nodded her agreement; her eyes widened in surprise.

"Your knowledge of spring flowers is impressive."

"Don't look so surprised; guys know a thing or two about flowers. Mom's flower gardens surrounded the house, and I helped her with them." His voice softened with the mention of his mother. "I like tulips. How 'bout lots and lots of tulips?"

"Tulips would be fantastic. See, you can do wedding planning."

"What else can I assist you with, darlin'? Seems I'm on a roll."

"What are your thoughts on colors for the decorations, flowers, tablecloths, and napkins?"

"I'm fine with any color as long as they aren't Green Bay Packer colors of green and gold." His smile warmed her. "Why not check with Edna on what colors the inn stocks and select one of them?"

"Practical, you are so smart." She made a note on her list. "Now let's discuss the rehearsal. Usually, a groom's dinner is held the night before the wedding after the rehearsal."

"What's a groom's dinner?"

"A dinner hosted by the groom and his fam—" Leigh stopped mid-word. Her thoughts raced forward; she would have commented on how the groom and his family usually host and pay for the groom's dinner. The only family Garrett had was her.

"The groom and his family do what, Leigh?" The words rumbled deep as he leaned closer.

"The groom…and…his family…usually host and pay for the groom's dinner. The dinner allows both families and members of the wedding party an opportunity for meeting each other. I shouldn't have brought it up; I'm sorry."

"Don't be sorry; I asked the question. Just because the answer doesn't fit my circumstances isn't your fault." He caressed her shoulder and pulled her closer. "The concept serves us though. Suppose we host a dinner at the inn the night before the wedding and invite Chief Martin and Candace, Matt, Deb, your parents, your brother, his wife, and your grandparents. That way they meet each other before the wedding. By the way, are your grandparents your mom's or your dad's parents?"

"They're Dad's."

"Thank God!"

Cocking her head, she almost questioned his remark before his reason for celebrating dawned on her.

"Not my mom's folks, which is a huge relief for you," she said.

"When you mentioned your grandparents this morning, I admit I did hope they were your dad's parents. The thought of dealing with your mom and an older version of her at our wedding didn't exactly thrill me."

His confession got a chuckle out of her.

"You have no idea how accurate you are with your description. Fortunately, Mom's parents live in Arizona now and don't travel, so you should be safe."

"That's a relief. What else do we need to discuss?"

"The ceremony itself such as who should officiate and our vows. Should we write our own or say the standard one?"

"Me? Write wedding vows? No way." He drank his beer after a shake of his head.

"I'm glad because I don't want to try writing them either. What else do we need on our list?"

"The training required for the lower priced marriage license. We can't take any training until I'm back. You can ask the minister of the local church about the training."

"Easily done when I check out the church. I love the thought of attending services on a regular basis with you. Maybe the local minister will agree to conduct our ceremony."

"Worth asking the question. I'm sorry so much is falling on your shoulders."

"Don't worry, all the tasks will keep me busy. Between house hunting and wedding planning, you'll be home before I'm ready." Afraid he'd recognize her act as more bravado than conviction, she put on a cheerful front. "Oh! I almost forgot invitations. We should discuss them and begin our guest list."

"The guest list is squarely on you. I only need two invitations: one for Chief Martin and Candace, the other for Matt; I'll ask him to be my best man."

"Should you call him tonight before you leave?"

"Guess I should, especially since you locked in your maid of honor." He picked at the label on his beer bottle. "I don't care about the invitations; I trust your judgment."

She eyed him as he drank his beer and timed her question for the most impact. "So, you won't mind if they're all hearts, flowers, and cupids, those little chubby naked angels?"

He choked on his beer.

She laughed and sipped her martini.

Their food arrived and delayed his response. He munched on his fries; a deep crease marred his forehead.

Leigh's nerves kicked in; either he actually considered her ridiculous question or planned retaliation. She played with her pasta dish until she couldn't stand the silence any longer.

"I'm joking about the invitations. My tastes don't fall toward something so tacky; you believe me, don't you?"

"Of course I do. The thought of little chubby naked angels generated visions of someone else naked." His words sounded in a slow drawl that sent a shiver through her body.

His eyes, piercing and full of promise, skewered her in place. He bit into his burger without taking his eyes off her.

She couldn't believe how his eating a burger acted

like foreplay. The slow, deliberate bite into the meat left her breasts aching to be lavished by his tongue and teeth in a similar fashion. The simple act of his tongue sweeping across his lips in search of crumbs or excess sauce heated her blood. She couldn't draw her eyes away from him, imagining her body in place of the burger. A strong desire to rip off her clothes battled against her good sense.

"Leigh, your pasta's getting cold."

"What?"

"Your pasta? Getting cold?"

"Oh, yeah." A shake of her head got her thoughts back in line with their conversation. "Where were we?"

"Invitations."

"Yeah, right. They should be in good taste, defined by simplicity, and state the invitation comes from you and me. We also must decide on the time for the ceremony. Would you prefer late afternoon or early evening?"

"Either sounds acceptable. The timing is a good discussion topic for you with the minister and Edna."

"I'll add timing to the list. Music typically plays before, during, and after the ceremony."

"More music than what plays while you walk down the aisle? The 'Wedding March,' right?

"I thought you were at a loss regarding weddings?" Leigh's eyes narrowed with her question.

"Well, they do appear in movies and on TV shows."

"Right. I prefer something other than the 'Wedding March' for when I walk down the aisle. Music plays before the ceremony, so people don't sit in silence. If we want, a song played or sung during the ceremony is acceptable. Something to reflect our feelings for one another. Why don't we each come up with a list of our favorite songs and select the ones we like best for the ceremony."

"I can work on my list while I'm gone. It'll give me something to do at night other than miss you," he confessed.

She enjoyed a bite of her pasta as she marveled at

his confession. Now she realized his nights would mirror hers: lonely, agonizing over their separation, and biding time until their reunion.

He ate the last of his burger and drained his beer. He declined a refill and asked for the bill.

"Hey! I might want dessert."

"When a tin of delicious cookies waits for us in our room and coffee is available in the lobby? Don't be ridiculous."

"How did I forget your precious snickerdoodles?"

She laughed while he shook his head. After she boxed up her leftover pasta, they departed.

***

They entered through the hotel's front entrance, got two cups of coffee, and climbed the stairs for the second floor. Once in their room and stretched out on the bed, Garrett offered the cookie tin to Leigh.

"Be sure you tell Edna how I shared the cookies with you."

"I promise." She munched on her cookie before reminding him, "You're supposed to call your friend, Matt."

"You're right, I forgot." He hopped off the bed, stuffed the last of his cookie in his mouth, and pulled his phone out of his jeans pocket. After punching in a number, he stood by the window. "Matt!" He smiled.

"Garrett! You old dog, how the hell are you?"

"Enjoying civilian life. Hey, I need a favor."

"Sure dude, anything."

"Would you be my best man?"

"What? Best man! What the heck have you been up to since you left?"

"It's a long story, but the highlight is I fell in love with the most fascinating woman I've ever met. Her name is Leigh Ramsey, and she agreed to marry me. Our wedding will be in Minnesota the last weekend of April, so will you be my best man?"

"How could I miss witnessing my best friend get married? I'll put in for leave tomorrow. Can I come out early and hang with you?"

"If you can swing the days off, yeah! A longer stay provides Leigh time for understanding the real you."

"Are you certain she could ever understand the real me?"

"For sure, she's intelligent with a great sense of humor." It felt right harassing his friend again. "We're looking for a house, but I doubt we'll be in one before the wedding. Rest assured, you'll have a standing invitation to visit anytime you can squeeze us into your schedule."

Leigh's eyebrows rose with interest. She enjoyed hearing Garrett talk with his friend and observing another side of him.

He continued his conversation while gazing outside at the snowbanks; they reminded him of the sand dunes from his first deployment when he and Matt met. "We put a hold on some rooms at the inn where we'll be married, so I'll email you the details. I'll be out-of-pocket awhile on a job for my new position but will call you when I'm back."

"Sounds like a plan. Hey, congrats, man. I'm pleased for you; you deserve some happiness considering all you've been through."

"Thanks, Matt. Talk with you later." He ended the call and focused on Leigh. "Guess I should ask you before I offer a standing invitation to someone."

"No, it's fine. Besides, he's your friend. I want plenty of time with him, so I can learn all your deep, dark secrets." She wore a huge grin and winked at him. "Turnabout is fair play."

As he walked toward her, his gaze intensified, and he leaned over her.

"You have cookie crumbs on your face." His voice

filled with promise. She moved a hand toward her cheek, but he stopped it from reaching its destination. "I'll deal with the crumbs."

Her anticipation spiked as he kissed her cheeks.

"Are there anymore?" She gasped for breath.

"A few more."

A shiver of expectation raced through her from the mere whisper of his voice in her ear. His lips brushed hers so gently she wondered if she imagined it. Without warning, his lips crushed against hers. His tongue ran across the seam of her lips, and she opened for him. Their tongues met and twirled together in expectation of what would come next.

He stretched out beside her on the bed. One hand fondled a breast while the other moved along the inside of a thigh headed for the junction of her legs.

A moan indicated her pleasure. She felt a smile on his lips and an increased intensity of his actions.

He undid her jeans and pulled them past her hips. His hand rubbed the material of her panties against her sensitive center.

The panties became wet from her response to him. Arching her back, she pushed her jeans farther down her legs and offered him fuller access to her hidden depths. She desired the weight of him on her body and the friction of skin-to-skin motion. She grabbed the sides of her sweater in an attempt to pull the bulk of it over her head but failed as his hand lay heavy on her breast.

He didn't plan on touching her skin with anything other than his lips and tongue until she ached for more. He kissed her jawline, nibbled an earlobe, and ran his tongue along the outer edge of the nearest ear focused on the sensitive spot behind it. His kisses grazed her cheek on his way to her lips. Once he reached his objective, the kiss he delivered left her panting. He nuzzled and kissed along her jawline intent on a new objective: her other ear.

"Garrett." She moaned as his tongue traced the outline of her ear. She gave up on words and surrendered herself to the passion he generated within her.

His hand on her breast moved under her sweater, but he only touched the satin of her bra. His actions concentrated on her nipples; strong fingers rubbed the material against first one and then the other nipple until each peaked.

She grew desperate for skin-to-skin touching.

"Enough!" She pushed him away, recognizing the satisfied expression on his face as he rolled away from her, but she didn't care. Her clothes needed to come off and his, too. She removed her clothes and cast them aside. Leigh stood by the bed, naked, and panting with need. "You're wearing too much."

"Are these the plans you came up with on the drive here?" he asked.

"First, your clothes are coming off. If you delay any longer, I'll rip them off."

"What do you need, darlin'?" he teased her, but his hoarse drawl suggested he knew the answer.

"I need you naked and making love to me." She pounced at him, but he rolled away with a laugh and stood out of her reach.

"Gotta be faster than that." He gave her bare butt a playful tap.

She missed trapping his hands in hers.

"Garrett! You might be gone for months. I need you making love to me over and over tonight, so I can survive on the memories until you return. Get over here!"

She knelt on the bed. Her golden mass of hair fell over her shoulders and masked her breasts. Dark nipples hardened from his attentions peeked out between curls. Her blue eyes reflected love and a desperate need for him.

His love for her consumed him. He acknowledged the truth of what she said and would hold tonight's memories close while away from her as well.

"Alright, I'm all yours." He stepped closer and spread his arms in surrender.

"You certainly took your time," she muttered as she reached for his shirt buttons.

She removed his flannel shirt and attacked the next layer, a Henley shirt. An impromptu plan of attack began with kisses up his throat and across his jaw until their lips met. Their tongues battled within his mouth. When her fingers located the bottom of his shirt, it flew across the room and landed in a heap by the door. Her hands glided along his body while her kisses covered his chest. She licked and nipped at his nipples, rewarded by a groan. She kissed her way lower and stopped at the waistband of his jeans.

Nimble fingers undid the button, but her hands slowed at his zipper. As her hand rubbed over the firm erection held captive by his jeans, a sense of empowerment thrilled her—she caused this physical reaction in him. The slow pull of his zipper teased. No shorts impeded her progress toward her objective; his going commando benefited her efforts.

"Are you having fun unwrapping?" His growl was low and soft.

"What a welcomed surprise. Thought I'd encounter additional wrapping before I finished."

She kissed the tip of his erection and pulled his jeans down his legs until she couldn't reach any further. Her head and arms hung over the edge of the bed and her butt raised in the air. "Can you help me with this? The jeans are stuck at your ankles."

He eyed her butt with intense interest. "Sure."

Ignoring the obvious purpose of her request, he placed kisses down her back as his hands rounded each of her butt cheeks.

"You misunderstood what I needed, but don't stop

doing what you're doing." She almost collapsed on the bed from pure satisfaction.

He stopped kissing her to rid himself of his remaining clothes.

She scrambled over the bed and pulled the covers down.

He stretched out and gathered her into his arms.

"We're making memories tonight," he promised.

She wasted no time in taking charge. Her hands roamed across his broad shoulders, down strong arms, over sculpted abs, past a trim waist, to narrow hips in an attempt to memorize his body by touch. She admired the strength of his tight, muscular butt. The butt she loved to watch whenever he walked away, although he wouldn't walk away from her tonight. Her hands glided across his back to his chest and lower. All the while she squeezed, lightly pinched, and gently raked her fingernails over his skin; she gained pleasure at the sound of his raspy groans.

Her lips moved down his body and followed her hands in a thorough exploration of him. She trailed a path of kisses over his chest, across his stomach, and along a hip.

After one hand brushed his erection, a short growl encouraged her further. Her hands wrapped around swollen-hard flesh, and she rejoiced at his sharp inhale of breath. With one hand around his shaft, the other traced his tip until moisture appeared. She wiped the drop away with a finger and rubbed the slickness on herself. When she released her hold on him, disappointment sounded in his sigh. She smiled. Her loving assault of his body had begun, and her plans included so much more. Repositioned lower and against his side, she took his erection in her mouth.

His hands entangled in her hair and massaged her head. He closed his eyes and surrendered to the sensations generated by her loving his body. His hands tightened on her hair in reaction to her mouth covering his erection. The use of her tongue and teeth destroyed his thoughts of taking this slow. As she moved her tongue along his length, he let loose of her hair and grabbed her by the shoulders.

"Come here."

Strong hands positioned her on top of him. He kissed her gently at first but deepened it with an urgency. A longing to kiss her forever built within him, but the knowledge of how this night may be their last filled him with regret. Tonight must be a memorable one. He intended to demonstrate the depth of his love for her, so no doubts shadowed her thoughts in the future.

His kiss took her breath away with its passion. She returned his kiss with her own show of urgency and an out of control need for him.

"Please, get inside of me now." Leigh's throaty demand sounded foreign to her.

In response, he rolled her below him. His warm hands caressed her thighs while they spread her legs. He entered her in a slow movement. Once he moved her legs over his shoulders, his hardened flesh went deeper and pushed forward until her body accepted all of him. He partially withdrew; at her whimper, he pounded into her.

His power thrilled her; she arched her back and encouraged him further. His rhythm drove her unaware of anything but him, and she matched him with each movement.

"I love you." His deep voice rumbled in his chest, and kisses traced her jaw to her mouth. His tongue demanded entrance, and she responded without hesitation.

Their lovemaking reached higher levels of sexual fulfillment than any time before, and they peaked together. He kissed her one last time before he collapsed beside her. He lay with an arm across his eyes and his chest heaving from exertion.

They lay wrapped together unable to speak until their breathing and heartbeats slowed.

She curled up with an arm across his body and left a

soft kiss on his chest. "I love you."

A strong arm came around her and pulled her closer. He murmured a heartfelt, "Same here, Leigh, same here." He nuzzled her hair a bit and inhaled her lily of the valley scent.

"Garrett?"

"Yes?"

"I'm ready for more. Are you?" Her voice trembled with desire.

He laughed. "Tell you what, you slide over here, and we'll discover if I'm ready for the rest of your plans. When we exhaust yours, we'll move on to mine."

She shifted on top of him, and their evening continued.

They loved each other throughout the night. Promises made and accepted. Tears flowed amid gentle caresses and passionate kisses. In the early morning hours, they lay intertwined, exhausted, and satisfied.

Garrett imagined their future as he gazed at the shadows in their hotel room. "I'll miss you so much. Hopefully, this separation won't be long."

"And I'll miss you. I promise to accomplish as much as possible, so we can enjoy ourselves when you're back."

"We'll finish whatever remains on your list together."

With an agreement reached, they relaxed in each other's arms and drifted into slumber. Their dreams were similar yet different. One dreamed of houses, weddings, and forever love while the other dreamed of danger, survival, and forever love.

CHAPTER FIVE

Garrett rose well before the morning dawned. Today his career as a Minnesota BCA Special Agent began. No way would he be late on his first day. He packed his bag for an immediate departure. Leigh still slept, so he stepped out of the room for coffee before he woke her. Upon his return, she surprised him by being in the shower. He took her coffee into the bathroom.

"Hey, darlin', I brought you some coffee. Can I bring you anything else?" He stuck his head around the shower curtain.

She turned and smiled at him.

The image of her standing in the water spray with droplets of water glistening on her body and in her hair imprinted on his soul. Attraction and desire for her thrummed to life within him. Realization of not having time for acting on those desires dampened his physical reaction.

"Coffee's plenty for now, thanks. I'll be done in a few minutes."

"Alright. We'll go down for breakfast when you're ready."

He ducked out of the bathroom and turned on the television. He hoped watching the morning news might calm his nerves—no such luck. While in the Air Force, he never experienced a case of nerves when reporting to new organizations after each reassignment or deployment. Today his nervousness caused tension across his shoulders and a severe tightness deep in his belly. His first ever civilian job began in a few hours, and the uncertainty of what the day held for them left him uneasy. His separation from Leigh so early in their relationship increased his anxiety.

Pacing might do the trick, he thought. That idea

worked as miserably as watching the news. The only positive aspect fell into occupying his time until Leigh finished in the bathroom. He stopped moving as soon as she stepped out. The nervousness disappeared, his love for her calmed him.

"Do I look okay? I'm not sure how I should dress for meeting your new boss and co-workers." She ran a hand over her hair, down her front, and ended on her pants leg.

His eyes followed her hand. She wore her long golden hair in a low ponytail, tied with a dark-pink ribbon coordinated with her pale-pink sweater. Maroon cords and short black boots completed her outfit for the day.

"You look stunning." His voice thick with emotion.

She feared embarrassing him by dressing inappropriately for his new workplace, so his words brought her instant relaxation.

"And you look so handsome and professional. I didn't realize you owned a suit."

The man before her radiated power and confidence. A crisp white shirt pulled taut across his broad shoulders; the stark whiteness was broken by a dark-gray silk tie. A five-button vest emphasized his trim waist. The charcoal-gray dress pants fit alarmingly well over his hips and sported a severe crease down each leg. The creases broke with precision at his shiny-black shoes. Stepping back for an improved view of him, she noted his sexy whisker stubble and focused on his shaggy blonde hair.

"Flaxen! The color is flaxen."

"What's flaxen?" His eyes narrowed.

"Your hair. Figuring out the right word for the color has been driving me crazy for days. Your hair is flaxen blonde."

"If you say so, but flaxen wasn't a color choice for my driver's license." He teased and caught her by the waist with both hands. "Let's eat breakfast and come back up before we leave."

"What time should we be at your office?"

They walked close together down the corridor.

"Nine o'clock, although, I prefer arriving early." He held the stairwell door for her.

"I'm hungry enough for one of those Belgian waffles this morning. How 'bout you?"

"I'll pass on the waffle. I'm in the mood for something warm and filling. Oatmeal works." Her nose wrinkled. "What? You don't like oatmeal?"

"On occasion I eat oatmeal, but not when waffles are available, especially Belgian waffles." She winked at him and led him into the breakfast area.

"You cook your waffle, and I'll fix our coffees." Always looking after her needs, he left her at the Belgian waffle machine.

After mixing their coffees and dishing up his oatmeal, he selected a table for two in a quiet section. His eyes followed Leigh while she exchanged greetings with other guests and the hotel staff. He recognized her as a spark of brightness in the morning and found her interaction with others fascinating. She giggled over something said and operated the machine for a few of the older guests. The latter action delayed her in making her own by two rounds of waffles.

"If you ate oatmeal, you'd be on seconds by now," he said when she joined him with her fresh waffle.

"Yes, but I met so many of the other guests and staff." Her smile lit up his morning. "This is worth waiting for." She ate a piece of crisp Belgian waffle drenched in maple syrup. "Hey!" she blurted out as he snatched a chunk of her waffle.

"Mmm. We may need a waffle maker for our house."

His smile struck deep within her heart, and the dragons circled in her stomach.

"So, what happens today?" She munched on her

waffle.

"I would expect an oath of office, receive my credentials and badge, and probably stacks of paperwork; after all, it's a government job."

"What sort of paperwork?"

"Benefit related such as health insurance, next of kin, and similar things." He almost said death benefits but stopped himself in time. Bad enough, he blurted out 'next of kin.' He didn't want her overly concerned for his safety.

"'Next of kin'? As in if you die?" Leigh's voice choked as she squeezed out the last word; the danger of his job had escaped her thoughts prior to this conversation. Her appetite disappeared.

"As in whom they should contact if I'm hurt." He spoke with quiet confidence, gazed into her blue eyes, and emphasized his words. He sensed her relaxing but noted she didn't finish her waffle. "I'll be briefed on the undercover assignment and maybe find out how long it should last. I'm not sure if the operation is under the BCA or a task force with other organizations."

"I'll find somewhere I can sit and work on our list while I wait until you finish." She pushed her plate away, most of her precious waffle remained in a puddle of syrup. "I can't eat anymore."

"Are you sure? You barely touched your waffle."

"What about you? You didn't finish your oatmeal."

"I suppose we're both uneasy with the uncertainties of the day. Let's head upstairs."

As they walked down the hallway, he caught her hand and held it against his leg, drawing her close. Neither spoke, each lost in their own thoughts and the physical connection they shared. When they entered their room, Leigh stopped moving at the sight of his packed bag.

"You're really leaving, aren't you?" Leigh stared; the bag brought home the reality of his assignment.

"It sounded like they need me to leave right away,

so I'll take this with us."

Unable to hold her stare and face the disappointment shadowing her eyes, he entered the bathroom. Perhaps brushing his teeth would buy him time before she confronted him further, but no such luck. She followed him.

"I thought we'd spend the whole day together, meeting with Nick and looking at houses." She hated the whine in her voice, but she couldn't control it.

He spit out the toothpaste and rinsed his mouth before he faced her. His eyes glittered icy blue instead of the warm brown she preferred.

"Leigh, I can't say what will or won't happen today, but I should be ready for anything. I need you to understand."

"I do, but I don't like it." She brushed her teeth with so much force, she winced.

"Leigh…" He resisted reaching for her by leaning against the sink's cabinet.

She spat out the toothpaste. "Garrett, I understand; believe me, I do. If you can't make our appointment with Nick, I'll be disappointed." Her raised hand stopped him before he said anything. "Fortunately, we discussed houses last night and created a list of our preferences, so I can handle the house hunting on my own. Let's go."

Surprised by her fast turnaround, he agreed.

After he helped her with her coat, he shrugged into his suit coat. He carried the packed bag slung over a shoulder, the weight banging into his leg with each step. She followed with their lists and notes on houses pressed against her chest. In moments, they sat in the Jeep headed for the BCA office.

***

In the parking lot, he turned the engine off and stared at the building. His lack of movement surprised her.

"What's up?" she asked.

"This feels different from reporting for a new assignment in the Air Force. A civilian job is a new dynamic, slightly scary but exhilarating, too."

"You'll do fantastic. They're lucky you're working for them." She leaned over and kissed his cheek. "I apologize for earlier; I didn't consider how emotional today must be for you. We're in this together and can survive the challenge of a separation. Let's go inside."

He loved her belief in him. They held hands as they walked into the building.

After identifying who they were, Garrett's new co-workers gave them a warm welcome. A flurry of names they'd never remember ended with directions to Special Agent in Charge, the SAIC, Henderson's office. Pleased by the acceptance of her presence with Garrett, Leigh relaxed by the time they reached his boss's office. Out of the door stepped a gray-haired man who looked too young for gray hair. He stood a couple inches shorter than Garrett with a huskier build. An air of authority radiated from the man.

"Garrett, great having you here." He shook hands with Garrett, a warm two-handed shake; he turned to Leigh. "And this must be your fiancée. I'm Joe Henderson." He shook hands with her.

"Yes, sir. This is Leigh Ramsey." Garrett snaked a reassuring arm around her.

"I'm happy to meet you." Leigh smiled and admired Joe Henderson's twinkling eyes.

"Come in and take a seat. Do you need anything to drink?"

They declined as they sat in comfortable upholstered chairs.

"Leigh, my wife, Janet, will be here soon. She'll show you around town while we ensure Garrett's squared away, but we'll conduct the oath of office before you go. We should be done with everything around noon, so I thought we might grab lunch together."

"Wonderful," Leigh said. "I appreciate your wife spending time with me."

"We previously scheduled an appointment with our realtor for this afternoon, so I hoped to join Leigh for the meeting." Garrett took advantage of the opening SAIC Henderson gave them when he mentioned events for the morning. "At least for a few hours," he added at the slight adjustment in his boss's expression. Leigh's appreciation for him raising the topic reflected in her face.

"I'm sure you'll have time for your meeting. I'll be honest with you both; I need Garrett in this operation tonight." SAIC Henderson turned to Leigh. Her lack of surprise pleased him. Maybe his new agent had chosen well for himself and his career. He hoped so; too many marriages went down in flames in this business.

"We anticipated I might leave today, sir, and discussed the possibility this morning."

"Outstanding! I can give you a few hours. I'll coordinate a pickup for…say…seven tonight, but you should be here by six-thirty. Not too long, but you'll be able to spend some time with your realtor."

"Thank you, Joe. We appreciate you working with us on this. He can easily return by six-thirty." Leigh marveled at the calm sound of her voice.

Garrett's eyes reflected his pride in her. She didn't care for the situation, but she accepted the inevitableness of their separation.

A knock on the door interrupted them. Henderson opened the door, and an attractive redhead walked in.

"Janet, this is Leigh Ramsey and our newest agent, Garrett Dane."

They stood and greeted his wife.

"Nice meeting you both." She approached Leigh first. "If you don't mind, I'll show you around the area while the guys do their thing. If I understood Joe correctly, you recently got engaged?"

"Yes. I'll be working on the wedding details while Garrett's on this assignment. Your husband mentioned you and I would spend time together today. I appreciate your kindness."

"Spending time with our new family members is my pleasure." Janet looked at Garrett. "Joe's been awaiting your arrival. Don't worry about Leigh; we'll watch over her for you."

"Thank you, ma'am."

Garrett hated leaving Leigh alone but learning his boss and his wife would look out for her brought him a bit of comfort.

"Let's get this show on the road." Joe clapped his hands for emphasis. "Janet, we'll do the oath of office first while Leigh's here. You two can kill a few hours while we finish up on paperwork and other details. Later we'll meet for lunch at your favorite burger place. They have an appointment with their realtor this afternoon, so I'm shooting for completion between twelve and one."

"Oh, I'm sure we can find something of interest until then. Call me when you're ready, and we'll join you at the restaurant." Janet ushered Leigh out the door and into a conference room.

Joe followed with Garrett. "My wife's like a tornado. She swoops in, spins everything up, and whisks the unassuming right along with her." He chuckled at his description of his wife. "Leigh's in good hands; Janet will keep a close eye on her while you're on this assignment."

"I appreciate your wife's efforts, sir, more than you can imagine." Garrett relaxed; the tension he suffered in the parking lot began to ease.

Joe called everyone into the conference room. After he officially introduced the newest member of their team and his fiancée, he swore in Garrett and handed over the credentials and badge of a BCA Special Agent.

"I am so proud of you!" Leigh hugged him close and kissed him while the others applauded their new co-worker.

"Thanks. Will you be okay?"

"Yeah, Janet's knowledge of the area will be helpful. I'm sure today will be fun."

"I'll see you later." He kissed her cheek before his boss clapped him on the shoulder.

"First, let's complete the paperwork and then discuss your assignment." They sat at the table, and Joe wasted no time in pushing papers at Garrett.

Leigh grabbed her things and followed Janet out the door.

"We'll be well acquainted with each other by the time they're ready for lunch." Janet pointed her in the direction of a massive SUV. "I'll show you around the area, but first a stop for coffee. You do drink coffee, don't you?"

"Who doesn't? Can we stop at a place where they sell food, so I can buy something to eat?" Leigh asked as she fastened her seat belt. The few bites of waffle from breakfast didn't last long, but she vowed a confession to Garrett would never pass her lips.

"Of course." Janet backed the SUV out of its parking space and edged out of the lot. "We'll stop at my favorite coffee shop. Are you familiar with the area?"

"Not at all. So far, everything is breathtaking."

"Where are you from?"

"I grew up in the Twin Cities, Eden Prairie to be exact. For the last four years, I lived in Chicago. I love being back in Minnesota."

"Chicago, how fun! Your family must prefer having you closer." Janet avoided main roads to reach the coffee shop near the BCA office. She negotiated the SUV into an open parking space.

Upon meeting Janet at the front of the vehicle, Leigh answered her question. "They're glad I returned. My best friend lives in Moorhead, so she's ecstatic over our living so close."

"After you." Janet held the coffee shop door open and followed Leigh inside.

"Wow! I love the aroma in here: baked goods and fresh coffee." Leigh studied the items on display.

"A mouthwatering combination." Janet spoke with the young woman at the counter. "Hi, Kelly, I'll take my usual."

"Already working on it." Kelly grabbed a cranberry-orange scone for her. "And for you, Miss?"

"One of those same scones would work for me with a latte, please." Leigh checked out the drink list and decided she and Garrett needed to come here one day. She joined Janet at a table near an inviting fireplace. After pulling off her coat and gloves, the heat from the fire warmed her back. "This is a lovely place; thanks for bringing me here."

"This is what I do with new family members of Joe's team, especially when they're new to the area. I love sharing the various discoveries I made around here. What types of things would you be interested in seeing?"

"How 'bout fun places such as reputable restaurants and unusual shopping spots? Oh! Bridal shops are high on my list of places to visit because I need a wedding dress."

"I'm sure we can find a bridal shop or two around here." Janet bit into her scone and sighed. "These are heavenly."

Leigh nodded her agreement as she enjoyed a bite of hers.

"How goes the wedding planning?"

"We took care of a few basics yesterday." Leigh shied away from discussing personal details. Her hesitancy surprised her at first. As she examined reasons for her apprehension, she recognized the implications of speaking freely to the wife of Garrett's boss. How much of what she said would find its way into SAIC Henderson's ear? No matter how much she enjoyed Janet's company, she must always keep Garrett's work relationship with her husband in mind. "We're planning a small wedding at the end of April. Garrett planned to discuss time off for the wedding and honeymoon with your husband today."

"If I can do anything for you, please ask." Janet smiled at Leigh before polishing off her scone. "If you're done, we can continue on our way. I'll show you some places here in Brainerd, afterward we'll check out Baxter. Another time, we'll explore the surrounding areas."

As they drove along, Janet carried on a running dialogue of her favorite places and stores in the area. A flurry of stories about the Henderson family, consisting of Joe, herself, two teenagers, two dogs, and a patient cat, made the morning fly by for Leigh. The stories brought on a fit of laughter, and she almost forgot Garrett wouldn't be coming home tonight or any night in the near future. Before they finished a rushed area tour, Janet's phone rang. She answered through the vehicle Bluetooth capability, so Leigh heard everything.

"Janet, we're done here. Are you and Leigh ready for lunch?"

Janet shot her a questioning look, and Leigh nodded. "Yes. We can reach the restaurant in ten minutes."

"I'll ask my newest Special Agent to drive, so he and Leigh can leave from there for their meeting with their realtor. Hopefully, you'll bring me back to my office."

"You buy me lunch, and I'll consider your request. Be with you soon. Bye!"

Leigh enjoyed the good-natured banter between the couple. She wondered how she and Garrett sounded when others listened to them.

"Hope you're hungry. This place has superb food with huge servings."

"Whatever I can't eat, I can bring with me since our

hotel room has a fridge and a microwave." Leigh steadied herself as Janet pulled a U-turn. "How many years have you and Joe been married?"

"We're going on twenty-two years. How long have you and Garrett been together?"

"As of today, ten days, ten unbelievable days!" A wave of love and warmth flowed over her as she remembered their short time together.

"Spoken like a woman in love." Janet glanced at her before focusing back on her driving. "I didn't miss how you watched him and your response whenever he touched you. And from what I saw on Garrett's face and in his actions, his love for you appeared as deep as yours for him, regardless of the length of time since you met. When love happens in ten days, weeks, months, or years, you grab hold and never let go. You're both very lucky."

"We truly are. Fate stepped in and brought us together."

Janet pulled into a parking space. She turned in her seat and placed a hand on Leigh's arm.

"I realize we scarcely know each other and on top of that, I'm the wife of Garrett's boss, but I hope we can be friends. If you need anything while Garrett's away or a shoulder to cry on, please call me." Leigh squirmed a bit in the directness of Janet's gaze. "I'm serious. I survived what you're heading into with him being gone on top of the worry of him working in law enforcement. At some point, you'll need someone to talk with. The appreciable difference between anyone you already count on as a friend and someone who has gone through what you're going through will show in the type of support you receive." She let her words sink in for a moment. "We can do coffee, lunch, shop, or just meet to talk."

"Thanks, I'm certain I'll need your guidance and assistance; this is all so new for me."

Leigh blinked back tears pooling in her eyes. Janet

hugged her.

"Let's go inside and find a table. The guys will be here soon." She gave Leigh's shoulder a squeeze and nodded toward the door of the restaurant.

***

By the time Joe and Garrett walked in, the ladies had already swapped phone numbers. Joe led the way to their table with Garrett trailing behind him.

While he approached her, Leigh admired his new attire from his hiking boots, the dark-brown cords hugging his long legs, and the heather-brown Henley under his leather jacket. She hadn't been able to tear her eyes away from him as he walked over and sat beside her.

When Garrett spotted Leigh appraising him on his way to the table, an immediate question entered his thoughts: should we skip the appointment with Nick and head back to our room instead?

"Hey, ladies. Sorry if we kept you waiting," said Joe.

"We've only been here a few minutes. You guys finished at the right time; we missed most of the lunch crowd." Janet lifted her face for a kiss. "Garrett, how does it feel being a BCA Special Agent?"

Garrett sat in the chair beside Leigh and found her hand under the table. "It fulfills a promise I made to myself, ma'am. I made my decision on a law enforcement career years ago and working for my home state is a dream come true."

"Please call me Janet. Ma'am makes me feel old." She smiled at him. "Leigh and I enjoyed ourselves today, and I have so much more to show her in the area. We'll be here for her while you're gone."

"Thank you, ma'am. Sorry, Janet," he amended at her frown. "Knowing she's not alone takes a huge load off my mind."

"You changed out of your suit," Leigh said.

"Yeah. I thought I might be overdressed for the rest of my day, so we stopped at the hotel before coming here."

"Let's eat, so these two can do some house hunting." Joe picked up a menu as a signal the others should do the same.

After ordering their meals, they entered the typical conversation of those newly met, polite yet inquisitive.

Janet broached the wedding topic with one comment. "So, Garrett, Leigh told me you've known each other for only ten days."

"Yes, a definite case of love at first sight," Garrett admitted.

"Ten days!" Joe looked from Garrett to Leigh. "I would have never guessed. Are your families giving you any problems over your whirlwind romance?"

"None of my family are still alive, but Leigh's parents met with us this past weekend." Garrett ended the conversation topic without any further details. "She and I finalized a few decisions yesterday regarding our wedding plans and honeymoon. Those are the days off we discussed."

"Oh, sure, late April, early May, right?"

"Yes, sir."

"Guess I should approve your time off; difficult for a wedding to happen without a groom. What do you do, Leigh?"

"I worked as an investment advisor, but I'm in the midst of a career change to photography." Leigh squeezed Garrett's hand. The strength of his hand grounded her. The simple sensation of his thumb rubbing over the back of her hand sent warmth shooting through her.

"What subjects are you interested in for your photographs?" Janet asked.

"Wildlife and scenery. We'll research ways to reach magazines and people for sales." Leigh's comfort level sat higher with this topic. "We hope to find a house with space for a photography studio."

"Some of my friends are active in the local arts community. When you're ready, I'll introduce you to them. They often run exhibits." Janet pulled out a notebook and made a note for herself. "I'll call them and set some groundwork. They might offer additional suggestions for you, too."

"That would be wonderful. Thank you!" Leigh's voice reflected her excitement. "I'll call you once I gain some free time. I'm sure our realtor won't show me houses every day."

Their food arrived, so their attention focused on their meals.

"This is delicious. Thanks for the suggestion," Garrett said.

"You're welcome. I plan to show Leigh all my favorite haunts. Most are restaurants and even more are shops. So be warned," Janet said.

Garrett's laugh was genuine. "I consider myself forewarned."

"We stopped at a wonderful coffee shop, where I ate the best scone ever." As soon as the words were out of her mouth, Leigh realized she'd let the cat out of the bag. Garrett's eyebrows shot up, and his eyes glittered at her. "Yeah, I should eat oatmeal instead of Belgian waffles."

"I didn't say a thing." Garrett chuckled and ate another bite of his food.

"I love Belgian waffles. No way oatmeal competes with them." Joe defended Leigh's choice.

"Thanks for your support, Joe. We're buying a Belgian waffle machine, so I can make one anytime I want."

"She was amazing this morning. She helped other guests with their waffles before making her own." Garrett boasted of her generosity.

"Well, some couldn't read or follow the directions

for the machine. By helping them, I met other guests and the staff. Now I'll have someone I can eat with tomorrow morning since you won't be joining me." Leigh hated the loneliness wrapping around her heart after she said those words. She looked at Garrett and wondered if her words filled him with feelings of loneliness, too.

Until Leigh's last words, Garrett enjoyed his lunch. Her words combined with the details surrounding the operation he'd join tonight destroyed his appetite. His heart sank as he acknowledged to himself the very real chance, he might be unavailable for their chosen wedding date.

"I didn't realize how late it'd gotten. We should get going." Garrett tossed his napkin on his plate over the last of his food and looked for their waiter.

"You guys leave; we've got this." Joe stood and extended his hand. Garrett shook his boss's offered hand. "I'm glad you're here. You're an outstanding addition to our team. Leigh, I appreciate you sharing your fiancé so soon after your arrival. You call if you need anything, okay?"

"Yes, I will. Thanks for lunch, and thank you, Janet, for a fun morning." Leigh stood, nodded at Joe, and gave Janet a hug.

"Thank you, sir." Garrett smiled at his boss's wife. "Janet, it's been a pleasure meeting you. Thanks for being here for Leigh; you make my leaving her alone an easier task." He held Leigh's coat for her before he shrugged into his jacket, and they walked away, hand in hand.

"They're a sweet couple," Janet reflected as she watched them leave. "He appears agreeable and polite. Capable?"

"Highly. His well-rounded experience in the Air Force spoke well of his abilities and skills. While I briefed him, he asked intelligent questions and made suggestions the task force will consider for implementation. He'll do well." Joe faced his wife. "Poor timing for them, but this will be huge for his career. How'd she strike you? Can she face the challenges?"

"She's head over heels in love with him. Her eyes sparkle whenever she mentions him." Janet smiled at the memory. "I believe she'll do fine. I'll keep in touch but won't be too pushy. With her being busy house hunting and working on wedding plans, the time should fly by for her. The worse will be the nights, and she'll figure out a way for dealing with those."

"The separation won't be any easier for him. You're right. The nights are the worst." Joe gave her arm a gentle squeeze. "I hope they pull through and survive this life."

CHAPTER SIX

Garrett escorted Leigh to the Jeep. Neither spoke until buckled into their seat belts.

"I can't tell you the specifics, but the operation might take longer than we hoped for." He stared out the windshield. "Will you be okay on your own here?"

"I'll be fine. Janet and I exchanged numbers. I promised to call her if I need anything. Don't forget, there's also Deb and my family." She placed her hand on his chin and turned his head toward her. "Honest, I'll be okay, so don't worry over me. You take care of business and come back safe."

"Do you have any idea how much I love you?" He caressed her cheek.

"I assume as much as I love you. Can we meet with Nick now?"

"Yes, ma'am." He drove off in the direction of the realty office.

Leigh chattered on about her day with Janet and pointed out any place she recognized as they drove along.

"You enjoyed spending time with her today, didn't you?"

"How'd you guess?"

"Your nonstop talking since we left the restaurant gave you away."

She giggled. "You're right; I had fun."

"I'm glad you hit it off with her. Here we are."

They exited the Jeep and entered the office.

"Good afternoon. May I help you?" the receptionist asked as they approached his desk.

"We have an appointment with Nick."

"Your names?"

"Garrett Dane and Leigh Ramsey."

"Have a seat, and I'll inform him you're here. Help yourselves to coffee and water." A nod of his head indicated a comfortable waiting area.

"Thank you." Leigh focused on the coffee machine and decided a bit of caffeine might be necessary for them. "Garrett, I fixed you one." Leigh handed him a cup as she sat beside him. "I brought our lists and the magazine we made notes on last night."

"Thanks for remembering those. I'm a bit distracted by my expectations of everything happening today." He gave her a half-smile. "Before you drop me off, we'll find time for a talk."

"I hoped for more time; in fact, my preference is being in our room and—"

"Garrett. Leigh. I'm Nick. I've been looking forward to meeting you." A short bundle of energy greeted them. "Come on back; we can talk in my office. We'll discuss further what you're looking for, and I scheduled a couple of viewings for you. This way." He escorted them into a tidy office. "Please, make yourselves comfortable."

"We went through a magazine of listings, made notes on some of them, and created a list of features we're interested in," Garrett announced as they sat.

"Perfect, the information is valuable as I consider other listings. How much time do we have today?" Nick looked back and forth between them.

"We need to wind up by five," Garrett answered.

His eyes found Leigh's, his gaze an embrace. A chill of expectation ran down her spine. Maybe they'd finish early and enjoy some intimate time together before he left.

"Show me the properties you found interesting." Nick accepted the magazine from Leigh.

"This one is our favorite. It includes everything we're looking for in a house."

"I'll check if this one is still available. Here are the properties I'll show you today." Nick handed Garrett three printed sheets.

"These look promising. When can we begin?" Garrett glanced at the papers and turned them over to Leigh.

"Right away. Good news! From the looks of this, the property you identified is still available. I'll call the listing agent and ask if we can schedule a viewing for this afternoon. Come this way. I'll drive."

They joined him in his vehicle.

"Garrett, you ride up front with Nick," Leigh encouraged him. He nodded, opened the back door for her, and she climbed in. Before he shut the door, she gave his hand a squeeze.

Her heart skipped a beat at his smile for her. She relaxed into the softness of the leather upholstery, soon warmth radiated from the seat. Nick owned a sweet ride.

From the back seat, she watched Garrett and memorized images of him for her lonely nights ahead. At first, his hair caught her attention. She loved the flaxen color, how the length brushed his collar, and the errant lock that fell into his eyes. The silent assessment continued as she studied a slight bump in his nose and wondered if it had been broken or if the bump was natural.

She enjoyed listening to Garrett interact with Nick. His deep voice touched her soul. Now and then she caught a hint of the accent he picked up while stationed in the South. She adored how his accent strengthened as his romantic affections increased. Totally relaxed, she let the conversation in the front seat flow over her while she kept her eyes on Garrett.

"This first house is in a stupendous location with outbuildings and plenty of room." Nick initiated his sales pitch as they walked toward the house. The frowns on their faces upon seeing the house up close spoke volumes, so he added, "Of course the house is older and sat vacant for months, but the tremendous potential is worth consideration."

They looked at each other as Nick unlocked the front door, and they entered a dark entry. When he flipped a switch, the light transformed the dark entry into a dingy one. They walked through the house, looking in closets, checking out cupboards, and remarking on the color selections of walls and carpeting.

"We can walk out for a closer look at the outbuildings."

"Not necessary, Nick, this one isn't what we're looking for. This place requires more renovations than we're comfortable accepting." Garrett spoke for the two of them.

"No problem, we'll move on. I'm calling again about the house you picked out from the magazine listings, so go on into the truck. I left the keys in it, run the engine, and stay warm." The cell phone in his hand slapped against his ear, and he walked away talking.

"The house was horrible." Leigh laughed and Garrett joined her.

"I hope the next ones are in better condition." He gave her a hand into the vehicle. Before shutting the door, he leaned over for a kiss. His lips were gentle at first but became demanding. Their tongues tangled for a moment until he stepped back. She missed his nearness immediately.

"Nick's coming back." He shut her door and walked around the SUV.

Her eyes followed him; she loved his confident, fluid movements.

Nick stopped Garrett with an update from his calls.

"The next place is not far away, so we should be able to walk through the other two places today. Unfortunately, we can't view the house from the magazine. A newly accepted offer is on it, and they requested no showings. I'll search for similar listings on the market."

"Thanks for checking." Garrett glanced back at Leigh and shook his head.

They climbed into the SUV. Nick drove to the main road and sped off.

"Would you consider new construction?" Nick's eyes sought Leigh in the rearview mirror

"Do they build in the winter?" Leigh's interest piqued.

"Some houses are in the works if they dug the foundations before the hard freeze. We're approaching the construction season. If you build, you're buying the house of your dreams. There are a few furnished apartments in the local area available for lease on a monthly basis if you want out of the hotel for extra space until completion of a home. What do you think?"

Leigh and Garrett glanced at each other: interest showed in Leigh's eyes, concern in Garrett's.

"We never considered building. How much added responsibility would fall on Leigh's shoulders beyond what's necessary for looking at existing houses?" Garrett expressed his concern for her. "If Leigh's up for the challenge, we can definitely check into building."

His eyes caught Leigh's, and she melted at the total regard he had for her. Her long-ago ex-boyfriend, David, had never considered her needs or worried about her. "I'm leaning toward the idea of a house built specifically for us, Garrett. I'm sure whatever is involved wouldn't be too much for me." Leigh's eyes reflected her love and appreciation for him.

The realization of how much he appreciated her as well as loved her hit him hard. She seemed to handle their impending separation well, or she put up a brave front. He understood she did this for him, allowing him to concentrate on his work. His fiancée was an extraordinary woman, and he remembered how fortunate he'd been on the night she found him.

"Okay, we can check into new construction." Her wide smile rewarded him for his decision.

"I'll show you the last two houses, and then we'll return to my office. I work with some builders, so I'll prepare a package of material from them for your review." The SUV engine roared, and they headed for the next house.

"This one appears decent, but I don't care for the nearness of the power lines." Leigh spoke up when they approached the next house.

"So, we shouldn't stop?" Nick asked as he slowed his vehicle and looked at her in the rearview mirror.

"Nope." Leigh vigorously shook her head.

Garrett admired her certainty.

"Then, we're on to the last house." He threw the SUV in gear and headed off in a heartbeat.

"Nick, will these builders work on any land or only in certain areas?" Garrett's thoughts now leaned toward building their home.

"Both. Some of their sites might work for you; they're oversized lots with utilities. We can also search for other land available; after all, they're in the business of building houses."

Leigh chimed in with a thought. "Do any of them build log homes?"

"Sure. There are quite a few companies specializing in log homes and similar styles. I have materials on some of them and can provide a list of those with sterling reputations. Take your time, visit their showrooms, and determine which company you prefer. I'll help you with the negotiations and paperwork."

"Thanks, Nick." Leigh settled back in the seat and stared out the window at the scenery flying by. She itched to roam the countryside with her camera; ideas for photographs bombarded her mind. Working on her photography as well as house hunting and wedding planning should keep her busy while Garrett worked at his undercover assignment. If she stayed busy, time would fly by. Wouldn't it?

She glanced at Garrett who hadn't participated in the log home conversation. He stared at the passing scenery, but she doubted he saw any of it. She suspected his thoughts focused on his assignment. When the vehicle slowed and turned, she realized they already arrived at the last house for the day.

"This one is newer than the first house, only five years old. Lots of top-of-the-line features in this one. Shall we go in?" Nick encouraged them out of the warm SUV, into the afternoon chill, and up the walk.

"Here we are. Quite the impressive entry, don't you think?" Nick's exuberance amazed Leigh. She wondered how he generated so much enthusiasm over a house. He continued citing the selling points as she and Garrett wandered through the first level.

"Quite a fancy kitchen." Garrett took in the granite countertops, cherry cupboards, the spaciousness, and natural lighting.

"The appliances are high-end." Leigh's eyes had gotten huge.

"Don't drool," Garrett joked and laughed out loud when she glared at him.

"Upstairs are four bedrooms and two baths. Ready for a look?" Nick herded them along.

"All the money went into the kitchen," Garrett whispered while they wandered through the master bath.

"I agree. I expected an extravagant master bedroom and bath. The second bathroom at the cabin is fancier than this one." She paused before moving on, considering how their thoughts mirrored each other.

Garrett remembered their time together in a steamy shower at her family's cabin. He stood behind her. "This shower is too small for much fun. We need one like the one in the cabin with all the same features."

His throaty whisper and the brush of his lips against her ear surprised and delighted her. Her eyes closed; she got lost in the whirl of emotions he spun up within her. When she turned, he no longer stood near her.

Stopping at the doorway, he looked back, so he didn't miss the deep-pink blush on her cheeks. Oh, yeah, she remembered.

Nick interrupted their memories when he stepped in and announced, "With four bedrooms, one is easily adapted for your studio, Leigh, another as an office, and the last as a spare room for guests." He herded them along, nearing the end of their walk through of the house. "Out this window, you can visualize the size of the lot with plenty of room for a shed or even a separate photography studio."

After viewing the backyard, they returned to the first floor.

The long shadows prompted Garrett's check of his watch.

"We should call it a day, Nick. We have a few things to work out before I leave."

"I'll get you back to my office in twenty minutes." He ushered them out of the house, and soon they were speeding along their way. They discussed the pros and cons of the houses, so Nick gained a better understanding of what they desired in a house.

"Here we are," said Nick as he pulled into the parking lot. "I'll gather the information on builders for you, give me a minute."

Leigh slid out of the back seat, slammed the door, and walked with Nick around the SUV. "Can I have one of your cards?"

"Sure, here you are."

Because she paid more attention on entering Nick's number in her phone than where she walked, she bumped into Garrett's back.

"Whoops! Sorry."

"Not a problem, Leigh, no harm done." A broad smile broke across his face. He stepped aside, and she entered Nick's office.

She felt the warmth of a blush on her cheeks. Gracious! Would she ever stop responding to his smile? She hoped not.

"Here's information on builders." Nick handed Leigh a folder. "We can visit their sites later this week if you have time."

"I have nothing but time. How's tomorrow?"

"I'm busy tomorrow, but Thursday's clear. How's nine o'clock?"

"Thursday at nine works. Thanks." She shook hands with him and turned toward the door.

"Thanks, Nick. We appreciate your time and effort." Garrett shook his hand.

"My pleasure. While you're gone, Leigh and I will find the right house for you guys."

As they exited the building, Garrett reached for Leigh's hand.

"I thought we might enjoy an early supper; what do you say?"

"I say yes to a last meal together before you leave; we should have plenty of time for one." Leigh leaned into him, raised her face, and received the reward of a soft kiss. "Let's move, I'm cold out here."

He let out a short bark of laughter. "Alright, we're out of here!"

They drove off in his Jeep in search of a restaurant. In a matter of minutes, they sat beside each other at a high-top table.

"So…" Leigh couldn't continue. She wished for an ability to express the thoughts and feelings bombarding her, but words failed her. How to describe her loss from not having him near, her misery at being alone again, and her fear for his safety escaped her.

"So," Garrett repeated. He smiled his half-smile and held her hand. "There's no need for you to remain here all by yourself. Why not consider a visit with your family or your friend until I'm done?"

"No! I won't leave; how would you know where I was if I left? Besides, we created a long list of things I can do here."

He looked at her; he realized she wore a brave face for him and loved her for it. His eyes gazed into hers for a few moments before he responded.

"If you need anything, call SAIC Henderson. I can give you his number."

"Don't need his. I'll be more comfortable calling Janet if I need anything." She looked down at their hands, still clasped together. "I miss you already."

"I miss you, too. I'm sorry we ran out of time for a stop at the hotel." His eyebrows raised, his voice lowered, and he brushed her hand with his lips.

His words and the desire reflected in his eyes generated a flash of heat through her body. "We have many days and nights ahead of us. In fact, the first thing we'll do when you're back is—"

A waiter stopped at their table, interrupting her promises of future activities after this assignment. They each ordered a light supper.

"You were saying?" Garrett's interest in her plans sparkled in his eyes.

She leaned in close and whispered in his ear. "The first thing we'll do when you're back is make love like bunnies."

He laughed and gazed into her eyes. "Like bunnies?"

"Yeah, they must do it all the time; how else are there so many of them? We may not be seen for days." Her voice added a dramatic tone.

"Days?"

"Maybe weeks."

He had no clue how she maintained such a serious

look without cracking a smile. He couldn't stop smiling at her; he shook his head in disbelief.

"Days, maybe weeks, it is." He leaned over and kissed her. "Our kiss seals the deal."

Now she smiled back at him. He thought of how gorgeous she was. How lucky could he be? Damn lucky, obviously.

Their meals arrived, and they ate as they discussed what she planned to work on without him.

"If I have time, I'll check on those furnished apartments Nick told us about. It'd be less expensive than the hotel, and the idea of gaining space is appealing."

"Sounds like a good plan. Will you visit the builders tomorrow?"

"I believe so. What are your thoughts on a log home?"

"In the right location, they're impressive. Do you pine for one?" He smiled and raised his eyebrows at his play on words.

"'Pine for one'—you're so funny, a regular comedian. They intrigue me. I agree with you; they need the right setting. I'll talk with Nick; perhaps he can find properties for sale to show me."

"I'm sorry you're doing this by yourself." He pushed his plate aside. Snatching a French fry from her dwindling pile, he dragged it through her ketchup and popped it in his mouth.

"Hey!" She smacked his hand playfully but wiped a smear of ketchup from his lip with her napkin. "You should ask first. Practicing your table manners can be a personal task while you're away."

"I'll work on them, promise. It's almost six, we should head out." Garrett signaled for their bill and left cash on the table.

They bundled up again and left the restaurant.

"Come here, Leigh." His voice broke as he reached

for her.

He wrapped an arm around her and tugged her against his side as they walked toward his Jeep. She snuggled close beside him. They didn't talk but enjoyed their bodies rubbing against each other. He settled her into the passenger seat and kissed her. She moaned and wrapped her arms around his neck. Her lips parted and his tongue plunged into her mouth's moist warmth. His hand ran along the back of her neck and into her hair.

In slow motion, he pulled back. "Gotta get going."

"I know." She leaned against the seat back, closed her eyes, and released a long sigh. The door shut, and Garrett walked around the vehicle. "I'll miss you so much," Leigh whispered as she fought back tears.

"Drive the Jeep while I'm gone. I'll be more comfortable with you in a four-wheel drive vehicle; a lot of snow could still fall." He glanced at her as he drove. Now he understood what married Air Force Office of Special Investigations agents went through when they were on an undercover assignment or deployment.

The clock read 6:15 p.m. when they pulled into the parking lot of the BCA offices. Lights shone from SAIC Henderson's office. This would be the first real challenge of their fledgling relationship. Garrett didn't count meeting Leigh's parents, although her mother presented a challenge of sorts. But this tested their commitment to each other.

Garrett turned in the seat, so he faced her. A lump in his throat made saying the many things he longed to tell her difficult. "Leigh." The rough edge of his voice said more than any words he might utter.

She leaned into him; his arms wrapped around her. He held her tight, committing this moment to memory.

"They're waiting for you inside." She spoke into his chest.

"Yeah." He sighed out the word. His arms left her. He exited the Jeep and grabbed his duffle bag from the back seat. After he shut the door, he turned and found Leigh standing near him by the driver's door.

The bag dropped to the ground, and he gathered her in his arms. "I love you." He kissed her with an urgent passion. "You be careful and remember if you need anything—"

"I'll call Janet," she interrupted him. Her tears flowed, and her voice cracked. "I love you; don't you ever forget. Promise me you'll be careful; I insist you come back safe and sound."

"I promise to be careful." He held her close. "You should leave." He waited until she climbed behind the wheel. "I should have let you drive before, so you'd be familiar with the Jeep."

"I'll be fine. You concentrate on doing whatever it is you'll be doing and be careful. I love you." Her tears continued falling; she wiped them away with her hands.

"I love you, Leigh."

She received a single kiss on her cheek before he closed the door. Through bleary eyes, her gaze followed him as he strode toward the building. With his back straight and his strides long, he disappeared through the doors.

She sat alone in the Jeep, staring at the spot where he disappeared inside.

"Woman up, Ramsey. You've done plenty on your own before, so you can do this."

She wiped away the last of her tears and put the Jeep in gear. Once she reached the hotel, a long cry may ease the pain of their goodbye.

Garrett studied her from inside the building. He fought the urge to join her as she wiped tears from her cheeks. Disastrous idea, he told himself. It'd only delay their goodbye. Instead, he registered the sight of her talking to herself before driving away. With his duffle bag slung over a shoulder, he walked to Henderson's office. He said a short prayer for Leigh and himself as he approached the closed door. He needed to believe Leigh would be fine, so thoughts of her wouldn't distract him from his mission. Distractions were dangerous.

His knock on the door brought an answering shout. "Garrett, come on in and meet your partner for this adventure." He squared his shoulders and tucked memories of Leigh within his heart. The memories needed to remain locked away until this mission concluded, and he returned to her. He stepped into the office and shut the door behind him.

CHAPTER SEVEN

Joe sat behind his desk. "Karl, this is my newest agent, Garrett Dane. Garrett, we're working with the Drug Enforcement Administration, fondly known as the DEA, and this is their agent, Karl Frank, your partner on this assignment."

Each man sized up the other with one look and a shake of hands.

"I'm glad you're here. Joe told me your background and said he filled you in on the operation." Karl rested a hip on Joe's desk, looking as relaxed as Garrett wished he felt.

"Pleasure meeting you, sir. I understand what's required from me."

"Don't 'sir' me. Call me Karl. Do you have everything you need?"

"I do," Garrett responded before remembering the one item he needed. "Except for a bulletproof vest."

"I can give you one." Joe grabbed keys off his desk. "I'll be right back." He walked out and down the hall.

Karl broke the ice first. "Joe tells me you just got engaged. Congratulations."

"Yes, sir…ah…sorry. We're planning our wedding for the end of April." Garrett tried forcing an image of Leigh from his mind without success. "Are you married?"

"Divorced. This life isn't the easiest on a family, although my choice in wife material was questionable. My ex-wife was a demanding self-absorbed woman." Shaking his head, Karl scowled at Garrett. "Communication is key and never letting your wife take you for granted."

"I understand." Garrett shuffled his feet, anxious to begin.

The jingle of keys sounded outside the door. "Here ya go." Joe tossed him a Kevlar vest marked 'BCA.'

Garrett stuffed it in his duffle bag. "Now, I need you guys out of here, so I can head home and be with my family. Can't miss pot roast night." As Karl led Garrett toward the stairs, he called out, "Don't forget, I need him back safe and sound. You hear me?"

Karl waved a hand in reply.

"This way. I came in through the back entrance; the lighting is lower, and the lot isn't visible from the street." He lumbered down the staircase. Garrett stayed right behind him. "Did you eat dinner?"

"Yes, I did."

"We'll stop at the grocery store and restock a few things. You can purchase any food items you deem necessary." Karl indicated a nondescript sedan as his vehicle.

After tossing his duffle bag in the back seat, Garrett eyed his partner and asked, "Got peanut butter?"

Karl let out a laugh in reply. "Of course but maybe we should buy another jar."

"Make it a big one." Garrett smiled as he slid into the car.

After a short stop at a grocery store and a lengthy drive, Karl parked outside an old two-story farmhouse. From what Garrett distinguished in the moonlight, no hiding places existed near the house, so someone chose a good location for defensive purposes. The building itself looked as rundown as the car he rode in.

"Can you grab the last bag?" Karl hefted three grocery bags, and the keys jangled in his hand as he sought the house key.

"Sure," Garrett agreed and snatched up the last bag along with his duffle. He followed Karl into the house and squinted against the bright fluorescent light in the kitchen.

"Stow your things upstairs, first room on the right. We'll review my plans tonight and the role you'll be filling."

"Sure thing." Garrett climbed the stairs two at a time, entered his room, and dropped his bag on the floor with a dry laugh. "Déjà vu."

The sparsely furnished room reminded him of his first apartment; what a hellhole it had been. This room contained a mattress on the floor, a single wooden chair, and a worn chest of drawers. Threadbare curtains hung on the windows and rustled with every gust of wind outside. He peered in the closet and found a few wire hangers and plenty of cobwebs. With one last look at his home away from home, he strode out of the room and down the stairs.

In the kitchen, he found Karl unpacking groceries.

"I'll do the unpacking, so you can eat your dinner before it gets cold," Garrett offered and dug into the last two bags.

"Thanks, man. It does taste best while hot." Karl cut the roasted chicken in two and filled a plate. In seconds, he sat at the old wooden kitchen table and devoured his food. "When you're done, grab a plate. There's plenty of chicken and potato salad left. The store's deli is pretty darn impressive."

Garrett emptied the last bag and joined Karl at the table. "Thanks, but I'm not hungry. So, DEA?"

"Yeah, I signed up after college." Karl tossed a cleaned bone in the empty chicken carton. "You were in the Air Force?"

"Joined after high school. Spent four years in Security Forces and the last six years with the Office of Special Investigations."

"Why the Minnesota BCA?"

"Minnesota's home. I wanted to stay in law enforcement, and the BCA had a vacancy. I'm lucky they hired me."

"The way I understand the circumstances, you were the highest-qualified applicant. Not many of your competitors held a master's degree in criminal science, and your investigative experience made you the obvious choice."

"Thanks for sharing; I appreciate learning the reasons behind my selection." Karl's words humbled him. "So, what's the plan?"

In between bites of his dinner, Karl briefed Garrett on his current efforts to contact the owners of a local meth lab. The DEA suspected the organization supplied most dealers in northwestern Minnesota and eastern North Dakota. He hoped a meeting could be arranged soon. Garrett would act as his personal security guard and head of security for their organization.

"You should act all no-nonsense and scary, understand?" Karl licked his fingers after the leg bone joined the other cleaned bones.

"Easy enough." Garrett smiled at his partner. "When do you expect this meeting will happen?"

"I'm waiting on a call or a text. I hoped for this week, but now I'm thinking it'll be later." Karl stared out at the darkness of the evening and frowned. "My contact is a bit flaky, so I hope the delay is his screw up and not my cover being blown. I'm beat. We'll talk again tomorrow. Good night."

"Night." Garrett watched Karl trudge down the hallway toward the stairs. He thought the man looked tired and worn out. The downcast expression on Karl's face before going upstairs concerned him. In the morning, his first question would be what happened to the person he replaced. The second question was how long this operation had been running.

He locked up the house before climbing the stairs. On his way to the bathroom, a loud snore erupted from one of the bedrooms. Grateful for separate rooms, he closed the door.

After brushing the closet clear of cobwebs, he hung up a few shirts and placed the rest of his things in the dresser. Once changed into flannel pajama pants and a thermal top, he sat on the sole chair loading bullets into a spare magazine. With such an automatic task, his mind wandered and conjured up images of Leigh. He pictured her in their hotel room, lying in bed, watching TV, and eating his snickerdoodles. Damn! He should have packed them; his stomach growled in agreement.

He stretched out under cold sheets and light blankets. How he missed Leigh's warmth and company. He tried not thinking of her, yet her image appeared whenever his eyes closed. This would be a long night.

CHAPTER EIGHT

Once the door to their hotel room closed, Leigh threw herself on a bed. Her tears flowed and heart-wrenching sobs tore from deep within her chest. She hugged a pillow in place of Garrett and rocked herself. The ring of her phone halted her cries, but her tears continued falling. She looked at the display on her phone: *Mom. Wonderful.*

"Hi. What's up?"

"Leigh, you never called us back," her mom whined. "We were waiting to learn which hotel you're staying in. How is everything?"

"Sorry, we've been busy. We're at the Country Inn and Suites in Baxter. The countryside is magnificent up here, so I'm sure I'll produce some spectacular photographs."

"How wonderful for you. Is he there?"

"Did you just ask to talk with Garrett?"

"No, no, no. I simply wondered if you were alone yet. He's still leaving, right?"

"Yes, he left tonight." Leigh worked on steadying her voice; no way would she cry on the phone with her mother.

"You're holding up well. I expected tears if he's as important in your life as you've led us to believe."

Her mom's insinuation grated on her already stretched thin nerves. "He's my world, Mom. Did you want anything else?"

"We should schedule a time when we can discuss wedding plans."

"Garrett and I arranged a few things before he left, and I plan to work on others while he's away. How's next week for discussing invitations and my dress."

"I'll set aside time on my calendar. By the way, I worked with a superb printer on a club event. Their pricing is very reasonable."

Her mom kept talking; she loved this sort of thing. Leigh's challenge would be reining her in; otherwise, their wedding would become the wedding of the century with hundreds in attendance instead of the small wedding they wanted.

"Please don't do anything until we talk. Do you understand?" She broke into her mom's elaborating over colors, types of print, and varieties of paper stock.

"Why, of course, Leigh. One of my card club ladies mentioned a wonderful bridal shop. Supposedly, they have the newest styles. I picture you in a mermaid-style dress. They are sleek, one of the most popular styles, and should flatter your figure. We'll have so much fun shopping for your dress."

"To tell you the truth, I'm interested in a vintage dress and found a shop selling them in St. Paul." Leigh imagined her mom wrinkling her nose and shaking her head. "Do you suppose some of your friends might be aware of stores specializing in vintage dresses?"

"If you insist, I can check with them. When will you come home, so we can begin shopping? Soon, I hope."

"I'm not sure when I can drive down; I prefer staying nearby in case something happens with Garrett. Besides, I'm busy house hunting, and I might find us a furnished apartment. I'd rather not stay in a hotel while we wait on a house."

"How soon would you move into an apartment?"

"I'm not sure; our realtor only mentioned the possibility today when we discussed building a house."

Her mother gasped. "Building a house? Can you afford such an extravagant expense?"

"Yes, Garrett's already approved for a sizable loan."

"He is?"

Leigh laughed at her mom's incredulity over Garrett being approved for a home loan; her mom would faint over the dollar amount. "Yes, and he was working with a realtor before I met him."

"How expedient of him. I should go. I'll talk with you next week; will Monday work for you?"

"Sure. How's nine o'clock?"

"Works for me. Bye now."

"Bye." Leigh's voice broke, but her mom hadn't heard. She set her phone on the nightstand and stretched out on the bed. Her thoughts settled on Garrett. Where could he be? Could he trust his partner to have his back? Would he return safe and sound? She said a prayer for his safety and for her patience. Time to crawl into bed and cry herself to sleep. Tomorrow was soon enough to overcome her loneliness and fear.

CHAPTER NINE

Lois hung up the phone after talking with her daughter. Leigh still thought she found the love of her life in that disappointing young man. Such a foolish girl! Four years ago, she broke up with impeccable husband material, David Walker. *I can fix this*, she thought as she called her best friend.

"Claire! It's Lois."

"How marvelous hearing from you. How have you and Frank been?"

"We're good. Yesterday, we returned from a visit with Leigh."

"Oh, did you drive to Chicago?"

"She's no longer living in Chicago. We visited with her at our cabin, and David's name came up." She wouldn't share with Claire the negative context of the conversation. "How is he? Is he dating anyone?" Lois asked as though it was nothing other than a passing thought.

"He works long hours and hasn't had a steady girlfriend since he and Leigh broke up. With her back here, perhaps they'll reunite." Claire's voice vibrated with excitement. "How do we facilitate their becoming a couple again? Their breakup devastated us."

"The same for us." Lois exaggerated a bit because Frank had been pleased rather than dismayed. "We'd love for them to date again, but there's a minor problem."

"What kind of problem?"

"Well, she believes she's fallen in love with a young man she met at the cabin. Even though they've only known each other for a few days, they're engaged and plan to marry in less than a year. Did you hear me? After only a few days! You can imagine our surprise. They're staying together in the Brainerd area."

"You poor thing! What can I do to help?"

A smile broke across Lois's face. She needed Claire's assistance if her scheme for ending Leigh's engagement had a chance of success.

"The young man is gone for his work, so she's alone and vulnerable in an unfamiliar place. If David accidentally ran into her and spent time with her, he should win back her affections. I'm certain he only needs time with Leigh without anyone in his way. We agree they're made for one another. Once we put them together, they'll fall into each other's arms. Can you convince him spending a few days in the Brainerd area will be worth his time?"

"I'm sure I can. He's missed Leigh. We can invent some medical purpose for his appearance, so Leigh won't be suspicious of his being there. Once he arrives, David can pick up where he left off." Claire's voice trembled with anticipation. "Where's she staying?"

"At the Country Inn and Suites in Baxter. If he stays in the same hotel, he'll easily run into her."

"I'll talk with him tonight and call you in the morning with his decision. I believe this can work."

"It has to work." Lois smiled and looked at pictures of Leigh displayed on a shelf in the living room. "You and I will ensure our children are back together as they should be. I look forward to your call. Bye."

Her daughter would marry Claire's son, a wealthy doctor. After which, she'd be cared for properly and live in the stimulating urban environment of the Twin Cities. She would never allow Leigh to be stuck in rural Minnesota and married to a state employee. Never!

Frank came around the corner. "Were you talking with Claire Walker? We haven't seen them in ages. Are you planning an evening out?"

"We're in early discussions and will talk again tomorrow."

"I'm free any night this week. It'll be enjoyable

visiting with her and Don again."

"Yes, it will. Perhaps David will join us."

"David? Why would we want him tagging along?" Frank sat in his chair and grabbed a newspaper.

"Because he's a fine young man, and he's pleasant company." At Frank's snort of disgust, Lois huffed out of the room and headed for the kitchen, her sanctuary. Here she would plot and plan her crusade for ridding Leigh of her unacceptable fiancé.

CHAPTER TEN

Not quite awake, Leigh reached for Garrett, but cold sheets and emptiness met her reach. A sigh escaped her lips.

"Garrett, I hope you're safe today. I'll stay busy securing our future." She stretched and walked into the bathroom, preparing for her first day of being on her own since meeting him.

Dressed and ready for breakfast, Leigh ran down the stairs. The delicious aroma of Belgian waffles greeted her.

"Eat your heart out, Garrett; I'm having a waffle again today." With her spirits soaring, she hurried into the breakfast area. She greeted familiar guests and employees while she waited on her waffle.

"Excuse me. May I join you?" An elderly lady stood by Leigh's table for two. "We met yesterday, and you made me one of those delicious waffles."

"I remember and would appreciate your company." Leigh's smile brightened her face.

"Your strapping young man is missing this morning, so I hoped you wouldn't mind." Placing her tray on the table, the lady lowered herself in the chair across from Leigh.

"Your company is welcome." Leigh choked on her words; she blinked back tears threatening to fall down her cheeks. "He's gone for his work; I'm not sure how long he'll be away."

"So, you're here by yourself; you poor dear."

After a couple bites of waffle and sips of coffee, Leigh trusted her voice wouldn't contain the sadness within her at Garrett's absence. "I'm staying busy by planning our wedding."

"What a joyous chore for you, at least I would

assume it is."

"Yes, it is."

"May I see your ring?"

"Of course." Leigh extended her left hand across the table.

"My, how exquisite! The diamond is so clear and sparkles as if a fire glows inside it."

"Your description is lovely."

They sat in companionable silence as they ate. The weather forecast caught their attention.

"Such warm temperatures for February," Leigh remarked.

"Thank the groundhog. He didn't see his shadow this year, so we can expect an early spring."

"That's good news. An early spring works perfectly for our late April wedding."

"What a lovely time for a wedding. Nature is budding with new life, and you'll begin a new life together."

"You're right, spring's rebirth of nature adds a special meaning for our wedding, and we lucked into the timing."

"Ah, but everything happens for a reason."

"My fiancé says the same thing."

"He's a wise man. Well, I should return to our room; we leave today. Best of luck with your wedding plans."

"Thank you." Amazed at how an unexpected meeting with a stranger provided her a new perspective on their chosen wedding date, her spirits lightened. Instead of a miserable day of missing Garrett, she now foresaw an unparalleled day of happiness ahead. With a light step, she made her way down the hall.

After plotting out her day of visiting the log home builders, her thoughts flew to Garrett. What would he be doing this morning? Where did he stay? She missed sharing the morning with him. Then an idea struck. She should keep a journal and record each day's events and her thoughts whenever he traveled for work. The idea of keeping a journal excited her. With her list of builders tucked into a folder for safekeeping, she grabbed her purse and headed out for the Jeep.

Letting the vehicle warm up in the frigid morning, Garrett's scent wrapped about her and filled her mind with memories of him. *Please be careful, Garrett. I need you back with me.*

***

Garrett thought of Leigh from the moment he woke up. He stared at his reflection in the bathroom mirror; sleep-tousled hair and dark circles under his eyes spoke of a restless night. He tossed and turned all evening long, often waking with a start when his reach for Leigh met only cold sheets.

Aw, darlin', I hope you're doing well. Please realize how badly I miss you. I meant to keep you tucked away, but you refused to stay there. Your memory, your scent, your everything is a part of me now. Memories of you take hold of me when I least expect them, and I'm unable to fend them off. Could you at least let me get some sleep? He groaned his frustration and stripped for a shower.

As he descended the stairs, he found the first floor of the house cloaked in darkness. With a flip of a switch, the fluorescent bulb in the kitchen fixture surrounded him in harsh-cold artificial light. Tracking down the coffeemaker, he got coffee brewing.

"Where did I stash the peanut butter…aha!" After making toast, he sat at the table in the drab kitchen enjoying peanut butter toast with a mug of coffee.

"Did you make coffee yet?" Karl's question echoed throughout the near-empty house.

"Got a full pot," Garrett called back in response.

Shaking his head, he muttered, "Damn, exactly the same as my first apartment." He yelled out, "I'll pour you a mug."

A sudden rumble sounded like Karl fell down the stairs. He stumbled into the kitchen with an atrocious case of bed head and sweatpants riding low on his hips.

"Bless you; I can't do anything before my morning caffeine." He sat in the chair nearest the mug of coffee Garrett had poured for him. Sheer ecstasy showed on his face as he took his first sip. "Ah, this is perfection. Thanks."

Garrett acknowledged Karl's appreciation with a nod of his head as he drank his own coffee. "What happened with your last partner? Joe didn't say why he or she left."

Karl looked Garrett in the eyes as he responded, "Rest assured I didn't cause him any harm. George's family needed him home for a medical emergency; his wife's having problems with her pregnancy. With you arriving at the local BCA office, we decided we could let him be with her and bring you on board. Joe didn't provide an update for me on how she's doing when I picked you up. I'm worried about them. His absence may not register with the guy I've been working with. Should the guys with the meth lab question the sudden change, I'll satisfy their curiosity."

"Yeah, just wondering." Garrett paused before he asked his other question. "Why would the meeting be delayed?"

A sigh. "The last time I talked with James, my contact, he acted nervous over scheduling a meeting. As I said last night, he's kind of flaky. In my opinion, he uses too much of their product for his own good. He may have forgotten I asked for one, or they're being extra cautious. Our cover story is solid, so it shouldn't be causing any problems."

"Would any other law enforcement office be sniffing around and making them skittish?"

Karl's coffee mug landed with a loud thud on the table. "They'd be spooked if anything out of the ordinary began happening near them, but I doubt if anything did. Joe monitors police action nearby as does the task force, so they can head off any outside interest without jeopardizing our operation. He didn't mention anything last night."

"How long have you been working this?"

"Overall, nine months. The operation followed the usual process; I worked the dealers and tracked down their source. After we firmed up our cover with a few small buys, I built up the amount with each consecutive buy. This group has a sizable meth production, but we believe they're all locals without outside connections. I am so ready for the end of this operation."

"I'll admit I prefer ending this sooner rather than later. While I'm off doing this, my fiancée's working on our wedding plans and conducting our house hunting without my help. I'm unable to hold up my share of the bargain because I can't be with her. She understands, but we should accomplish those things together."

"I wouldn't sweat it. Weddings are all about the bride, so she'll have an easier time planning her dream wedding with you out of the way." He laughed. "I can tell by your glare you don't believe me. All women developed the wedding of their dreams long before they said yes to a proposal. Trust me, you're doing her a favor by not being around to interfere."

Garrett decided against pointing out how Karl's marital status made his advice suspect at best. "Alright, I can agree with what you're saying about weddings, but she's handling all the house hunting, too."

"Same concept holds true. She won't be compromising with you on anything like the size of her closet. Oh yeah, don't ever consider it as 'our' closet. Shoot! If you're lucky, she'll give you a little closet space in a bedroom at the end of the hall. You figure I'm crazy, I don't know her, and she wouldn't do such a selfish thing. Hah! Time will prove me right. You wait and see." Karl embodied the look of an old sage as he held Garrett's eyes.

"I still feel rotten," Garrett muttered.

"Don't you ever say those words around her!" he exploded and shook his head as if Garrett broke a cardinal rule. The vehemence of his reaction surprised Garrett into silence. "A woman will manipulate those feelings against you. Anytime she asks for something you don't agree with, her weapon of choice to use against you will be how she conducted the house hunting all by herself. She'll forever coerce you to her way because of one thing—guilt. Your guilt will be wielded as the reason why she deserves whatever she desires." A finger pointed at Garrett as Karl made his point. "Mark my word!"

"I'll keep your words of wisdom in mind." Garrett crossed the kitchen, grabbed the coffee pot, and warmed the liquid in his mug. "Ready for a refill?"

"Nah, I'm going upstairs for a shower. I'll call James later and find out what's up. Maybe ask to meet with him tonight; he drinks Jack and Coke and doesn't know when to stop." Karl winked at Garrett. "An exploitable weakness. A meeting will be my opportunity for introducing you. I'd rather not spring you on him the day we meet the guy in charge." The scrape of chair legs against the dingy vinyl floor announced Karl's departure.

Garrett sipped coffee and bit into his toast. Relief flooded his senses as Karl headed upstairs; he sat back with a sigh. The man held curious views on women and marriage, all quite jaded by his divorce. He mentally vowed to never again discuss marriage with his partner.

While he washed up the few dishes from breakfast, a memory of doing dishes with Leigh came to mind. The strength of the memory surprised him, so again his thoughts focused on her. Today, she planned to visit the log home builders, but after today her plans were a question mark. He wondered if she'd stay in Baxter or leave to visit with her friend or her parents. He hated the emptiness in his heart at the thought of her not being nearby. Obviously, this assignment presented him one of his most difficult challenges.

CHAPTER ELEVEN

Lois paced in her kitchen.

"What's got you all riled up this morning?" Frank's cheery voice crossed the kitchen as he walked in for a second cup of coffee.

"I'm waiting on Claire's call." She stopped pacing and forced a smile.

"Did you ever talk with Leigh since they reached Brainerd?" The muffin he munched muffled his question.

"Use a napkin, Frank. Yes, I spoke with her last night."

"How're they doing?"

"They aren't doing anything. He's gone already, so she's all alone and forced to do everything by herself: wedding planning and house hunting." Dismay dripped from her words.

"We knew Garrett's job would take him away occasionally. Leigh seemed okay with it." Frank snatched another muffin and left for his den. "A mighty fine muffin, Lois, thanks."

"You're welcome; I'm glad you're eating them." The housephone rang, so she called out, "I'll get it; it's probably Claire." She reached for the receiver. "Hello?"

"Good news, Lois! David agreed this is a marvelous idea. In fact, he's so excited he's taking Friday off. He leaves Thursday after work for Baxter. I made him a room reservation at the same hotel where Leigh's staying. He can stay through the weekend. Being near Leigh again has him anxious, but he's certain they can pick up where they left off!"

"Excellent! Thanks, Claire. I'm sure he'll charm her back into his arms. Why don't you and Don join us for dinner on Friday?"

"Wonderful, Friday works for us."

"Alright. Come over around five-thirty. Let's not mention anything regarding our plan for David and Leigh's reunion; we should wait on their announcement."

"Certainly, mum's the word."

"Thanks again for making this happen. I should let you go; see you Friday. Bye."

"If I hear anything from David once he's there, I'll phone you. Bye now."

As Lois hung up the phone, a thin smile cut across her face. Her scheme began sooner than she thought possible. With any luck, Leigh would dump her fiancé this weekend. Upon his return, all he'd find would be his pitiful ring and a goodbye note. By Sunday Leigh would be back where she belonged with David. Ah, the future looked brighter already.

CHAPTER TWELVE

Sitting alone in the same bar where Garrett and she had last eaten together brought bittersweet ramifications for Leigh. She missed being near him, so she hoped dinner here might recapture her feelings from their last meal. It didn't.

She opened her new journal, pulled a pen from her purse, drank some of her Gin Buck, and began writing.

Wednesday, February 12th. My dearest Garrett, I have never kept a diary or journal, but I plan on recording everything I do whenever you're away from me. This morning I missed you so much. Since I promised I could do this, today I visited all the log cabin builders on Nick's list. Most were a bust, but one—OMG—their homes are so impressive! It's not only the homes though. It's the people working there; they were so down-to-earth and knowledgeable. I realize it sounds silly, but I could tell they were family...a loving family, unlike Mom and you. (Joking!)

They have property out toward Nisswa, so Nick and I are checking out their lots tomorrow. I believe this is what we should do. All the options have me excited but also concerned over how I'll ever select from them all and the many floor plans available. Our house—NO! Our <u>home</u> will be gorgeous, functional, and meet all our needs. Oh, you'll fall in love with the master suite options, and the bathroom can be all we want it to be if you catch my gist (hint, hint)!

I talked with Mom last night and scheduled time with her next week for discussing invitations and maybe my dress. I haven't decided how much assistance to accept from her. During that call, I'll break the news regarding the date we've decided on and how we scheduled it at the

Aspen Inn. I'm sure you wish me well with the discussion. I also recognize you'll be pleased with not participating in the call; you are such a lucky duck.

Speaking of the Aspen Inn, I called Edna this afternoon. Gosh, she is one in a million! I told her about our decision on tulips; she thought it would look heavenly. Of all the colors of linens she has, we decided on peach for the tables. It would be appropriate for Deb's dress; she loves the color. Edna will email me some suggestions for wedding music, too!

I'll call Deb tonight after supper. I returned to the bar we ate at last night and am drinking a Gin Buck. Yeah, I remembered, and the flavor is delicious! Of course sitting alone is not the same as being here with you. Until tomorrow. Love you. Leigh ♥ ♥

With her meal over and leftovers in a box, Leigh drove to the hotel. After a stop in the lobby for a cup of coffee, she entered their room and broke into the snickerdoodles. A smile crossed her lips as she bit into one. *I wonder when Garrett realized he forgot his treasured snickerdoodles. Ha! He was so ate up over these cookies.* She laughed out loud at her play on words. Intent on recording her thoughts, she opened her journal.

P.S. I'm back in our room, enjoying coffee and your snickerdoodles! Thanks for leaving them/forgetting them. Yummy!!

She glanced at the clock; time for calling her best friend, Deb. Leigh stopped her musing over Garrett and dialed her friend, who picked up on the second ring.

"Leigh! How are you? Where are you?"

"Hey, Deb. I'm in Baxter, staying busy and missing Garrett." Her voice cracked, and she found herself blinking back tears.

"Oh, Leigh. You sound so lonely, what can I do?"

"Can you come join me for the weekend?"

"Weather permitting, I'm there!" Deb's enthusiasm

buoyed Leigh's spirits.

"Super! We're in the Country Inn and Suites, and you can stay with me in our room. What should we discuss first? Wedding plans or house hunting?"

"I'd rather you tell me all about Garrett, but I'm sure your story is best told in person. Swear you'll tell me everything this weekend."

"I swear. So, for our wedding you'll need a peach dress."

"I love the color peach! Are there stores in the area where we can shop for bridesmaid's dresses?"

"I remembered your love of the color. How could I forget? You wore it every day our last year in college. I made a list of the bridal shops in the area. This weekend will be so much fun!"

"What about your dress?"

"I'm leaning toward a vintage dress if I can find one. I told Mom my preference yesterday."

"How'd that go over?"

"Well, she thought I should wear something called a mermaid dress. I asked her to check with her lady friends for a place selling vintage wedding dresses. She prefers to work through her friends and connections, so hopefully they'll identify some shops in the Cities."

"What will Garrett wear?"

"We decided on a black cutaway tuxedo, and he'll look rather dashing in one." Her voice softened and a sigh ended her sentence.

"Earth to Leigh!" Deb's laughter flowed out of the phone. "I sure hope you took plenty of pictures, so I can judge for myself how gorgeous he is."

Shock hit Leigh. "Would you believe I didn't take any since we met? Wow! I'm correcting my lapse as soon as he's back."

"How hilarious, and you call yourself a photographer! Were you too busy doing other things?" The inflection of Deb's voice made it clear what things she imagined kept Leigh from taking pictures of Garrett.

"We were busy with other things a lot of the time, but the thought of pulling out my camera for pictures never occurred to me. My gosh, we discussed photography, lots of times. What if something bad happens, and he doesn't come back to me? Without pictures, my memory of him will disappear over time." Tears formed in her eyes, and her voice broke with volatile emotions ready to burst loose.

Deb recognized the impending crisis in Leigh's voice and tried heading it off.

"He'll be fine. Don't fixate on such a terrible thing. You'll take so many pictures of the two of you within days of his return, your worry about this slight oversight will prove to be ridiculous."

Deb's message came through and calmed her.

"Thanks, you're right; he'll be fine. So, when can you come for a visit? Friday or Saturday?"

"I'll wait for Saturday morning—safer driving with all the critters." Her excitement bubbled over.

"Another thing we can do is walk through the model homes of the builder I chose to build our house!" Leigh's delight in her friend's visit sounded in her voice.

"You plan to build a house?"

"Not just a house, a log house. They're exquisite. Wait until you see the available floor plans; your input on them will be helpful." The thought of reviewing the many choices with a friend brought her massive relief. "Tomorrow our realtor and I are looking at land for the house."

"Sounds as though we'll have a fun and busy weekend!" Deb's smile sounded in her tone. "I should go. Expect me late Saturday morning."

"Great! Bye, Deb, and thanks."

"This is what friends do for each other. Bye!"

Ending her call, Leigh reached for another cookie.

Too early for bed, so wedding planning called to her. She grabbed her notebook and an extra cookie before researching the dress shops again and the local United Church of Christ.

After she finished her research, she pulled out her journal.

P.P.S. Had a fun call with Deb tonight. She'll come for a visit this weekend, so I'll have a host of tales I can write about. Disconcerting observation tonight: I don't have any pictures of you! I'll immediately correct the oversight when you're back. I'm photographing you every day so be prepared! Oh, I have information on the local church and will visit the minister this week. I plan to talk Deb into attending church with me on Sunday before she leaves. Time for bed. I love you! Leigh ♥♥

CHAPTER THIRTEEN

Garrett and Karl entered the dark bar in search of James, their contact for the meth group. A few folks eyed them as they weaved between tables until they reached the bar; others dismissed them at once and turned back to their drinks.

"Two Goldens," Karl ordered from the bartender. Grasping the cold bottles, he pointed Garrett toward a table in the back.

"Is he here?" Garrett asked as he took a chair.

"Nah, too early for him. He should stumble in within the hour." Karl turned the chair, sat on it backwards, and rested his arms across the back. "Sit back and enjoy your beer."

Garrett sat with his back to a wall. The cold beer hit the spot. "They draw quite the assortment of clientele in here. Suppose others from the group come in?"

"I doubt it. James comes in alone, sits alone, and leaves by himself. No one ever followed him out. My guess is he lives near here, but the so-called business is located somewhere else." Karl drained his beer with one long gulp. "Ready for another one?"

"Almost. I got this round." Garrett strode to the bar, caught the bartender's eye, and got two bottles. As he turned toward Karl, he spied a short man with greasy long hair skulking in the direction of their table. Assuming the man would be James, Garrett slowed his speed and walked up behind the man, who greeted Karl. "Is this guy bothering you, Keith?" Garrett used Karl's cover name and sounded as menacing as possible.

James spun around, fear and surprise reflected in his eyes.

"No, this is the gentleman we've been waiting on; I

hope we can establish a business arrangement with his company. Want your usual, James?" Amusement showed in Karl's eyes; he enjoyed his partner's silent approach and the other man's reaction. After James's shaky nod, he directed Garrett, "A Jack and Coke for our friend."

As he waited for the drink, Garrett assessed the other patrons in search of anyone interested in James and Karl. A man and woman across the room stared at the men with keen interest. The man wore his long hair pulled into a ponytail and wore a suspicious expression. The woman looked bored but alert. When they spoke, their eyes never strayed from James and Karl. His investigative instincts kicked in, so he noted their descriptions and committed their faces to memory. Drink ready, he ferried it back to the table and set the glass in front of James.

"If your organization is interested, I'm ready for a huge purchase. I can find a home for your product—all of it. Before I throw a sizable amount of money your way, I need some introductions." Karl pushed for the meeting they needed for a successful conclusion of their operation.

"Keith, your references checked out, but my boss isn't sold on you and your organization yet." James downed his drink, held up the empty glass, and grinned at Karl. "Could do with a refill."

Karl nodded; Garrett grabbed the empties from the table and returned to the bar. A gaunt woman with long black hair sidled next to him.

"Hi there, haven't seen you before." She looked him up and down, and her tongue ran over her lips.

Garrett's stomach lurched, and he repressed a shudder. "You're right." Ignoring the woman, he ordered the drinks. The bartender must have taken pity on him as the beers and drink appeared quickly. Smiling his thanks, he left the bartender a sizable tip and walked away, leaving a disappointed black-haired woman in his wake.

Karl worked his charms on James over the

following two hours. The Jack and Cokes flowed freely, and James became a jovial drunk much to Garrett's relief.

"So, we return three days from now and meet again. Will any of the others come out?" As they all stood, Karl clapped James on his back and the force made him stumble. "Sorry, you okay?"

"Yeah, I tripped over something." James drew himself upright, his eyes darted from Karl to Garrett and back to Karl. "I'll brief them on what we discussed tonight, and in three days I'll be back here if they're interested. I'd say your offer sounds promising."

"I'll warm up the car." Garrett pulled on his jacket and left.

The cold seeped into his bones as he jogged to their vehicle. While the car warmed up, he watched the bar exits. The man and woman he spotted in the bar earlier, left through a side entrance, entered a pickup, but didn't leave. When James and Karl walked out the bar's front door, instinct told him not to move. James shook his head at something Karl said, probably declined a ride home. They shook hands and walked away. A smile crossed Garrett's face when James climbed into the pickup with the couple, and they drove off. After he picked up Karl, he tailed the truck.

"What's up?" Karl fell against the back of his seat as Garrett sped out of the lot.

"James rode off with a man and woman who were extremely interested in your meeting." Garrett concentrated on his driving, watching the taillights in the distance. "They left the bar after I got in the car, but they didn't leave. After James joined them, they pulled out. Thought we should tail them and find out where they go. Unless you prefer doing something else tonight?"

"This is perfect. How the heck did you spot them?" Karl grabbed a pair of binoculars from the back seat. "Drive closer, so I can read the license plate number.

Impressive work, Garrett!"

Self-satisfaction flared within him as he drove into the night. How he wished he could share this moment with Leigh. Realizing his train of thought would send him spiraling out of control, he clamped down on his thoughts of Leigh and saved them for later when he was alone.

"They're turning, probably James's place. Continue straight, turn the corner, and come back around, so we can sit at the intersection. I noted down the plate number and the address of this place." Karl's enthusiasm reflected the possibility of the man and woman being the key to their operation.

Garrett parked the car, and they waited for the truck to leave. With lights off, their vehicle blended into the evening.

"Tonight's meeting with James struck me as positive." Garrett glanced at his partner.

"Our discussion proved promising. He received my proposals with enthusiasm, so our pressing worked miracles. If this couple runs the organization, perhaps they came round tonight to check me out in person before agreeing to meet." Hopefulness sounded in Karl's voice. "Knock on wood, we'll finish within the week."

Garrett nodded while watching the driveway the truck had disappeared down. As time dragged by, a snore rattled the car's interior, and the suddenness of it startled Garrett.

"No reason for both of us to lose sleep," he muttered after glancing at Karl.

Karl's head lolled to one side, and his hands lay across his chest.

The late-night dip in temperature chilled the car. Garrett started the engine and warmed the interior, removing some of the evening chill. As he turned the key in the ignition, he spotted headlights reflecting off the snow along the driveway.

"Hey, they're moving again." He jostled Karl's shoulder.

"What? Who?" Karl woke with a start, blinking himself awake.

"Let's hope they're headed home." Once the pickup passed through the intersection, Garrett turned on the lights and eased the car on the road. They were headed farther into the country. "Should I tail them all the way? No traffic out this far, so they might be suspicious of our headlights."

"Follow them until they turn again and then continue straight. We can drive out tomorrow and search for their location." Karl squinted at the taillights as though it helped him see better. "Too bad we didn't bring a night vision capability."

"What's the process for having the license number checked out?"

"We established a drop box for information exchanges. We'll stop there tomorrow morning and tour the countryside afterward. They're turning right. Change in plans; hang a left, so I can keep an eye on them." Karl climbed into the back seat and peered through the rear window. "Slow down, you're kicking up too much dust."

"How's this?" Garrett eased off the gas pedal and let the car coast.

"Perfect. Turn off the lights when I tell you." The silence built as Karl concentrated on their target. "Now!"

The lights went off, followed by the car rolling to a dead stop. Garrett shifted the car into park, turned around, and faced Karl.

"They went down a hill when you turned off the lights, but their lights never appeared again. My guess is they turned left at the bottom of the hill; otherwise, I would've seen them off on the far right." He faced Garrett and smiled. "You got my blood pumping. Best lead we've had since this began, well done. We're finished for tonight, so head for the house. We'll sort out the info in the morning."

"Sounds good."

Garrett turned the car around and Karl stretched out in the back seat. Snores filled the car as he drove down the country road. Mindless driving brought Leigh into his thoughts. Tonight marked their second night apart; he hoped she fared better in the sleep department than he did. Maybe sleep would be his tonight instead of restlessness.

The clock on the dash showed just after three in the morning when he parked the car in the driveway. His eyelids were heavy when he woke Karl and herded him into the house. Today seemed successful, but things often appeared different in the harsh reality of a new day.

CHAPTER FOURTEEN

The hotel phone rang, startling her awake.

"Hello? Hello?"

"This is your six-thirty wake-up call," an automated voice told Leigh, who promptly hung up.

"What was I thinking last night? Six-thirty in the morning? I didn't do this early when I worked."

Leigh rolled over and snuggled into the warmth of the covers. She recaptured her dream of Garrett losing a game of Strip Crazy Eights. He drew another card because he had no play. His belt had been lost on the last draw, and now his jeans would come off. The button slipped free; the zipper came down lower, lower, and…an alarm sounded near her head and wouldn't stop. The dream faded away. Drat! Her cell phone alarm blared. The dream and sleep abandoned, she grabbed her phone and turned on a light.

After a stretch, she struggled out of bed and stumbled to the bathroom. As the water warmed for her shower, she remembered the reason for an early wake-up call: time to talk with her brother, Alex, and tell him about her engagement. If her parents already told him, then some damage control might be needed, especially if Mom had done all the talking. A morning meeting with Nick to view properties completed her required tasks for the day.

While in the shower, she considered what to say to Alex, but her thoughts turned to Garrett. Was he okay? Did he need anything? Did he miss her as much as she missed him? Argh! Maybe asking Janet to meet her for coffee and a chat would be a smart idea. Thank goodness, Deb would join her for the weekend, and her best friend's presence would ease her emotional upheaval. As she dried her hair, she decided on eating breakfast in the room and write a bit in her journal before she called Alex.

Her tray held oatmeal, juice, coffee, and a banana. A smile broke across her face as she pulled out her journal.

Thursday, February 13th. Dearest Garrett, Breakfast featured oatmeal today; I smiled as I brought it up to our room thinking how you would approve of my selection. This morning I'm calling Alex and then looking at properties with Nick. I'll tell you about the call and property search later. I plan to call Janet today; I need a pep talk. Dreamed of you last night, we were playing Strip Crazy Eights, and you were losing. How I wish I could win in real life. I miss you so much and fantazise about you throughout the day. Later. Leigh ♥♥

Seven-thirty, Alex would be in his office by now. Leigh's nervousness increased with each ring.

"Hey, kiddo! How are you?" Since he married Tina, Alex always sounded content. Over the last five years, Leigh envied his relationship with his wife. Now a future with Garrett offered her a chance for similar happiness.

"I'm good. How are things with you and Tina?" The question delayed her purpose for the call; she wasn't sure how to broach the subject with her older brother.

"Five-star all the way! We're trying for a baby. What do you say to becoming an aunt?"

"I say it's about time. I can't wait for your announcement that a baby is on the way. Promise you'll tell me before Mom and Dad."

"Sure. So, what's up with you?"

"Well, I met someone special."

"Yeah?" The way he drew out the word meant he either doubted her or waited for details.

"Yeah." Playing her cards close to her chest, she waited on his request for further information.

"Hmm…you're not bursting out with info, so this must be serious. How serious, Leigh?"

"Very serious. He asked me to marry him, and I said yes."

"My baby sister is engaged? How the heck did this happen? Last I heard you weren't seeing anyone."

Leigh imagined his eyebrows almost meeting in the middle of his forehead. A giggle escaped. "We met at the cabin, and...do you believe in love at first sight?"

"Aha, and who is this guy? Do I know him? What does he do?" Because of his concern for her and fear of her being heartbroken, Alex fired questions at his sister. "Are you familiar with his background? Are you sure he's right for you? Did you tell Mom and Dad yet?"

She laughed, loving how concerned he sounded. "This guy, as you called him, is an Air Force veteran and works for the BCA, so he's one of the good guys."

"Well, okay. Now answer my other questions."

"I'm sure, more than sure. You never met him, but Mom and Dad did last weekend at the cabin."

"And?"

"Dad approves of him. Especially after they bonded over snowmobiling, pool, and beer. They beat Dad's buddies at pool, so you can imagine how ecstatic he is with him. But Mom dislikes him for some reason; the degree of rudeness she demonstrated toward him shocked me. Truth be told, I believe she hates him. Over the course of the weekend, she never once said his name and continually brought up David Walker."

"David, really? Mom always did like him. She can be tough, Leigh; been there, done that. I had a girlfriend she didn't care for, and we lasted a week before ending our relationship." At her sudden intake of air, he wisely added, "But you're stronger willed than me. Of course if I hadn't broken off the relationship, I wouldn't have met Tina."

"Wrong spin on the situation." She spat out the words. "Although, if I had married David Walker four years ago, Garrett and I wouldn't be getting married at the end of April. Mom's not stopping us from being together."

"His name is Garrett? Can I talk with him?"

"No."

"No?"

"Only because he's not here; he's on an assignment for work."

"So when will I meet him?"

"As soon as he's back whenever that is."

"He'll be back before the wedding, won't he?"

"I hope so."

"Is this a joke or for real?"

She laughed. "No joke, why would I fake it?"

"You love playing jokes on me is why." He realized her voice held a vibrancy that had been missing for a long time, also hope and joy. "So, you're marrying a guy you only just met?"

"Yup."

"As soon as I tell Tina, she'll call you for the details you'd never consider sharing with me." Alex sounded elated for her. "Where are you now?"

"Staying in Baxter and looking for a house."

"Dang! A house? Are you becoming a little Suzy Homemaker?" Laughter choked out his words.

"Not yet, but stranger things have happened." Leigh's happiness rippled over the phone connection.

"You said the wedding will be the end of April?"

"Yes, so mark your calendar."

"Where are you having it?"

"Less than an hour's drive from the cabin, at the Aspen Inn."

"I stayed there once! Nice place but small. Holding your wedding there limits the number of guests you can invite."

"The size of the inn is what makes it a perfect location for us. We want an intimate occasion for us and our guests." Leigh's joy bubbled out of her. "Alex, I need to go; I meet with our realtor this morning. Love you."

"I love you, too. I'm happy for you and can't wait

to meet Garrett."

"Bye. Give Tina my love and best of luck in the baby department!"

"I will and thanks. Bye, sis." He disconnected.

Leigh put down her phone and pumped her fist. "Yes!" With Alex on their side, that made two in favor of their marriage and one against it. The increased odds lifted her spirits for the day. She had enough time to grab some coffee before leaving for Nick's office. *Garrett may your day be successful. Be safe. I love you and miss you.* With her wish and prayer for him in her heart, she stepped out of the room, ready for the day.

CHAPTER FIFTEEN

The morning came way too early for Garrett. As the driver for their late-night excursion, he stayed awake the entire time, whereas Karl dozed off a couple different times. The knowledge gained looked promising and could aid their investigation, so the long evening was worth a few hours of sleep.

"Garrett, come on man! Time's a wasting. I'll buy you a breakfast sandwich when we reach town." Karl beat on the bedroom door, startling Garrett awake.

"I'll be down in a couple of minutes. I hope you made coffee." Garrett staggered into the bathroom. Cold water splashed on his face cleared his vision. A quick wash and a fast brushing of his teeth had him ready to face the day's challenges. After throwing on the same clothes from the previous day, he shot down the stairs.

"Here's your coffee." Karl tossed a travel cup at Garrett, who caught it with one hand. "Let's go. I'll drive because you don't look so hot."

"Not enough sleep." Garrett sank into the passenger seat. Desperate for a much-needed caffeine fix, he tipped the travel cup and welcomed a long drink of hot coffee. "I couldn't fall asleep for hours—tossed and turned until the sun came up."

"My guess is you're missing your fiancée, especially how she's all soft and warm when you cozy up with her at night." Karl laughed as he shifted his eyes from the road to Garrett and back again.

"Don't go there." Garrett glared at him.

"Hey! I'm just saying, once you've been sharing your bed on a regular basis, you find sleeping alone again difficult. Lighten up. Jeez."

"Sorry." Garrett rubbed his eyes and drank more coffee in hopes of waking up further. "What's on the docket for today?"

"We'll stop by the drop box and leave the truck information. With work stuff completed, I'll buy you breakfast. Afterward, we drive back in the country and see if we can figure out where they went last night." Karl glanced at Garrett as he slowed down at the city limits.

"Practical plan, especially the breakfast part." Garrett laughed and finished his coffee.

They stopped at the storage site serving as their drop box. After depositing the information with their data request, Karl cruised through a nearby drive-through for the promised breakfast sandwich. They devoured the food as they retraced their route from the previous evening.

"This is where they turned off." Garrett pointed at the upcoming intersection.

"You sure? It was awfully dark last night."

"I'm sure. I marked it with the old willow tree."

"We've passed plenty of willows already, yet this one stands out for you?"

"This one has a cottonwood leaning against it, none of the others did." Garrett maintained his composure even though Karl questioned his observation skills.

"Okay, I'm only checking. Let's figure out what road they turned down." Karl gunned the engine, making the car slide around the corner. "Yeehaw! Hang on partner."

Garrett clung to the dash and the armrest of his door. A memory of his best friend from high school and him performing the exact maneuver on gravel roads captivated him. A grin replaced the grimace on his face. Karl corrected for the tailspin, and they continued barreling down the road.

"Your driving reminds me of my escapades in high school."

"Hey, I outperform anyone from high school; I've trained with the best drivers on pursuit tactics," Karl bragged as he stomped on the accelerator.

"Right."

"You know, some people consider sarcasm a poor form of effective communication." Karl battled the steering wheel as the car skidded around another curve.

"Right." Garrett focused on the countryside rather than respond to Karl's jab. "They probably turned at the bottom of this hill."

"Yeah, once we drive up and over, we'll go with our best guess. Lucky thing we can take all day if need be."

Their day consisted of driving the back roads and checking out every farmstead and home they came across. They noted a few possible sites for further investigation.

"These are enough possibilities for today," Karl announced as shadows blended into darkness and dusk settled across the land. "How do sloppy joes sound for supper?"

"I doubt if I'll care whether they're edible or not; my breakfast sandwich ran out hours ago."

"Should have ordered an extra one. If you recall, I did offer you two."

"Yes, you did. Next time I'll accept your offer."

"Ah but next time you'll be buying." Karl laughed as he turned the car in the direction of their house.

Garrett shook his head at Karl and smiled. He stared out his window as the snow-covered fields zipped by while they drove along. The sun sank low on the horizon turning the clouds a brilliant red. He imagined what a spectacular picture it would be. Perhaps Leigh saw it and captured it with her camera. He sighed and rested his forehead on the side window. *Leigh, I miss you so much*, he thought as his eyes closed. This assignment wouldn't be over soon enough.

CHAPTER SIXTEEN

It'd been a long exhausting day for Leigh. She sat in a restaurant at a booth along the windows and perused the menu. While she debated the choices in her head, a brilliant sunset caught her eye. Wow! Spectacular reds dominated her view. Unfortunately, she didn't bring her camera with her, but then she thought of how her smartphone's camera took high-quality photos.

"Would you care for something to drink?" the perky waitress asked as she placed a basket of chips and salsa on the table.

"A glass of water and a margarita, please. I'll be right back." After she pulled on her coat, she walked outside.

The joy of taking pictures again shocked her. The last time she used her camera was the day before meeting Garrett. Had only twelve days passed since she found him in the backyard of the cabin? Unbelievable! The myriad of emotions and adventures she experienced over the short time being with him amazed her. They ranged from horrendous to captivating, exhilarating, and momentous. As she viewed the pictures, she thought of Garrett and how thoughts of him filled her days usually when something seen or said sparked a memory.

Oh, Garrett, how I wish we stood here together and enjoyed this sunset. She took in a deep breath of cold air, cast one last look at the setting sun, and hurried back into the restaurant.

A margarita and water waited for her. She settled into the booth and pulled out her journal. As she sipped the margarita, she found where she stopped writing that morning.

Continuation, Thursday, February 13th. I took my first pictures since before I met you. Do you realize we met only twelve days ago? Back to the pictures, they're of a radiant red sunset. I wish we could have shared the sunset, but our future will hold so many we can share together, right? Tonight, I used the camera on my phone, but I'll carry my camera with me each day from now on.

I had a fabulous call with Alex this morning and told him I was engaged. At first, he thought I was joking. Later, he could hear the truth and love in my voice, so he can't wait to meet you. Best of all, he'll support us, so now the score is two for us and one against us! Mom is outnumbered. Hooray!

Nick and I drove all over the countryside looking at land for sale, and there were two properties I found captivating. Both are good-sized, and one has a creek running through it. Tomorrow Nick's busy, so I'll visit the church and meet with the minister.

I had an enjoyable chat with Janet, and tomorrow we're having coffee. She's invited me to their home for supper tomorrow. It's meatloaf night! I promised to bring wine and a dessert.

The waitress returned and took her food order. Leigh gazed out the window. Somewhere out there her fiancé faced unknown dangers, so she said a short prayer for his safety. A sigh escaped as she turned back to her journal.

I miss you so much. Thoughts of you torment me, and I dread the night as it is the loneliest time of day for me. I miss cuddling with you. I miss falling asleep in your arms and waking beside you. I miss your kisses. I miss how your touch sends me to heights I never reached before. I seriously miss making love to you. I miss the intensity of our lovemaking. I miss the exquisite sensation I experience when you first enter me. I miss the way your eyes turn a deep warm brown as your passion heightens. I miss your *sexy little smile; it shows how ready you are to make love to me. Oh, and I miss your accent! Yes, you have a slight one you must have picked up down South. The drawl is stronger when you seduce me and make love to me. I miss kissing you. I miss your scent and your taste. I miss undressing you and running my hands over your <u>exceptionally sexy body</u>. I miss holding your hand. I miss your sense of humor. I even miss playing Strip Crazy Eights!*

When you return, your office may report us as missing persons because you and I are not surfacing for a terribly long time.

I love you so much. You're in my prayers every day, and I ask for your safety and success. Yours always. Leigh

♥♥♥

With the delivery of her dinner, she set aside her writing. The journal aided her in dealing with Garrett's absence, bringing him close through her written words.

As she sipped the last of her drink, her phone sounded the ringtone for Deb.

"Hi! What's up?" Leigh whispered, so she wouldn't disturb the other diners.

"I hate doing this, but I can't come for a visit. Something came up, so we'll have to pick another time. I'm sorry." Deb's voice quivered.

"If you can't be here, you can't. We'll visit together another time." Leigh hoped her disappointment wouldn't be obvious to her friend.

"Has Garrett been able to contact you?"

"No, but he didn't expect he'd have any opportunities to call during his assignment."

"Well, you should do something fun this weekend: do some shopping, see a movie, or get drunk."

"Shopping yes, movie maybe, but get drunk no way." Leigh laughed quietly. "You know, drunk isn't something I do; besides too much alcohol would only depress me more than I already am with him not being here."

"Just promise me you'll do something fun this weekend," Deb demanded.

"I promise to do something fun. Be good."

"You, too. Bye." Deb disconnected.

Leigh released a sigh. Her planned weekend blew up with a phone call. What to do now? A movie or shopping might serve as distractions. *Perhaps Janet's available for shopping on Saturday.* On Sunday, church services loomed as her only activity. Attend by herself? Why not? Shouldn't be scared of being in church by yourself, should you?

After paying her bill, she trudged out to the Jeep. Besides the fun she had when she drove it, Garrett's essence surrounded her and comforted her when she sat in it. She needed that comfort right now.

Once in their room, Leigh decided on a long soak in the tub. She dug out her favorite bath oil from her suitcase. The scent of lily of the valley filled the bathroom; as the hot water wrapped around her, the disappointments of the day dissipated. The harsh ring of the room telephone broke into her musings.

"Who the heck would be calling me on the hotel phone?" Leigh struggled out of the tub, wrapped a towel around her wet body, and ran for the phone. "Hello?"

"Leigh?"

"Garrett? Garrett, is it really you?" Her heart pounded in her chest and not from racing across the room.

"Yes, darlin'." He sighed. "I don't have much time."

"Hearing your voice is wonderful! Why are you calling this phone? How are you?"

"I couldn't remember your number. When I saw this pay phone, I figured why not call? I'm fine, but I miss you. You'd be surprised how often I think of you." His voice cracked, and he released another long sigh. "I'm not sleeping well; guess I got used to you lying beside me."

"I'm sorry. I don't sleep well either. You're in my thoughts all the time. In fact, I'm writing a journal for you and recording everything I do during my days including my thoughts."

"Whatever you write will be fascinating, and I look forward to reading it. Why did you take so long to answer the phone?"

"I was soaking in the tub."

"Are you telling me you're naked?" His voice dropped low and sounded way too sexy.

"Nope, got a towel wrapped around me, but I can drop it for you."

"No, no, I'm okay; I doubt I can handle a reasonable conversation while a mental image of you naked on the other end of this connection consumes my brain cells. I imagine you smell of lily of the valley, right?"

"Yes! How'd you guess?" His question amazed her; he never mentioned the fragrance she wore.

"Appears my observation skills kicked in before I left." Ecstatic over having impressed her, Garrett tried downplaying his remark. "My mom grew a big patch of lily of the valley along one side of our house. The scent always reminds me of times with her."

"I'll be sure I never run out of it. Oh, Janet invited me for dinner with the family tomorrow. How's your work going? Making any progress?"

"We think we made some headway last night. Whoops! Gotta go; my partner concluded his flirting with the bartender." Garrett took a deep breath. "I love you."

"You be careful. Thanks so much for calling; this is what I needed tonight. I love you, too." Leigh's voice trembled with emotion.

"I'll be as careful as I can be." Reluctant to hang up, Garrett kept an eye on Karl. The sign to leave came too soon. "Bye, darlin'."

"Goodbye, Garrett." The line went dead.

Her hand shook as she placed the receiver in the cradle. Her longing for him spiked and tears pooled in her eyes. She walked into the bathroom, dried off, got her pajamas on, and crawled into bed. With a lingering glance at the empty side of the bed where Garrett had slept, she pulled out her journal.

P.S. You called me tonight. My heart sang with happiness when I heard your voice. Now I ache for your arms around me. The bed is cold and empty without you in it. I'm reassured you're safe. You not sleeping well concerns me; you need your rest. How can you be ready for whatever may happen if you're tired? Maybe you should do something strenuous and wear yourself out, so you'll fall asleep. Or try drinking milk in the evening. You need to do something. Crap! Now I'm worrying over your sleeping habits. ☹

I'm relieved I'll be with Janet tomorrow. I hope she'll have ideas on how I can move beyond this blue funk I exist in without you.

I should turn out the lights and get some sleep. I'm checking the church out tomorrow and meeting with the minister, may even attend services on Sunday.

I love you, miss you, and I will be here for you when you're done. Leigh XXOO (Those are kisses and hugs for you...you can collect on them when you're back with interest!)

CHAPTER SEVENTEEN

Garrett gathered her in his arms and held her close. She looked in his eyes; they radiated a warm brown.

"I love you, Leigh. Prepare yourself; I'm showing you how endless my love is for you." His hands ran down her body as his lips moved toward her breasts…

Brrinnggg!

Garrett disappeared as she woke. Dang wake-up call! The dream Garrett had been breathtaking. The phone call with him last night probably prompted her dream. Leigh stretched and closed her eyes in hopes of bringing back the sensation of his arms around her. No luck.

Time for a shower and breakfast. Leigh turned on the shower; the hot water reactivated the scent of her bath oil from the evening before. A smile creased her face.

Garrett not only recognized but remembered her lily of the valley scent. He surprised her by remembering, and the fact he did pleased her to no end. He paid attention to her, unlike someone else who would remain nameless.

After the shower, she dried her hair and let it fall about her shoulders. The brown cords and cream turtleneck sweater she wore afforded comfort during today's activities. Ready for breakfast, Leigh pulled on hiking boots to complete her ensemble. Belgian waffles called her name, although in her head Garrett spouted off how oatmeal would be the healthier choice. The resultant smile stretched wide.

At the breakfast area, she headed for the waffle machine.

"Leigh? Leigh Ramsey?"

She stopped mid-step, recognizing the voice! A voice from her past. As she turned to face the speaker, her smile dissolved into a frown.

"David? What are you doing here?" She couldn't

believe her ex-boyfriend stood by the juice dispenser.

"Leigh, it is you!" David walked to her; his arms slipped around her, and he drew her close into a familiar hug. "Is that a different perfume, very flowery." His head dipped to kiss her on the lips. Her senses returned in time, and she turned her head. David dropped his hands and suggested, "Rather than stand here in the middle of the room, let's eat breakfast together."

"Ah...sure."

Leigh's thoughts ran at a crazy speed. Why was he here? A new perfume? Not hardly. Flowery? He had no clue, unlike her fiancé. Thank heaven Garrett's not around. We're only talking breakfast. Breathe! She dished up oatmeal as a reminder of Garrett and sat at a table for four in the center of the room. She wouldn't sit with David at a table for two in a quiet spot.

David joined her at the table. "I can't believe this. What a surprise seeing you here. The last time we saw each other was four years ago." He dropped his voice lower. "Four miserable years; I missed you, Leigh, more than you can imagine."

"You never contacted me. If you missed me, why didn't you call?" Leigh couldn't stop from asking and hated her need for an answer.

"My shame overwhelmed me, and I doubted you'd accept a call or read a letter from me. Soon too much time had passed."

David sounded sincere, but did whatever he claimed to be true matter anymore? No, not since Garrett entered her life. With his black hair styled to perfection and dark-blue eyes, some women might describe him as drop-dead gorgeous, especially in the tailored suit he wore. He no longer turned her head or sped up her heart with a mere look. Those days were long gone.

"What are you doing here?" Leigh found it hard to believe happenstance brought him to her hotel.

"I'm here for a meeting and will check out some vacation homes. Why are you here? Last I heard you lived in Chicago." David worked his way through a Belgian waffle.

"I moved to this area." Leigh refused to speak of Garrett with her ex-boyfriend.

"Here? As an investment advisor?" David acted surprised.

"No, I'm switching careers to photography." Leigh pushed aside her oatmeal and prepared to leave.

"Why did you decide on such a radical career change? Can you make a living with photography? You built an outstanding career with investments and did so well financially. Why throw your successful career away for a…a hobby?"

Not surprised in David's response, Leigh acknowledged to herself the difference between David and Garrett; one questioned her wisdom and the other supported her dream. No doubt her chances for a happy future had shifted in a positive direction after leaving David and meeting Garrett.

"Yes, I believe I can make a living with photography, besides it's more than a hobby, it's my passion." She stood. "David, I need to go or be late for my appointments this morning."

"Of course. Why don't we get together for dinner tonight? We can catch up with what's happened in our lives." David followed her into the hallway.

"Not tonight, I have a dinner engagement." Leigh stopped walking and faced him.

"What about lunch? My meeting is over by noon. Please, meet me for lunch." David snatched hold of her hands.

"Fine, lunch. Where should we meet?" Leigh decided a midday meal would be better with him than dinner.

"Let's meet here, so I can change out of my suit. How does twelve-thirty sound?"

David's face beamed with either happiness or satisfaction, Leigh couldn't decide which, and the indecision concerned her. "Works for me." She extracted her hands from his and headed down the hall, putting distance between them.

"See you then, Leigh," David called out after her. He added to himself, "You can run, but you can't hide, sweetheart."

Back in her room, Leigh leaned against the closed door. Why was David here? The story of a meeting and looking for a vacation home didn't ring true. Suspicions swirled in her mind. Restless in her unease over David's appearance, she moved about the room. She needed to discover his real reason for being here and with luck, today would be the last time she saw him.

As she sat in the Jeep, a peacefulness replaced Leigh's anxiety. The engine roared to life, and she turned up the heat and defroster. Pulling out of the parking lot, she recited the route to the church. Depending on how long the stop took, she might be able to check out a bridal shop before coffee with Janet.

***

Garrett's conversation the previous night with Leigh had lifted his spirits, but a long sleepless night followed. Giving up on sleep, he showered and wandered into the kitchen.

Later, he sat in the living room with no lights on. The dark and silence soothed him as he drank coffee and admired the reddish-pink sunrise. Retrieval of the information on the truck they followed the other night was their first action today. If the registered address matched any location they identified yesterday, surveillance of the site would occupy the rest of their day.

The biggest frustration remained a meeting with the

heads of this meth production crew since James had yet to call. The end of the operation and his return to Leigh depended on the meeting happening…soon.

His thoughts moved to Leigh. She sounded well last night. The intense loss he endured by missing her surprised him. His mind visualized the many things he missed: her kisses, her hair, holding her close, falling asleep with her head on his shoulder, waking beside her, and making love with her. He repositioned himself on the chair, a tad uncomfortable after his body reacted to thoughts of his fiancée. He smiled; Leigh would savor his getting a hard-on simply from thoughts of her.

"Why are you sitting in the dark?"

Karl's voice echoed in the near-empty living room and startled Garrett out of his contemplative mode.

"Doing some thinking." Garrett sipped his coffee, covering his discomfort for having been caught unaware. "I'm confident the address from the plate will match one of the spots we identified yesterday. If so, we scout it out today and identify the location of the operation without a meeting."

"How long have you been sitting there in the dark?" Karl got himself a mug of coffee and sat on the couch. His green eyes pierced Garrett. "I think your thoughts centered more on your fiancée than work."

"Thoughts of her crossed my mind but work comes first. When are we leaving for town?" Garrett directed the conversation away from Leigh.

"Anytime you're ready."

"I'm ready as soon as I pour a coffee to go."

"Pour two and I'll warm up the car." Karl dumped the last of the coffee from his mug, grabbed his coat from a hook at the back door, and disappeared into the cold morning.

They took off once Garrett buckled in.

"We'll check if the info on the plates is back first. If

so, we'll grab breakfast on the road and reconnoiter the address. Should the location match one of the spots on our list, I'll buy you lunch." Karl drank some of his coffee. "But you're buying breakfast."

"Only one sandwich. You'll need room for lunch." Garrett smiled as he raised the cup to his lips.

"You gettin' all cocky on me?" Karl laughed after a glance at Garrett.

"Not cocky, confident; huge difference." Garrett looked out the side window at the fields flying by and sipped his coffee.

"Right. We'll soon find out." Karl slowed as he prepared for a turn. "I'll pick up any information left for us. You keep watch."

"Will do."

Karl left the car running as he stepped into the storage area. Garrett stood outside the warm interior of the car as he stretched his legs and eliminated kinks from his shoulders. He didn't spot anyone taking interest in their activities. Karl returned before the cold set into Garrett's limbs. The smile on Karl's face told him everything.

"Okay, so you can display all kinds of confidence and know-it-all attitude," Karl called out as he got back in the car.

"The address is one of our spots?" Garrett had been hopeful but prepared himself for disappointment.

"Yes, turn on the GPS and plug in this location. We'll cruise by and employ our covert-observation skills for a few hours. I stuck a camera on the floor behind me." The car spun out of the parking lot headed back the way they came. "You might reach the altar on time, Garrett!"

He didn't respond, except for a smile. He dragged the camera into the front seat and checked the settings. Charged and ready, he kept hold of it as Karl selected a drive-through for breakfast sandwiches on the go.

With the camera in his lap, Garrett's thoughts flew

to Leigh, and his love for her swelled within him. Talking with her last night had cheered him and recharged his resolve for a safe return to her arms. He'd been proud of her for contacting Janet and accepting a dinner invitation from the Hendersons. He hoped her visit with the Henderson family would increase her understanding of how their relationship could succeed even when assignments took him away from her. Truth be told, seeing how the Hendersons' marriage had succeeded eased his mind, too.

"Hey! Dig out your money, partner, you're paying for this!"

Karl's voice jolted him out of his reflective state. He pulled some bills from his wallet and handed them over. Soon they sped along, and GPS directions guided them as they munched on their breakfast.

"There, on the left." Garrett pointed out a cluster of buildings set back from the road. "This is number three on our list. We're good, Karl."

They congratulated themselves with a high five.

"Not only are we good, but we're nearing the conclusion of the operation. I'm not certain whether we collected enough details for a search warrant of the property, but we'll hand over everything to the task force and let them work the legal angle. We'll find a location to monitor the place for a couple of hours, snap a few pictures, and figure out what we can of their activities. Afterward, I'm buying you lunch."

"And I'll let you." Garrett's pride in his contribution to the operation sent his spirits soaring. If this panned out, he might be home with Leigh sooner than expected.

They spent three hours parked on a country lane masked by trees; their chosen observation point worked well for their purpose. A weathered house stood on one side of the property with three oversized outbuildings on the other side. What looked like dedicated generators supported two of the buildings. Garrett drew a diagram of the site and annotated their educated guesses regarding the purpose for each building.

"Bet they use tons of power. Did you spot the fuel tank over there?" Karl gripped Garrett's shoulder as he pointed at the farmstead. "Probably for generators."

"And what might be a water tank sits next to the largest of the three buildings. With power and water, my hunch is they grow marijuana in there."

"Solid hunch from what I see; put our assumptions on your diagram. I'll add a couple extra shots, and we'll leave." Karl snapped close-ups of the fuel and water tanks. His hand clamped over Garrett's arm. "Let's go."

Garrett finalized his notations and followed Karl to the car.

"I'll incorporate approximate distances on these tonight; if they offer us a meeting, the diagram and pictures will be handy for our backup." Garrett dropped his papers in the back seat and buckled up.

"I'm impressed with your thoroughness. Joe selected well for this assignment, and I'll be sure I tell him."

"Thanks. Can we carve out a little time for target practice later?"

"See? You're full of ideas. I created a firing range on our property, so we can shoot off some of this high. But first you deserve something special for lunch, my treat!" Karl put his foot down, and the car sped away.

Garrett leaned back and looked out the side window. Unable to share this triumphant knowledge of having done his job well with Leigh, he wished she enjoyed a day as successful as his.

***

Leigh pulled in front of the coffee shop, ecstatic over her visit at the church and ready for time with Janet. She spotted Janet's SUV in the parking lot, so she scanned the inside of the shop until she located her.

"Janet!" Leigh reached her new friend and received a warm, solid hug. "I'm so pleased you could meet me for coffee. Did you order already?"

"Not yet." Janet's smile brightened her face. "I'm glad you called."

"I promised Garrett to call you if I needed anything. This is my treat today."

"How sweet of you. Thank you."

They got coffees and scones and sat near the fireplace.

"How's everything going?" Janet evaluated Leigh for signs of not coping with being alone in a strange place.

"So far, everything is clicking along. Our realtor and I are looking at property, so Garrett and I can build a log home."

"I meant how are you handling Garrett being gone?" Janet's eyes pierced through Leigh's resolve to appear confident and unaffected by her fiancé's assignment. "I won't pass anything you say to Joe unless you ask me to tell him. If I believe he should hear something, I'll tell you before sharing the information with him. Agreed?"

Leigh considered Janet's words. "I can live with those terms." She sighed. "I'm so worried about Garrett. I understand he's done this before, and he's trained for all aspects of law enforcement. But I can't stop worrying. Tell me I'm acting normal."

"Of course you are. I would imagine you cry yourself to sleep most nights." At Leigh's nod, Janet continued. "Anything reminding you of him brings tears to your eyes."

"Yes. I drive his Jeep everywhere; not only does it remind me of him, but his scent surrounds me when I'm sitting inside." Leigh blinked back the tears pooled in her eyes.

"I hold Joe's pillow close to me on nights when he

travels." Janet grasped Leigh's hands in hers. "You're in love, and he's in harm's way; you're acting totally normal. I'd be concerned if tears didn't fill your eyes now."

"Will the being alone and waiting ever be easier?"

"Only if you fall out of love with him. Given the way you two look at each other, I suggest stocking up on boxes of tissue."

"He called me last night," Leigh admitted, a slight blush colored her cheeks.

Janet didn't appear surprised.

"Whatever bar they were in had a payphone, so he placed a call through the hotel switchboard. We spoke for a short time, but hearing his voice improved my spirits."

"I'm sure the same is true for Garrett."

"Yes, he did sound cheered by our conversation. He told me he's not sleeping well, so now I'm worried he won't be as sharp as he should be when the time comes to act."

"He's missing you." Janet squeezed Leigh's hands in encouragement. "The same thing happens to Joe whenever he travels. I guess, they don't need as much rest as we do. Personally, I believe the reason is because they don't work as hard as we women do every day!"

Leigh laughed at Janet's premise.

"Finding out my reactions are normal offers me hope I'll survive this separation. I purchased a journal and record each day's events; I'll do this whenever Garrett's away. When I'm writing, I find myself imagining he's with me and I'm talking to him. Sometimes I can hear him responding to what I write."

"What a marvelous idea! Journaling is a wonderful method of dealing with stress. Would you mind my telling the other spouses?"

"Not at all." Leigh's delight sparkled in her eyes. The tone of her voice had lightened, and her tears had dried.

"Back to your log home. Did you select a builder

yet?"

"Well, I'm fond of one company, but I prefer having Garrett's input. The decision is a big one, more involved than simply buying a house. A working relationship with them is critical, so both of us must be comfortable with them and confident in their abilities." Leigh sipped her coffee but chewed on her lip as she waited for Janet's response.

"I understand what you're saying, but the fallout from not deciding until he's back further delays your house." Janet placed a hand on Leigh's arm. "Garrett trusts your judgment; otherwise, he would never give you a power of attorney. Be confident in your instincts."

Leigh looked at her, warmed by the concern reflected in the eyes locked on her own. She considered what Janet said and understood the underlying message: she must push forward and finalize decisions for their future whenever Garrett's assignments took him away from home.

"You're right. My heart told me the same thing, but spending his money makes me uncomfortable." Leigh placed her hand over Janet's hand resting on her arm. A moment of connection sparked between the two women. She appreciated the friendship offered by the wife of Garrett's boss. When the moment passed, their attention turned to their coffees and scones.

"Did you visit any of the local bridal shops yet?"

"I'll check them out this afternoon. Well, as many as I can. I planned on looking for a vintage dress. My Internet searches showed many new dresses styled with a vintage look, so I hope I can find one or two in stock.

"I wish you luck in your search. Will you also shop in the Cities?"

"It depends on what I find here. My maid of honor lives in Moorhead, so I may drive up and shop with her in Fargo. We could look for her dress at the same time." Leigh blew on her coffee before drinking.

"I recommend shopping around; you can't rush your choice. I remember when I shopped for my dress. I drove my mother crazy! We visited every bridal shop in a four-county area. I always had my nose in bridal magazines, clipping pictures, and making a wedding scrapbook of ideas. I acted rather manic over the whole thing." She laughed and shook her head.

Janet's laughter became contagious, and Leigh joined her, laughing felt wondrous.

"I honestly don't know whether I want my mom shopping with me or not," Leigh confessed. At Janet's raised eyebrows, she continued. "When I told her I was engaged, she jumped to a wild conclusion I accepted a proposal from my ex-boyfriend from four years ago. He's the son of Mom and Dad's best friends. As a result, she didn't accept our engagement too well and developed an unreasonable hatred of Garrett."

"Oh." Janet looked at her. "I'm sorry, Leigh. That must be challenging for you."

"As long as Garrett's mine, I'm fine."

"If you care for help on your search for a wedding dress, I'm offering my assistance."

Janet's heartfelt offer warmed Leigh.

"You're generous with your time, and your company is welcomed and appreciated."

"I can't today, but I'm available tomorrow."

"Works for me. I'll check some of them this afternoon, and we'll do serious shopping tomorrow." Leigh stood and gave Janet a hug. "I'll be by tonight for dinner."

"Come anytime. Dinner's at six-thirty. We'll plan our attack of bridal shops after we eat.

"Sounds perfect. Bye!"

Leigh climbed in the Jeep and drove to the hotel. Later she'd suffer through lunch with David.

Why was he here? There was no reason for his

interest in her, yet he was in Baxter. Was her mom behind his appearance? Memories besieged her: Mom assuming her good news had been David returning into her life, Mom's cruelness toward Garrett, Mom verifying Garrett had left for his assignment, and Mom practically demanding their hotel information. If she asked David why he was here, would he answer honestly?

Back in her room, she sat at the desk with her journal before her.

Friday, February 14th. Happy Valentine's Day, Garrett! I'm sad we're separated for our first Valentine's Day, but we'll enjoy others together. Note for next year: I love dark chocolate with caramel or toffee centers! Breakfast brought me a surprise: David Walker is staying in the hotel. Yes, that David. ☹ I sat with him for breakfast to be polite. It wasn't long before I confirmed your superiority over him in all categories. He said he was here for a meeting and to search for a vacation home, but I doubt his story. He pressed me to join him for dinner tonight, but I told him I couldn't. Thankfully, I have a dinner engagement with the Hendersons. Yes, you're right, I don't need an excuse, so should he ask again, I'll decline.

I had a delightful time with Janet at coffee, and she offered to join me when I shop for my wedding dress. She and Joe should be on our guest list. OMG! They would be our first guests: not yours and not mine, but "ours". We'll soon have a cluster of "our" friends; it has an encouraging ring to it.

I stopped at the church today and visited with the minister. She is an interim minister as they're searching for a new one. I met the church secretary and a few of the members who were folding programs for Sunday's service. They were so friendly and welcoming; I promised I'd return Sunday. As soon as you're back, we can schedule the marriage class, so we can pay the discounted price for our license. Oh! Almost forgot the most noteworthy tidbit of news; she'll officiate our wedding. She may finish her interim duties before then, but she lives in the area. I believe you would approve of her. We discussed Bible verses for the ceremony. I'm fond of two. The first is from the Song of Solomon 8:6, New Living Translation (NLT). It talks of love and fierce passion. How else would you describe what we have? I jotted it down, so here it is for your consideration: "Set me as a seal upon your heart, as a seal upon your arm, for love is strong as death, passion fierce as the grave. Its flashes are flashes of fire, a raging flame." The second is 1 Corinthians 13:7 NLT. "Love never gives up, never loses faith, is always hopeful, and endures through every circumstance." This is us, too! We have lots to discuss upon your return to include joining the church. I truly look forward to belonging there. We can participate in their many activities.

    I need to end this for now. I'll write again tonight after this lunch thing with David, bridal shops, and dinner at the Hendersons.

    Please be aware of the endlessness of my love for you. Some nights you join me in my dreams; those are the best nights. I miss your arms around me and your strength. Love and kisses. Leigh XX ♥♥

    Setting aside her journal, she jumped when her phone rang. A quick glance at the screen cheered her.

    "Tina! How's my favorite sister-in-law?"

    "I'm your only sister-in-law, Leigh." Tina's dry remark matched her sense of humor. "I'm fine, but you've been holding out on me. Why did I find out about your engagement from your brother? And why didn't I hear about this guy before?"

    "I only met him almost two weeks ago, so I had no time to share details with you."

    "I'm sure you told your friend, Deb." Her pout sounded over the phone. "So, tell me everything."

    "Tina, I told Deb when I asked her to be my maid of

honor, but she hasn't learned any of the details yet," Leigh confessed. "You'll be the first, so what can I tell you?"

"How'd you meet him?"

"He fell into the backyard of the cabin while I stayed there."

"Fell?"

"Yup. He saw the cabin lights through the trees."

"Had he been snowmobiling and got lost?"

"No, a crazed escaped prisoner shot him."

"What?"

"Garrett had arrested the guy when he was in the Air Force. He threatened to kill Garrett in retribution; somehow, he showed up in Minnesota and tried to fulfill his threat."

"Way too much excitement for me. When did you and he, you know, do it?"

"You're shameless, you do realize that? The first night, it was wonderful!"

"So, who made the first move?"

"Duh! He'd been shot, so I did."

"Good for you. He must have enjoyed it."

"He didn't complain. The next day a blizzard snowed us in, so we stayed inside all…day…long."

"Oh là là! I suppose a fire burned as bright and heated as you two did in each other's arms, and the wine flowed freely."

"You know me too well," Leigh admitted. "We played cards."

"What? Strip poker?"

"Nope."

"I thought by the tone of your voice stripping would have been involved." Tina sounded disappointed.

"We played his made-up game, Strip Crazy Eights! I lost but losing at his card game was pleasurable."

"Hmm, I may need the rules for the game." Tina laughed.

"You'll have a blast playing; maybe I'll get a niece or nephew out of the game. We played a rematch while at the Aspen Inn, and I lost again. Garrett's very lucky at cards."

"Garrett. Nice name. What's his last name, where's he from, and what's he like?"

"Dane. He's from western Minnesota, a strong man with strength of purpose. He's loving, playful, and better looking than anyone I ever met."

"Can you text me a picture of him?"

"Sorry, we were having so much fun I never took any pictures of him."

"From the sounds of it, you wouldn't share any you may have taken," she teased.

"True, but you'll meet him soon enough. Our wedding will be the last weekend of April."

"Not much time for planning. Do you need any help?"

"I'm good for now, but I'll keep your offer in mind."

"So is the crazed guy still after him?"

"No, Garrett's an expert shot."

"That doesn't make—wait…you mean Garrett killed the guy?"

"Well, the guy did have a gun on me."

"Oh. My. God. I'm not delving any further into that portion of your story." Tina took a deep breath. "Alex said he works for the BCA?"

"Yes. He's on an assignment, so he's not with me." Leigh sighed. "I miss him so much and worry about him."

"I'll keep him and you in my prayers."

"Thanks. I should go. I have an appointment."

"Call me anytime. I'm here for you."

"I will. Thanks for calling. Love you."

"Love you, too. Bye."

The call ended, and Leigh realized she wore a smile

on her face. If they made a trip to the Cities, a stay with Alex and Tina would ensure a fun visit and a less confrontational one than a stay with her parents.

Time to meet David and figure out his true reason for being here. With her shoulders set, Leigh grabbed her coat and purse. If she let David drive, she could focus on him and his reactions to her questions.

As she came down the front steps, she spotted him near the desk with his back to her. As always, his dark hair showed the styling of an expensive salon. She expected his hands would be immaculate and soft with manicured nails, not like the hard-working hands of her fiancé. He wore tailored pants and a cashmere sweater. Nothing but the best for David Walker. At the sound of her on the stairs, he turned. His smile broadened, but his eyes remained calculating when he met her at the bottom step.

"Prompt as ever, and you look fantastic!" He leaned down for a kiss.

She flinched. The last thing she desired would be David's lips on hers or anywhere. She pretended she missed noticing his attempt and moved around him while thrusting an arm in her coat. "Where shall we go for lunch? Do you mind driving?"

David recovered smoothly and pulled on his coat. "I'm delighted to drive us. This way."

He caught up her arm before she evaded him and pulled her close. She opted against fighting the closeness. As they approached a sporty Mercedes coupe, he guided Leigh to the passenger door.

"Here you are, my dear." David held the door with a flourish.

"Thank you." Leigh slid into the car and noted the new car smell and luxurious interior. So different from Garrett's Jeep, yet she found herself missing the familiarity of it.

David hurried around the car and dropped into the

driver's seat. "I learned of a charming restaurant nearby, so I thought we could eat there today."

"Wherever. How did your meeting go?" She shifted in her seat to watch his reaction.

"Hmm? Oh, fine, but I prefer not talking about work. Tell me what you did over the last four years."

His smile set her on edge.

"I worked investments in Chicago, but I returned to Minnesota about a month ago." Leigh had no intentions of listing the various ways his actions decimated her self-confidence as a woman.

"I can't believe four years of your life merited such a short description." David drove with ease and confidence. One hand on the steering wheel and one on the shift, sitting conspicuously near Leigh's left leg. "I missed you." His voice dropped to a sexy rumble, and his hand touched her thigh.

Leigh jumped when his hand caressed her knee. "Remove your hand, David." She delivered a cold and humorless demand as she glared at her former boyfriend.

"You needn't sound so unwelcoming, Leigh. After all, we are old family friends." He squeezed her knee before sliding his hand back to the shift. "Ah, here's the restaurant."

He pulled into the parking lot, taking up two spaces and facing the road. He grinned at her and said, "This should be fun. It's been a long time since we last ate together." Exiting the car, he walked around to her side.

Before he reached her door, she exited, letting her hair blow in the wind rather than waste time pulling on her stocking hat. She wouldn't allow him other opportunities to touch her. "Let's go." She marched off in the direction of the front door hoping she left him behind.

"Your wish is my command." David not only caught up with her, but his arm went around her waist, and he gathered her against his body. He steered her toward the door and rushed her inside.

CHAPTER EIGHTEEN

"This place is famous for their ribs," Karl declared after he parked the car. "Since lunch is on me, don't go crazy and order the most expensive thing on the menu."

Garrett looked over the car roof at Karl and laughed. "What about the next most expensive item?"

"Maybe I should order for both of us." As Karl moved around the car, his partner stood frozen in the same spot and focused on something across the road. "Garrett? Are you listening to me?"

A flash of golden hair caught his eye; Garrett stared off in the distance, too stunned to move. "Leigh?" Her name, a ghost of a whisper on his lips. All his senses focused on the woman across the highway.

"Hey! What's the matter?" Karl's vision followed his partner's stare and zeroed in on a couple entering a restaurant. He spent more time assessing the golden-haired beauty than the man holding her close. He stood near Garrett. "Who are they?"

Garrett didn't respond until after the couple disappeared into the restaurant. With his brows drawn down and his jaw clenched, he radiated anger. "The woman is my fiancée, but I don't recognize the guy with his hands on her." He couldn't move. *I must be in a state of shock. Who'd be holding her so close? The man should be me and no other.* He fought against the flare of jealousy.

"They appeared way more than friendly." On the receiving end of Garrett's glare, Karl continued in a more supportive way. "Well, come on. Let's investigate." He opened Garrett's door to their car.

"I can't go inside." He turned on Karl.

"But I can." He winked and shoved Garrett into the car. "I'll wander in, order us some food, and eavesdrop on them for a bit. I'll find out who he is for you."

Garrett buckled up and sat in a daze. Spotting Leigh should send him soaring with high spirits, but the sight of her in another man's arms sent him in a downward spiral. A reasonable explanation must exist; she would never betray him.

Karl zipped the car across the highway and into a parking space in the restaurant's lot. "Stay down. I'll be back as soon as I figure out what's happening." He clapped Garrett on the shoulder and slipped out of the car.

Garrett slouched in the car seat, fought the urge to sulk, and battled his desire to charge into the restaurant to confront...what? Confront his fear of losing the love of his life if he was being honest with himself. One hand ran through his hair and a moment afterwards the other followed suit. His thoughts surged through his memories of his short time with Leigh. Could he survive losing her?

She said she loved me last night on the phone, so the circumstances can't be what they appear to be. Why is she with a guy? Who the hell is he? What's taking Karl so long? "Come on, Karl," he muttered.

***

"David, don't you ever touch me again!" Leigh turned on him as he closed the restaurant door.

"I just offered you support as you walked over the slippery sidewalk. I don't understand why you're so upset." His eyes searched hers with no sign of remorse in them.

"You manhandled me. I didn't appreciate your arms around me." Anger sparked in her eyes; she stood stiff and away from him.

"You did at one time." He softened his voice and reached for her hand.

She jerked her hand away from him. "Four years ago, David. Four long years." Irritation seethed within her. She supposed he thought himself charming, but she found him insincere and revolting. "Do not touch me again."

The hostess approached them, so any retort he planned went unspoken. Arriving at their booth, Leigh pulled off her coat and filled half the seat with its bulkiness before she slid into the remaining space. A slight frown flashed across his face, so she congratulated herself on the smooth maneuver.

"How can I resist touching you when you're as delectable as ever?" David sat across from her with his hands on the table. His fingers tapped the surface.

"Why are you here? You in the same hotel as I am didn't happen by sheer chance." She leaned forward and glared at him.

"Why, Leigh, you wound me. So suspicious." He shook his head. "I'm simply here for a meeting, my administrative assistant made the hotel reservation, and the time frame lets me use the weekend to shop for property."

"You're not a fisherman, so why buy here? I envision you purchasing a condo in downtown Minneapolis instead of something around here." Leigh stared at him as though she could extract a confession from him.

"Why can't you accept the proposition I changed and would prefer spending time up here rather than in the hustle and bustle of a city? Or that I rethought my life and desperately yearn for you in it again?"

His eyes glittered with some deep emotion. *Deceit? Definitely not honesty.*

"I doubt every word you said. Besides, you're too late." Leigh smiled as she thought of Garrett and how he surpassed David in so many ways.

"Not until you're married." David leered at her as he leaned over the table.

"You're wrong. It is too late because I'm in love and engaged to a man who loves me."

"My mom mentioned your engagement. However, you're not married yet, so I have time on my side.

Engagements often end before the wedding." He snatched hold of her hand and ran a thumb over her palm. "So, where is your fiancé? When can I meet him and size up my competition?"

"You aren't meeting him, David; he's working and not here. There is no competition because there will never again be an us." Leigh extracted her hand from his grasp. "We should order."

David cast his eyes over her as she reviewed the menu. Four years had been generous to her; she looked hotter than he remembered. He decided to continue his pursuit of her regardless of what she claimed.

The waitress arrived for their orders.

"Order anything, sweetheart; lunch is my treat." David beamed at her.

"Separate checks, please," Leigh instructed the waitress as she glared at him. "I'll have the soup and sandwich combo with chili and chicken salad. Please bring me water with lemon. Thank you."

"I'll take the chicken penne, Italian dressing for the salad, and a Seven and Seven. Thanks." David smiled at the waitress, winked, and ogled her as she walked away.

Unable to stop herself, she compared David's interactions with waitresses to Garrett's. Garrett would smile and be friendly, but never flirt with one or ogle them as they walked away. She shook her head.

"What's wrong?" David caught the shake of her head.

"You'll never change, so I'm counting my blessings."

"Are you counting your blessings because I showed up?" A dazzling smile displayed bleached teeth against his tanned face. "Listen to your heart, sweetheart; your heart says we belong together."

"I'm counting my blessings for breaking up with you before it was too late. My heart doesn't say anything about you, David, and don't call me sweetheart." Leigh leaned back in the booth, putting as much space as possible between them.

"I always considered you as my sweetheart; you're mine and only mine. I acted like a fool when I lost you and changed after losing you. I deserve a second chance, so you can fall in love with the new me."

"Yes, you were a fool, but you saved me from marrying you. I'll never be yours and doubt you changed. I moved on to someone better and will soon marry him. So, I suggest you move on, too," she hissed at him.

"Moving on isn't my intention because you're the only one for me. Our parents were heartbroken when you left me."

Leigh snorted her disagreement.

"I'll make amends. We should be together in this life. You and me against the world, remember?" David continued hammering at her defenses. "All of our parents desire us as a couple again. Our friends thought we were perfect together and will be excited for us when you return with me. Please, I deserve another chance."

"Not hardly." She sat with her arms crossed.

"You can't seriously be marrying some guy you just met."

"How did you learn when we met?"

"Our parents remain best friends. Your mother's distressed over your impetuous engagement. She's concerned for your happiness and your safety."

Leigh leaned forward and braced herself on the tabletop. She pinned him with an accusing look.

"My safety? How ridiculous. Garrett treats me with love, respect, and kindness; he would never treat me as you did." She wouldn't elaborate on how his actions devastated her and affected her for more than a year after their breakup.

"Ah, Leigh, you should forgive me for being young and stupid. I didn't appreciate your special qualities or the beauty of our relationship." Taking advantage of her hands laying on the table, he grabbed one and lifted it to his lips before she realized his intent.

She noted how his eyes gleamed with some emotion, maybe lust, unable to believe it might be love. When his lips touched her hand, a vicious shiver ran down her spine. She wrested her hand out of his grasp.

"David, I may forgive you one day, but I will never be yours again. Get used to it." Her tone sounded flat and threatening. She thought a chuckle erupted from the booth behind her, where a single man had been seated.

The waitress appeared with their drinks. While Leigh nodded her thanks, David accepted his glass and ensured his fingers brushed against the waitress's fingers. He mouthed his thanks, and a blush rose in the woman's cheeks.

"You aren't aware how uncontrolled your flirting becomes whenever a beautiful woman is nearby, are you?"

"The flirting is harmless, Leigh. I only do it for improved service."

"Yeah, sure you do."

They sat in stiff silence. Leigh's eyes roamed the restaurant, uninterested in her lunch companion. David waited for her eyes to land on him. His disappointment at her disregard for him increased his desire to seduce her.

He reached out toward her. "Leigh, you can't ignore me forever. Give me your hand; don't you remember how we would hold hands all the time?"

She glared at him, frowned, shook her head, and kept her hands in her lap. The delivery of their food forced him to move his hand. Leigh shifted her dishes into defensive positions to block any future advances on his part. After the departure of the waitress, he tried a different tactic.

"The day before you broke up with me, I bought an engagement ring. Your parents approved of my marrying you, and the purchase of the ring was my last step before I proposed."

Leigh's gaze reached his eyes in search of the truth or an indication of a lie. When his eyes locked on hers, he produced a dark-blue velvet box from his coat pocket. With a swift movement of his thumb, he revealed the gaudiest engagement ring she ever set her eyes on.

"This ring features a three-carat diamond with a few rubies thrown in for added richness. All yours when you say yes and return with me to where you belong. Obviously, our parents will be delighted when you accept your destiny." He slid the box toward her, sat back, and sipped his drink.

Leigh glanced from the ring to David twice before she dipped a spoon into her chili. "No. If you paid any attention during our two years together, a gaudy ring wouldn't be on the table as your offer to me."

A deep chuckle sounded from the man behind her. He received an order of food to go soon after their meals arrived. She heard him gather his things and leave the booth. His departure was like the loss of an ally. Her eyes followed him as he walked past. Once beyond David, he turned, smiled, and gave her a thumbs-up. How odd to see a stranger signal his approval of her rejection of David's overtures and to experience such strong appreciation for the man's support.

"You prefer wearing a minuscule diamond instead of this?" The tone of David's voice made his annoyance quite evident. "You aren't your mother's daughter, Leigh."

"Correct, I'm my father's daughter, who thinks for herself and falls in love without any assistance from her mom. Did she send you here?"

"Of course not. I came to attend a meeting and look for property." David drained his cocktail and sought the waitress's attention for another. "I'll be here through Sunday. Would you spend time with me tomorrow during the day?"

"Nope, I'll be shopping for my wedding dress with a friend all day." Leigh polished off her sandwich with a smile on her face.

"Since you're busy during the day, join me for dinner." At the shake of her head, he pleaded, "Why can't two friends enjoy a meal together? Is your fiancé a control freak and won't allow you out at night?" The sneer in his voice echoed in his eyes.

"No, he isn't, not that it's any of your business. Why bother spending time together? Just accept the fact you're out of my life forever." Leigh shrugged as she pushed away her dishes.

The waitress appeared with David's fresh drink and cleared her empty dishes. Her actions interrupted their conversation for which Leigh was thankful. His words and attitude put her on edge, and the slight break in talking allowed her head to clear.

"Leigh, we're old friends; we grew up together…you're not frightened of me, are you?" He focused on her eyes. "You are! Why? Hmm. Because deep down you wish to be with me rather than your fiancé and that realization frightens you. I believe your secret desire is to be part of my life in the Twin Cities instead of leading a dismal life out here. With me, you'll enjoy endless opportunities for social outings, the best of everything like designer dresses and exquisite jewelry, not to mention travel to exotic locations around the world. Your life married to this guy couldn't possibly compare with what I can offer you." David sat back, sipped his drink, and studied her over the rim of his glass.

Leigh listened to his ramblings and thought how his arguments mirrored her mother's. She caught the eye of the waitress and indicated they needed their bills. She endured enough of his nonsense. How she wished she drove herself instead of riding with him.

"My secret desire has nothing to do with you and

everything to do with my fiancé. I'm not frightened of you. What you offer is nothing I want, let alone desire. My doubts of your story about looking for property are now confirmed by your own words describing life here as dismal. You're a liar, David. Why don't you save yourself the cost of a hotel room and go home?"

When their bills arrived, David regarded her before he picked up his bill.

"I'm staying, and you should reconsider dinner tomorrow night." He leaned toward her with a smile on his lips, yet his eyes turned cold and ruthless. "Expectations for us exist, and they will be met."

Unable to contain a shiver, she yearned for Garrett to walk in and pull her into his arms where she'd be safe and protected. "I'm calling a cab."

"Don't be ridiculous, I'll drive you back to the hotel." He tossed a hundred-dollar bill on the table, stood, and glared down at her.

"No, you won't. You should return to the Cities today." Leigh gathered her things and walked toward the bar area.

"Stop!" The word came harsh and forceful. He grabbed her arm.

"David, you're hurting me. Let me go!"

He released her arm but grasped her waist and dragged her against him.

"You can run off in a cab now, but you will have dinner with me tomorrow." His lips crushed against hers. With her lips pressed together, she prevented his tongue from an invasion of her mouth. He released her with a slight push and sent her against the wood of the booth. "Seven o'clock. I'll meet you at your room. Oh yeah, I can find you, Leigh. I can always find you." He stormed away from her and exited the restaurant.

She stood stunned and embarrassed as other diners stared at her. Somehow, she restrained her tears and marched straight to the bar.

"Excuse me, can you help me find a number for a cab service?" Leigh asked the bartender, her voice shaking.

"Sure, I keep a business card around for these types of situations. Pardon me for commenting, but I suggest you search for a different boyfriend." She held out a card.

Leigh's cheeks heated and colored to a deep red. "Oh, he's the ex-boyfriend, I upgraded since him."

"Good for you." She left to serve other customers.

"Yeah, I upgraded big time," Leigh muttered as she dialed the cab company.

***

After an hour of jitters and second-guessing on Garrett's part, Karl appeared with two carry-out bags and drinks. He juggled everything when he entered the car.

"What took you so long?" Garrett demanded as soon as the driver's door opened.

"I ordered a drink while I reviewed the menu, so I could sit by them." Karl handed Garrett the bags which he dropped to the floor. "I admire your taste in fiancées."

"What did you find out?" Garrett struggled with the chaos in his head. "So help me if you don't talk soon, I'll punch you in your smiling face."

Karl laughed. "You got it bad, man! Okay, okay. I sat in the booth behind them, so I watched and listened to their conversation. Don't worry, they didn't sit all cozy together, but on opposite sides of the booth. She didn't sound thrilled being with him, but he continually made moves on her. She turned him down on every play."

The car engine purred to life, and Karl drove out of the lot to the highway leading out of town.

"Did you catch a name?" Garrett leaned on the dash; his hands fisted to ward off throttling the man who withheld the information he ached to hear.

"A name?" Karl chuckled after hearing Garrett's

growl of frustration. "Only the guy's first name."

"And?" Garrett prompted, irked at his partner playing with him.

"David."

"David? Are you sure?" Garrett's stomach clenched.

"Yeah, I'm positive. You recognize the name but not the man?" Karl stomped on the gas when they left city limits.

"David is the name of her ex-boyfriend." Garrett spoke through gritted teeth. Anger ran through his blood, and his breathing came fast. Unwilling to lose control, he took deep breaths to calm himself.

Karl glanced at Garrett and gauged when he had gotten control of his emotions before speaking again. "How long ago did they break up?"

"Four years. He's a doctor and works in the Cities." Garrett ran a hand through his hair while he stared out the side window. He didn't notice the scenery flashing by as Karl drove them back to the house.

"So, why's he here?" Karl's eyes narrowed as he pondered the puzzle presented to them.

"Because Leigh's here, but how did he find her? Damn!" Garrett's head fell back on the seat, his eyes closed. He swallowed against the lump in his throat.

"What?" Karl threw a worried look at the man beside him, his voice demanded a response. "What?"

A sigh came out as Garrett raised his head, opened his eyes, and stared unseeing out the windshield. "Leigh's mom. She prefers him as Leigh's husband, so more than likely she's behind his appearance."

"Rather extreme, isn't it?"

"Not for Lois. With me out of the picture, he gains a clear shot at Leigh, and I'm helpless to prevent anything." Garrett's opinion of his future mother-in-law dropped to a new low.

"Unless we complete this operation in the next day

or two, and you return home to her." Karl smiled at Garrett. "Let's find James tonight and push for a meeting. What do you say?"

"I want this over, but we can't screw up the mission for my personal issues." Garrett shook his head. "Thanks for the consideration though. I appreciate the thought."

"Garrett, we're beyond time for grabbing the reins in the negotiations with these guys. We're offering plenty for their product. If they believe we're tired of them stalling and we're taking our business elsewhere, they'll commit." Karl's smile took on a devilish cast. "Time to play hardball."

"You're the boss. I'll buy the first round tonight." Garrett grinned. Ready for action, he agreed with Karl's decision. Should their operation successfully conclude, he wouldn't complain. He hated the image of Leigh with her waste of an ex-boyfriend. *Stay strong, darlin', and please wait for me* became a mantra in his head as they continued toward their house.

CHAPTER NINETEEN

Leigh trudged up the stairs to the second floor and her room. She slumped against the door, spent, and frazzled. A long soak in the tub might revive her.

As the hot water flowed, she added lily of the valley bath oil, so the floral scent filled the sparse bathroom. As she sunk into the water, her eyes closed, and a sigh escaped her. Memories of the sensual bath she shared with Garrett at the Aspen Inn floated before her. Tension eased from her body as the heat chased away the day's challenges. The ring of her cell phone broke into her relaxation, and the name on the display deflated her improved mood.

"Mom, how's everything?"

"Everything's fine. How are you?"

"Getting things done for our wedding. I met with a minister today at the church we plan to join, and she introduced me to some members. Everyone was very welcoming. On Sunday, I'll attend morning services."

"I'm surprised; you never mentioned any interest in church before. Anything else happen?"

She wants information on whether David succeeded. "Yes, I met Janet for coffee today; she's the wife of Garrett's boss. I'm having supper tonight with her and the family. Tomorrow she and I will see what wedding dresses the local shops stock. Hopefully, I'll find my dress up here."

"Nothing else happened?"

"Nothing of interest." With her voice calm, she refrained from discussing lunch with David; Mom could obtain her information directly from him or his mother.

"Oh. Being in a new town, I imagined your days filled with the excitement of new discoveries." Deflated spirits gave her mom's voice a whiny quality.

"I'll have plenty of excitement when Garrett's back."

"By the way, I can't keep our appointment next week for discussing invitations."

"That's fine. I'll handle ordering them on my own."

"Why don't you come home for a few days? We can visit the printer I mentioned and check out bridal shops down here."

"I'm staying close for Garrett's sake since there's no telling when he'll return. People are married up here all the time, and I doubt they drive to the Cities for everything. Did you want anything else?"

"No, nothing." Her mom sounded disappointed.

"Please tell Dad I love him. Bye."

Leigh ended the connection and mulled over their call. David's appearance must be the result of her mother's manipulations. The lengths she employed against her relationship with Garrett astounded her. At least her mom bowed out of the invitations. Thank goodness Garrett missed her mom's attempt at destroying their engagement. Such a plot wouldn't improve their fractured relationship.

The cooled water drove her from the tub. Time remained for visiting a bridal shop or two before picking up a bottle of wine and dessert for supper with the Hendersons. She wouldn't let the horrid lunch with David or an inquisitive call from her mom interrupt her day any further.

The afternoon flew by. She visited two bridal shops and the experience of shopping for wedding dresses drained her. Although she learned many current styles were designed with a vintage flair, she didn't find one. She developed an attack plan to prevent her search from becoming Garrett's analogy of hunting for Christmas trees. She'd record pluses and minuses for each dress and ask Janet to take pictures of her in the various dresses.

"What would be a proper dessert for teenagers...chocolate cake? A red wine goes with meatloaf, so I'll find a Shiraz." Leigh discussed her options with herself as she drove in search of her contributions for the night's dinner. She hoped Joe had an update on Garrett's assignment. Should she tell them of her run-in with David? No, she could handle him on her own.

In a half hour, she parked in front of the address Janet provided her. What an adorable home! Even buried in snow, the house radiated hominess. She noted the fenced backyard and remembered the family included two dogs. Grabbing her purchases, she made her way up the walk to the door.

"Leigh! Welcome. Let me take those." Joe opened the door as she climbed the steps.

"Thanks. I hope everyone eats chocolate cake."

"What all-American family doesn't love chocolate cake?" Janet gave Leigh a hug. "No problem finding the house?"

"None whatsoever," Leigh answered as Joe took her coat.

"Follow me." Janet led her through a living room, past a dining room, and into a large country-style kitchen.

"Your home is lovely." Leigh settled on a bar stool at the kitchen island.

"The floor plan works well for us. The boys use the family room in the basement while Joe and I enjoy the living room up here. I don't concern myself with their mess, and they're solely responsible for the cleanup of their space. Although, the possibility of something nasty growing downstairs worries me, so I send Joe down for periodic health checks." Janet broke into laughter, and Leigh joined her.

Joe walked around the corner, returning from the discussed family room. "I should receive a medal or hazard pay for venturing into their play area," he quipped good-naturedly. "I asked the boys to come up and meet you. Be prepared, the dogs will come up with them."

Shortly after Joe's warning, a thundering noise raced up the stairwell. The first arrivals were two black labs. They found Leigh as soon as they entered the kitchen.

"Well, hello! Aren't you two adorable?" She hopped off the stool and greeted the dogs. Their tails beat against the island as they jostled for position near her. "Who's who?"

"The smaller one is Hitch, and the bigger one is Butch. And these two are our sons, Josh and Jared." Joe stood between two tall brown-haired teenagers, one wearing glasses and the other with a full set of braces. "Boys, this is Miss Ramsey. She's engaged to the newest member of my team."

"Hi," they said together.

"I'm pleased to meet you." Leigh smiled at them. "I brought dessert, so I hope you like chocolate cake."

"Wow! That's my favorite," Josh shouted.

"Who doesn't like chocolate cake?" Jared asked seriously.

"Then I'm glad I selected this over cheesecake." Leigh laughed in response.

"We like cheesecake, too, especially with fruit over the top," Josh volunteered.

"You can bring cheesecake when you come over for dinner again," Jared suggested.

"Boys! You do not put in requests!" Janet scolded while she restrained a smile.

"I'll remember you like cheesecake," Leigh promised with a wink.

"Alright, you can head back down and take the dogs with you." Joe's authoritative order sent the boys and dogs in motion down to the family room.

"What a crew; how old are they?" Leigh regained her seat on the bar stool.

"Josh is sixteen and Jared is fourteen. They're well-behaved kids for teenagers, and their friends are very responsible for which I'm thankful." Janet's eyes sparkled as she spoke of her sons.

"Garrett and I plan on having children, at least three. We never discussed pets. After meeting your two, I can see us with one or two dogs," Leigh speculated.

"The dogs are great company when Joe travels. Don't discount cats though. I wouldn't trade Snowball for anything." At Leigh's raised eyebrows, Janet added, "Snowball's our cat. She's around somewhere, so you may or may not see her. Would you care for something to drink?"

"A glass of wine would be delightful."

"Joe, can you open the wine?"

"Already started, Jan." He arrived with a corkscrew and the bottle of Shiraz.

"I should finish the side dishes, so why don't you two relax in the living room?"

"Can I help with dinner?" Leigh asked.

"Thanks, but no. You're a guest, and I'll be done in no time." Janet shooed them out of the kitchen.

Joe preceded Leigh into the living room. "Make yourself comfortable."

"Thank you. I appreciate this evening; a home feels so normal compared to the hotel and restaurants." Leigh sat in an overstuffed chair near him.

"We're happy having you over. I promised Garrett we'd watch out for you, so why not get together now and then?" Joe's voice gentled to a reassuring tone. "He's doing well and making a difference on his assignment."

"Really?" His comment caught her attention. She sat forward; her eyes begged for additional information.

"Yes, he identified a man and a woman they suspect are in charge of the group he and his partner are tasked to bring down. His observation skills did the trick. We now have names and a location we can focus on; meanwhile, they're seeking a meeting with them. With any luck, this could wrap up soon." Joe noticed a smile broke across Leigh's face. "What's so funny?"

"Once I commented on Garrett's lack of observation skills when he didn't notice a girl flirting with him." A slight blush colored her cheeks over sharing the personal moment. "I'm glad his skills are working for him now."

Joe laughed. "Leigh, I believe when it comes to women, his eyes only see you and zone out all others. I saw the way he looks at you; he won't stray."

Her blush deepened with his words, and he chuckled.

"What are you two discussing?" Janet walked in after hearing Joe's laughter. "What did you say? Leigh's blushing as red as an apple."

By now Leigh's laughter joined Joe's. "I'm fine. He reassured me of Garrett's being true to me as well as the quality of his observation skills."

"I'm sure I'm missing a pivotal piece of this conversation, but as long as he's behaving, I won't say another word." She sat by her husband and gave him a playful glare.

"He's been the consummate host, don't worry." After controlling her laughter, Leigh continued. "I visited a couple of the bridal shops this afternoon, and I'm relieved you're joining me tomorrow. This will be a demanding task. I came up with a strategy for shopping. We record our impressions for each dress, and you photograph me wearing each one."

"Sounds like a solid plan. The notes and photographs will make your decision process easier." Janet sipped her wine. "This wine is delicious."

"Garrett introduced me to Shiraz wines. I can't believe I never tried one before." Leigh remembered how the wine tasting at the Aspen Inn served as a prelude to Garrett's proposal. "Are you sure I can't help with dinner or set the table?"

"No, thank you. We're informal and dish up right in the kitchen, so the boys have fewer dishes to wash. Joe, did you update her on Garrett's status?"

"Yup, mission accomplished." He gave her a smart salute.

"We hope his assignment is completed soon."

"I miss him so much but learning he's making a difference means my missing him is worth my loneliness." Leigh smiled and sipped her wine. "Will he be given similar assignments, Joe?"

"The task force in charge of this operation is a standing organization but staffed out of a different BCA office. His arrival came at the right time. He filled an empty position created by a man leaving for a medical emergency with his family. This might be a onetime deal, but I'm not comfortable saying he'll never be tasked again. He has a knack for this type of work." Aware his answer fell short of the one Leigh hoped for, Joe's eyes sought out his wife for assistance.

Before Janet could add anything, Leigh spoke up in a soft voice. "I understand and appreciate your honesty. Law enforcement is Garrett's life, and I understood what came with him and his career choice when I accepted his proposal. Whenever he's home, we'll celebrate our time together."

"Your understanding and support will strengthen your marriage." Janet shared a warm look with Joe. "Supper should be ready, so you two can join me in the kitchen."

"Dinner smells delicious. Eating a home-cooked meal is a real treat." Leigh sniffed the aromas with appreciation.

"It's nothing fancy, only meatloaf," Janet mumbled, seemingly embarrassed by the simple meal.

"The dinner is more than the food; this is a touch of home. I can't wait until we have a kitchen, so I can cook for Garrett," Leigh admitted.

"Don't feed him too much; I prefer my team lean and mean," Joe joked with her as they filled their plates.

Leigh laughed in response. "I'll keep your preferences in mind, but no promises."

Janet called her sons upstairs, but only Butch and Hitch appeared. "You two, outside." The dogs escaped through the back door.

"I hope you didn't send them out because of me." Leigh gazed at the two black labs jumping through the snowdrifts.

"They'll be back in soon; besides they enjoy playing in the snow." Joe set his filled plate on the long wooden table in the kitchen and walked to the back door, where two snow-covered black dogs had appeared.

While they ate, the discussion covered pets, recipes, Leigh's house hunting, and the local area.

The ring of Joe's cell phone interrupted the conversation.

"Excuse me." He rose and continue speaking as he walked into the living room. "Henderson…yes, I can be there. Give me forty-five minutes." His voice carried into the kitchen, but the words were no longer discernible.

"Many nights he receives business calls, but he stays for the entire meal as often as he can. I suggest you work with Garrett on a similar arrangement. Most of the newer agents respond as soon as they receive a call, but more times than not they can wait until they finish whatever they were doing." As her husband walked away, Janet used the interruption as a mentoring opportunity. "The job can be a struggle and requires patience over the many demands on him and his time. He'll figure it out but ensure you and your relationship remain a priority."

"I understand. He let me have my way many times, so he's been receptive to my needs and desires, plus my suggestions." Leigh appreciated Janet's guidance, certain her wisdom and experience would be invaluable in the future.

"I'm needed at work for an hour or so after dinner," Joe informed Janet as he returned from the living room. "Boys, upstairs, now! I'm leaving for the office when I finish eating."

Sounds of the boys rushing up the stairs echoed in the stairway.

"Easy guys, or else Miss Ramsey will think you don't have any manners at all." The warning in Joe's tone brought the boys under control as they continued into the kitchen.

"Yes, Dad," they agreed in unison. They filled their plates and sat at the table. The older one, Josh, braved sitting beside Leigh.

"Why are you going in?" Josh asked before he stuffed a fork piled high with mashed potatoes into his mouth.

"I received some reports to review and forward on before the morning." Joe evaded details with an expertise developed over the years.

Leigh wondered if the reports dealt with Garrett's work, but she decided against being too inquisitive. She watched the boys devour their meal and enjoyed the sense of family around her. This is what she wished for Garrett and her: a loving family with quality time spent together. Her thoughts drifted to him, and she recited her constant prayer for his success and safe return.

***

Hours before then, the subject of her prayer sat in the back of a crowded bar with Karl as they awaited James's arrival.

"Guess who walked in the door." Karl waved at the man they spent over an hour waiting on.

"I'll bring him a drink with our refills." Garrett

strode to the bar. "Two more Goldens and add a Jack and Coke." As he waited on the drinks, James joined Karl. The man wore a broad smile and gestured with wild abandon, so perhaps a favorable decision had been made regarding them. Garrett searched for the couple who traveled with James the other evening but didn't see them. When his order appeared before him, he returned to the table.

"James, thanks for meeting us tonight." Karl clapped the man on his back and almost toppled him over. "Here's a drink for you."

Garrett set the drinks in front of everyone. He loomed over James, fully engaged in his security role. "I see you're carrying a weapon."

"How do you know?" James twisted to his right.

"Knowing is my job. Sit and keep your hands on the table where I can see them." Garrett's hands clamped down on James's shoulders and guided him into a chair. Once James positioned himself with his hands around his drink glass, Garrett took a seat across from him.

"I believe you can ease back a bit," Karl directed Garrett. "He's here for negotiations, nothing more. Am I correct?"

"Yes, I'm here for negotiations. The gun's for self-protection." James still clutched his glass with both hands.

"Fine." Garrett sat back and drank some of his beer. Perhaps he should feel guilty for intimidating the man, but it distracted him from thoughts of Leigh with David.

"I appreciate your joining us, James. We either negotiate a deal tonight or I pull back my offer." Karl stared down their target.

"I understand, and I spoke with my employer before coming. He approved working with you, so I'm here to finalize terms." James downed the drink and pushed the empty glass in Garrett's direction.

"Excellent, let's talk details." Karl rubbed his hands together and nodded at Garrett. "Get the man a refill, and I need one, too."

"Sure thing."

Garrett scooped up the empty glass. Once at the bar, he leaned against the wooden edge and followed the negotiations with interest. Karl maintained a low profile during the heated discussion. As the two men's heads drew closer together, he decided they must be nearing the end of their dealmaking. Sure enough, Karl's head popped up, and his smile said mission accomplished. And that meant, they were in with their targeted crew. With fresh drinks in hand, he rejoined them.

"Ah, here we go." Karl clapped James on the back. "Let's drink to our new partnership. Here's to success!"

"To success!" James tapped his glass against their beer bottles. "Is tomorrow night too soon for your purchase? Seven o'clock?"

"Seven? Yeah, I can rearrange my schedule and secure the payment by then." Karl's voice dropped, and he became all business.

"Super! As I said, we're ready for this exclusive deal with you." James tossed down his drink and looked expectantly at Garrett.

"James, I can't tell you how excited we are over doing business with your organization," Karl continued.

"Once your references checked out, we were anxious to finalize this relationship, too. My employers need a distribution network for our product; our emphasis is production. In fact, we grow some spectacular weed if you're interested." He pushed his empty glass in Garrett's direction.

"If the quality is there, I might be. If you add a sample in our first order, I'll complete a comparison and get back with you on my decision." Karl disregarded James's apparent need for another drink.

"Sure, Keith, no problem. Here, let me buy this round." He slid a fifty-dollar bill to Garrett. "You don't mind going up for our drinks, do you?"

"Nope." Garrett kept his voice level and his movements smooth as he rose. Clasping the money and empties in his hands, he returned once again to the bar. "Another round."

The bartender nodded his acknowledgment of the order as he drew a beer. Garrett took this opportunity to observe the other customers. His instincts worked overtime as his gaze surveyed the crowd.

Two young women, a drink away from drunken stupors, sat at one table. Two men at the next table aided in their endeavor. The flirting between the tables increased with each sip of liquor. He predicted they'd share a table soon, pair off into couples, and enjoy wild sex throughout the evening. Another woman sat alone in a dark booth, but people continually stopped by for a short visit. Either she was a popular lady or a dealer, and his money was on the latter option.

"Here you go. Did you have a tab?"

"Nope." The fifty passed hands, and he left a sizable tip. As he approached the table, Karl laughed at something James said.

"Took you long enough; we're parched." Karl reached for his beer and took a long swallow.

"Yeah, dude, parched." James laughed until Garrett leveled a glare at him. "Dang, Keith, you need a guy who smiles every once in a while."

"I don't pay him to smile." Karl enjoyed the interplay between James and Garrett. "He's the head of my security and worth every penny I pay him."

"Security? He doesn't look big enough," James blurted out but ducked his head in response to another glare sent his way.

"Size isn't significant; I pay for his intellect and fighting skills." Karl drank more of his beer and stared directly in the man's eyes. His voice dropped to a lethal calm. "Plus, he's downright deadly with any weapon."

James broke out in a sweat and glanced in Garrett's direction. The man capturing his attention sat back and coolly assessed him.

"N-no offense. I always thought big burly guys worked in security." James's voice cracked.

"Those guys provide intimidation through a show of force. Whether they can provide actual security is questionable. I prefer having confidence that my man can handle any situation. Exceptional security is why my organization is successful."

"I see. Well, I should be going and ensure everything is ready for you tomorrow." James downed his drink and offered his hand. "Keith, we expect this will be a profitable relationship."

"Absolutely. We'll meet you here tomorrow night as agreed. Working with you has been a pleasure."

Garrett played his role by sitting back and assessing them as the other two men stood and James took his leave.

"Right! Let's ensure our organization's ready, too." Karl drained his beer and clapped Garrett on the shoulder. "Let's roll."

They walked out of the bar re-energized by their accomplishment, eager for a successful completion of the assignment. Karl tossed the keys to Garrett and slid into the passenger seat.

"You drive, and I'll complete some calls. We'll drop off our photos and maps with Joe. He'll pass the info to the task force, and they'll coordinate the support we need for tomorrow." Karl noted Garrett's raised eyebrow. "Yeah, we got the location right, the meeting is at the farmstead we picked out the other day. We proved to be a high-performance duo, partner."

"Good thing I finished the drawings after lunch. What's your recommendation for this going down?"

"The outbuildings work as direct cover for the

support team, but they're a distance from the farmhouse. We'll be on our own until they reach us. The road we parked on for our surveillance should work as a staging area for our backup, close enough for a fast response in case of a shoot-out."

"Sounds like a solid plan. I don't recall seeing much security around the place."

"I think most people on-site are workers, so the advantage is ours. Let me call Joe." Karl pulled out his cell and dialed in a number. "The meeting is scheduled, so can we meet you at the office tonight?...Forty-five minutes?...Sure. We'll bring the photos and diagrams of the location for the task force...Tomorrow night at seven....Yeah, setting up a meeting has been a long time coming, but we succeeded, thanks to your boy...We'll be there." He ended the call.

"So back to the house, grab our stuff, and head for the office?" Garrett glanced at Karl.

"That's the plan. Joe prefers having dinner with his family whenever he can, so he asked for forty-five minutes. We couldn't reach his office much before then anyway."

"Leigh joined them for dinner tonight." Garrett's voice softened with thoughts of her.

"At Joe's?"

"Yeah, they promised to keep an eye on her. She's become friends with Janet."

"Janet's the type of woman you want her being friends with. She can provide guidance and insight into the life Leigh will live as your wife. Her influence will be huge in Leigh's understanding of the lifestyle she's signed up for. Their relationship might prevent a divorce from happening in your future." Karl's typical gruff tone softened to a low rumble.

He bristled over Karl's last remark but chose to ignore it. "I appreciate their watching over her; their involvement made the separation easier for me." Garrett wrestled with the steering wheel as the car bumped down the road.

"We're nearing the end, and you'll be back in the arms of your hot fiancée soon." At Garrett's glare, Karl added, "She's hot. You can't deny the fact, so don't crucify me for speaking the truth."

A smile formed on Garrett's lips before he responded. "She is hot, but I prefer you don't leer at me when you say it."

"You'll introduce us, won't you? After all, we've worked together, ate together, drank together, slept together…in the same house, not the same bed."

"Thanks for clarifying the sleeping together part. I'll let you know what I decide." With a shake of his head, Garrett focused on driving rather than his comedic partner. An introduction to Leigh would happen once this ended, but he found devilish pleasure in letting the man wonder.

As they neared the house, Karl tossed out instructions. "You gather your diagrams, and I'll grab the camera. We'll head for our meeting with Joe as soon as we pull everything together."

"Don't let me forget to make copies of the diagrams while we're at the office." Garrett stopped the car but left the engine running.

Moments later they raced back to the car. Karl thrust the camera at Garrett. "You hold everything, and I'll drive."

"Can this come together in less than twenty-four hours?" Garrett juggled papers and camera as he reached for the door handle.

"Shouldn't be a problem. The task force can act fast. They'll coordinate with local law enforcement and ensure all the capability we need is available." Karl backed down the driveway too fast, jerked the wheel, and spun out on the road. "Because we've seen the property firsthand, they'll accept our recommendations. They'll be close by if the action goes south, but I'm sure you and I can handle this group."

"Thanks for your confidence. Could you slow down before you put us in the ditch?"

Karl laughed. "Don't you trust me?"

"Sure, I trust you. But I'm not convinced you're the safest driver in the DEA." Garrett smiled as he relayed his doubts.

Karl snorted. "We'll arrive safe and sound. You sit back and watch a trained professional handle the driving."

With a shrug of his shoulders, Garrett did as instructed, but his gaze strayed to the side window in hopes of reducing his involuntary cringes and stomping on imaginary brakes. When the office came into view, he failed at repressing a sigh of relief. After the car came to an abrupt stop, Garrett considered kissing the ground when he exited the vehicle. He doubted Karl would appreciate the humor in the act, so he dismissed the thought.

"Did you let out a sigh of relief when we stopped? At least you didn't kiss the ground like my last partner." He spotted the telltale smile on Garrett's lips. "You considered doing the same damn thing, didn't you? Everybody's a critic. Come on."

They started toward the rear door when a car pulled in and parked beside them. SAIC Henderson stepped out.

"Greetings, guys! Garrett, you look a bit pale. Obviously, Karl drove in his typical breakneck style." Joe clapped Garrett on the back and laughed.

"As if you drive any better. Let us in, so we can get out of the cold." Karl punched Joe in the arm and pulled him close to share a confidential assessment. "You did alright bringing him on board. He's sharp, real sharp."

"Thought you might approve of him, and I appreciate the feedback." Joe unlocked the door and led them through the dark hallways.

Garrett hung back from the other two men, giving

them privacy for whatever information they shared. The interactions between them exhibited a different side of each man.

They settled into Joe's office.

"If we'll be here for a while, I can brew coffee," Joe offered.

"Not necessary, we won't take long. Garrett, bring over your drawings." Karl took immediate charge of their discussion. "This is the location for the meeting, probably in the house for the transaction. We took pictures of the entire site, so you can download them."

"The cluster of buildings will provide cover for a support team. What type of communications capability do you use?" Joe reviewed the drawings.

"All the high-tech stuff. We'll conduct a communications check with the task force tomorrow." Karl pointed at the drawing of the overall area. "The road to the north offers cover. We used this spot as our vantage point when we observed the farmstead and took the pictures. How fast can you download them?" He removed the chip from the camera.

Joe turned on his computer. In a short time, they studied the photos.

"James confirmed they expanded with a marijuana growing operation, so we guessed correctly, Garrett." Karl smiled as he pointed out one of the pictures. "This larger building with extra generators and a water supply is where we suspect they grow the plants."

"Where do you think the meth production happens? Wherever they cook meth is the most volatile location." Joe scanned the other pictures while glancing at the drawings.

"This building is the most likely." Garrett pointed out a building on his drawing. "The sophisticated ventilation system screams meth production."

"With such an elaborate setup, this group's operation must date back a few years." Joe leaned back in his chair with a thoughtful expression on his face.

"Or else they invested their life savings. However they financed their operation, they're serious about seizing a sizable market share for themselves." Karl sat back, arms behind his head, and stared at Joe. "We meet them at seven tomorrow night for the buy. Tell the task force we need realistic funds to convince them. I agreed on one point two million."

"They'll love putting that amount together in less than twenty-four hours. Won't I be the popular one?" Joe sighed.

"Better you than me." Karl smiled.

"I'll email the task force your photos and drawings and call them to ensure they read the message tonight. Should I advise them of your plans for a communications check in the morning?"

"It'd help if you would." Karl thumped him on his back.

Joe tapped a few keys on his computer keyboard before looking at them. "Outstanding work, guys!"

Karl and Garrett looked at each other and grinned. They were near the end of their operation.

"Where can I make copies of the drawings?" Garrett picked up the papers.

"Copier is on your right and around the corner." Joe pointed in the general direction.

"Okay, I'll be right back." Garrett slipped out of the room.

"Today's been a tough day for the kid." Karl listened as Garrett walked off. "He spotted his fiancée walking into a restaurant with her ex-boyfriend at lunch."

"Leigh didn't mention anything about an ex-boyfriend at supper tonight." Joe's eyes widened, and his mouth dropped open.

"Not exactly something you share with your fiancé's boss, is it? He didn't recognize the guy, so I went inside the restaurant and scoped out the situation. To her credit, she didn't appear entranced with her lunch date. We have no idea what he's doing here or how long he's staying."

"Jan's shopping with her tomorrow for wedding dresses, so the wedding is still on."

"Mention their plans to him. The knowledge may ease his mind a bit."

"Sure. You're proving to be a caring partner, Karl, even if your lousy driving skills threaten their lives on a daily basis."

"Gee, thanks for the backhanded compliment." Karl's laugh drifted out of the office and down the hall to Garrett as he returned from the copier.

"Here you are, sir." Garrett handed Joe the originals.

"Alright, I'll send the email before leaving tonight. You guys rest up for tomorrow." Joe settled behind his computer. He couldn't ignore Karl's bobbing head serving as a silent reminder for him to say something of Leigh to his agent. "Garrett, hold on a minute."

"I'll be in the car," Karl advised Garrett. He walked out the door with a wave for Joe.

Unable to come up with an operational reason for being asked to stay behind, Garrett's thoughts centered immediately on Leigh. If something happened to her, he wasn't sure how he'd react.

Joe chose his words with care. "Leigh came over for supper tonight. She remains positive regarding your assignment and was in good spirits. After meeting our dogs, she'll be looking for puppies, so consider yourself forewarned. She and Jan are shopping tomorrow for her wedding dress."

"Thank you, sir, I appreciate the update. I can't help but worry about her." Garrett's face reflected his relief.

"Well, you should be with her tomorrow night. Best catch up with Karl, or he may leave you behind."

"Yes, sir." Garrett took off at a jog.

Joe sat for a moment staring at the spot vacated by Garrett. He held a short debate in his head over sharing this news with Jan. After deciding she should be aware of what happened in case Leigh shared any concerns, he continued with his work. The sooner he completed his email and made a few calls, the sooner he returned home.

Garrett caught up with Karl on the stairs.

"So, good news from your boss?"

"What? Oh, yeah, he mentioned having Leigh over for supper."

"And?"

"She's still positive about my job, and the two ladies are shopping tomorrow for her wedding dress."

"Then the ex-boyfriend shouldn't be a problem." Karl prompted him to the obvious conclusion.

"No, I suppose he shouldn't be, but I'm sure her mom will develop other schemes."

"Her mom sounds as though she's one crafty bitch." Karl walked to the driver's side of the car.

"Yeah, you summed her up fairly well." Garrett held his partner's eyes. His fingers tapped against the door frame in a show of his agitation. "You ready?"

"Yup, let's go."

They slipped into the car. Garrett buckled up as Karl brought the engine to life.

"I need something sweet. What would you say to some coffee and a cookie or two?" Karl glanced at Garrett, unable to determine his thoughts.

"I can't say no to coffee and cookies."

They drove off in search of an evening treat.

***

Leigh reached her room without a run-in with David. She avoided the lobby, fearful he might be waiting there in hopes of catching her when she returned.

She pulled out her journal and the last of the

snickerdoodles. After she prepared a small pot of decaf coffee to brew, she let the coffeepot do its thing as she washed up and donned her nightshirt. With coffee and cookies nearby, she poured out her heart and mind to her fiancé.

Continuation, Friday, February 14th. My dearest Garrett, How I miss you! My life truly improved when you fell into it. I'm certain because I now have you to compare David to, and there is no comparison! He falls short in every way, to include sexual prowess. (Thought you'd enjoy reading that.)

Lunch with David was horrendous. How did I not realize what manner of man he was? Now my eyes are wide open. He acted so sure of himself as if he expected me to fall into his arms. He wants to have dinner with me tomorrow. Somehow, he knows what room I'm in and plans on picking me up at my room. Maybe I should renege? I haven't decided. He got forceful today and kissed me as I tried to walk past him in the restaurant. The kiss was hard and demanding. I should have slapped him, but he shocked me into a stupor. I refused to ride back to the hotel with him.

The funniest thing happened; there was a gentleman who sat in the booth behind us. He heard most of our conversation and chuckled at some of my responses. As he walked away, he gave me a thumbs-up sign. It appeared he approved of my actions. Unfortunately, he left before the kiss; otherwise, I bet he'd have intervened.

Then Mom called to find out if anything exciting had happened. I didn't mention David or the lunch. I'm convinced she had a hand in David's being here. On the bright side, she said she didn't have time for our scheduled appointment to discuss invitations, so I'm forging ahead without her involvement. Her loss and our gain!

I visited a couple of bridal shops today. It will be a challenging decision, and your Christmas tree analogy is accurate. Janet is joining me tomorrow. I'm bringing my notebook for notes and will take pictures, so I'll be prepared for a wise decision. I wonder what the chances are for falling in love at first sight with a wedding dress; can it happen twice in one lifetime—love at first sight?

I had a fun time at the Hendersons tonight. Their boys are typical teenagers, and their dogs are adorable. I didn't meet their cat, but Janet says to not underestimate them as family pets. We need a dog or two, especially if we have a lot of property for them to run on. What breed would you want? Are you a hunter? If so, should the dog be a hunting dog? Have you had pets before? We never did. Mom said they were too messy; I think I missed out.

I understand you're doing well and making a difference on your assignment. I'm so proud of you!

Because of the late hour, I'm having decaf coffee with the last of your snickerdoodles. LOL! You didn't eat as many of them as you expected; too bad, so sad. I, on the other hand, have enjoyed them. Don't worry. As soon as we have a kitchen, I'll bake you some—I promise.

I hope my dreams are of you tonight, and I further hope you're in a playful mood! Yes, I'm talking sex. I'd rather be with you in person, but these days I'll have fun with dream Garrett. I love you with all my heart. Leigh

♥♥♥

The ring of her phone surprised her. The ringtone told her the caller's identity.

"Dad!"

"Hi, Leigh. Hope I didn't wake you." He sounded hesitant.

"No, I've been writing in my journal. What's up?"

"How's Garrett?"

"He's doing well and making a difference. I miss him."

"He'll be back soon, honey." Her dad's voice softened. "I called as a favor to our friends, Claire and Don Walker."

"Oh? A favor to the Walkers?" Leigh sat upright; her voice sounded brittle in her ears.

"David's up there looking at some property, and they asked if you could spend some time with him, possibly join him for dinner."

"I ran into him this morning at breakfast. He's staying at this hotel."

"What a coincidence."

"I'm not sure it is a coincidence." Leigh confided her suspicions.

"I'm sure it is. They had no idea you were up there; we had dinner with them tonight. They expressed surprise when we informed them you had returned to Minnesota."

"Did you tell them about my engagement?"

"Well, no, your mother didn't feel it was wise to discuss the topic with them, considering the past relationship between David and you. Because of her response to Garrett at the cabin, I agreed." His voice dropped lower and quieter as though preventing his wife from overhearing their conversation.

"Yet David knew of my engagement. You're playing right into her hand, Dad. This is Mom's attempt at breaking up Garrett and me. I doubt any other explanation exists." Leigh's flat delivery demonstrated her disgust.

"I can't believe your mother would stoop to such lengths. David probably noticed the engagement ring you wear, nothing more sinister. Agree on a dinner with David and be done with it." Her dad didn't argue often, but he could be persistent.

"Please don't ask me to spend time with him."

"Leigh, his parents are our closest friends, and I doubt your schedule is so busy you can't do this for me. I'm only talking about one dinner. I'll tell his parents you're pleased to join him. Do this for me?"

Her dad rarely asked her for anything, so she couldn't deny him. "I'll do it, but only because you asked."

"Thanks, honey. Good night."

"Night, Dad." She ended the call and stared at her phone. Why did he not see this as a ploy by her mother to arrange time together for David and her? A feeling of betrayal sank her spirits; she plopped on the bed. How she ached for Garrett's arms wrapped around her. She sprang from the bed, sat at the desk, and searched through her journal for the end of her last entry.

P.S. I believe my dad has fallen victim to a ploy for reuniting David and me. He called and asked, as a favor to him, for me to have dinner with David tomorrow. He and Mom had dinner with David's parents tonight. Of course they didn't inform the Walkers of our engagement. I can understand Dad's reasoning for Mom would have been most critical of you.

I will suffer through this for Dad. You cannot come back to me soon enough! Leigh OXOXXX

After closing her journal with a sigh, Leigh turned off the desk lamp. Tears flowed as she climbed into the empty bed. Dinner with David was not a pleasant thought after what transpired at lunch. She grabbed what she thought of as Garrett's pillow and hugged it close. *Oh, Garrett, please come back to me soon. I need you.*

The pillow muffled her sobs as she cried herself to sleep.

CHAPTER TWENTY

The morning dawned overcast with a promise of snow. Garrett woke early and packed his things. When he dressed, he allowed room for the bulletproof vest under his clothes. Their strategy didn't include anyone being killed, least of all Karl or him.

Later he sat in the kitchen, a mug of coffee by an elbow and supplies to clean his gun spread before him. A loud thump upstairs drew his eyes to the ceiling. Either his partner fell out of bed or started packing his stuff. He shook his head as his attention returned to his SIG. This assignment turned into an enjoyable one because Karl proved to be a reliable partner, who knew his business and provided entertainment at times.

"Garrett, you got coffee made?" Karl's rough call echoed off the empty walls.

"Yes!" Garrett hollered back. He pulled out a mug and poured another coffee. He set it on the table as the man rumbled down the stairs.

"What an acceptable husband you'll be for Leigh if you do this for her every morning." Karl slouched in a chair and inhaled the coffee aroma before he took a sip. He hadn't showered yet and his hair stuck up in odd tufts scattered around his head. "Noticed you packed already, so you're eager to head home? Can't say as I blame you, what with her ex-boyfriend hanging around."

"Thanks for reminding me."

"As if you forgot. Remember, I witnessed your reaction to the sight of them together. You would have torn him apart limb from limb if he stood within reach." Karl eyed him over the mug as he drank his coffee.

"Yeah, well, I don't need my weaknesses thrown in my face. I recall every second of him walking with her, and how I envisioned racing over there, breaking his arms, and punching him out for touching her. Not too adult of me," Garrett confessed with self-disgust.

"You're human, man, don't sweat it." Karl clapped him on the shoulder. "As long as you don't act on those urges, you're golden. Tell you what. As your penance, you cook breakfast while I clean up."

Garrett laughed. "Sure thing, Father Karl. Don't take forever."

"Be back in a flash." He bounded up the stairs, and the water flowed in the shower seconds later.

Garrett finished with his gun and set it aside. He laid the copies of his drawings on the table, so they could review their strategy for the evening after breakfast. He anticipated a long day as they waited on their meeting. He pulled out a variety of items from the refrigerator for their breakfast. He decided on cooking a massive egg scramble consisting of the last of their food; as he worked, his thoughts focused on Leigh.

Did David's appearance have her reconsidering the decision to marry him? Did his thoughts show a weakness in his belief of Leigh's commitment to their relationship? No, they reflected his disbelief in the possibility of being loved for himself. Never had a woman touched his soul or captured his heart as Leigh had with one look.

Was Lois behind David's appearance? Would she forever crusade against him? If she did, he'd never trust her. Would his distrust of her mother affect Leigh? Would she eventually resent his attitude toward her mother?

Stop!! he cautioned himself. *You're letting David's sudden appearance mess with your head. Leigh loves you; remember she told you how he had treated her. She'd never return to him and leave you behind*, he reminded himself.

"Smells delicious. Not only will you be a passable husband for Leigh, but you can cook for her! Do you clean, too?"

Garrett scowled at him. "You're not funny, Karl. If

you plan on eating breakfast, walk away." He jabbed the bacon with the fork in his hand and flipped the shriveled strip. "I'll call you when the food's ready."

"Jeez, lighten up. I told you, she didn't accept any of the crap he offered her. She's not cheating on you with the guy."

"Didn't I say walk away if you want breakfast?" Garrett turned on his partner brandishing the fork he used on the bacon.

"Yeah, but I ignored you and plan to stay in the kitchen."

"Sorry, I'm wallowing in self-pity with a touch of self-doubt thrown in. And I can't do either properly with someone watching." Garrett tried not laughing but failed.

Karl relaxed and joined him in laughing. "Your knack for playing a bad ass is unnerving. No wonder you scare James."

"In other words, I played my part well." He pulled out the bacon and tossed in onions and mushrooms. "I thought another review of the plans for tonight might be a smart idea. Will the task force contact us soon?"

"If they don't, we can call. I'll break out our communications gear and schedule a sound check with them. Tonight, we wear our vests and carry our weapons," Karl advised. With a loud sniff, he added, "The aroma of whatever you're cooking is making me salivate like a damn St. Bernard. Can I help with anything?"

"Make the toast. Four pieces should do." Garrett cracked eggs and whipped them up. As he scrambled the eggs, he asked, "Do you expect they'll be heavily armed?"

"No. Since we only spotted a couple armed guards while we had them under surveillance, I doubt they added anymore. According to James, they debated on whether they needed guns or not."

"I suppose he's a proponent for guns." Garrett kept his eyes on the scramble.

"You spotted him carrying a concealed weapon the first time we met, right?" At Garrett's nod, Karl continued. "James bears watching, he's the wild card when this goes down."

"If I can intimidate him enough, he may not be a factor." Garrett plated the food as he spoke.

"I like the way you think. Intimidation might work. You already scare the crap out of him. I almost laughed out loud last night when he told me I should hire a guy who smiled. Did you see his reaction when I told him I didn't pay you to smile? Thank goodness I didn't break into giggles. Do me a favor and maintain the same attitude with him tonight. On second thought, kick it up a notch." Karl added toast to each plate, took one, and walked to the table.

"Sure, I'll ensure James is off kilter." Garrett's eyes held an evil glint. He grabbed the remaining plate and joined Karl at the table. "I'm harboring a high level of angst and playing my security role with him will be a welcomed way to wear the level down."

"Angst?" Deep in thought, Karl dug into his portion of the breakfast scramble, but his eyes remained focused on Garrett.

"Yeah. With David in town and so close to Leigh, plenty of angst built up. James is my legitimate opportunity for relieving most of what's bottled up inside." Garrett's devilish smile showed his eagerness for the evening activities.

"Now I almost feel sorry for him." Karl tried for a sober face without any success. He scooped up the last of his scramble. "Let's review your drawings and strategize on different ways this might go down. After we tweak our plan, I'll call the task force and schedule a few things."

"Okay." Garrett collected their dirty dishes and placed them in the sink. After refreshing his coffee, he joined Karl at the table, but thoughts of Leigh momentarily distracted him. He hoped to be with her soon and planned on showing her how desperately he missed her while away. If they were lucky, the hotel had well-constructed beds because they would put them through some rigorous exercise.

***

Leigh braved the breakfast area first thing in the morning. She breathed a sigh of relief when there was no sign of David. Reflecting back on their time together, he never rose early, so she decided she had time for a Belgian waffle. Janet walked in from the lobby as Leigh indulged in the last golden piece dripping in syrup.

"Your waffle looked delicious," Janet remarked as she sat with Leigh.

"They aren't merely delicious; they're downright decadent!" Leigh smacked her lips for emphasis. "Garrett tried mine our first morning here, and he promised a Belgian waffle machine will be one of our first purchases."

"Instead of buying one, you should add it to your gift registry. Are you registered anywhere yet?"

"Oh crap! Now I need to add create a gift registry on our to-do list for the wedding." Leigh pulled a notebook out of her tote bag and wrote the item at the bottom of her list. "Here I thought I made a dent in our list, but now I lengthened the darn thing."

Janet laughed. "You'll survive. In fact, you may get some assistance with completing your list soon."

"Well, yeah, you shopping with me for my dress is a big help and—you're not talking of our shopping together. You mean something else, don't you?" Her friend's smile spread across her face. At her nod, the one thing Leigh longed for popped into her mind. "Garrett's coming home. His assignment is done?"

"Joe okayed my telling you. With luck, the operation ends tonight." Janet had been thrilled when her husband shared his news and approved her telling Leigh.

She knew no further details and didn't ask for any.

Leigh hugged Janet; her excitement couldn't be contained. She danced with joy, but her exuberance crashed about her when a greeting sounded from behind her.

"Good morning, Leigh. I hope your excitement is for me." David swaggered toward the two women.

"David!" Leigh stood still; her eyes darted from him to Janet and back again. She didn't address his ridiculous comment. "Janet, this is David Walker, a family friend. David, this is Janet Henderson, she's my friend and the wife of my fiancé's boss."

"How do you do?" Janet gazed into his eyes and noted a slyness in them.

"I'm well, especially after seeing Leigh; my morning is off to a wondrous start. Do you ladies need anything?" He slipped into his charming mode.

"No, we're leaving." Leigh grabbed her coat and gathered her things.

"Off for some shopping?" He followed them to the door.

Leigh turned on him. "Yes. We're shopping for my wedding dress. By the way, my father called last night and asked me for a favor, so I'll join you for dinner tonight. His request is the one and only reason I'm doing this. Meet me in the lobby." She didn't wait for his response but spun round and joined Janet outside.

"Hmm, you're making this challenging, Leigh. No telling how the evening unfolds," David muttered to himself.

He smiled as she rushed into her friend's vehicle. His scheme continued tonight with him reminding her of the love they once shared. Full of self-confidence, he entered the breakfast area intent on enjoying his meal. Leigh may believe she's preparing for a wedding to this mysterious fiancé of hers, but in the end the wedding she prepared for would be theirs.

***

Once Janet navigated her SUV on the road, she glanced at Leigh. "He's a family friend?"

Leigh held her eyes for a moment before looking out the windshield with a sigh. "David's parents and mine are best friends. He showed up yesterday at breakfast. He asked me out for dinner, but I declined because I was having dinner with you and your family. Instead, I joined him for lunch which I thought would be a safer option."

"Safer?"

Leigh wondered how much information she should provide Janet, then she realized the benefit of having an ally nearby. "Yes, safer as in broad daylight. He claims he came here for a meeting and to search for a vacation home, but I don't believe him. When he demanded I join him for dinner tonight, I wondered if my mother orchestrated his being here. After my dad called and asked me to join David for dinner as a personal favor, I'm positive she's behind his appearance."

"All this for a family friend?" Janet's eyebrows drew together.

"No," Leigh paused before confessing, "because he's my ex-boyfriend."

"Your ex-boyfriend..." Janet repeated. She remembered Joe's comment of Garrett having caught a glimpse of Leigh walking into a restaurant with a man whose arm had been around her. Later he found out the man was Leigh's former boyfriend. "Ah...Garrett saw you entering the restaurant with David yesterday."

"He what? How?" Leigh faced Janet, her eyes wide and uncertainty sounded in her voice.

"He and his partner were in town for lunch. They were across the street, but he spotted you."

"Just my luck his observation skills kicked into gear," Leigh muttered. "Wait! He never met David, so how did he identify who walked in with me?"

"His partner went inside to discover what was going on, and he got a first name. Garrett figured out the rest."

"Oh my gosh, he must be so upset!" Leigh leaned back in the seat. "This could be bad, right? He'll be distracted. What if he's hurt or killed?"

"Leigh, relax. He'll be fine." Janet smiled as she glanced at her passenger.

"Relax? This is awful, really, really awful! David put his arm around me and pulled me close against his body. At a distance, the appearance of intimacy presented the wrong impression! He probably thinks I'm cheating on him. This is worse than awful; this is catastrophic!" Leigh spoke fast and squirmed in her seat.

"His partner told him of your displeasure with your lunch partner." Janet parked in front of the first bridal shop. "Leigh don't worry; he doesn't doubt your love for him. Joe told Garrett we're shopping for your wedding dress today, so he's aware of you continuing with the wedding plans. Now, are you ready for some serious shopping?"

Leigh stared at Janet. She took a deep breath and a shaky release followed. "I can handle this. Thanks."

They walked into the shop, and Leigh's wedding dress adventure began. Three hours after setting foot in the bridal shop, they tumbled into Janet's SUV.

"This will be so difficult, but so much fun! Who would think they served champagne in a bridal shop?" Leigh giggled as she buckled up her seat belt.

"I enjoyed the experience, too. Should we grab some lunch before our next stop?" Janet settled into her seat.

"Lunch is a good idea; I think I'm a little tipsy. Is a restaurant either near here or before the next shop?" Leigh dropped her notebook into her tote bag.

"I know of an unusual restaurant on our way. We'll stop there, review your notes while we eat, and be prepared for whatever we run across at the next shop." Janet pulled out on the street and drove through the traffic with ease. The traffic volume diminished to a rare car when she stopped at a quaint restaurant located off the beaten path. "We're here. Not much more than a hole-in-the-wall, but the food is the best."

"Works for me." Leigh hastened out of the vehicle. She enjoyed out-of-the-way places, and Janet apparently knew them all. "This is cute!" She admired the rustic décor. The owner must be a huge fan of taxidermy based on the various wildlife and fish mounts displayed throughout the restaurant.

They sat in a booth near a window overlooking a few sparse pine trees and guarded by a stuffed goose. After they ordered beverages, Leigh pulled out her notebook and phone.

"All the dresses I tried on were pretty, but I noted pluses and minuses for each one." Leigh scrolled through the photographs Janet had taken of her in the many dresses she'd tried on.

"In other words, none of them wowed you." Janet reviewed the notes they wrote at the shop. Her eyes caught Leigh's, and they shared a smile.

"You're right, no wow with any of them. When you shopped for your dress, how did you decide on the one you bought? Did you see it on the hanger and say this is the one? Or was it when you saw your reflection in the mirror?"

"I picked out my dream dress in a magazine, so my mother and I tracked down a bridal shop carrying it in their inventory." Janet's voice softened to a dreamy quality as she focused on the past. "The dress had lace everywhere and a long train with a matching lace veil. When I found it on the rack, I actually shrieked and couldn't wait to put it on. I had tears in my eyes all the way into the dressing room."

"Did you feel like a princess?"

"Hah! The thing turned out to be the most uncomfortable dress ever, and the weight of the veil made my head hurt moments after I tried it on. I was so disappointed."

Leigh couldn't believe what she heard. "How terrible having your dream crushed. What did you do?"

"I cried for a day, and then we resumed our shopping." Janet sighed and smiled. "Two days later I found a satin dress, the fit and style blew my mind away, and we stopped looking."

"So, what you're telling me is don't give up. I shouldn't be disappointed after one shop."

"Correct. Remember, the salesclerk said they're receiving new stock next week, so we can return and check them out. We'll find you the ideal dress." Janet squeezed Leigh's hand. "You'll see. Let's order, so we can continue shopping."

Once the waiter left with their orders, they reviewed their notes in conjunction with the pictures.

"This first one flattered your figure," Janet offered, "but our notes don't agree with the fit."

"I didn't care for the neckline, too revealing. If I bend over to visit with people at a table, their view of my upper body almost matches Garrett's view in the privacy of our room." Leigh enlarged the photo and showed Janet what she meant.

"Understand. We'll mark this dress as a no. Let's be sure we mention the neckline issue at each of the shops, so they eliminate similar dresses." She marked the entry and turned to their notes on the second dress. "This one sounds promising: an appropriate neckline, short train, but no lace. Is not having lace a terrible thing?"

"I should decide whether I want lace or not. Part of me considers lace as romantic, and the other part believes it's too much. Perhaps when I see the right one, I'll know.

We can mark dress number two as a maybe." Leigh sounded less than enthusiastic. "I should rename these pictures with their corresponding number."

"Add your rating as a reminder, so you don't need to pull out your notes all the time," Janet suggested.

"Great idea. The name will be a time-saver. I'll label these first two now." Leigh fiddled with her phone. "Here's dress number three."

"I didn't care for this one."

Janet's frankness surprised Leigh but pleased her.

"Neither did I; way too much dress for me." Janet marked the notebook as she labeled the picture. "Thanks for your honesty. I appreciate your help with the shopping, and I'm glad you don't hold back your thoughts. Your insights are priceless."

"What sort of friend would I be if I let you commit a fashion faux pas?" Her voice and expression reflected a seriousness; however, Janet's sparkling eyes said otherwise.

"I do consider you a friend. I understand the difficulty with you being the wife of Garrett's boss, but I believe we can make the situation work. Ooh, here comes our food." Leigh set her phone aside in eager anticipation of her lunch.

"Only two dresses left from the first shop for our review." Janet read through their notes before sliding the notebook away when a plate appeared in front of her. "This looks delicious, thank you." The waitress returned her smile.

"I'll mark them as 'maybe'. The champagne color is intriguing on the fourth dress, and the appliqués on the fifth looked rich and expensive." Leigh handed Janet her phone before reaching for the ketchup. "Do you agree?"

"Yes, good call on the maybe rating. Which one did you prefer?" Janet asked before biting into her sandwich.

"The last dress; it showed off my curves without hugging them too closely." Leigh lifted her eyebrows for a short moment and wore a sly smile.

"I'm sure Garrett would appreciate a display of curves, although you don't want him drooling at the altar. I suggest your dress color be champagne or ivory rather than white. Those colors complimented your coloring."

Leigh considered Janet's opinion as she ate her burger. "I agree, or even a pale pink color."

"What will Garrett wear?"

"We decided on a cutaway tuxedo for him. He has a contact in the Cities for a rental, but we can check for one around here. I saved the picture of one from a website. If you touch at the top and select downloads…" Leigh waited while Janet manipulated her phone.

"This one?" At Leigh's nod, she studied the details. "Oh my! Garrett would be fabulous in one of these. As I recall, he's tall, broad shouldered, and handsome."

"Nothing wrong with your recollection. I can't wait to see him in one."

The remainder of their lunch conversation focused on the boys, the dogs, and Leigh's house hunting. By the time they paid their bills, they had moved on to Leigh's ex-boyfriend.

"David is here for the entire weekend?" Janet asked as she settled behind the steering wheel.

"Yes. I never planned on joining him for dinner tonight, but when my dad asked me to go as a favor to him, I couldn't decline." Leigh dropped her tote by her feet and buckled her seat belt. "Since agreeing with my dad, I realized this is something I must do. Otherwise, David may continue believing there's hope for him. I can't imagine why he assumes I'd consider being with him again after he cheated on me." While on this shopping excursion, Leigh came to the realization she not only liked Janet as a friend, but she trusted her and valued her counsel. "I broke up with him and hid in Chicago for four years."

"This all happened four years ago?" Amazement

reflected in Janet's face.

"Yes."

"Did he reach out to you during those years?"

"Not once, hence my suspicions regarding my mom's involvement in his being here."

"What time is your dinner?"

"Seven, we'll meet in the lobby. I don't know what restaurant he decided on, but hopefully not a romantic one."

"If he plays to win, I'm sure his selected restaurant will be one with a romantic ambiance. You should dress down for your date…er…appointment." Janet corrected herself at Leigh's pained expression.

"Exceptional idea, jeans and a bulky sweater would be the opposite of what he's expecting. If I text you a 911 message, will you call and fake an emergency?"

"Of course. Enough with this depressing topic, let's continue our shopping." Janet headed for the next shop.

Four straight hours passed with numerous dresses selected and pros and cons documented. Exhaustion overcame each of them.

"How 'bout returning to my hotel? Usually, coffee's available in the lobby, and we can review the dresses."

Janet glanced at the clock in the dash before answering. "I wish I could, but I should head home for the boys. Joe's coming home late, so I promised them pizza and a movie. Sorry. If you don't understand my notes, call me."

"Today has been fun. Thank you."

"You're welcome. We can schedule another date for visiting the other shops."

"Wonderful." Leigh settled back and gazed out at the darkening scenery.

Janet followed Leigh's directions and stopped at one of the side doors of the hotel.

"I hope you'll enjoy an exhilarating evening with

Garrett later. His return will make up for your dinner. After you figure out your schedule, contact me to plan our next shopping trip." She hugged Leigh.

"I will. Thanks again. Don't forget I may text you a 911 for a needed departure from dinner." Leigh left the vehicle, waved, and hurried through the door. She climbed the stairs with a spring in her step. Janet's reminder of Garrett's probable return filled her with happiness and an expectation of a night of sexual bliss. Enough time for her to enjoy a shower and pen a last journal entry before she met David in the lobby.

A short time later, she sat wrapped in her robe with the journal opened in front of her. Thoughts of Garrett's return excited her, so she decided writing would calm her.

Saturday, February 15th. Garrett, my love, I learned you may be done with your assignment tonight! I am hopeful it ends successfully and safely for you and your partner. The thought of being with you again has me excited but concerned. Will what we had before you left be gone, extinguished as a lit candle burns down and goes out? Or (my hope) will our love be stronger? Will your sexy smile still make me melt in your arms? Will everything be fresh and vibrant? Will a mere touch send us into a fit of unleashed passion? Will people be concerned when they don't see or hear from us for days on end as we make up for lost time? We shall soon have answers to these speculations and ones I haven't even imagined.

Janet also disclosed how you saw me with David at lunch. I pray seeing David with me didn't make you doubt my love for you. I now suspect the gentleman I wrote of previously was your partner. I was concerned when she told me. Why? I worried your seeing me with him would be hurtful for you and your concentration would be less than it should be because of it, putting you at risk. Surely you can compartmentalize these things and maintain your focus. OMG! Now realization strikes me...if you never had this type of relationship, then you never had to compartmentalize on an assignment. Now my fear for your safety has increased! You must be safe for I need you. You are my life now, and all I think of throughout the day. Everything I am revolves around you...love is supposed to work this way, right?

Time is ticking away until I have dinner with David. I am not looking forward to this, but I will persevere for Dad. Janet and I have worked out a deal where I can text her 911 and she'll call me with a message, so I can leave. Yes, it's a brilliant plan...thank you.

I do hope you'll return tonight, I long to hold you and make love to you all night long. If we get out of bed on Monday, we can meet with the builders; I think you'll like them as much as I do! We can also look at apartments and move out of the hotel. We should find a place for ordering our invitations. You being back so soon allows for your involvement in all the wedding planning...lucky you! Or is it lucky me??

Gosh! In reviewing my list, it seems as if I've not done much, but I have stayed busy since you left. So, I must have accomplished something. What have I done; you ask? I have laid groundwork, so I/we will have an easier time completing our list!

Speaking of planning, my wedding dress hunt continues. Janet and I visited two shops. I found a few pretty dresses, but none jumped out at me or as Janet says, they didn't "wow" me. She and I will continue our shopping, and no, you can't be there for this. Why not? Because the groom is not to set eyes on the bride in her wedding dress before the ceremony, it's unlucky. We shouldn't seek out extra trouble!

I haven't told Mom and Dad of our wedding plans yet. Guess I hoped you'd be with me for this unseemly task. Whenever you're ready, we'll call them.

Well, time for me to change for dinner. Don't worry; I'm wearing the bulkiest sweater I have with me and thick cords. I'm not looking sexy for him; my sexy look is exclusively yours and yours alone.

I'll love you forever, Garrett. Yours always, Leigh XXOO ♥♥

***

Leigh waited impatiently for David in the front lobby. She wanted this meal over before the dang thing began.

"Leigh, I hoped you might wear something a little dressier." David sauntered into the lobby a few minutes after seven, looking her up and down.

"Tonight is a simple dinner out with a family friend, nothing more. I saw no need for dressing up." Leigh stiffened as he walked toward her.

"Perhaps I can adjust your attitude later." David turned on the charm. "Let me help with your coat." He snatched her coat away from her reaching hands. "Here you are. Relax, I won't bite…at least not yet." He whispered the last words in her ear and kissed her cheek. He laughed at her flinch.

"David, I don't appreciate your actions. Stop, please." She backed away from him as she spoke; a tremor ran through her when she noted the glimmer in his eyes. She remembered the look from their time together; he would be a handful tonight. At one time his charm broke down her defenses but no longer.

"I can't restrain myself. Believe me when I say I'm a changed man and I still love you." As he spoke, he advanced on her and reached for her shoulders.

"I couldn't care less whether you changed or not." Leigh stood her ground and tried to shrug his hands away. She refused to cower from him or appear intimidated. "We've been finished as a couple for four years. I moved on, and you should, too."

"Don't you realize how deeply your parents desire our being a couple again? How can you disappoint them?" David placed his hands on her arms pulling her closer.

"Yes, my mother wants us together, but not my dad. He approves of my relationship with Garrett. You're sorely misinformed if you heard anything different." Leigh's defiance blazed in her eyes and radiated through her stiff posture.

With a sigh, he dropped his hands. "If you check with your parents, you'll find they view your engagement negatively. Circumstances change." He pulled out his gloves and tugged them on. "We should depart now, so we're not late. I'll drive as I'm familiar with the way."

"No, I'll follow you." Leigh stood firm on her plan.

"Don't be ridiculous," he countered. "I won't kidnap you. Besides my mother asked to say hi and you can call her on my phone while I drive."

"Why can't I talk with her right now?"

"If we don't leave now, we'll lose our reservation." David grabbed hold of her elbow and rushed her out the door.

Not desiring to make a scene, Leigh allowed him to escort her out of the hotel. Talk with his mother? To say hi? Doubtful. If she used the call to emphasize her engagement and disinterest in David, she might defeat whatever he planned for tonight.

"Alright, I'll ride with you." She jerked her arm from his grasp. "Hand me your phone."

He smiled at his successful maneuvering of Leigh against her wishes. Plans for the evening remained on track.

"Here." He held out his phone. "Her number's listed under 'Mom.'"

"How original." Leigh slid into the car, buckled in, and placed the call before David settled behind the steering wheel.

"David?" Claire Walker answered the phone as

though she waited for a call.

"No, Mrs. Walker, it's Leigh Ramsey. David said you asked to say hi." Leigh marveled at how she controlled her voice to sound friendly and upbeat.

"Oh, Leigh, how gracious of you to call. Yes, I did ask. We're so happy you returned to Minnesota." Claire's excitement filtered into her voice.

"Thanks, Mrs. Walker. I like being back."

"Will you stay with your parents until you find a place to live?"

Leigh hesitated only a moment. "No, I'll be living in the Brainerd area."

"Brainerd? You still plan to live up there?

"Yes, this is where my fiancé works, so I'll live with him."

"You're still with your fiancé?"

"Yes, why wouldn't I be?"

"Well, we…er…I…ah…I hoped seeing David again would spur second thoughts on your part. You've known him your whole life compared to the short time since you met this other person." Claire sounded nervous.

"No, Mrs. Walker, my marriage hasn't been called off. In fact, we're finalizing plans." Leigh smiled as she spoke, sensing victory over her mother's manipulations. "Would you care to talk with David?"

"David? Ah, no, I'll speak with him later." Frustrated, Claire saw no reason to continue the conversation.

"Okay. Please say hi to your husband for me."

"Yes, I will. Bye."

"Bye." With a flick of her finger, Leigh ended the call and dumped the phone in a cup holder. "She'll talk with you later. Is this the restaurant?"

David pulled into a parking lot, but he appeared disgruntled over their arrival. "Yes, this is it."

Leigh's spirits rose after deflecting his mother's

expectations. His mother knew of her whereabouts and engagement. Apparently, her mother had been busy colluding with Mrs. Walker and David since her parents returned home from the cabin. Her dad had been tricked into asking her for a favor. Leigh's resolve to exclude her mother from any wedding planning became firmly ingrained within her. She checked her watch and wished she knew the time schedule for Garrett's operation.

CHAPTER TWENTY-ONE

Garrett glanced at the two men in the front seat, then returned his gaze to the evening darkness. Karl drove them through the countryside bound for the farmstead.

He reflected on their meeting with James a short while ago and strained against laughing. He took pleasure in looming over the guy in his security role for Karl. The man jumped at his first touch, so Garrett used rough motions as he patted him down. When he relieved James of his pistol, he delivered an extreme frown. Relief showed in James's face as he inched his way toward his car. Karl stopped him in his tracks by insisting he ride with them. Ah, the life of drug dealers; the stress alone must shorten their lifespan.

Clouds dimmed the night sky, which would cover the supporting teams as they moved into position amid the various outbuildings. A flawless sound check with the task force promised smooth communications, and Karl confirmed their plans for the evening. With any luck, their night would end with no shots fired.

Since James appeared nervous, Garrett leaned forward determined on finding out why.

"James." He kept his voice low, but powerful. A smile developed at the man's involuntary jump. "You're acting nervous; should I be concerned?"

"No, not at all. I don't usually ride, I mean, I'm typically the driver, not the passenger. In fact, I get car sick if I'm in the back seat." James rattled off the words.

"Glad you're in the front seat," Karl commented. He glanced at Garrett in the rearview mirror and winked.

Garrett clamped one hand on James's shoulder. "I'll keep an eye on you at all times. If any trouble befalls my boss, you're the first to receive my wrath."

"What? No, everything's cool." James leaned towards Karl. "Wrath? Who talks like that?"

Karl laughed. "He does, and you should believe him. He's worth every thousand I pay him. Is there anything you didn't tell us?"

"No. We meet at the farmhouse where the office is located. Your product is all packaged up for you. They agreed to kick in a sample of our weed, so you can try it out before ordering any. If you're interested, you can tour the facilities. The couple in charge of everything built quite the operation."

"Who are they?" Karl probed for information.

"Dennis and Janis Dexter; they were college sweethearts. He majored in hydroponics and her interest has always been chemistry. They run a sweet operation." James slumped in the seat and stared out the windshield.

"How do you stay off the radar of law enforcement?" Karl pushed for greater insight into their operation.

"We thoroughly vet all buyers via connections," James responded with an air of mystery.

"Connections? Are you telling me someone from local, state, or federal government is on your payroll?" Karl asked.

"Nothing so complicated. We employ an IT genius who hacks systems for us; she accesses all types of information. We used her abilities to check you out, but she couldn't find anything on your security guy. Not being able to track his information frustrated her all to pieces. Can you tell me what his story is?" James dropped his volume to a hoarse whisper.

"Ha! I haven't even learned all parts of his past. If you're so curious, you ask him." Karl nodded toward the back seat and on cue Garrett checked the magazine in his gun. The metallic sounds echoed in the car's silence, and James flinched again.

"No worries as long as you trust him," he stuttered.

"With my life, James. With my life." Karl smiled, darted a look at the man in the passenger seat and returned his eyes to the road.

Garrett sat back and relaxed for the first time since he saw Leigh with her ex-boyfriend. Nothing took the edge off quite as well as scaring the crap out of someone. He holstered his weapon and gazed out the window at the dark landscape flying by as Karl drove at his normal breakneck speed.

If their strategy worked, this mission would wrap up in a few hours, and Leigh would be in his arms tonight. Too often as he tried sleeping, she invaded his thoughts wearing sexy lingerie or nothing at all. Those nights usually involved cold showers. He endured too many of them since Leigh entered his life, so he planned on a shared hot shower after their reunion. He created a mental list of intimate acts for her consideration. They would be busy as they worked through his list.

The slowing of the vehicle for a turn ended his musing. He shifted into work mode—ready for action.

"What does the operation use for security? Armed sentries?" Karl ferreted out information for their mission. His words and James's reply would be heard by the team positioned near the farmstead and ready to advance on their location after the sale concluded.

"No need, we use sensors and surveillance cameras throughout the property. Our IT gal set up a monitoring system, and any breach sends her and the dorm a warning. The guys store their weapons in there, and they respond to any threat."

"What's the distance between the dorm and the production area?" Karl needed the identification of the dorm location for their team to neutralize the threat. "Can they respond fast and prevent thieves from stealing your product?"

"The dorm is a pole barn south of the farmhouse. Their response time is five or ten minutes unless they partied before turning in." James chuckled at his last comment.

"Rather fascinating concept of security. The response plan sounds haphazard and sloppy," Garrett offered his assessment. "Do they party often?"

James shrugged his shoulders. "Well, they party on Friday and Saturday nights, holidays and any special occasions."

"I'll need a complete review of the security, so I can ensure my investment is safeguarded." Karl maintained his business persona for James. He didn't want him suspicious of their questions.

"What types of weapons do they use, and what's their skill level? How many guards are we talking about?" Garrett jumped in and played his security role. "Are they strictly security or do they perform other duties? Boss, I suspect they might need to be trained better. I can schedule time with them."

"You'll train us?" James glanced back at Garrett but focused his question at Karl.

"Yes, we would. Our actions are all about the protection of our investment, so can you answer his questions?"

"Rifles and shotguns mostly because the guys are hunters. Most of them work other tasks, but four guys work only security. Two guard the entrance all the time, and two protect any delivery we make away from the farm," James responded.

"No automatic weapons?" Garrett knew the answer would assist the team when they moved in on the operation.

"None. Would you procure some for us?" James sounded hungry for anything and everything Karl offered.

"Yeah, automatic weapons are a specialty of ours." Karl nodded and caught Garrett's eyes in the rearview mirror. They gathered useful info without raising any suspicions over their questions.

Dim lights from the farmstead came into view. James waved at the two guards as they turned into the driveway.

"Head for the farmhouse and park by the garage." James pointed at the area for their vehicle.

"Sure." Karl braked, eased behind a parked truck, and blocked it in.

"Alright, let's grab the money and complete this transaction, so we can party!" James clapped his hands and exited the car.

Karl climbed out and met Garrett at the back of the car.

"Stay alert. This should be over fast." Karl popped the trunk and pulled out an overnight bag.

"No problem. I spotted a couple dark figures near the barn." Garrett spoke quietly, so his voice wouldn't carry.

"I'm sure most of the teams are in position. Let's do this." Karl closed the trunk and followed James to the front porch.

Garrett brought up the rear and scanned the farmhouse for unexpected dangers. It had seen better days; dingy yellow paint peeled off the sections visible in the low lighting. Dirty windows without curtains flooded the sagging porch with dim light. Lawn furniture poked out from under mounds of dirty snow. A narrow path had been cleared from the driveway, through the yard, up the steps, across the porch, and to the front door.

James rapped on the door, and it opened without hesitation. A rancid meat odor with a strong garlic and onion aroma wafted out; Karl and Garrett fought a gag reflex. They followed James inside, but neither could imagine spending longer than necessary in the stench.

They stopped in what functioned as a living room and sales area. A yellowed-white leather couch sat against the far wall with a matching chair nearby. A long table stood nearest them, blocking access to the other rooms. A large bundle took up most of the table, and a short rotund man stood behind it with both hands resting on the bundle. A tall man with shoulder-length hair and the beginning of a potbelly stood before them.

Garrett eyed the men and noted the lack of telltale bulges from concealed weapons. He listened for sounds of other occupants in the house, but only the sizzle of something frying in the back held his interest. Obviously, the sizzle originated the sickening odor that filled the house, so someone must be in the kitchen—the wife? He recognized the tall man as the one he spotted at the bar.

"Keith, let me introduce the owner of this flourishing operation, Dennis." James hopped around eager to share his news. "Dennis, this is Keith. Wait till you hear what he can do for us!"

"I'm pleased to meet you, Keith. And this is?" Dennis extended his hand to Karl but nodded toward Garrett.

"Gareth, my head of security. Shall we complete this? We're conducting other business later tonight." Karl shook hands with Dennis.

Garrett nodded in Dennis's direction at his introduction but maintained his grim scowl staying in character until the arrest.

"Sure. Your product is over there if you want to inspect it. Show the man." Dennis motioned to the bundle.

James led Karl to the table, but Garrett stood back with their suitcase of money. A considerable amount of real cash filled the suitcase, but most of the money was fake. The bills looked real enough to fool anyone except currency experts and should withstand a close inspection by this group.

"You followed my specifications for the packaging, a sign of first-rate quality control. I'm impressed by your attention to detail." Karl completed his inspection of the contents of the bundle and nodded at Garrett. "Give him the money."

He handed over the suitcase. As Dennis knelt and unzipped the case, Garrett stood over him ready for action if things went wrong. Dennis rifled through the stack of bills, his lips moving as he counted the stacks.

Once his count ended, Dennis stood and smiled. "It's all here. Thanks. This will be a profitable relationship for both of us. The smaller package is a sample of our new product; thought you might enjoy some for personal use." He winked at Karl.

"A free sample of your weed? Thanks, I appreciate your generosity. James mentioned you built quite the operation here." Karl picked up the package and tucked it in a pocket. "Been a pleasure doing business with you. Just one more thing."

Karl spoke the words designated for kicking off the sweep of the farmstead.

"What?" Dennis asked as he zipped up the suitcase of money.

"You're all under arrest for production and sale of illegal drugs." Karl flashed his DEA credentials, gazed at the men in the room, registered Garrett's nod, and eyed the two men nearest him, confident his partner covered Dennis.

"What? No way!" James wailed as Karl grabbed him and zip tied his hands behind his back.

The other man pushed the bundle at Karl and headed for the front door. Karl intercepted him, grabbed him by the shoulders, spun him round, and crashed his face into the table. With an arm pressed against the man's shoulders, Karl zipped his wrists together. Sounds from the rest of the team's progress blared in his earpiece. He stared where Garrett and Dennis last stood but saw empty space. His eyes caught movement in the dining room.

At Karl's announcement Dennis froze for a moment,

grabbed the suitcase of money, and ran toward the dining room. Garrett glanced at his partner and verified Karl controlled the other two men before he pursued his man. He launched himself at Dennis in a flying tackle; both men crashed into the wooden dinette set. Surrounded by broken chair parts, Garrett rolled and got on his knees. He held Dennis by the collar.

"Garrett! On your left!"

Karl's warning caught Garrett's attention, and in a split-second he located the danger. A black object swung down at his head; his instincts screamed deflect and protect. His left arm came up, and he ducked.

Crack!

Tears blurred his sight. Instant pain radiated through his left arm. His mind cried out—focus, the threat is still there! To stand, Garrett used his right hand for leverage on the table since his left arm hung at his side useless for defense. He focused on the black object, a cast iron skillet. He remembered his mother using one in their kitchen for almost every meal. The memory came and went when he recognized the woman holding the skillet like a baseball bat. She must be the wife; he recognized her from the bar.

A crazed look flashed in the woman's eyes. Garrett noted her huge pupils with no hint of the iris color showing. She prepared for another swing, so he smashed his right fist into her face. The frying pan dropped with a dull thud followed by her body. She lay crumpled on the floor. The sight of blood spewing from her nose didn't faze him: a broken nose for a broken arm seemed a fair exchange.

He turned toward where he last confronted Dennis. A blur of motion preceded pain across his abdomen below his bulletproof vest. He stepped back as Dennis came into focus.

"You hurt Janis! I'm gonna kill you!" Dennis wielded a long knife.

Blood dripped from the blade, and Garrett realized

it was his blood.

"Don't be stupid, Dennis. Her nose is broken. She's not dead. Put the knife down." Garrett moved away from Janis's sprawled body, drawing Dennis's view away from his wife crumpled on the floor and covered in blood.

"No, you're paying for Janis and all this." Dennis pointed the knife in Garrett's direction.

"I don't have time for this." He drew his gun; Dennis would be dead before he stuck the knife in him again.

"Just shoot!" Karl's voice boomed across the room. Dennis glanced at him. "He already wounded you; it'll be a clean shoot. Do it! Shoot him!"

As Karl's words sunk in, Dennis's hand shook, and he bit his lips.

"Your choice: drop the knife or die." The dark shape of the gun melded in Garrett's one-handed grip, so they appeared as one. Man and weapon forged together as a single instrument of death. Anger and hostility flashed in icy-blue eyes locked onto his opponent. "What's it going to be, Dennis: a nine-millimeter slug in your brain or a comfy jail cell? You have five seconds…four…three…"

Dennis's eyes danced between Karl and Garrett. Whatever reflected in Garrett's eyes made him turn pale and drop the knife.

"Put your hands on your head." Garrett leaned against the wall as he kept his gun aimed at Dennis. "Karl, can you do the honors?"

"My pleasure, partner." Karl stepped behind Dennis and bound his hands behind his back. He sat him in the one remaining chair, kicked the knife in Garrett's direction, and squatted by Janis, binding her hands behind her back. He keyed his earpiece and barked out, "I need a couple of ambulances, one for a wounded agent and one for a prisoner. Need back up in the house, *now*!" He stood near Garrett, who still leaned against the wall. "You look like shit."

"Makes sense because I feel like shit." Garrett grimaced when he laughed at Karl's observation.

Two officers in dark uniforms and helmets rushed into the house in response to Karl's demand for back up.

"Keep an eye on these four. The woman on the floor needs the ambulance; her nose is probably broken. The knife and frying pan are evidence; be sure they're bagged. Oh, and so is this." Karl pulled the small package from his pocket and handed it to the nearest officer. "Garrett, you need out of this stench." Karl supported his right side and walked him out of the house into the cold. "The fresh air is an improvement. How did they stand the stink?"

"The better question is how anyone eats something that stinks so bad?" Garrett's voice weakened as he struggled to stay upright.

"Where are my ambulances?" Karl demanded of the voices talking over his earpiece.

"Ten minutes out. They responded to a multiple vehicle accident on Highway 371. A first aid kit is on its way," an anonymous voice answered.

Karl sat Garrett in the front passenger seat of their car. He hurried around to the other side and turned the engine over. "I'll warm you up shortly." No response. "Garrett!" He checked on his partner.

Garrett flinched at Karl's voice and closed his eyes against the resulting pain. "I'm still with you."

"I'll find some towels. We need to stop the blood flow before you bleed all over my car." Karl hopped out of the car and raced into the house. He took the stairs two at a time. "Towels, towels...if I were spare towels, where would I be? Bathroom!" He found a linen closet, removed three towels, and rushed out of the house.

"Here's the first aid kit. Where did you need it?" Another black-uniformed officer appeared in front of the farmhouse.

"Follow me." Karl jogged towards the car.

Garrett saw Karl head back from the house, so he didn't react when the door swung open. The heater had kicked in a few minutes back, but now the chill of the winter evening battled the warmth in the car.

"We brought a first aid kit, and I found some towels." Karl turned to the officer with the kit. "I need sterile pads directly on the bleeding, and we'll pile these towels on top."

Karl created a pressure pad and slowed the blood flow from Garrett's knife wound. He shut the passenger door and paused a moment as he looked down on his partner sprawled in the front seat. Pulling off bloody gloves, his voice cut through the night, "Where the hell are my ambulances? You said ten minutes."

"They're up the road, should arrive in less than two," the anonymous voice stated in a calm manner, a stark contrast to the frantic timbre of Karl's demand.

"About time," Karl muttered as he glanced around for the first time.

Portable lights lit up the farmstead. Those arrested were herded into vans for transport to the county jail. Crime scene technicians bustled throughout the area and processed evidence with their usual efficiency. The evening ended as a huge success, so why didn't he feel satisfaction? Because his partner sat in the car covered in blood from a knife injury. At least he was only wounded and would heal.

Had Joe said he wanted Garrett back safe and sound or in one piece? Well, Garrett didn't get sliced in two and should be fine, so he could stand before Joe and not face unpleasant consequences. With phone in hand, he searched for Joe's number, but the wail of an ambulance siren distracted him. First order of business, ensure Garrett and the woman received medical care. Afterward, call Joe. He waved the first ambulance over near his car and met the paramedics as they bailed out.

"Passenger door, front seat. Broken left arm and a knife wound to the abdomen. Guys, he's my partner, so take good care of him. Garrett, I'll be with you at the hospital. I'll call Joe and ask him to reach Leigh. You'll be okay." A nod from Garrett indicated he heard and understood Karl's words. The paramedics swooped in, so Karl stepped aside. The second ambulance pulled in for the woman with a broken nose. As he waved it down, he pulled out his phone and dialed.

"Henderson."

"Karl here. Can you do me a favor?"

"First things first, how'd it go?" A peripheral member of the task force, Joe played no active role in the night's operation.

"Huge success! We got everyone with no shots fired." Karl covered the mouthpiece as he directed the second team of paramedics. "Inside you'll find a woman with a broken nose. Be sure an officer stays with her."

"What's going on? No shots fired, but a woman is injured?"

"Yeah, your boy punched her out." Karl relaxed a bit, the adrenaline rush dissipating.

"Garrett did what?"

Karl chuckled; he enjoyed any opportunity to spin up Joe. "He punched out the wife of the leader of this group. I'm sure he broke her nose; blood spurted everywhere."

"Let me talk to him—wait a minute, you chuckled. What aren't you telling me?"

"She was about to swing a cast iron skillet at his head for a second time when he punched her. You should have seen him. Cool and confident—the skillet dropped and so did she."

"And where is he?"

"Ah…he's leaving now." The ambulance crew loaded Garrett and turned on the lights and sirens as they drove away.

"I hear sirens."

"That'd be his ride, and the reason for the favor." Karl winced at the verbal abuse coming over the phone. "Relax, it's nothing life threatening."

"What happened?"

"A broken arm from the afore mentioned skillet, and the husband's retaliation with a knife."

"A knife? Where were you during this?"

"Hey, I dealt with two other guys. I warned him of the skillet, so only his left arm is broken and not his head." Karl watched as paramedics assisted the woman into the ambulance. "Joe, can you tell Leigh and ensure she meets him at the hospital?"

"Telling Leigh is your favor? Of course Janet will track her down. She'll be there." Joe paused before continuing. "Congratulations, Karl."

"Thanks. The success of this operation relied on your assistance. Garrett's a hell of an agent. He did you and the BCA proud."

"See you at the hospital?"

"I'll be there as soon as I can." Karl tucked his phone in a pocket and looked around. Surely there was someone here capable of overseeing the cleanup, so he could depart for the hospital. He walked off in search of the unfortunate person.

CHAPTER TWENTY-TWO

Leigh and David sat at a table for two tucked into a dark corner of the restaurant's dining room. A fire burned nearby and threw a warm glow across the entire room. White linen tablecloths, candles, flowers, and soft music added a romantic ambiance.

David ordered for them. The appetizers tasted superb and her wine exquisite. He had a flair for selecting first-class restaurants. While they awaited their entrées, he refilled her glass.

"This is a wonderful restaurant. I'll be sure Garrett and I come here; the setting is quite romantic." Leigh celebrated the flash of irritation in his eyes generated by her words.

"Romance is exactly why I brought you here to ensure the proper mood for our first dinner together in four years." His leveled stare unnerved her. "Not to provide ideas for you and your sham of a fiancé."

"My engagement is no sham; however, your being here is." She held his eyes.

"How can you say such a thing? I care for you, our parents are best friends, they expect us to be together. And why shouldn't we? We're sexually compatible, and I can provide you anything you desire. Why delay the inevitable? Break off your engagement and return to the Cities with me tomorrow."

Leigh's jaw dropped open. "You can't be serious. I'll never leave Garrett."

"Why not after he deserted you two weeks into a relationship? No telling what he's been up to while he's been away. With time on his own, he probably reconsidered this ridiculous whirlwind romance of yours. How can you presume things will be the same for you when he's back?" David caught her left hand and twisted her engagement ring. "This ring doesn't do you justice but does reflect your relationship with him: small, cheap, and no grandeur. Ours on the other hand would be spectacular, filled with grand opportunities." A velvet box appeared in front of her. "This is a reflection of what our life together will be." A diamond ring sparkled at her. The center diamond was larger than the three-carat diamond from yesterday, and a cluster of smaller-sized diamonds encircled it. "I heard what you said at lunch. The diamonds in place of the rubies are more elegant. Say yes, Leigh. Come home with me and make our families happy."

Speechless, Leigh gaped at the monstrosity in the box. She focused on his expression of victorious expectation.

"David, you can't expect me to end my engagement."

"Oh, but I do. Put away your foolish ideas of a marriage with anyone other than me. Let's make sure this ring fits." David pulled on her engagement ring.

"No! Let go of my ring and my hand." Leigh pulled back her hand as she closed her fist; no way would he remove the ring placed on her hand by Garrett.

"You're acting childish. The ring is coming off." His voice dropped with a threatening tone. "Put my ring on instead."

"*I'm* acting childish? You're crazy if you assume I'd marry you after what you did four years ago. You betrayed me, and I thank God you did. If not for you cheating on me, we might be married now with me living a miserable existence. Instead I met the love of my life, and we'll marry soon. Meanwhile you'll still be the sorry SOB you've always been. I'm going to the ladies' room. Excuse me." She grabbed her purse and stormed away.

David pulled out his phone and called his mother.

"How'd it go?"

"Coming up here was a waste of my time, she's not interested. I'm heading back first thing tomorrow."

"What's wrong with her?"

"She claims to be in love, but what happens after her fiancé returns may not be what she expects. I suggested things between them may not be the same when he returns. Hopefully my words will stimulate a change in her way of viewing their relationship."

"What a brilliant idea. I'm sorry this weekend didn't work out as we hoped. I'll stay in touch with Lois; she'll be checking on how things go with Leigh."

"Things will work out, Mom. The situation just needs time to play out. I'll stop by the house tomorrow night."

"Okay."

David tucked his phone into a pocket. His eyes found their waitress, and he smiled at her. She smiled back.

***

Leigh stared at her reflection in the mirror. Irritation with David breached any level she experienced before. How dare he try pulling off her engagement ring! Of course he selected another hideous ring. Worst of all he implied Garrett had been unfaithful. Being a cheater himself, he painted Garrett with a similar brush. His words angered her because of the insult to Garrett's character. She didn't doubt her fiancé's fidelity. He was honorable and loved her. As she fumed, her phone rang Janet's ringtone.

"Hi, Janet. Is there a problem?" Her heartbeat sped up when she recognized the ringtone. "Did something happen with Garrett? Is he not coming home tonight?"

"Leigh, are you with David?" Janet's calm composure came over the phone connection.

"Well, we're still at dinner, but I'm in the ladies' room now. Why? What's up?"

"Garrett was injured—"

"What?" Light-headed and weak-kneed, she gripped the counter and leaned against it for support.

"The injuries aren't life threatening, but he's on the way to a local hospital. I don't know which one, but Joe's working on learning the details. Once he finds out, I'll text you the name. Do you need a ride? I can pick you up."

"No, I'll call a cab. Will you and Joe be there?"

"Yes, we'll meet you at the hospital. He'll be fine, but he'll need you to be strong. Do you understand what I'm saying?"

"I do. I'll see you at the hospital. Thanks for calling."

"See you soon."

Thankful for having the foresight to save a local taxi service number in her phone, she called for immediate pickup. Time to finish things with David.

"I thought you fell in," he joked without standing when she returned.

"I received a phone call. Something came up, and I'm leaving."

"Leigh, you needn't create a phony crisis. I'll drive home in the morning, but you should consider what I said. If you change your mind, I'll be waiting for you. Now join me for dinner."

"David, I realize this is a foreign concept for you, but Garrett and I love each other. He would never cheat on me as you did. He's an honorable man. Something you could never understand. Now, if you'll excuse me, I should watch for my cab. Give your parents my best and never come back." She grabbed her things and marched toward the front door.

David watched her walk away. Perhaps her mother underestimated Leigh's commitment to her engagement. Whatever. He waved down the waitress.

"Something more, sir?"

"I'll take a Scotch on the rocks, and if you cancel the lady's order, your tip will reflect my appreciation."

"I'll do what I can. I can't believe anyone would walk out on you."

"She's just a friend. Something came up, so she had to leave. Unfortunately I'll be all alone tonight." He tried for his best sad look.

"I'm off in two hours. I'd be happy to spend time with you, so you're not all by yourself." She winked at him before walking away.

David enjoyed the view of her hips swaying and leaned back in his chair. Apparently, the night wouldn't be a complete wash after all.

CHAPTER TWENTY-THREE

Leigh hopped out of the cab and raced into the ER. Her heart pounded in her chest so fiercely it hurt. A hand on her shoulder made her jump.

"Leigh." Janet drew her into a hug. "He's okay; the waiting room is this way."

"What happened to him?" She clung to her friend as they walked down the hall.

"Karl can answer your questions; he was with Garrett through everything. The doctor's stitching him up, so you can't see him yet."

"Stitching him up?" Leigh stopped walking.

"Come on, keep moving."

Janet pulled her forward into a smaller waiting area where Joe and another man stood together in deep conversation.

"Leigh, he'll be fine." Joe wrapped her in a supportive hug. "This is Karl Frank with the DEA; he partnered with Garrett on this operation."

In automatic mode, she extended Karl a hand. "I'm so pleased to meet you."

"Garrett spoke of you a lot. He's quite the guy and did a phenomenal job." Karl recognized the concern in her eyes as he shook her hand. Garrett was a lucky man.

"Can someone please tell me what happened?" Leigh fought back tears.

Janet led her to a chair, and Leigh collapsed in it, grateful for the support. Karl sat on one side of her with Janet on the other, and Joe stood looking down the hallway.

"He sustained a broken arm and a knife wound." Karl began the story. When her eyes widened at his words, he hurried along. "The cut runs across his abdomen; the blade struck below his vest. They told us the knife didn't hit anything vital, so they're cleaning the wound area and stitching it closed."

She nodded her head. "When can I see him?"

"They'll get us when they're done." Joe's calm tone eased some of the tension in the room.

"Did anyone else get injured?"

"Only Garrett unless you count the wife with a broken nose." At her startled response, Karl continued. "We completed our transaction, announced they were under arrest, and confronted three guys. I took two, and Garrett chased down the third, the head guy. His wife surprised us by coming out of the kitchen with a cast iron skillet in her hands. She swung it at Garrett's head. I called out a warning, and he raised his left arm to deflect her swing. All I heard was a crack."

Leigh's stomach lurched, and she paled. Janet held her hand and wrapped an arm around her shoulders.

"I'm not sure how he managed with his arm broken, but when she wound up for another swipe at his head, he broke her nose with one punch. She dropped the pan and followed it to the floor. When Garrett turned around, the husband cut him across the abdomen with a kitchen knife. After he pulled his gun, the guy saw the wisdom of dropping the knife. I got him out of there and administered first aid until the ambulance arrived."

"Thanks for telling me what happened and for taking care of him."

Leigh's hug surprised Karl, but he enjoyed himself.

A doctor walked in and addressed them, "Are you all here for Special Agent Dane?"

"Yes," they responded in unison.

"We've cleaned his wound; fortunately, no organs were damaged. The arm break appears clean, but we called in an ortho specialist to set the bone. He received pain medication for the procedure, so he's not overly coherent. You can visit him for a short while. A nurse will escort you, but only two at a time, please."

"Thanks, doctor. We appreciate everything you and your team did for him." Joe shook his hand before the man escaped back into the ER. "Leigh, if you don't mind, Karl and I will see him first. You and Janet can follow, so you can stay longer."

"Sure, you guys go ahead." Stunned, Leigh appreciated the additional time to prepare herself and leverage Janet's support in settling her raging emotions.

The nurse arrived and escorted the men down the hall.

"Should you call anyone? Your folks or a friend?"

"My folks?" Leigh released a heartless laugh. "No, I don't need to call them or anyone. I'm grateful for you and Joe being here. You're the only support I need."

"Once you get him home, call if you need anything."

"I hope the hotel will be comfortable enough for him."

"I'm sure the hotel will be fine." Janet spotted tears in Leigh's eyes, so handed her a tissue and wrapped her in another hug. "You should finish your crying before you see him. Let's go to the ladies' room, so you can freshen up."

"I am so thankful for you being with me." Leigh relaxed in her friend's hug before her tears fell.

***

Down the hall, the nurse left the men outside the room where Garrett lay and went in to check on his alertness.

"There are two men here for a visit. Are you up to seeing them?"

Garrett tried to focus on the nurse but settled instead on the IV needle in his hand. He hated needles. Where'd the nurse come from? Did she ask him something? She seemed to be waiting for an answer.

"I'm sorry, did you say something?"

A gentle smile crossed her lips. "Yes, you have visitors." She left the room and Joe and Karl joined him.

"Hey, you don't look like death warmed over anymore. How ya feeling?" Karl stopped at the foot of the bed.

"Thanks to whatever they pumped into me I feel great." Garrett spoke slowly and tried not to slur his words.

"You performed well. An impressive performance to start off your career." Joe clapped him on the right shoulder.

"Thank you, sir, but I just did my job."

"And you did it very well. By the way, you did break Janis's nose. She spouted off about brutality charges, but when I showed her and her attorney pictures of the skillet and your broken arm, she shut up. Their response was priceless!" Karl chuckled at the memory.

"Glad you enjoyed it. Does Leigh know what happened?" Nerves dug into his stomach. How would she react? He failed to keep his promise to be careful.

"Jan told her, and she's here. The doctor only allowed two visitors at a time, so they'll come in after we leave," Joe reassured him. "She handled the news well, and Janet will be there for her while you recuperate."

A long sigh was Garrett's initial response. "Thank you, sir; I appreciate everything your wife's done for her." His eyes closed and slowly opened as he fought drowsiness.

"Hey, we're out of here, so Leigh can come in before you fall asleep." Karl jerked his head at Joe.

They stepped out, and Joe caught the nurse's eye. "There are two ladies waiting to visit with him next. One's his fiancée, so she'll stay longer with him."

"No problem." She walked with them down the corridor to the waiting area.

Leigh jumped up when they walked through the door. Joe thought she appeared more composed and glanced at his wife. Janet nodded as she placed an arm around Leigh's shoulders.

"Ladies, your turn," the nurse said.

Leigh's gratefulness for Janet's calming influence couldn't be expressed. Janet had held her as she sobbed away her fear for what might have happened.

As she stepped through the open door, Leigh held her breath unsure of what to expect.

"Oh, Garrett!" She ran to his side, her hands found his face, and her lips landed on his before she could stop herself. His lips parted, and their tongues explored each other. Her fear of his injuries dissipated with his immediate response. A hard object ran along her back, and startled her, so she broke away from their kiss.

"Sorry, it's a temporary splint until the ortho doc shows up." Garrett's eyes didn't stray from her. He wanted to touch her and breathe in her scent.

"I'm so thankful nothing worse happened. The staff here provide excellent care." Janet doubted either Leigh or Garrett remembered her presence in the small space.

"Thank you, ma'am. I appreciate you being here for Leigh while I worked."

Janet marveled at the sight of their reunion and their almost frantic touching as if to confirm the reality of the other. Her smile radiated her understanding. "Joe and I are here for you both. If you need anything, call us. Okay?"

"Of course. Thanks again." Leigh hugged her friend.

"I'll leave you two now. We're happy you're back, Garrett." She departed before they realized her intention.

As Janet slipped out of the room, Leigh closed her eyes and took a deep breath. When she turned back around, her heart raced at an erratic pace. Alone at last. She stepped back to his side and did a visual check of him. Was his face thinner? The brilliance of his eyes appeared duller, probably because of drugs and pain.

"I hope you didn't worry too much when you got the call." Garrett struggled against the drug induced drowsiness.

"Worried doesn't cover how I reacted."

"If I had been as careful as I promised to be, we wouldn't be in a hospital. Sorry for that." Garrett reached out to run his fingers through her hair. "You are more gorgeous than I remembered. How is that possible?" His voice lowered as he spoke, and his eyes closed as he inhaled. "I missed running my fingers in the softness of your hair."

"I missed everything about you. Is there room for me?"

His eyes widened. "Here? In bed?"

"Yes. I doubt the hospital staff would approve of us making love in the ER, but I'll risk cuddling." She kicked off her boots and moved to the side of the bed.

In pleased disbelief, his eyes followed her every move; his body tensed and hardened in response to the combination of her words and actions. He shifted to his right, grimacing as the stitches protested the motion. "There's nothing I'd prefer more than you in bed with me."

She stretched out on top of the blankets and cuddled with him. His broken left arm angled down her back and held her close. Her head rested on his shoulder, and his right hand stroked her hair.

"I missed you terribly. My thoughts always centered on you." Her body relaxed for the first time in days. "I love you."

"You're my world." The hand stroking her hair slowed as the drugs and exhaustion took over.

"As you are for me." She looked up; his eyes closed as his breathing softened. "Heal, Garrett, you're home with me." She relaxed as she listened to his breathing.

***

Later the nurse checked on her patient. She planned on telling him the ortho specialist was delayed. She stopped short at the sight of the young couple asleep in each other's arms. With no reason to disturb them until the ortho doctor showed up, she closed the door and searched out the others who visited earlier with the young agent.

"The ortho specialist is delayed by an emergency, so Special Agent Dane's release will be much later than expected. My advice is for you to go home for the night."

"How's he doing?" Joe asked.

"He's resting comfortably."

"How is his fiancée?" Janet's concern for Leigh showed in her face.

"She's resting comfortably, too." The nurse smiled and departed the waiting area.

"Totally out of it, and he's in bed with a good-looking woman. Unbelievable!" Karl shook his head in disbelief. "Guess I'll head out. Joe, I'll work with Garrett anytime. Thanks again for throwing him into the thick of things."

"Your confidence in him speaks highly of his abilities. Send us something in writing from your agency for his personnel file." Joe shook hands with Karl.

"Of course I will. He's a strong force in action." Karl turned for the door. "I expect he'll be the star of your team."

"I think you're right." Joe grabbed his coat. "Let's head home, Janet. You can call Leigh tomorrow morning and ask if they need anything."

"Their reunion touched my heart. They only had eyes for each other. Oh, to be young and in love." Janet shrugged into her coat and searched her pockets for her gloves.

"And what's wrong with older and in love?" His arms circled her waist, and he pulled her close for a kiss.

"Obviously, nothing at all." Janet's cheeks warmed from a blush. She took his hand in hers, and they walked to the exit.

***

The hum of machines, groans of pain, and an antiseptic odor assailed her senses, totally inappropriate and unexpected for the hotel. As she woke, she remembered being in the hospital ER with Garrett and in bed with him no less! After blinking the sleep from her eyes, she gazed at the love of her life still sleeping beside her. She scrambled off the bed and circled the room in search of her boots. As she finger combed her hair, the door flew open, and a doctor bustled into the room.

"I'm here for Garrett Dane." He carried an X-ray.

"You found him. Are you the ortho specialist?" Leigh peered at the man.

"I am. And you are…?" He eyed her suspiciously.

"I'm Leigh Ramsey, his fiancée." The man's brusqueness made her uncomfortable. She wished for the return of the friendlier nurse.

"Well, I need you out of here while I conduct my exam." He stopped at the bed.

"I'm not leaving his side." She glared at the doctor, lifted her chin, and placed a hand over Garrett's arm, resting atop the covers.

"Miss, you cannot stay here; there are privacy concerns and requirements I must follow, so you must leave. Otherwise, I can't treat him." The doctor returned her glare. "Do I need security to escort you out?"

"You wouldn't dare," Leigh challenged him.

He stepped out and bellowed, "Nurse!"

The nurse from earlier rushed in. "Doctor, what's the matter?"

"Call security. I want this woman removed." He pointed at Leigh, adamant in his resolve to evict her.

"I'm sorry, but she stays. The patient completed the necessary forms allowing his fiancée's presence with him at all times and to be consulted on any treatment." She showed the doctor the forms in Garrett's chart.

"Very well. As long as you're here, please assist me." The doctor didn't hesitate further and went right to work.

Leigh stepped out of the way as the doctor began his physical exam of the broken left arm. When the splint came off, Garrett roused. He jerked his arm out of the doctor's hands, cringing with the effort.

"Who are you?" Garrett grimaced over the throbbing pain in his arm.

"Sorry, Dr. Staples. I'm here for the ortho consult. You received a simple fracture of your ulna. The fracture isn't quite aligned properly, so I'll correct the alignment by manual manipulation. I don't think you need a cast, so we'll use a sturdier splint. Be sure you always wear the splint with a few exceptions. Are you ready? Perhaps you might want additional painkillers before I set it?"

"No. Just go ahead, doc." His eyes sought out Leigh.

"As you wish. Nurse, hold his upper arm. On three, I'll pull the bone in place. One, two, three."

Garrett gritted his teeth against the sudden pain. His eyes instantly teared and closed.

"Ah, flawless alignment! Your arm should heal perfectly." Dr. Staples appeared pleased with his work. He replaced the temporary splint. "Don't leave until you receive the sturdier replacement."

"Thanks, doc." The imprint of the skillet remained visible on his arm. Lucky for him, the wife hadn't swung the hot one.

"You'll need checkups to ensure the healing is progressing without a cast. I'll see you again in a few weeks. Good night." He walked out, presumably off to another patient or home.

"He's quite the charmer," Leigh observed from her vantage point in a far corner.

"He's the best there is when it deals with bones. The splint for you should arrive soon. Let me free you from your IV, and I'll check all the orders placed and any prescriptions for you. Your clothes are in the bundle under your bed." The nurse removed the needle and bustled out.

"Can you find the bag, Leigh? No reason we should wait on changing me out of this hospital gown." Garrett swung his legs over the side of the bed and cursed his way to an upright position.

"Slow down. You're pale from your sudden movement, and would you please let me help when you want to move?"

"Sorry, I'm anxious to leave."

"I'm equally anxious for you to be home, but I won't accept you being in worse shape because of us rushing you out of here." Leigh crouched beside the bed and gathered the bag in her arms. "All your clothes are here, except for a shirt."

"Figures, my shirt and sweater took the brunt of the knife wound between being cut and the blood. Karl probably grabbed both as evidence." Garrett reached for his jeans. "Not much blood on these, at least not a gross amount. I'll need your help to put them on though; the cut hurts like hell when I bend over."

"Give me those." She took the jeans from his hands. "This is weird; usually I'm pulling these off, not putting them on." Leigh talked him through her actions as she worked on dressing him.

"Thanks, darlin'." He watched her struggle with his socks and boots, and his love for her flowed through him. She never flinched over his wounds, and her climbing in bed had surprised and pleased him. She felt so right beside him; he easily fell asleep with her in his arms. Sure, the drugs pushed him along, but he credited her presence for the underlying peace he experienced.

"Okay, let's get you standing, so I can pull this all the way up." She stood and met his eyes. The turbulence reflected in them stopped her. "Oh, Garrett. I missed you so much. There will never be anyone else for me, but you." She leaned into him and brushed her lips against his.

His right hand found the nape of her neck and moved into her hair. The broken left arm frustrated him until he placed the hard length against her back and urged her body closer against him. His tongue grazed against the seam of her lips and found its way between them. Her tongue met his and their kiss deepened. Her moan, followed by his groan, escalated the heat of the kiss. Her hands roamed his body.

"Ow!" Garrett jerked backwards.

"Oh my gosh! I'm sorry; I forgot about your stitches." Shocked by his outburst, Leigh stepped back. "Are you okay?"

"Yeah, I'm fine. We'll figure out how to deal with my injuries." He looked embarrassed by his reaction.

"Perhaps we should stick to getting you dressed." Leigh busied herself by arranging his shorts and jeans in preparation of pulling them over his hips.

They had grappled his jeans to his waist when the nurse returned.

"Been busy, I see." Her gaze didn't miss Garrett's partially dressed form and Leigh's hold on him.

"He's missing a shirt. Can you find something for him to wear?" Leigh asked as she pulled his jacket out of the bag.

"Certainly, I'll find you something. Here are your orders. You'll find two follow-up appointments: one for removing the stitches and the other for your arm. Wound care instructions are included and what you should watch for over the course of healing. I'll review all of this with you before you leave. Also, you have prescriptions for an antibiotic and a painkiller. Both can be filled at the hospital pharmacy on your way out. Let me find a shirt." She slipped away.

"We're almost out of here. How are you doing?"

"Tired, probably from the meds they gave me." He leaned against the bed and paged through the papers. "Hmm, looks as though we'll be limited in the bedroom. Sorry." He handed her the sheet of instructions and pointed at a section.

"'Limit activities straining the stitched area...limit movements for at least two weeks...internal healing is slow and can take months after external healing is complete.' This doesn't sound promising." Dejected, Leigh sat beside him.

"Should we ask the nurse?"

"Asking about limitations on our sexual activities is personal. I'd be embarrassed to ask."

"But we should be sure, shouldn't we?" His eyebrows rose and his smile kick-started the dragons in her stomach from the grounded status they entered when he left.

"Well," she returned his smile, "perhaps we should check with her before we leave."

The nurse returned with a scrubs top. "This should fit, and I met Jerry with your splint. He'll instruct you on the proper use of it."

Leigh received instruction and practiced putting the splint on Garrett's arm and removing it until she became confident in doing all the steps. She cringed at his suffering through her practice attempts and admired the grim determination he displayed by trying to hide his pain. Once she succeeded to properly align the permanent splint twice, Jerry announced her training complete, handed over a sling, and left. The nurse returned and reviewed his discharge orders and care instructions.

"Do you have any questions?"

Garrett glanced at Leigh, and she stared at her feet. The awkwardness of the question they planned to ask loomed between them. Each hoped the other would broach the subject. Because he first identified the issue, Garrett cleared his throat and took a stab at their question.

"We wondered whether we can…that is, if we can, ah…"

The nurse took pity on him. "Limit your sexual activity until the stitches come out and strive for less robust activities. You," she stabbed a finger at Garrett, "will experience pain if you go too far or do too much. Listen to your body. You'll know when you should stop. Just be sure you heed what your body tells you."

"I will. Thank you." Garrett's cheeks and neck flushed deep red. Now glad he asked, or rather attempted to ask, they knew the answer although it didn't match what their surging desires demanded.

"Bottom line, follow the orders from your doctors and keep all your appointments. A volunteer is on his way with a wheelchair. Stop at the pharmacy on your way out, and cabs are outside the front door if you need one. Best of luck." She hurried out.

"Finally. Ready to go, darlin'?" Garrett couldn't wait for alone time with her.

"I'm past ready." She gathered up the paperwork and grabbed his jacket. "You dressed in maroon scrubs is sexy; we're keeping it."

"Are we playing doctor later?" His voice dripped with suggestion.

She gazed into his eyes; they radiated his need for her. A glance down showed an erection straining against his jeans. "Might be fun, but I think you had your fill of doctors for one night. Where the heck is the wheelchair?" Anxious for their return to the hotel and a semblance of normalcy, she glanced at her watch. After two in the morning; where had the evening gone?

A young man appeared with a wheelchair. "Special Agent Dane? I'm here with your ride. Let me help you into this thing."

After a stop at the pharmacy, they reached the front doors, and Leigh secured them a cab.

Once he set the wheelchair brakes, he helped Garrett to the car. "Assisting you tonight has been my pleasure. Everyone's talking about what you did. A cousin of mine got hooked on meth and killed himself in a car accident as a result. Thanks for taking them down." He offered his hand before backing away from the car door.

"You're welcome. Thanks for your assistance." The young man's heartfelt words of appreciation pierced Garrett's composure. "That's why I do this, Leigh, for people like him." He strained against a lump in his throat.

She cuddled beside him. "I understand your feelings. You're committed to your work, and I plan on supporting you in all ways."

"In all ways?" His voice softened, and he leaned against her. His right hand followed the inseam of her cords up one leg.

"Ooh! I doubt we reach the hotel fast enough."

She raised her face and captured his lips as her hands roamed through his hair. When his tongue flicked across her lips, she opened her mouth for him. They explored areas recently relegated to memories during their lonely nights. Tonight they would pick up where they left off in their relationship. They lost themselves in a rolling passion as the cab drove through the stillness of early morning.

"Country Inn and Suites," the driver announced as he stopped before a side entrance.

Leigh paid the fare before rushing around the vehicle to assist Garrett out of the back seat.

"Wait a minute, the keycard is buried in my purse." Before she opened the door, a voice called out.

"Why, Leigh Ramsey! What are you doing? Sneaking in some lucky guy you'll share your body with while your fiancé is away?" David smiled at her as he sauntered toward them. He cast a disdainful frown at Garrett. "Won't your mother rejoice when she learns you found someone else? Scrubs! Did you find yourself a doctor or just an orderly?" His smile turned ugly as he stepped closer.

Garrett had been leaning against the building but drew to his full height and sized up the man approaching them.

"You can drag your mind out of the gutter and offer an apology to her now. Or you can continue talking trash and apologize after I beat you senseless."

His eyes flashed an icy-blue warning. After looking the guy over, Garrett didn't doubt his ability to defeat the man even with a broken arm and stitches across his middle. Widening his stance, his right hand clenched into a tight fist.

Leigh stepped between the men. "Now is not the time for hostility! David, this is my fiancé, Garrett Dane. Garrett, this is—"

"David Walker." Garrett completed the introduction for Leigh. "You're a bigger asshole than I expected. You owe Leigh an apology."

"So, the missing fiancé returned. Impeccable timing on your part. In another couple of days and nights, she'd be back in my arms to stay." David's lewd smile and exaggerated emphasis on the word nights suggested things already happened between Leigh and him.

"That's doubtful. You blew your chance four years ago when you cheated on her. Because you acted like the biggest fool ever, I met her. She's part of my life, so I'm grateful you're a fool. You'll never hurt her again because I won't allow you the opportunity." Garrett confronted David and pinned him where he stood with an icy glare. "I'll repeat myself once, Walker. You owe Leigh an apology, and after you're finished, get out of our sight."

David backed away from Garrett's stance. He looked at Leigh, who stood beside the tall man, who radiated lethal power. One swallow, a second, and he spoke, "Leigh, I'm sorry for suggesting you cheated on your fiancé and slept with me. If you'll excuse me, I'll leave you alone."

He turned and hurried toward the front of the building.

A long exhale followed by a gulp of air brought Garrett's attention back to her.

"Are you alright?" He pulled her close against his right side.

"I am. An apology from him never sounded so sincere. Thank you." She burrowed into his side. "Would you have fought him?"

"Hell yeah, and I would have beaten him."

"With a broken arm and stitches across your abdomen?"

"Without a doubt. Can we move inside now? I maxed out on excitement hours ago."

"What are we waiting for?" Leigh slid the keycard into the lock, and they disappeared through the closing door, bound for their room.

CHAPTER TWENTY-FOUR

Closing the door behind her, Leigh trembled with excitement at being alone with Garrett for the first time in what felt like months. He seemed taller than she remembered and more masculine than before.

"Here, I'll do the undressing." She pulled his jacket off in seconds. "Should we leave the shirt on?"

"No, the bandages protect the stitches." The shirt rose over his head.

"Now for your belt and jeans." Her hands undid the buckle and drew his jeans down to his knees. "How I missed you." She stroked his erection pressing against his shorts and drew a low groan from him.

"Quit wasting time and undress me."

She kissed his chest and wrapped her fingers around the waistband of his shorts. As she pushed them down, she followed the movement and ended on her knees.

A light kiss fell on the tip of his erection, and he groaned again. He caressed her head and ran his fingers through her hair.

She pushed his clothes down to his ankles.

"Sit before you fall over."

Her soft and commanding voice forced compliance from him without hesitation. She tackled his boots and removed each one, followed by socks, and drew off his jeans and shorts. She stood and viewed the man whose image haunted her dreams over the past week. Other than the splint and bandages, he wore nothing but a smile for her. His sexy half-smile weakened her knees and stirred her fantasies.

"You're wearing way too much, darlin'."

She kicked off her boots while undoing her cords. Soon they slid down her legs and stopped at her feet. She yanked the sweater over her head and stepped away from her cords.

One of her satin and lace lingerie sets hid her private areas. He caressed one lace encased breast. A rosy bud showed through the material of her bra, so he thumbed the nipple until it peaked.

She pushed him back on the bed. At his slight grimace, she jumped back.

"Did I hurt you?"

"It's nothing I can't stand. Are you joining me in nakedness?" His smile reflected his desire for her.

"I am." Her bra and panties disappeared, and she flipped off the lights before climbing in bed with him. "Whoops, I almost forgot."

"Forgot what? Where are you going?"

A click sounded, a sliver of light appeared, everything went dark again, and another click sounded. The covers moved and Leigh's warm body cuddled beside him.

"What did you do?"

"I put out the 'do not disturb' sign. I'm certain we'll sleep in."

"Smart. Now let's figure out how we satisfy our needs without going too far. I can't be too active, but I can do this."

His actions began when his right hand glided along her side and paused at a breast. His one-handed action won him a whimper. After the satisfying response, he shifted focus to her other breast until another whimper sounded. With his right hand, he blazed a hot trail down her body to the soft curls of hair at the juncture of her thighs. He found her moist when he plunged one finger within her and garnered a heated gasp in response.

His abilities with one hand delighted her as her sexual need heightened. She arched her back and pressed against his hand, a silent demand for more.

He whispered words of love before slipping a

second finger within her.

Her body responded as though she became his puppet on strings. His actions drove her over the edge of passion's heights, muscles tightened on his fingers, her hips moved of their own accord, and she cried out. Her senses overloaded when her climax hit and wave upon wave of pleasure washed over her.

"Wow!" She panted in exhaustion. "All my dreams came true, and you accomplished it one-handed. I can't wait until your arm heals."

He chuckled, a deep throaty sound. "I may not be experiencing the pleasure of your attentions for a couple weeks, but I love watching you lost in a passionate response." He kissed her brow and tasted the saltiness of sweat-soaked skin.

"I missed you so much. I wondered if we'd still enjoy what we had before you left." His body tensed in reaction to her words, but she continued. "For a fleeting moment, I worried we couldn't recapture what we built at the Aspen Inn."

"And your decision is what?"

His cautious tone carried through the darkness of the room.

"I wasted time worrying. We forged something special, and this is our destiny. I love you."

"You are my one and only, Leigh. I'm amazed every time I realize you said yes when I proposed. You are my life. I live for you." The tension her initial words created eased, and he drew her close.

"Sweet dreams, Garrett." She nestled into his side, away from his stitches.

"You, too, darlin'." He relaxed against the pillows, closed his eyes, and welcomed the peace of much-needed sleep.

***

Agonized sounds of pain woke her. Garrett groaned in his sleep. She rose from the bed and stumbled over their discarded clothes as she sought out his pain pills in the bathroom. Armed with two pills and a glass of water, she stood by his side of the bed. The light from the bathroom illuminated the grimace on his face. Setting the glass of water down, she leaned over him.

"Garrett? Garrett? You need your pills—" His splinted arm came up with sudden force, connecting with her face under the right eye. She stumbled backward.

Garrett's eyes blinked open. In his dream, he was back in the farmhouse, and Karl called out his name in a warning. Repeating what happened in the dingy farmhouse, his left arm flew up and struck something. As his focus improved, he spotted Leigh with a hand on her face.

"Leigh! Ah, crap. I hit you, didn't I? You need something cold on your eye right away, so the swelling stays down." He strained against the pain in his abdomen and reached for her.

"No, you stay down." She pinned him against the bed with her hands on his shoulders. "Your moaning woke me, so I brought you two pain pills."

"I don't want any; I won't get hooked on them."

"You will not become dependent on painkillers by taking two on your first night after being sliced open. Remember, your nurse said you'll need them for at least the first couple of days to heal." She held out her hand holding the pills.

"Leigh, I worked with a guy who got hooked on these. He couldn't control himself; soon he needed something stronger and moved on to illegal drugs until he killed himself with an overdose. I'm not taking them." He shook his head. "You need some ice for your eye."

"I'll go for ice if you take your pills."

"You can't blackmail me into taking them."

"Sure I can. Take them if only for my well-being; I need my rest. I promise I won't let you become addicted." She handed him the pills and glass of water.

"Okay, I'll take them for you and because the pain's excruciating." He tossed down the pills and handed her the empty glass. "Your turn; ice, now!"

She threw on some clothes, grabbed the ice bucket, and trudged out. She returned with a load of ice.

"Put some in a washcloth and hold it on your eye." Garrett yawned as he directed her.

"I got it. Back under the covers, you're falling asleep as we talk." She smiled as he fought the sleep beating him down. She wondered if a much younger Garrett fought sleep in the same way and imagined him as a little cutie fighting his bedtime. At another time she'd ask him about Dane family photos. "Come on, I'll tuck you in."

After he settled under the covers, she sat with the ice pack on her eye. She wondered if a black eye would result from the collision with the splint. Funny how her first black eye might come from her fiancé. Almost laughing, she sobered at the thought of her mother going off on ridiculous tangents if she learned Garrett gave her a black eye. Grateful for not scheduling a visit with her mother in the near future she shook off her concerns.

An hour or so later sleep beckoned, so she dropped the ice pack in the bathroom sink. Pulling off the few items of clothes she wore, she left everything where they fell. She climbed into bed with Garrett and curled up behind him away from his injuries. The pills worked, and he slept peacefully. He needed rest to help heal his body. She understood his worry of dependency on pain medications, and she loved him for his caution. As her eyes closed, his breathing became her lullaby and sleep overcame her.

CHAPTER TWENTY-FIVE

A crack of light spilled into their room. Leigh stirred; welcomed heat radiated along her side and a hand cupped one breast. How she missed waking up this way. The time was eight-thirty. She could shoot down for some breakfast items and return before Garrett woke.

She extracted herself from his hand and rolled off the bed. Donning discarded clothes from the night before, she hurried out the door and reached the breakfast area in minutes. She loaded a tray with juice, fruit, yogurt, and a couple of decadent donuts, grabbed napkins, and turned for the return trip to their room.

"Good morning, Leigh. I didn't expect to run into you this morning." David appeared in the doorway with a suitcase by his side.

"Leaving I see. Good. Have a safe drive home." She tried to walk past him, but he moved in her way.

"Looks like things got a bit rough last night between you and your fiancé." He held her chin and turned her head for a clear view of her bruised right eye. "So, he didn't care for our seeing each other in his absence?"

She jerked her head from his hand and stepped around him.

"Not that our relationship is any of your business, but this is from an accident with his splint. A simple case of my leaning over, him jerking awake, and the splint catching my cheek near the eye. And clear away any misconceptions in your head that you and I in any way dated each other while you were here. I acted politely by joining you for lunch the first day and never intended on joining you for dinner until my dad asked me to do it as a favor to him.

Excuse me, but I'm going back up to Garrett."

"Don't kid yourself and consider this over. When I want something, I seize it for keeps…never forget," he called after her.

She spun around and faced him; her eyes narrowed.

"I'm not some inanimate object you can grab up and take possession of. I'm a person, David, with free will, and I made my decision regarding you a long time ago. I share a love and a life with my fiancé you'll never understand. Return to your life in the Cities and leave us to ours out here."

She stomped away with thoughts of the man upstairs in bed.

David considered her words and dismissed them. He cheered her well-timed black eye. No doubt the incident happened as she claimed, but her parents didn't need the true story. His smile held a cruel edge as he walked to his car. A fabricated tale of her violent fiancé whispered to his mother guaranteed the version she shared with Leigh's parents to be worse. Her parents would demand the prosecution of her abusive fiancé. He laughed; such a twisted injustice would serve the guy right for threatening him.

***

Leigh hurried back to their room. Why did she have to run into David of all people? She shook off the remnants of her disgust of him. Today should be the last time she ever laid eyes on him, and the thought made her smile.

Upon entering their room, she sensed something ominous happened in her absence. She set the tray on the desk and glanced around the room. Not a thing out of place, but she couldn't shake the sense of something being wrong. She looked at Garrett. Shock overwhelmed her at the sight of the grimace on his face and his white-knuckled grip on the covers.

"Leigh?"

"Garrett, I'm here. I went down for a few breakfast items. What's the matter?"

"We should go back to the hospital." A deep groan sounded before he opened one eye.

She rushed to the bed. "Why? What's the problem?"

Both eyes were closed again. "The wound's on fire and hurts like hell." Overcome with pain, he gritted his teeth and fisted the blankets. "Ah, shit." He clutched his abdomen and strained against the pain.

She winced in sympathy for him; the distortion of his features announced each wave of pain. Then she noticed beads of sweat on his forehead. She placed the back of one hand on his brow. "Garrett, you're burning up. Should I drive you or call for an ambulance?"

"I had my fill of ambulances unless you'd rather not drive?"

"No, I can drive us. Here, let me give you a hand."

Together they got him upright and dressed. Worry about him heightened at the intense heat radiating from his body. Her concern increased as though it matched the rise in his temperature. The disagreeable confrontation with David was forgotten.

***

Upon reaching the ER, the medical staff whisked Garrett away. She stared at the doors he disappeared through; tears rolled down her cheeks. The sheer weight of being alone and frightened of losing him threatened to overwhelm her. Her former self would react in a weak manner but not the woman she became since Garrett fell into her life. He was a fighter, and she would match his courage. She wiped away her tears and called the one person she knew would support her through this.

"Janet? Garrett's back in the ER; something's not right." A stray tear traced down her cheek.

"We'll be right there."

Janet's immediate response and abrupt ending of the call brought her untold comfort. She and Joe would be with her, and their support would lead her through the latest challenge in her life. The shared knowledge of the dangers faced by their men drew the women together and wove a strong bond between them. Leigh collapsed in a chair, surprised by her shaking.

A nurse informed her Garrett had been moved to a surgical suite. The doctor planned to reopen his wound for a thorough cleaning. The description of the procedure made her nauseous. A separate waiting room outside the surgical area afforded her a place to wait for word of his progress. After she texted the new location to Janet, she searched out the other waiting area.

Time dragged. She had never suffered through a loved one needing emergency medical care. This was a reality of his profession, and she needed to handle all aspects of her new life beside him. She thought of the church she visited and planned on attending for Sunday services. Today was Sunday she realized. She wouldn't be attending today, but a need for the support offered by a church family grew within her. She and Garrett would attend church together next Sunday, and this week schedule their marriage training. Her faith in his recovery battled against her fears.

***

"Leigh!" Janet gathered her into a hug, and Joe waited in the doorway.

"Thank you so much for coming. I'm so scared…" Unable to continue, she struggled with her negative thoughts. "He described the wound as being on fire and doubled over in pain. Heat radiated off him, so his fever must be dangerously high. He lost consciousness before we got here."

"It sounds as though a severe infection set in. Don't you agree, Joe?" Janet's eyes reached her husband's.

"Based on Karl's description of the house where his injury occurred, the knife was probably filthy. Knife wounds hold challenges for the medical teams when they clean them. Treating him in a sterile environment is a smart move. He'll pull through; he's strong and has the best reason for living." At Leigh's puzzled look, he added, "You're his reason for living."

A doctor stepped into the room. "Miss Ramsey?"

"Yes?" She moved near the doctor but held Janet's hand.

"He's fighting an infection. We opened the wound and cleaned the area a bit deeper into the surrounding tissue. He's stitched up, but his temperature remains elevated. We're focused on treatment of the fever and pumped him with fluids and antibiotics. As soon as his temperature is down, you can see him." He turned away, but came back, staring at her face. "Do you need your eye checked out? The discoloration looks fairly new."

"No thanks, I'm fine. It happened early this morning, an accidental collision with his splint."

Her cheeks heated. She stared directly in his eyes—a dare to dispute her story.

"If the swelling doesn't reduce or trouble with your vision occurs seek medical care immediately. You can continue waiting here. When he's ready for visitors, someone will come for you. Excuse me." He stopped on his way out. "Joe? I didn't notice you standing there. How are you?"

"Been better. When my newest agent is back in the hospital a few hours after his release, I'm not happy. With you on his case, I'm confident he'll pull through." The men shook hands as the women stood by.

"In case you don't recall, this is my wife, Janet." He pointed at her. "Jan, you must remember Rob McNair. His boys played on the softball team I coached."

"Oh, yes. Your boys came home with ours a couple times."

"Believe me, my wife and I appreciated the boys being out of the house for a few evenings. As I recall, we hadn't enjoyed a date night in forever."

Leigh found their interaction fascinating, and her fears lessened after learning Joe knew Garrett's doctor. The men's conversation flowed over her and reminded her of the warmth of friendships. It was such a small world, and now she and Garrett were part of this one.

"So, Garrett Dane is one of yours? Nothing identified him as a BCA agent. I'll keep a close eye on him for you." With a wave of his hand, he disappeared out the door.

"Hmm, Rob McNair. Leigh, Garrett's in skilled hands." He frowned at her. "Your eye is colorful; how did you say it happened?"

She dreaded Joe assuming Garrett hit her; surely, he wouldn't jump to the same conclusion as David.

"His moaning woke me up. When I leaned over and said his name, his arm came up and the splint caught me below my eye. He didn't intentionally hit me; in fact, he was asleep at the time." Her eyes pleaded for his belief in her story.

Joe said nothing right away and looked deep in thought. "Sounds as though he relived the incident in the farmhouse."

"Really?" Leigh's relief showed in her face.

"Yes, him reliving the circumstances of how he broke his arm and later was knifed doesn't surprise me. I suspect he was dreaming the whole incident. When you said his name, it fit in with Karl calling out his name in warning. He probably raised his arm the same way he deflected the skillet away from his head. Only this time instead of a skillet, it was you or more accurately your face.

Anyway, you should always allow him space when you're waking him, especially after an assignment like this one."

He noted her reaction of relief on her face, no sign of fear at all. Yes, Garrett had done well when he chose Leigh for his life partner.

"I got a black eye in much the same way." Janet shared her similar experience. "I bet you're hungry. Can I bring you something from the cafeteria?"

"Why don't you both go down? I'll stay here and wait for any news," Joe offered. "Bring me back a coffee?"

"I am hungry; our breakfast is still sitting in our hotel room," Leigh admitted.

They left Joe in the waiting room, rifling through outdated hunting magazines.

***

Janet wondered why Leigh looked so concerned over the discussion of her black eye. Perhaps while they spent time over breakfast, she would offer a hint or explanation as to what weighed so heavily on her.

"Let's eat down here; you need a break," she suggested.

"I do. Last night and this morning have been difficult for me. First, a horrendous supper with David, followed by Garrett being hurt, and now this."

"I'm an excellent listener if you need one."

"What I need is this drama behind me."

"Get yourself some food, I'll grab a coffee and find us a table somewhere private."

Leigh nodded, took a tray, and selected oatmeal in honor of Garrett's usual preference. After selecting a couple of items for Janet and Joe, she made it through the line. The demands of the last day had drained her, and she appreciated Janet's being with her.

"I bought a donut for you and one for Joe. I can't eat by myself."

"You shouldn't have, but thanks." Janet hesitated before posing the question needling her. "How horrendous was your dinner with David?"

A long sigh was her initial response. "David offered me another gaudy ring at dinner." Janet's jaw dropped. "Yeah, my reaction exactly until he tried to pull off my engagement ring. He suggested Garrett cheated on me during his time away. He claimed our parents want us back together. Dad bonded with Garrett and approved of our marriage, but David implied he changed his mind. For some reason, my mom desires I marry David. On the way to the restaurant, he had me call his mother. The conversation went beyond bizarre. Her responses to everything I said were quizzical. I'm sure she and my mom are scheming together. I planned on sending you a 911 text, so I had an excuse to leave. Your call gave me a reason for leaving before I texted you."

Leigh played with her oatmeal before eating some. The warmth tracked all the way to her stomach.

"He sounds so full of himself. Would he try anything else?"

"I wouldn't be surprised. We met him at the hotel early this morning when we returned from the hospital."

"He was out late."

"You're right. With all the innuendos hurled about and the male posturing going on, I never connected the lateness of the hour with him returning to the hotel. I'm sure he hooked up with someone from the restaurant. He's a flirt and enjoys a conquest." Leigh ate another spoonful of oatmeal. "He assumed I picked up a doctor for the evening because Garrett wore the top from a set of scrubs. When I introduced them, David implied he and I were on track for a reunion. Garrett didn't believe him and forced an apology for his innuendos about me."

"Of course Garrett wouldn't believe such a story."

"This morning when I went downstairs for breakfast,

I ran into David."

"Of all the luck. What happened?"

"He spotted my black eye and assumed Garrett hit me because of my seeing him. I told him it was an accident, but I'm sure he'll spread his version all around. My mom will freak out, and no telling what she'll do with a story so demeaning of Garrett's character." Leigh let her spoon drop in her bowl as she released a sigh.

"Have you called your parents yet?"

"No. When I got into our room, Garrett needed medical attention, so we ended up here."

"Maybe you should call your father and talk with him, at least inform him of Garrett's condition."

"Yes, if I don't tell him now, and he finds out later, he'll be upset. Thanks, Janet. It's a relief sharing my worries with someone."

"I appreciate you confiding in me. Do you mind if I warn Joe about David's version of how you received a black eye in case something comes up at work?"

"No. In all honesty, I feared you might think the same as David did this morning. My relief from your belief in what I said was immense. We should probably go back up."

"Refill your coffee while I do the same and buy a cup for Joe."

When they walked into the surgical waiting area, Joe looked up from a magazine.

"You're looking better, Leigh. No word yet on Garrett's condition, so I planned to search out an update in a couple minutes." Janet handed him his coffee and the donut. "Thanks, honey."

"I only bought you coffee. The donut's from Leigh." Janet sat in the chair beside him.

"Thanks, but you didn't need to do this," Joe said.

"Yes, I did. You and Janet are so supportive, and you gave up your Sunday morning for us." Leigh sat across from them; tears threatened to fall.

"This is what I do for my folks. Speaking of my folks, I'm off in search of information on Garrett's condition. I'll be back."

Joe's departure reminded Leigh of a bloodhound on the trail of its target.

"He'll come back with an update; his talent is subterfuge. Of course his acquaintance with Garrett's doctor will help." Janet's pride in her husband sounded in her voice.

"Once we get an update, I'll call my dad." Leigh shuffled through the magazines for something of interest and settled on one about fishing.

Joe returned with an unreadable expression on his face. Leigh jumped to her feet.

"They're still battling the fever. His temperature remains higher than they hoped it would be by now, so they're working on cooling his body."

"Isn't a high fever dangerous?" Her voice wavered.

"One can be." Joe didn't mince any words. "Dr. McNair said he'd stop in and update you personally, Leigh."

She nodded. What she remembered of high fevers frightened her. If a fever remained too high for too long, brain damage or death might occur. Sudden light-headedness hit, she swayed on her feet.

"Leigh, sit down and put your head between your knees before you pass out." Janet sat beside her and coaxed her head down. "Joe, get some water."

In minutes, the faintness lessened.

"A high fever can cause brain damage and death, right?" Leigh asked.

"Only positive thoughts from now on, you hear me?" Janet admonished her.

Dr. McNair walked into the waiting room; they huddled around him.

"How is he?" Leigh asked, thankful for Janet's nearness in case of unsatisfactory news.

"We lowered his temperature a few degrees. It's still higher than where I want it, so we'll continue our efforts to cool him down. I'm admitting him to monitor his condition overnight. Once he's settled in his room, you can visit with him; I estimate an hour, two at the most."

"Thank you, doctor." Leigh relaxed for the first time in hours.

"Thanks, Rob, I know you're doing all you can for him." Joe shook hands and walked out with the doctor.

"He'll be fine, Leigh. You should call your dad and tell him what happened," Janet prompted.

"You and Joe don't need to stay any longer; you should be home with your boys. I'll call when he's in a room. I'll be forever grateful for you being here."

"How could we not be here for you?" Janet wrapped Leigh in a warm hug.

"Where'd Joe go?"

"He walked out with Dr. McNair; he'll return soon."

In the hall, Joe stood with Dr. McNair deep in conversation.

"How's he really doing, Rob?" Joe asked.

"They were smart coming in right away. The knife used on him must have been filthy. An infection set in and resulted in the fever. Antibiotics didn't do a thing to decrease his temperature. The high fever concerned me. In fact, it went up a few degrees after he arrived, so we had him in cool wraps. His temperature only dropped two degrees, and I want the number down another two before we send him to a room. He'll experience quite a bit of pain across the abdomen for a couple of days, and he'll continue having residual pain for a couple of weeks." Rob ran a hand over his face. "He's a fighter and strong, so he should pull through well enough."

"How soon could he be back to work?"

"You're anxious for his return, huh? A lot depends on how fast his body heals itself. The stitches stay in for two weeks, but it'll be months before the wound heals internally. Give him until the stitches are out. By then he should be moving well, but nothing strenuous for at least a month. Start him on light duty." An urgent sound came from his pocket. "I'm needed in the ER. Great seeing you, Joe."

"Same here. Thanks for taking care of my guy." Joe clapped Rob on the shoulder and returned to the waiting area.

"There you are!" Janet smiled at Joe when he rejoined the two women.

"Are we leaving?" He watched Janet put on her coat and hand him his jacket.

"We are. Leigh's confident she can handle things from now on and said we should enjoy the rest of our day with the boys." Janet hugged her. "Remember, call if you need anything."

"I will. Thanks again for coming." She hesitated before hugging Joe. "I'm so grateful you're his boss."

"I'm the lucky one. He did a bang-up job for us." Joe returned her hug. "I won't expect him at work until his stitches are out, I believe that's in two weeks. Your job is to ensure he follows the doctor's orders. Can you do that?"

"I can and will." Leigh followed them to the door. "Please tell the boys and the dogs hi for me."

"We will."

They walked down the hall holding hands.

"Where were you?" Janet watched her husband's expression.

"I asked Rob about Garrett's condition. They did the right thing by coming in when they did. He should pull through, but he'll be in a lot of pain. His stitches will be out in two weeks. I'm sure Leigh will have her hands full nursing him; he doesn't strike me as the kind of patient who'll take it easy for weeks on end."

"I'm glad you're giving him plenty of time for recovery. They can spend the time house hunting and completing their wedding plans. Those poor kids have faced many challenges so early in their relationship."

"But they'll tough it out and survive."

"How can you be so sure?" Janet gazed up at him.

"Garrett's fearless and loves her. He made a wise choice in Leigh, who's smart and understands what's required of him in his career. She strikes me as a woman who'll face all challenges with courage and conviction. She proved herself by dealing with his undercover assignment so soon after they arrived at a new location and with no immediate friends in the area. And you saw her at the hospital last night and this morning, sure she needed our support, but she didn't shy away from anything. They complement each other, and together they're stronger."

"My word, you have never been so outspoken before."

"I like them. They're a welcome addition to my team." Joe smiled and wrapped an arm around her.

"Leigh plans to call her dad and inform him of what happened. She believes her mother played a significant part in her ex-boyfriend's appearance. He didn't play nice while he was here."

Joe stopped walking. "He wasn't violent with her, was he?"

"No, nothing so extreme. He tried winning her back, but it didn't happen. He came upon them as they entered the hotel early this morning." She started him walking again.

"I'm certain the confrontation could have turned ugly in a heartbeat. Garrett never met the guy, but he's protective of her."

"Yes, well, their meeting ended with an apology from David for implying Leigh had been unfaithful to

Garrett. This morning David saw Leigh's black eye and assumed Garrett hit her for seeing him. She feared we'd assume the same."

"I wondered why she appeared apprehensive when she told us what happened, and now I understand."

"She's convinced David will spread a story of how Garrett beat her, and he'll make a point of telling her mother. She has no idea what her mother would do with the false information."

"I guess her mom's not a fan of Garrett's?"

"Not in the least. Leigh fears her mom may create trouble for him and wanted you to be aware of the situation in case she succeeds."

"I hear you. Let's drive home and find out what the kids have been doing while we've been here." He held the car door for her.

"I hope they slept in."

"We can only hope, Jan."

CHAPTER TWENTY-SIX

Leigh pulled out her phone, sighed, and dialed her dad.

"Leigh! How are you? Is Garrett back?" One question reinforced her dad's acceptance of her fiancé.

"Garrett's back, but I'm scared." She decided against holding anything back. "He's in the hospital."

"Hospital? What happened? Should we come up?"

"No, you don't need to come. Neither of us would want Mom here."

Leigh's bluntness shocked her dad. "What are you saying?"

"I believe Mom's the reason David showed up. The true purpose for his appearance was to make up with me and break my engagement with Garrett. He brought an engagement ring with him and even had me talk with his mom. She didn't express any surprise at me being in the Brainerd area. Mom set us up!"

"Honey, I don't have an explanation, but I can't believe your mom would orchestrate anything like this."

"Think about it. She hates Garrett and will do anything to prevent us from marrying." Leigh paced the waiting area. "And if you hear a story of Garrett hitting me, don't believe it."

"Hitting you? What the heck is going on?"

"First, let me explain why Garrett's in the hospital, and you'll understand my last comment."

A heavy sigh came over the phone. "Alright, give me the whole story."

"He's been on an undercover assignment for his work. Last night his assignment ended with arrests, but he suffered a couple of injuries: a broken arm and a knife wound across his abdomen. When we entered the hotel last night, we ran into David. The guys exchanged words.

David implied he and I would be back together in a few more days. Garrett took exception to his implication as to my behavior and forced an apology out of David. You would have enjoyed seeing him in action, Dad."

"He's a good man, honey. Did he get physical with David?"

"No, but he intimidated him. Garrett told me he could beat David even with a broken arm and stitches!"

"I agree, but we're off topic. Continue with your story."

"Last night while he slept, I got hit under an eye by his splint, so I have a black eye. This morning I saw David in the hotel breakfast area. He assumed Garrett hit me because I spent time with him. I'm sure he'll exaggerate the story when he's home, so don't believe anything you're told by him or his mom." Leigh took a deep breath.

"I understand. No way would Garrett harm you, so I'll stop any false stories I hear. You said he's in the hospital, but you were at the hotel this morning. What happened?"

"His knife wound developed a bad infection. This morning, he woke up with severe pain and a high fever, so I brought him to the ER. The fever remains high, so the doctor's admitting him."

"Are you sure you don't need anything? If I ask Alex, he'll drive up to be with you."

"No, Dad. I'm fine. If I can, I'll stay with Garrett, so I won't be around the hotel."

"Sounds as though you have everything in hand. I always knew you were strong, and now you're showing Garrett your strength. If you change your mind about needing anything, you call me."

"Thanks, Dad. I should go. Love you!" Leigh's spirits soared higher.

"I love you, too. Give Garrett my best wishes for a speedy recovery."

"I will. Bye."

The conversation with her dad provided her needed reassurance of his belief in Garrett and a degree of relief from his promise to quell rumors generated by David.

"Hi, are you waiting for Garrett Dane?" A nurse had entered during Leigh's musings over her dad's comments.

"Yes. Has he improved?" Leigh jumped at the nurse's question.

He smiled and nodded. "His fever is down, so we're moving him to a private room. I'll show you the way and explain what we're doing for him."

Leigh grabbed her coat and followed him down a hall and around a corner.

"This is his room, and here he comes. If you'll wait here until we move him to the bed, I'll call you in when he's settled."

Leigh nodded. When Garrett rolled by, her smile faltered. The image of his pale coloring against the white bedding combined with his closed eyes shocked her. An IV ran up to multiple bags hanging from the bed. She closed her eyes and willed herself into remembering him as he had been the night before: loving, playful, and active.

"You can come in now."

Leigh stepped inside a comfortable-sized room with an actual view out the window.

"He's on fluids, antibiotics, and a painkiller. This is a self-dosing mechanism and provides the painkiller as he needs some. As soon as he experiences pain, he should push this button rather than waiting until the pain increases."

"He has issues with using painkillers. He knew someone who got dependent on them, turned to illegal drugs, and died of an overdose."

"For the first couple of days, he shouldn't worry. Once he tolerates the pain, he can stop taking them. With him being aware of the possibility of addiction, he should be safe."

"If he's moaning in his sleep, can I do the self-dosing?"

"Sure, he'll thank you for it." He smiled at her.

"How long am I allowed to stay with him?"

"As long as you like. The chair isn't the most comfortable, but people do spend nights in them. Here's the call button and controls for the bed. He'll be out for a couple of hours if you need anything from home or something to eat."

"Thank you."

"No problem. He should be fine and might be released as early as tomorrow."

When the nurse left the room, the rush of varied emotions stunned her. Gratefulness for the medical care, lingering fear for Garrett, and exhaustion from the stress of the unknown washed over her and threatened to overwhelm her. Squaring her shoulders, she walked to the bed.

Unable to quell the urge to touch him, she pushed a lock of hair off his forehead and behind an ear.

"Oh, Garrett, I love you so much. Please wake up, so I can gaze into your eyes, all warm brown as they were last night."

She placed her hand on his chest, leaned over, and kissed him. Now what? Stay? Go? Her stomach rumbled and decided for her.

"I'm going for some lunch; I won't be long."

She kissed his forehead and walked out. While she walked, she texted Janet an update.

After she returned with a sandwich and milk, she sat in front of the window with an unobstructed view of Garrett and a direct path to his self-medication mechanism. When he moaned and thrashed a bit, she reached his side in seconds. She placed a hand on his forehead in fear of an increase in his fever. Relief coursed through her when he felt cooler than when she left for lunch. Moments after she administered the painkiller, he became restful. She finished her lunch without realizing it for her focus never strayed from Garrett.

***

The sunlight filtered through the window. Garrett broke out of the lethargy of medicine and exhaustion. When he opened his eyes, he discovered he was alone in a hospital room and no longer in the ER. A wave of panic washed over him. *Where's Leigh? Why isn't she here? Did a return trip to the hospital overwhelm her? Did she decide my job created too much chaos for her? Did she run into David Walker's open arms?* Emotions wreaked havoc with him, he closed his eyes against the devastating thoughts of losing her.

The sudden flush of a toilet drew his attention to a closed door in the room. Could it be…?

The door opened and out walked Leigh. The sunlight bathed her in a golden glow, and a huge smile broke across her face. His worries disappeared as the vision before him warmed his heart.

"You're awake!"

"And you're still here."

She rushed to his side. "Of course I'm here. Where else would I be?"

Without voicing his fears, he reached out for her hand. "I love you."

She kissed him. "And I love you."

"What happened?"

"You don't remember?"

"The last thing I remember is driving here." He coughed and grimaced.

"How bad is your pain? I can give you some medicine if you want." She registered his contorted features and the fisting of blankets. The pain must be intense, she thought. A check of his brow dispelled her fear of the return of the fever.

He caught one hand in his. "I'll be fine once you kiss me again."

Her wish and prayers had been granted; he'd woken up. She complied with his request as her fears for him vanished. On automatic for the kiss, she leaned over him and closed her eyes. He wrapped his right arm around her, drew her closer, and breached her mouth with his tongue. Her moans echoed in the room; her need for him intensified by her fears of losing him. Their kiss stoked her desire for him.

Garrett broke off their kiss. "You taste delicious. If we continue this, you'll be with me in this bed and not for sleep."

Leigh giggled. "I'm sure the hospital frowns on the activity you're thinking about, and I doubt your doctor or nurse would approve."

"Perhaps they won't, but I do." A warning of his intentions showed in the glint of mischief in his eyes. He placed a hand on one breast and rested the splinted arm across her back, holding her against him.

"You're feeling better, aren't you?" She removed his hand from her breast, squirmed away, and gazed down at him.

"Better than at the hotel or on the way here. Tell me what happened after we arrived? This isn't the ER."

The intensity of his focus on her and his dazzling smile made her knees weak.

"Your doctor admitted you, so they can monitor your condition. Your wound became infected and caused a high fever. They opened the wound and cleaned deeper in a surgical suite this time." She looked away for a moment, turning back with tears in her eyes. "The antibiotics didn't work fast enough, so they used other methods for battling your fever. You could have died!"

"But I didn't. Please, don't focus on 'could haves.'"

He wiped away her tears with a gentle touch.

"You're right of course." She took a deep breath to regain her resolve. "Joe and Janet came and stayed with me until your fever dropped. Joe's giving you two weeks off, so you can heal."

"Lots of wedding and house stuff can be accomplished in two weeks. Right?"

"Yes, but nothing too demanding until you heal more. We can tackle things like our marriage training, buying our license, deciding on a property, and selecting a house plan."

"Sounds as though we'll be busy." As she rattled off items to work on, he focused on her rather than on what she said. His attention lingered on her sparkling eyes, flushed cheeks, and peaked nipples pressed against her light sweater. All courtesy of his earlier actions and their kiss. The kiss held everything he remembered: passion, love, and a promise for their future. Uh-oh, she was staring at him, waiting for a response. *Oops, should have been listening.* "What?"

"I asked if you needed anything, but now I wonder whether you're okay."

"I don't need anything but you, and I'm fine. You distracted me." He smiled at her and patted the bed. "Join me."

"As enticing as your offer is, I'll pass for now. Before I forget, my dad sends his best."

"You talked with your folks?"

"Only Dad. I informed him of what happened up here and warned him."

"Warned him about what?"

"I expect David will spread a story of you beating me."

"Me? Beat you? Why would he come up with such a wild story?"

"When I went downstairs this morning, he and I met

in the lobby. Of course he commented on my black eye."

"And David, being who he is, won't hesitate to spread a false story if it ruins me and furthers his agenda."

"Exactly. Mom would pounce on anything denigrating you, and no telling what she would do with such information." Leigh ran her fingers through his hair. "You don't have to cut your hair when you report for work, do you?"

"Wow! Abrupt switch in topics, but not discussing your mother or your ex-boyfriend is a relief." He smiled, and her returning smile sent his stomach spinning. "I don't have a clue how short my hair should be for work. Joe gave me a stack of regulations and stuff, and one of them probably includes information on a dress code and personal appearance standards. We should pick up all the paperwork once I'm out of here. Do you remember how the men in the office looked?"

She shook her head. "Don't recall. Will you shave your beard?" Her fingers traced his jaw.

"As soon as I lay my hands on a razor, I'm shaving all this away, permanently." He caught her hand.

"Until the next time," she added, her voice low and sultry.

"If there is a next time." He kissed her fingers and pulled her closer. "Let's not worry over an imaginary assignment."

He brushed his lips across hers and didn't wait long for her response.

One of her hands snaked along the back of his head and held him in place. She plunged her tongue past his lips and stroked against his tongue.

Restricted from performing the physical act of loving her, he responded in ways to demonstrate his love for her. His splinted arm held her against him while he ran his right hand along her side to a breast. He needed her in bed with him and being hospitalized made fulfillment of his needs impossible. As his frustration grew, his kiss sought her complete surrender.

Leigh moaned as his hand caressed her breast. Dang hospital bed! Her desire for him soared higher than before, probably due to the limitations. He'd better improve and be released tomorrow. They needed privacy.

A knock on the door went unnoticed as did the sweeping open action. They responded to a cough and separated so fast Leigh fell into the chair.

"Sorry for the interruption, but I need to check your vitals." The nurse failed at hiding his smile. "Are you okay, miss? Your landing sounded hard."

"I'm fine. Fortunately, I can't die of embarrassment." She let loose a low chuckle.

"Well said. I'm your day nurse, Neil. Obviously, you're feeling better." He reviewed Garrett's chart as he spoke.

"Obviously." Garrett grinned as the nurse completed notations in the chart. "Will the doctor stop in today?"

"Dr. McNair visits all his patients before leaving for home each night, so he'll be by later. Do you need anything? Perhaps lunch, you missed the meal service. I can order you something light."

"I am hungry, thanks." Garrett grimaced as a pain struck across his abdomen.

"Time for another dose of the painkiller," Leigh urged.

"Are you having pain across your wound area?" Neil, all business, studied Garrett's eyes.

"Some but not unbearable." Garrett minimized his pain.

"The pain will only worsen. You should self-medicate by pushing this button. Go ahead; try it out," Neil coached.

"I prefer not—"

"Garrett, you need something for your pain, at least today and tomorrow," Leigh pleaded.

"Your fiancée told me of your reluctance over taking painkillers. With your awareness, you shouldn't worry about addiction. For today and tomorrow, the relief gained from the painkillers will aid in your recovery. Afterward, you do whatever you're comfortable with for the pain."

"Fine." Garrett surrendered and let Neil show him how to use the mechanism. The painkiller flowed into him. "It works fast, doesn't it?"

"Yes," Leigh and Neil answered him.

Their knowing smiles irritated him. "Thanks for not adding 'we told you so' to your responses, at least not out loud."

Neil laughed. "Caustic sense of humor. I admire your attitude after everything you went through. I'll order your lunch and stop by later." He departed with a wave of his hand.

"Neil's a super nurse. He's the one who brought me to you, explained everything they did, what they were giving you through the IV, and how the self-medication thing worked." Her cheeks changed hue to a light pink. "While you were out, I medicated you a couple of times."

"You did?"

"Well, you groaned a lot, so I punched the button. You rested easier afterward." What she didn't expect was a smile in response to her confession.

"Thanks for watching out for me." There was no doubting his sincerity. "Where are the bed controls? I'd like to sit up."

"Here." She manipulated the bed and adjusted his pillows. "Comfortable?"

"Yes." He caught her shoulders and held her in place. "Have I told you lately I love you?" His throaty voice and darkened eyes demonstrated the emotions building within him.

The desire in his eyes and the delivery of his question launched the dragons in her stomach. Her knees weakened, so she leaned against the bed for support. He took immediate advantage of her position by pulling her into a hug followed by a kiss.

"I love you, Leigh Ramsey, and cannot wait until you're Mrs. Leigh Dane."

"That's the first time I heard my soon to be married name spoken out loud; how appropriate the first time would be from your lips." She returned his kiss.

A knock at the door stopped him from kissing her again.

Leigh stepped back as a young woman carried a tray into the room.

"Hi. I brought lunch for Mr. Dane." She set the tray on a rolling table and slid it in front of him. "Enjoy your meal." She walked out and the door closed behind her.

"Let's find out what Neil ordered for you." Leigh uncovered the dishes. "Hmm, tomato soup, crackers, and the requisite hospital Jell-O. Yummy!"

"Tomato soup is one of my favorites." Garrett crushed the crackers into his soup. Once the soup thickened enough, he took a spoonful.

Leigh shook her head. "Having a bit of soup with your crackers?"

"This is the only way you should eat tomato soup. Didn't this conversation come up before at the cabin?"

A slight snort sounded as she sat in the chair. A check of emails on her phone provided a distraction while he ate. When eating sounds stopped, she looked up.

"Would you care for some of my Jell-O?" He tried for a sexy look, but figured the splint, IV, and hospital gown detracted too much for success.

"Thanks, it's been years since I ate Jell-O." She slid her chair nearer the bed and received her first spoonful. "I forgot how fun Jell-O is to eat."

"I can imagine us eating Jell-O in our home. Of course whipped cream and nudity will be involved." Garrett's wicked grin announced the seriousness of his description.

Finding her voice was a challenge. Images in her mind's eye, inspired by his words, delayed her response.

"I never ate Jell-O naked, but I'm game."

"We'll discover plenty of interesting firsts to explore together."

Another spoonful hovered in front of her. She ran her tongue over the wiggling orange mass. When she grasped his hand, she explored the Jell-O piled high on the spoon with the tip of her tongue

He emitted a groan and fidgeted in the bed.

She scraped the Jell-O from the spoon with her teeth, swallowed, smacked her lips, and drew the spoon and his hand toward her mouth. She licked the spoon front and back before releasing his hand. The spoon clattered against the tray.

"We are definitely stocking Jell-O in our house." Garrett's voice sounded raspy.

She laughed, wickedly satisfied by his reaction. Her phone rang. After a glance at the display, she didn't hesitate to answer.

"Hi, Janet. Were the boys and dogs okay?"

"They were fine, watching TV, and eating cereal. How's Garrett's condition?"

"He's awake and having a late lunch." Leigh stood by the window, but kept an eye on him as he finished the Jell-O.

"Sounds encouraging; have you seen the doctor again?"

"No, but the nurse told us he checks on his patients before he leaves for the night."

"Hopefully, he releases Garrett tomorrow. Let him

know his gun, vest, and credentials are in Joe's care. Eventually he should stop by the office to review his partner's report."

"I'll tell him. Thank Joe for us."

"Be sure you rest up, too. Buh-bye."

Leigh pocketed her phone and found an inquisitive Garrett staring at her.

"She wanted to check on how you were and shared a message for you from Joe. He has your stuff, including your gun, and you need to review Karl's report whenever we stop at your office during your time off." She rolled the table tray away and sat back in the chair. "Do you need anything?"

"Nope, I'm fine. Lunch hit the spot."

"Are you tired? Do you want your bed down?" Leigh asked.

"A little drowsy. You can put the bed down but not all the way."

She nodded and pushed the controls until they found a comfortable position.

"Did I tell you your doctor knows Joe? The doctor's boys had him as a softball coach. Small world, huh?"

"I guess." A yawn punctuated his response. "Did you find a wedding dress?"

"Not yet. Janet's shopping with me; I like her a lot. We should send them a wedding invitation. They can take the last open room we reserved at the Aspen Inn. They might enjoy meeting Chief Martin and his wife."

Another yawn. "I agree. I'm…going to…sleep now…darlin'." His eyes closed and his breaths became soft and regular.

"Rest well, Garrett. I need you healed." She pushed a stray lock of hair away from his eyes. Settling into the chair, she picked up a discarded magazine and whiled away the time reading.

***

Later, another knock and Dr. McNair entered the room.

"Hello again. How's our patient?" He looked through Garrett's chart.

"He was awake for a few hours this afternoon and ate a light lunch."

"Has he had much pain?"

"While he slept, he groaned and thrashed a bit, but after I used the self-dosing mechanism, he settled down. After he woke up, he experienced some pain. The nurse showed him how the self-medicating mechanism works, and he used it a couple times."

"His temperature fell another degree and is nearly normal, which reassures me he's on the right track. If this continues, we may be able to send him home tomorrow morning," he suggested with a smile.

"Tomorrow is what I'm hoping for."

"Have a pleasant evening."

"You, too, thanks."

The doctor's words lifted her spirits; tomorrow Garrett may be home. She liked the hopeful sound of taking him home regardless of home being a hotel room for now.

She thought of the many challenges they had faced since their first meeting. Surely, they were due for an easier time from here on out, but memories of David and his threats loomed over their happiness. Well, maybe they'd enjoy some downtime before another challenge reared its ugly head. She stood at the foot of the bed and watched Garrett sleep. The hour approached dinnertime, and she realized she was hungry. If he woke up before she returned, her coat on the chair offered reassurance she'd return. Before she left, Neil popped in.

"I'm taking orders for supper; you can buy one also."

"Sounds perfect." She made selections for them.

"Did the doctor come by?" Neil busied himself with

checking the IV and entering chart notes.

"Yes, Dr. McNair seemed pleased with his progress and said if his temperature continues to drop, Garrett might be released tomorrow morning."

"Promising news for sure. The night shift will be on soon. You have a quiet evening."

She admired how Neil completed his duties; his visit lasted a mere five minutes.

"Leigh?" Garrett struggled awake.

She bent over the bed, remembered Joe's warning, and moved away from the side. "I'm here." She touched his feet while watching him wake.

Blinking cleared the haze, and she came into focus. "There you are!" He smiled at her. "I dreamed of you."

She walked around the bed and held his hand. "Did you?"

"Yeah. But soon you disappeared, and I stood in the farmhouse where Karl and I arrested everyone, but the people changed. The head of the organization turned into David, and your mom wielded the frying pan. Strange dream, don't you think?"

"Bizarre is the more accurate term." She sat on the bed. "You need happier and less violent dreams."

"I agree; got something in mind?" His expression looked hopeful, and his right hand grazed her hip.

"I have ideas, but…" she paused and slapped his hand, "…we'll wait until you're out of the hospital."

"Are you sure?" His eyebrows raised as he snaked a hand up her side, stopping at the back of her neck. He drew her closer and almost had his lips on hers when her phone rang. He dropped his hand as he muttered, "Damn cell phones."

She laughed. "Hi, Alex! How's everything in the baby-making business?"

"Working at it and putting in lots and lots of practice time," Alex joked back. "Sis, can I ask you something?"

"Of course ask away."

"Before I ask, are you with Garrett?"

"Yes, I'm in his hospital room. Why?" She met Garrett's questioning gaze and shrugged her shoulders.

"His hospital room? What happened?"

"An infection and high fever, but he's better now. We hope he'll be released tomorrow. What's your question?" She hopped off the bed and crossed to the window.

A deep breath sounded over the phone. "Did he hit you?"

"Who? Garrett?" Her voice exploded out, and she stood still. "No! Why would you ask such a ridiculous question? Did David talk with you?"

Garrett closed his eyes and his head fell back against his pillow. *A new drama begins.*

"He called this afternoon and told me he saw you this morning with a black eye. David figured Garrett didn't like you seeing him and got violent with you. I can drive up tonight and bring you home. You shouldn't stay with him, Leigh. Don't be a victim."

"Victim? I'm not a victim. You shouldn't believe a word David says. Garrett did *not* hit me last night and would never be violent toward me."

"So, you don't have a black eye?" Alex remained unconvinced.

"I do because of an accident. Shall I tell you all the bedroom details on what happened?"

She became more animated as her conversation continued and gestured with abandon. Garrett snuck a peek now and then, but mostly he kept his eyes closed. He resigned himself into accepting how David's vicious rumor would spring up when and where they least expected.

"No, but how do I know for sure you're not one of those willing victims?"

"Because I'm telling you and your source is unreliable. I can't believe you let David influence you. You don't even like him!"

"No, I don't like him, but he sounded sincere and concerned for your safety. As a doctor, he's aware of responses to abuse."

"Did he tell you that in support of his story? Please believe me and not him." She stopped at Garrett's bedside.

"Suppose I reserve judgement until I meet him when you come for a visit?"

"Why can't you just believe me?"

"Because I love you and want you safe."

"I am safe because of Garrett. Tell you what. He has two weeks off for healing, so we'll visit you and Tina during that time."

"I can live with that. Bye, Leigh"

The call ended, and she stared at the blank screen for a moment.

"Well, David didn't waste any time spreading lies." She turned toward Garrett and thought she might cry at the despair in his eyes. "Alex agreed to withhold judgement until he meets you."

"If I ever run into David again, he'll regret his lying ways," Garrett grumbled.

"You'll do no such thing. You're above seeking revenge on someone like him."

"Of course I won't but saying the words out loud was satisfying. Who else will David spew his lies at besides your brother? Will he tell your mom?"

"He'll share his lies with our old crowd, I suppose. I doubt if he tells Mom directly; he'll let his own mother pass on the news." Leigh racked her brain for ways David could harm them.

"Your mom would announce the story to the world, right?" Ever since her call, his body had tensed and put undue pressure on his abdomen. The pain in his wound area intensified so much, he self-medicated.

Leigh noticed him use the machine. His action amazed and concerned her because his pain increased during the call.

"I thought Mom might spread David's lie to your boss, so I informed Janet. She'll tell Joe." Leigh expected fury from him, but surprisingly he appeared thoughtful. *Must be the drugs.*

"Just another challenge for us to weather through. If I ever catch David Walker near you again, I'm not sure how I'll react."

"Be the bigger man, Garrett; you are already. Maybe I should call my mom."

"Why?"

"Make her understand her plot with David failed. And how David's story won't cause us any trouble because the whole thing is fiction." She chewed on her lower lip as she thought out the conversation.

"You may have a point, but only if you're convinced talking with her is the right thing. Your mom can be aggravating, and you experienced enough strife lately." He worried over her pacing again. "So maybe we shouldn't rattle her cage."

She stopped pacing and faced him. "What do you mean?"

"We don't contact her just to bring up the subject and see what she says."

She studied his face in search of his honest feelings. "Do you truly believe what you're suggesting?"

"I do."

"I guess waiting a few days won't hurt." Her expression lightened.

"Probably a smarter choice. Besides, we're dealing with so many other things, a confrontation with your mom would be overkill."

"I'm glad you suggested not contacting her because

I really don't want to deal with Mom now." Her smile widened. "To help get our minds off unpleasant things, let's watch TV until dinner. Speaking of dinner, I'm eating with you tonight. Surprise!"

"Nice. I'll enjoy eating with you again even in a hospital."

Leigh grabbed the TV controller and tuned in a movie. "This looks entertaining." Settled in the chair beside the bed, she laid a hand on his arm. Being together felt so right.

While the movie played, Garrett dozed.

A yawn signaled his waking in time for the ending. "Must have been quite the movie. I enjoyed the action in the end. Sorry I fell asleep."

"No problem. I smell food, so dinner should arrive soon."

"I only smell you." Proving his point, he leaned toward her and breathed deeply. He loved her lily of the valley scent.

"You're being silly!" Leigh laughed, but one look in his eyes stopped her laughter. The same desire building inside her reflected in his eyes. "Garrett..." She leaned toward him.

His lips brushed her hair. When she raised her head, he kissed her forehead, her temples, her nose, and her lips. A hunger for her raced through his system.

Being confined in the hospital bed frustrated him. His mind plotted how to draw her further within the confines of the bed. Maybe if he moved his splinted arm around her and pressed...she moved in closer. Success! The pain from his abdomen eased a bit as he sat back and welcomed her into his arms. Now he could move further with the business of seduction; his lips moved over hers with a gentle touch. The intensity increased with each breath, and soon he ravaged her lips with his.

Garrett's kisses ignited a passionate response in

Leigh. She framed his face with her hands as she returned his kisses. Fears of losing him increased her need for closeness. Because his splint and IV limited his maneuverability, she took over all the moves. She snaked her arms around his neck and leaned into him. She covered his face with kisses, ran her tongue around his ear, rained kisses down his neck, along his jaw, and found her way back to his lips. At the sound of his groan, she smiled.

Neither of them heard the door open.

"Excuse me!"

They looked in the direction of the spoken words. Dismay over the interruption overwhelmed embarrassment for them. It took a moment before they figured out the reason for the intrusion: dinner.

"Guess you were right about the food." Garrett's glazed eyes drifted from Leigh to the food service worker at the door and returned to Leigh.

"Told ya." Leigh ran a hand along his neck to his jaw before she sat in the chair.

"I brought your dinners if you're ready for them." The smile on the worker's face couldn't be any broader.

"We are, please bring them in," Leigh said.

The young worker set a tray on the rolling table for Garrett and one on the stationary table for Leigh.

"Thank you," Leigh called out to the worker as the door closed. "I do believe we embarrassed him." She couldn't repress a giggle.

"I agree." Garrett checked his tray contents. "This doesn't look too gross for hospital food."

"Mine's tasty. I made the selections, so I hope you enjoy yours." Leigh gobbled down her food in need of a distraction from her fiancé.

"Nice selection, darlin'. This is better than expected." Garrett's pace slowed as he spent his time watching Leigh rather than eating his dinner. She mesmerized him, and he wanted to be with her forever.

"Oh! We need a picture record of this." Leigh pulled out her phone.

"Of eating hospital food?" Garrett sped up his eating.

"No, our first hospital stay." The flash from her phone illuminated the room. "Hold up your splint."

Garrett did as she requested and followed up with a pose displaying his IV.

"Love it, you're a natural. I need a picture of your stitches."

"The stitches aren't visible, only bandages."

"Bandages work. Once you're home, I'll take one with the bandages off." Undeterred by his words, she adjusted his hospital gown. "This is quite the shot; not only did I capture the bandages, but your sculpted abs are on display, too." She looked at his bare chest and tried not to drool.

"How 'bout a shot of your black eye?"

Agreeing with his suggestion, she took a picture of herself. Upon review, she rejected it and tried another one. Satisfied, she deleted the first one.

"Here, they turned out well." She held out her phone for him.

"Don't I look a bit sickly? Yours is cute."

"Thanks, and sickly fits because you're the one in the hospital. I really like the one showing off your bandages." A deep purring sound demonstrated her pleasure with his bare-chested look.

"Leigh, stop."

She purred louder.

"Please?" He smiled.

She continued purring and rubbed her head against his chest.

"Leigh, please! Laughing is painful. Stop it." He struggled against a laugh building within him; a wince showed how he failed at repressing it.

"Fine, I'll stop." She stood near the bed, but she wore a devious smile. "For now."

"These stitches aren't coming out soon enough," he grumbled.

"I promise I'll be sensible and in control, so you won't laugh." She kissed his brow before snatching up the TV controller. "Let's find something to watch."

"You should sleep in the hotel tonight." When she opened her mouth in protest, he rushed on with his reasoning. "A chair is no bed. You can return in the morning."

"I don't mind sleeping in the chair if it's the only way I can be near you."

"I'm not going anywhere, darlin'. I'll be here in the morning. You look worn out."

"Alright, I'll sleep at the hotel tonight, but I'll be back by eight tomorrow morning. But first, we watch some TV together; there must be something worth watching on tonight." She checked the channels and found another action movie. "Here we go! I love Bruce Willis movies."

"Me, too."

She found she could lay her head on his thigh and still see the TV. Soon, his fingers tangled in her hair, and she enjoyed intense pleasure from the simple action.

Staff collected their dinner trays, and the night nurse checked on him during the movie. As the movie credits rolled, he yawned.

"You're tired. I should go." She turned off the TV.

"I am sleepy. How are you?" He stifled another yawn.

"Fine. I'll see you in the morning." She pulled on her coat. As she leaned over his bed, she gave him a long goodbye kiss. "Sweet dreams."

"Good night. I love you." His gaze followed her to the door.

"Love you, too. Good night." The sound of her

steps down the hall reached the room until the door shut.

He closed his eyes, wishing he could have walked out with her. He prayed his condition improved enough overnight for his release in the morning. Sleep wrapped around him, and he dreamed of the love of his life with no violence involved.

***

Leigh stumbled into their room, too edgy for sleep. She decided on a warm shower, followed by one final journal entry, and at last bed.

Sunday, February 16th. My dearest Garrett, I am thankful you are healthier now than you were this morning. Your condition scared me—I was terrified you might die. Janet didn't hesitate to tell me they would join me at the hospital when I called. She and Joe were supportive and always there for me. I told Joe I'm glad he's your boss, and I truly am. I pray you're resting well and will be bright-eyed and bushy-tailed when I return in the morning. You mean everything to me, and I would be lost without you. Please never leave me. I love you dearly, now and forever. Leigh ♥♥♥

One last sigh escaped as she closed her journal. After crawling into bed, she hugged a pillow as she fell asleep.

***

Late in the evening, Garrett woke when someone touched his hand. He couldn't distinguish the person's features in the dim light of his room.

"Who are you? What are you doing in here?" Garrett's senses shot to high alert; something wasn't right.

"I'm Leonard, a janitor. I'm emptying the trash." He spoke softly and hurried out the door.

Unable to shake off the unease and suspicion over his late-night visitor, he fumbled for the call button and rang for a nurse.

"Yes, Mr. Dane, do you need something?"

"Do janitors normally come through the rooms at night?" Garrett shifted into his investigator mode.

"Yes, but they won't be around for a few hours. Why?"

"I woke up when someone touched my hand. He claimed to be a janitor named Leonard. He walked out before I pushed the call button. Did you see him?" His unease increased.

"No one walked by the station. Your room is near a stairwell though. I'm changing out your meds in case he put something in them. Do you feel okay?" He nodded. She disconnected the bags from his IV. "I'll be right back with a change in meds, and I'll call security."

"Thank you." As he waited on security, his unease continued building.

In less than fifteen minutes, a man dressed in a uniform entered his room.

"Agent Dane, I'm Todd Kramer from hospital security. I understand you had an unexpected visitor?"

"Yes. He claimed to be a janitor."

"Can you describe him?"

"Your height, but I couldn't make out his features in the dim lighting. Are there surveillance cameras in the hospital?"

"Yes, I'll check them as soon as I return to the security center."

"Todd, I need a print of any facial shots you retrieve off the surveillance footage. My office can work on identifying this guy; his visit may be related to a case I was working."

"Understand. The arrests were the primary discussion topics when you came in yesterday. After the lady with the broken nose showed up in restraints, we were lucky we accomplished any work. You brought us plenty of excitement last night."

"Yeah, I suppose, but I would have preferred less excitement."

"I understand your perspective. Let me find out what I can for you." Todd hastened out.

Garrett wondered if he should call his boss. Without any information available, a call this early in the morning would be futile. Once he got pictures from Todd, a call or stop at the office in the morning should suffice. No longer tired, he left the lights on and searched his memory for every detail about his late-night visitor.

CHAPTER TWENTY-SEVEN

Brring! Brring!

Leigh fumbled with the room's telephone.

"Good morning, this is your six-thirty wake-up call."

Once she slammed the receiver back in the cradle, she plopped over in the bed, never fully waking.

Much later, her eyes opened, she stretched, and remembered the importance of the day. Garrett would be released from the hospital this morning; she knew it. He looked so healthy last night. She rolled over to check the time…eight o'clock!

Crap! She was late. She stumbled into the bathroom, planning a swift wash up and leaving right away, but the sight of her hair and face changed her mind. To borrow a cowboy saying, she looked as though she'd been ridden hard and put up wet. She hopped in the shower, waking up further under the spray of water.

As she braided her hair, she decided to wear one of her sexiest lingerie sets, a soft blue sweater, and dark cords. After pulling on boots and her jacket, she flew out the door.

Monday morning traffic slowed her progress to the hospital. She turned the corner into his room at nine-thirty, but an empty bed greeted her. Fear struck her hard, where had he gone? Had his condition worsened overnight? She jumped back when the bathroom door swung open. A clean-shaven Garrett emerged, and her heart skipped a beat.

"Garrett! You're up and dressed." She didn't believe how he could be any more handsome, but without his whiskers covering his features, his square jawline and tempting lips held her attention.

"You slept in this morning. I knew you were overtired last night." He pulled her into his arms being careful of the splint.

"You shaved." She ran a hand over his smooth cheeks.

When he smiled, dimples she'd never noticed dug into his cheeks, and she fell in love with him all over again.

"Neil tracked down a razor and shave cream I could use. I'm feeling almost like me again."

Her embarrassment over arriving late disappeared when his rugged body pressed against her. She sensed rather than saw his head duck down for a kiss. Her thoughts spun, caught in a whirlwind of emotions.

His kiss went from gentle to fierce in a heartbeat and moved from loving to demanding in seconds. It felt so right having Leigh beside him; he'd missed her being this close. He longed for skin-to-skin contact and growled his frustration at their standing in a hospital room rather than being alone at the hotel. He cupped her butt with a strong hand and drew her closer. An erection strained against his jeans, so he ground against her to physically communicate his desire for her. A soft moan told him she'd received his message.

Leigh broke away first. Breathless, it took her a moment to speak. "Since you're dressed, you're coming home today?"

"Yup, Dr. McNair stopped in first thing, checked me out, and released me. Neil's collecting the paperwork for us." He kept her in his embrace, in no hurry to release her.

"Best news I've heard all day. Did you have breakfast?"

"Only a fruit cup." He kissed her again before releasing her. "Should we eat something here in the hospital before we leave?"

"Here works for me. Do we need to wait for Neil?"

"No waiting required, I'm here," Neil announced as he walked into the room. "These are your care instructions and should match what you had before. A new appointment for removing the stitches is one day later than the previous one. Your follow-up for your arm remained the same. Last thing I need from you is a signature and you're out of here."

Garrett signed his name without hesitation. "Easy enough."

"Here are your copies. Caring for you has been a pleasure, and I hope you don't have a return performance. Have an exceptional day." With his typical efficiency, Neil bustled out.

With papers in hand, Garrett did a quick scan of the room for anything they'd forgotten. "I'm ready, let's go."

"Breakfast here we come." She grabbed his right hand and led him to the cafeteria. She continued stealing glances at him, marveling in the change of his appearance resulting from shave cream and a razor. He appeared younger and more deliciously tempting than before.

***

"Can you do anything today or should you rest?"

"Hmm?" Garrett put down the papers he'd been staring at since they'd arrived at the table with their breakfast trays. "After a stop at my office, we can do anything on your list."

"Right. You have a report to review, and we should pick up the paperwork from your first day."

"Plus, I'll be asking for Joe's assistance with this." He set a grainy black-and-white picture in front of her.

"Who's this?" Leigh picked up the picture and studied it. She raised questioning eyes to his.

"I don't have a clue." At her puzzled look, he sighed. "Last night this guy came into my room while I slept. I woke when he touched my hand. He claimed he was a janitor before he left my room. Hospital security got these pictures off their security camera footage."

"What was he looking for in your room?" Her eyes

were wide, and breakfast forgotten.

He shrugged. "My first thought was he could be related to the drug operation Karl and I shut down. The nurse changed out the meds hanging for my IV in case he'd messed with them, but I was fine."

"He looks slightly familiar, but I have no idea why." Leigh handed him the picture. "I'm not hungry anymore."

"Sorry I ruined your appetite. I should have waited on this." He stacked the picture on top of his other paperwork.

"No problem, I'll survive." She smiled at him. "Let's go, so we can figure this out."

***

As they walked to the Jeep, her mind wrestled with why the man in the picture looked familiar. Who the heck was he?

They drove in silence, each wrapped in their own thoughts. When she stopped in a parking space, Garrett broke out of his musings over the photograph with a jump.

"Dang! Hadn't realized we arrived."

"Too deep in thought?"

"Yeah, I'm trying to place the guy in the picture."

"Does he remind you of anyone?"

"I have a vague feeling saying I know him, but I've got nothing." He sank against the seat, threw his head back, and closed his eyes. "Who is he, and why did he come into my hospital room?"

"Come on, let's head inside and talk with Joe."

Leigh slid out of the Jeep and joined him at his door. Hand in hand they walked into the building and to the office.

"Garrett! Leigh! I didn't expect to see you today." Joe met them a short distance in the office, he'd been conversing with another agent. He gave Leigh a hug and clapped Garrett on his right shoulder. "You look better than the last time I saw you."

"I'm much stronger, sir. I need your assistance with identifying a guy who was in my room last night."

Joe's jaw dropped. "A stranger entered your room? Did he do anything?"

"No, sir, it didn't appear he did. Not sure of his purpose for being there." Garrett shifted his weight back and forth uncomfortable discussing this in front of his new team members.

"Let's finish this in my office."

They settled around Joe's desk.

"So, what do you have on this guy?" Joe asked.

"Just these pictures from the hospital security cameras. I don't recognize him, but he looks familiar." Garrett handed over two pictures. "I thought perhaps he was involved in the drug operation Karl and I shut down, but Leigh says he reminds her of someone, too."

"Hmm, he's no one I recognize." Joe's intent stare cut from the picture to Leigh. "Who does he remind you of?"

"I can't come up with a name." Leigh believed any suspect would crack under Joe's scrutiny. She found his unblinking stare disconcerting.

"I'll identify him. In the meantime, you stay watchful, and this may come in handy." He reached into a drawer and pulled out Garrett's gun, badge, and credentials. "I have your bag, too. Your holster's in it."

"Thank you, sir." Garrett slid his badge and credentials into a jacket pocket. He checked his gun and slipped it into the back of his waistband.

"You should have called me last night." His tone sounded admonishing yet gentle.

"I thought it'd be too late, sir. It was around three in the morning, and we didn't have any information."

"Don't ever worry over the lateness of the hour; I should always be informed of anything or anyone threatening my agents." Joe walked them toward the door. "Now get out of here; tackle the things on Leigh's list." He poked Garrett on the chest. "You, get well. Leigh, don't put up with any crap from him. You're in charge of his recovery."

"You'll be the first person I call if he becomes unruly." Leigh laughed.

"Oh, Jan wants you two over for dinner on Saturday, and the boys requested you supply dessert. They said you'd remember what you should bring."

"Cheesecake. We'll be there. A home-cooked meal will be welcome; he needs a healthy diet." She rapped Garrett on the back. "I'll call her later, so we can schedule our next shopping trip."

"Shopping with you was a discussion topic at dinner last night, she's waiting for your call. Don't forget dinner on Saturday." Joe handed Garrett his duffle bag before turning back at the sound of his ringing phone.

Garrett led the way to his own desk.

"This is where you'll be working when you're in the area?" Leigh absorbed the aesthetics of his workplace.

"Uh-huh, this is it." He gathered up the papers from his orientation.

"Do you have things to decorate it?" Leigh had already decided she'd photograph them and frame it for his desk as an engagement gift for him. Her mind shifted into photographer mode and generated ideas for the picture.

"Decorate? I may have a couple of things from my Air Force days I'll put out. Ready to go?"

"Yes."

As they exited, many of his new co-workers congratulated him on his successful assignment and wished him well on his recovery. Leigh watched his interaction with them and marveled at his modest acceptance of their praises and well-wishes.

Once outside and in the Jeep, she looked over at

him with pride shining in her eyes.

"I enjoyed hearing your co-workers say such complimentary things to you. Did it embarrass you being the center of attention?"

"Not too much, but mostly I'm optimistic they realize I can handle this job and deserved the position." He fiddled with his seat belt. "What's on the docket for today?

"A stop by the church to schedule our classes. Then you can meet the log home builder and walk through their models. I'll call Nick and find out if he can show us the two properties I selected. You can help choose between them. I planned on finalizing my decisions this week on the property and the model, so now you can do it with me. I'm glad these will be our decisions instead of mine alone."

"I'm happy I'm here for you, but I'm certain your decisions would have been right for us." He smiled at her before a clouded expression crossed his face. "Should we verify the minister is available to meet with us before we drive over?"

"If she's busy, we'll schedule an appointment with the secretary. You'll be familiar with the church this way, and we can attend services this Sunday. I planned on attending this past Sunday, but you interrupted those plans." She slapped the Jeep into drive and had them cruising on their way.

"I'll enjoy going to church with you." He settled back and absently gazed at businesses and homes as they flew by while his mind worked on the mystery man in the pictures.

The morning continued in a whirl of activity. By the time they'd toured all the log home models, Garrett's movements had slowed.

She saw him flinch in pain as he settled in the Jeep.

"We should stop for today and go to the hotel. You need some rest."

"No, I'm fine. We have our meeting with Nick

scheduled. I want to see the properties, so we can decide on one and make an offer."

"Then we'll have lunch before we continue. You need a break."

"I have a break, don't need another one." He held up his splinted left arm.

She smiled at his sense of humor, relieved it was intact after his ordeal. "Ha. Ha. Ha. I've been too aggressive today and pushed you too far on your first morning out of the hospital. Are you really okay?"

"Yeah, but a stop for lunch is a good idea."

As she drove toward Nick's office, she kept an eye out for a restaurant. Spotting one, she zipped into the parking lot. After she turned off the Jeep, she placed a hand on his forehead.

"Well, your fever's not back, but you should take some pain medication when we're inside."

He nodded as he worked at exiting the Jeep. Lightheadedness hit when he stood, so he appreciated Leigh's support by his side as they walked to the restaurant. Without her assistance, he figured he would have stumbled and crashed to the ground.

They accepted an offered booth, and she took charge of removing his winter gear. Her heart broke at the appearance of pain on his face as he pulled his arm out of his jacket and sat in the booth.

"Here, let me do it for you," she offered when he fumbled with his pill bottle.

"No, I've got it." He held the bottle with the fingers of his left hand, wrenching the top with his right. One moment the lid came off, and the next the contents skidded across the tabletop.

They corralled the pills with their arms, and Leigh put them back in the bottle.

"You should have seen your face!" She tried to stifle a giggle. "All your feelings reflected on your face one after the other. Here's how it played out: determination, frustration, surprise, defeat, and resignation. Your eyes were huge when the pills went flying out!" Her giggles escaped.

"Not resignation, Leigh, regret." He smiled at her, so she wouldn't worry her giggles upset him. "I regret not accepting your offer to open the bottle. I never relied on anyone before, so I'm doing poorly at letting you assist me with things. I'm fortunate you're here for me. Thank you." He tossed down a couple pills.

"I will always be here for you. I shouldn't have planned so much activity for today."

"I'll be fine after this. You were right, I needed a break."

"The visit with Nick shouldn't take too long with only two properties to check out. I'm not sure how much time we'll spend on the paperwork for an offer, but we can call it quits afterward."

"Then back to our hotel, right?" His eye color signified the direction of his thoughts.

With his eyes fixed on her, she wished they could return to their room, but the property decision shouldn't wait. The waitress appearing for their orders delayed her response.

"I can tell what you're thinking, but we can't do too much yet. Remember, the first nurse said we should wait until your stitches were out."

"We didn't pay much attention to her instructions as I recall. I can't wait two weeks before making love with you. In fact, I'm not waiting long after we return to our room." His smoldering look kicked in her own lust-filled thoughts. He continued in a taut voice. "I'm desperate for the feel of you around me, for the pleasure of plunging into your hot wetness, and for the joy of hearing you cry out my name after your own sweet release."

"Shh, don't talk so loud." She placed one of her

fingers to his lips as her cheeks went a deep-crimson color.

Garrett wished he'd thought of putting his finger against her lips; they were so lush. When his thoughts traveled on to what she could do with his finger, he shook his head to clear his thoughts.

"I have an idea on how we might speed up our two-week timeframe," Leigh suggested.

"Go on, I'm all ears."

They leaned over the table in a conspiratorial manner.

"Well, we start slow with you pleasuring me and then I pleasure you. With each night we move on a bit further and further until we can go all the way."

"Sounds provocative. Like a physical therapy program for having sex. Can we test it out after lunch?" He raised his eyebrows and winked at her.

The delivery of their food interrupted their banter.

"Since we have an appointment with Nick, we'll have to wait. You shouldn't have agreed with my calling him if you wanted to return to the hotel."

"My agreement came before you divulged your intriguing sex physical therapy program."

"You'll wait until we're done this afternoon, and then we can test it."

"Okay, I'm holding you to it." He turned his attention to his bowl of chili and blew gently on it in hopes of cooling it.

Leigh watched him blowing on his chili, and she thought of how he could be blowing on various overheated parts of her anatomy. Cursing herself for calling Nick, she tackled her sandwich in search of any distraction from her erotic thoughts.

After she paid the lunch bill, they were back in the Jeep headed for Nick's office. Both were quiet, lost in their own thoughts.

With the Jeep in park, she turned off the ignition

and wished she could turn off her thoughts of Garrett making love to her as easily.

"Let's go!" She hurried around the Jeep and joined Garrett as they walked into the realty office.

"Hi, Leigh. Welcome back, Garrett!" Nick shook hands with them as they entered his office. He picked up a folder. "I'm ready; let's pick out some property."

He walked them out to his vehicle.

"Leigh, you ride up front, and I'll slide in the back," Garrett offered.

"Okay." She hopped into the front seat and dragged on her seat belt. "We checked out the models before coming, so Garrett has an idea of them all."

"Smart planning." Within moments, Nick had them on their way and destined for the first property. He glanced at Garrett in the rearview mirror. "There's a pair of binoculars back there; they'll make viewing the property easier. Has Leigh described them for you?"

"No, we haven't discussed them."

"Here's the first one." Nick pulled over his vehicle. "This is two and a half acres. The property lines are the fence on the North and the tree line on the South. The other line is way back in the distance; it's not visible from here." He handed over a printout of the property information.

Garrett and Leigh took their time viewing the property through the binoculars.

"Ready for number two on the list?" At their nods, Nick headed for the other property. "Here's the information for this next one. The acreage is more than the first parcel."

Garrett assessed the passing scenery with interest. Homes within view dwindled in number, and they drove farther from a main road.

When Nick stopped the vehicle, Garrett gazed out and saw home. This was it, no question. Here they could build a future for themselves, their children, and even a couple of dogs. "How many acres is this?"

"Slightly over five. Plenty of trees with a creek running through the property on the west end. You can barely make out the fence through the trees marking the back property line." Nick entered his sales mode.

"Who's responsible for plowing the roads?" Garrett asked.

"The county does the plowing, but these will be low on the priority list. The main road would be cleared well before this one. If you had a tractor with a blade on it, neighbors may chip in on your gas cost to plow the road."

"You'd need the road cleared to get to work, wouldn't you? I hadn't even thought of how or when the roads would be plowed," Leigh confessed.

"Don't forget the Jeep is four-wheel drive. We'll probably buy snowmobiles, so I'd have that as a transportation option. A tractor would come in handy, especially if we added a mower attachment for the summer."

"Having a tractor would be fun, and I could drive it if you teach me how." Leigh's excitement bubbled out.

Garrett envisioned Leigh driving the tractor; in his vision, she wore a bikini as enticing as her lingerie. He imagined the sweet fragrance of fresh cut grass and fantasized of them rolling around in the cut grass and moving on to more intimate activities. He squashed his daydreaming before he got carried away any further.

"We could build a pole barn for storing any equipment we buy and include room for a studio," he suggested.

She turned in the seat and gazed into his eyes. She loved how he thought of her needs before she did. "An at-home studio sounds wonderful, so you like this one?"

"I do. Nick, can you give us a minute to discuss the properties?"

"Sure. I have a couple of calls I can make." Nick had his phone to his ear before the door closed behind him.

"Both of the properties are nice. Which do you prefer?" Garrett asked.

"This one. We could build a blind near the creek for wildlife, and we won't be on top of our neighbors."

"I could build a gun range to practice my shooting and even teach you to shoot if you're interested."

"Then have we decided on this one?" Her face lit up with excitement.

"Yeah, this is the one. Can you signal Nick?"

She honked the horn and waved him back to the vehicle.

"You decided already?"

Garrett nodded at Leigh for her to share their decision.

"We want this one." She beamed at Garrett as she spoke.

"Alright, we'll do up a purchase agreement when we're back in the office. I'll need a check for the earnest money." Nick had them bouncing down the country roads as though he drove them every day.

"Not a problem," Garrett said. He settled back and let his daydreams run wild.

Once back in Nick's office, they completed the purchase agreement with his guidance. Writing out the check made it seem more real to them.

"I'll ensure the purchase agreement is received by the property owners this afternoon. I'll call you as soon as I hear back from them. It's a fitting choice. I'm sure you'll enjoy the location."

"Thanks, Nick. We look forward to hearing from you." Garrett shook his hand.

"Thanks for everything." Leigh gave Nick a hug before walking out.

Once at the Jeep, Garrett uttered one demand. "Leigh. Hotel. Now."

He had never been so demanding, so she toyed with

him. "Sorry, I came up with an additional item we should address this afternoon." Her innocent look did nothing toward ending the glare he had for her. "We should checkout a printer I located in town for the wedding invitations. Time's short. The invitations must be printed and then mailed out. No time to waste." She had no intention of driving them anywhere but their hotel, yet she had fun watching him fume.

"No." He led her to the driver's side of the Jeep. "One day won't make much of a difference." He opened the door and waited until she climbed in. He slammed the door shut and stalked to the passenger side. After he buckled in, his terse phrasing continued. "Drive."

"Even though your conversation skills have dropped to zero, your body is speaking to me loud and clear." She dropped her gaze to his lap. Her laughter caught him off guard. "No printer for us today, Garrett. The hotel's fine by me, but you needn't be such a Neanderthal about it." She spun the tires leaving the parking lot.

"My apologies for my Neanderthal behavior; I'll work on harnessing it." His voice cracked. "How soon until we're back?"

"Not soon enough." She drove toward the hotel, all the while wishing she knew a shortcut.

When she pulled into the hotel parking lot, an enormous sigh came from Garrett.

"That was the longest drive in history." He reached for the door handle.

"If not for all those red lights, we'd been here a long time ago." Leigh patted his shoulder. "We're here now!" She exited the Jeep and joined him for the short walk into the hotel.

As soon as their room door shut behind them, Garrett pulled Leigh into his arms.

"I've been waiting forever for this." He gathered her in his arms and ran kisses down her neck, along her jaw, to her lips.

She gasped as his kisses moved along, but when his lips crushed hers, she melted against him for a moment. Dual tasking, she participated in his kiss while unbuttoning and unzipping their winter coats. She broke away from their kiss, pulling off their outerwear, and letting them drop by their feet.

"Come this way, Garrett."

She grabbed his belt and pulled him nearer the bed. She drew off his shirt with slow movements, being wary of his splinted arm.

"Are you working from a plan or are you flying by the seat of your pants?" Garrett ran his right hand down her back, stopping when he cupped her butt. He drew her closer, so her body pressed against his erection. He ground into her as he growled in her ear. "You feel so right against me."

"Would you stop it? You're interfering with the removal of your clothes."

"Here, I can do a few things to help." He leaned back, pulled out the gun tucked into his waistband, and undid his jeans.

Leigh hooked her thumbs over the waistband and pushed down. Upon the release of his erection, she couldn't resist running her tongue along the length and kissing the tip. She smiled at his groan. After a struggle with his boots and socks, she removed them and followed with his jeans and shorts.

Success! He stood naked before her, and she admired him for a short while. Normally, she loved looking at him, except now the view included the white bandage covering his knife wound. She hoped for strength when they changed it. She hadn't seen the actual wound, but a disturbing picture settled in her head of how it would look. With determination, she dragged her eyes from the bandage.

"Stay where you are, and I'll bring your pills." She disappeared into the bathroom.

No way I'm following the nurse's orders. I will be inside her tonight, Garrett thought while he cursed his unfortunate luck at receiving a knife wound across the abdomen.

"Here you are."

Garrett looked up and nearly fell over; Leigh stepped out of the bathroom clad only in skimpy lingerie with her golden hair tumbled over her shoulders. Scraps of lace framed her breasts with rosy nipples visible behind a sheer insert. Her panties were a minute patch of lace covering the spot he'd target with his growing erection. He couldn't drag his eyes away from her.

"Wow! You are…"

She popped his pills in his mouth and handed him a glass of water.

"…sexier than ever." He tossed the empty glass away and drew her close. "No sex therapy tonight cause we're not waiting two weeks, Leigh."

"As long as you stop if you're in pain."

"If it's unbearable, I'll stop." He agreed because his pain tolerance was unusually high.

He dipped his head, nibbled on her neck, and continued with kisses upward to her lips. His demanding kiss garnered a low moan in reward for his actions. With his splinted left arm pressed behind her, he held her close. He palmed one breast with his right hand, rubbing against the scrap of lace until the nipple peaked. His mouth abandoned her lips and trailed kisses down her throat in a quest to capture her other breast.

"I cannot wait until I regain full use of my left hand, so I can do justice to your body," he growled with frustration.

"You're doing fine with one hand and a mouth." She sighed.

"I'm certain I can kick it up a notch."

His attentions centered on one breast and freed his

hand for a languid slide down her side and over her stomach. He stopped at the tiny patch of lace between her legs, shoved it aside, and plunged a finger within her warm moistness.

"Oh! Garrett!" She leaned against him as her eyes closed from sheer bliss.

"You are so ready for me, Leigh."

He added a second finger into her slickness and drew them in and out.

Her moans grew louder as his actions sped up. Muscles tightened on his fingers when she climaxed.

While tremor after tremor ravaged her body, he held her close. Before she collapsed, he guided her limp body toward the bed, tearing off her bra and panties before he laid her across it.

"You do magic things with one hand," she panted.

"You're so responsive. I love watching you explode from my affections." He kissed her forehead and brushed a lock of hair away from her face. "I'm fascinated by your response to me."

"It's your turn as soon as I catch my breath." She smiled at him and then closed her eyes.

"I'll be right here waiting for you." He ran his fingers down her body in a soft caress, tracing circles over her stomach.

When she recovered, she knelt over him and gazed down at his magnificent body.

His eyes blazed with heated passion as she hovered above him. He reached out for one breast, fondling it, and rolled the nipple between two fingers.

In response, she grasped his erection, ran her hand up and down, and thumbed the tip.

He groaned as she played with him.

She watched for any indication of pain. She slid down past his bandages to fully engage with his sizable erection. Her tongue replaced her hand, and he groaned aloud. When she took him in her mouth, he gasped, closed his eyes, and abandoned her breasts.

He should stop her before an explosion happened. Their lovemaking needed to end with him encased in her moistness and to experience the climax with her.

"Leigh. Stop. Please." He placed his hand on her head.

She raised her head and looked at him. "Are you in pain?"

"No. Come up here, so we can make love."

"We're not supposed to. Remember what the nurse said, we probably already pushed the limits. There will be no popping of stitches or ER trips. Besides, we are making love."

"I promise no more hospitals. If I experience any pain, I'll tell you." His eyes pleaded with her. "I need you around me, so I must be inside you."

"I'm only agreeing because I need you there, too." She straddled his hips below his bandages.

He guided her over his erection, and his breath caught as she lowered herself. When her buttocks reached his hips, she covered him completely and his desires were realized. A shift of her hips produced a deep moan.

She rose slightly and then came back down. She repeated the motion over and over, going further and further up before sliding down. By adding a roll of her hips as she moved up and down, a strong pulsing began inside her.

He grabbed her hips and thrust into her, burying deeper within her warmth. Her muscles tightened around him as she found her release while he reached his. His pain was minimal and so worth the sensations consuming him.

She sat back, still straddling his hips, and her hands on her thighs.

"Are you okay?" Concern showed in her eyes.

"I'm fine, no damage." He was winded but

exhilarated.

"No damage, huh?" She rounded her hips and felt his response inside. "So, we can do it again?"

"It seems so, darlin'." His smile could have been an arrow piercing her heart.

They forged ahead with their lovemaking, taking things slow and being careful of his wound. At times, he found the pleasure of her touch overcame his pain while at others the pain intensified his awareness of her. They pleasured each other as well as joining together in celebration of their reunion.

In the end, they were a tangle of limbs and bedding. Garrett lay stretched across the bed with his head on a pillow, an arm over his eyes, and his chest heaving. Leigh curled around him with her head at the foot of the bed; her eyes focused on him while her body recovered from her last orgasm.

"Let's stay in tonight," Leigh said after she caught her breath.

"Supper?" He gasped out the word.

"Pizza; they'll deliver here."

"Pepperoni and mushroom or everything?"

"Everything."

"You have the number?"

"In my phone."

"Got your phone?"

"Nope, gotta find it."

"Need any help?"

"Maybe."

No movement.

"Find your phone?"

"Not yet."

Still no movement.

"Leigh."

"Yes?"

"I'm hungry."

"Working on it."
No movement.
"Should I call?"
"You can."
"Hand me your phone."
"Haven't found it yet."
"Hand it over when you do."
No movement.
"Starving here."
An unladylike snort responded.
"Leigh?"
"Garrett."
"Please?"
"Oh, alright." She struggled upright in search of her phone.

"While you're up, can you fluff my pillow?" He laughed as a pillow flew across the room and hit him in the face.

CHAPTER TWENTY-EIGHT

With the pizza ordered at last, Leigh pulled on a pair of flannel pajamas. The softness enveloped her in warmth.

"We should change your bandages." She rummaged through his stack of papers and located the care instructions Neil had given them.

"He gave me supplies for doing this. You'll find the bag on the table," Garrett said as he rose from the bed. He reached into his duffle bag and pulled out flannel bottoms and a thermal Henley. "Meet you in the bathroom."

She admired him as he walked away. *I will never tire of the sight of him.*

After hearing the toilet flush, she carried the bag of supplies and instructions into the bathroom but stopped short at the door. The image of him standing in the middle of the room stopped her with one look. He wore flannel pajama bottoms, and they rode low on his hips. Disheveled hair and his whiskers from the day added a rakish quality she never noticed before. It took a moment and a few deep breaths before she moved farther into the room.

"Taking the tape off may be painful." She reached for one edge with trembling fingers.

"I'll pull it off while you review the steps." His fingers brushed hers before they each moved onto their task.

"Okay."

Still distracted by his image burned into her mind, she read the instructions twice before comprehending the meaning. As the hot water ran in the sink, she looked back at him and gasped at the ugly red gash running across his abdomen, the black stitches adding a wicked contrast. She sat on the side of the tub when a wave of nausea hit her stomach.

"Oh, Garrett."

Her whispering of his name stopped him cold. Her compassion tore through him, and the tears in her eyes almost sent him to the floor.

Wrapping his arms around her would feel so right, but the wound would be in her face. He turned his back on her, taking the stitches out of her line of sight.

"Maybe I should do this myself."

A hard swallow was followed by her hands on his back. "No, I can do this for you. I just wasn't prepared for how it looked; I'm fine."

"Only if you're sure."

She turned him around and gazed into his eyes. "I'm sure."

Working together, they cleaned and bandaged the wound.

"See? I told you I could do it. I even remembered we needed a picture for a complete set of our first BCA adventure together."

"You did well. I'm fortunate you're my home nurse." He kissed her in thanks.

"Kisses are my favorite form of payment for services rendered."

"Hmm, I'll remember your preference for the future."

"I also read you can remove your splint for a shower, but you must be careful of your arm."

"Should the bandages stay dry? Maybe I'll forego showers until the stitches are out."

"Doubt if I could stand the stink." She laughed at his hurt expression.

"I didn't say I wouldn't wash up."

"I couldn't resist kidding you. Having you back is wonderful, and I'm making up for lost opportunities."

"You do realize I'd be tickling you now if not for the stitches?"

"Yeah, I figured as much." She led him out of the

bathroom. "Here, I'll arrange the pillows for you, so you can sit in bed."

"Thanks. How long for the pizza?"

"It should be here anytime now." She watched him climb into bed; each grimace tugged at her heart. "I have my journal here, so you can read it whenever you're ready."

"Does it contain all your exploits without me and your deepest, darkest thoughts?"

She handed him the leather-bound book. "Nothing deep or dark included, but I did write down many of my thoughts and concerns. I'll write in this whenever an assignment takes you away from me. Writing made me feel closer to you as if you shared in everything I did. Do I sound silly?"

He considered his answer before he responded. "Not silly, but remarkably generous. This took your time and energy. This is sharing yourself with me, and I love you for doing it."

Her cheeks reddened with his compliment. The ringing of the room phone saved her for the moment.

"I bet our pizza is here." She answered the phone and confirmed her suspicions.

While she prepared to get their supper, he considered the mystery of her journal. What did she share with him? Did they have similar thoughts while separated? What would her journal hold of her interactions with her ex-boyfriend? His anger rolled through whenever something prompted thoughts of the scumbag. Why Leigh dated the guy bewildered him; he decided she'd been blinded by the family-friend facade clinging about Walker. He'd be forever thankful she'd broken up with the guy before becoming his wife. He marveled at her strength of character when she stood up to Walker and her mother.

She was his perfect match, his soul mate, his one and only love, and he thanked his lucky stars for bringing her into his life. If he hadn't been attacked by Jonas Klein, he never would have met Leigh and…damn, Jonas Klein! The picture: the guy in the picture reminded him of Jonas Klein. It couldn't be a coincidence. His eyes darted in Leigh's direction. She had slippers and a robe on, what the heck?

"What are you doing?"

"I'm going downstairs for the pizza. Are you okay? You look pale."

"I'm fine; I'll wait on your journal until you're back."

"Okay. I won't be long." She kissed him on the forehead before walking out the door.

The instant she left, he got off the bed and had his phone in hand, dialing his boss.

"Henderson."

"Sir, it's Garrett."

"Surprised you're calling; did something happen?"

"I figured out why the guy in the picture looked familiar."

"Why?"

"He looks like Jonas Klein, so I suspect he's a relative."

"Klein's the guy from your last Air Force case, the one who hunted you down and attacked you?"

"Yes, sir. I killed him when he grabbed Leigh and held a gun on her. It explains why both of us thought he looked familiar. Klein was from Georgia, so that's a starting point."

"I'll work on it first thing tomorrow." Joe could be heard scribbling notes. "If he's a relative of Klein's, then chances are he's seeking revenge. You be careful."

"I will, sir."

"As soon as I learn anything, I'll contact you."

"Thank you."

"Have you told Leigh your suspicions yet?"

"Not yet. This just dawned on me a second ago."

"Don't waste time in telling her," Joe advised.

"I understand and will tell her this evening. Goodbye, sir."

"Bye, Garrett. I wish you luck."

After the call ended, he stood in the middle of the room, threw his head back, and closed his eyes. He wondered: *Why? Why is this happening? Please don't force us through this again.*

The door opened...in walked Leigh, carrying a pizza box and a liter bottle of cola.

"You're out of bed!"

"Call of nature," he lied, while he thought, *I'll tell her later, so we can eat in peace.* "I can help serve up supper."

"No, you climb back in bed, and I'll bring everything over there." She sat their supper on the table. "They brought plates for us, and we have glasses here in the room." She dumped her robe on a chair and kicked off her slippers before disappearing into the bathroom and reappearing with two glasses in hand.

"It smells delicious!" He hoped his tone sounded light.

"Here you go." She handed him a plate loaded with pizza and set a glass of cola near him. She sat on the second bed across from him with her plate. "I love pizza."

"One of my favorite foods, but I haven't had any in a long time."

"I would have thought you'd have eaten lots of pizza while you were with Karl."

"Actually, we either cooked or ate food from the grocery store deli most of the time."

"I'm surprised. Who did the cooking?"

"We took turns." He noted her intense interest in his answer. "Are you looking for a way to shirk cooking meals once we have a kitchen?"

"No. I'm wondering how helpful you'll be with the

cooking chores. I'm familiar with your cleaning abilities."

"I'm very handy in the kitchen." His response rumbled out of his chest, and he looked at her through his eyelashes.

"Somehow, I don't have the feeling you meant cooking with your last admission. Lucky me!"

They ate a few slices of pizza in silence.

"Regarding my journal, there are only a few entries in it since you weren't gone too long for which I'm thankful."

"I am, too. Should I read the entries out loud?" He wiped his hands and opened the book.

"Sure, then I'll know where you're at."

"Okay, here we go." He set aside his plate and gazed at the first entry. "*Wednesday, February 12th. My dearest Garret.*' The way you begin this has a comforting ring to it. Will you say the words for me?"

Leigh approached him and bent down. "My. Dearest. Garrett." A kiss came after each word; she added what could only be described as pregnant pauses between each word.

"If you continue, this journal reading will be over in a hurry." He smiled at her before refocusing on her journal. "'*I have never kept a diary or journal, but I plan on recording everything I do whenever you're away from me. This morning I missed you so much. Since I promised I could do this, today I visited all the log cabin builders on Nick's list. Most were a bust, but one—OMG—their homes are so impressive! It's not only the homes though. It's the people working there; they were so down-to-earth and knowledgeable. I realize it sounds silly, but I could tell they were family...a loving family, unlike Mom and you. (Joking!)*'"

He laughed out loud, but it stopped with a wince. "I never realized how funny you can be. I agree with your assessment of them and their model homes. Continuing on.

'*They have property out toward Nisswa, so Nick and I are checking out their lots tomorrow. I believe this is what we should do. All the options have me excited but also concerned over how I'll ever select from them all and the many floor plans available. Our house—NO! Our home will be gorgeous, functional, and meet all our needs. Oh, you'll fall in love with the master suite options, and the bathroom can be all we want it to be if you catch my gist (hint, hint)!*' Tomorrow we can review those options after I put you in the proper mindset. If you catch my gist." His eyebrows raised, and he bucked his hips ever so slightly.

Leigh choked on her bite of pizza. "If you're promising what I think you are, I should stick the 'do not disturb' sign on the door later."

"It may be best if we tape it in place. Back to your journal. '*I talked with Mom last night and scheduled time with her next week for discussing invitations and maybe my dress. I haven't decided how much assistance to accept from her. During that call, I'll break the news regarding the date we've decided on and how we scheduled it at the Aspen Inn. I'm sure you wish me well with the discussion. I also recognize you'll be pleased with not participating in the call; you are such a lucky duck.*' Quack. Quack. Even though I'm back, I'll evade the discussion with your parents and remain a lucky duck."

"You're not playing fair, but we shouldn't both suffer. You can make up for being a lucky duck by cheering me up afterwards."

"You've got a deal. Continuing with your journal. '*Speaking of the Aspen Inn, I called Edna this afternoon. Gosh, she is one in a million! I told her about our decision on tulips; she thought it would look heavenly. Of all the colors of linens she has, we decided on peach for the tables. It would be appropriate for Deb's dress; she loves the color. Edna will email me some suggestions for wedding music, too!*' Peach? Can we incorporate peaches into the menu and the cake? I came up with a few suggestions of songs for the wedding, but we can discuss them later. Did you receive the music suggestions yet?"

"Wow! I hadn't even thought about the peach connection. You have a natural talent for this wedding planning. We can discuss your idea with Edna. No music email, but I haven't checked it today. I had lots of critical issues on my plate."

"I hear what you're saying. I'm glad I'm back in time for so many decisions—seriously, I am." He wore a broad smile and held up his right hand as though swearing to his honesty. "Let's continue reading before I'm in deeper trouble. *'I'll call Deb tonight after supper. I returned to the bar we ate at last night and am drinking a Gin Buck. Yeah, I remembered, and the flavor is delicious! Of course sitting alone is not the same as being here with you. Until tomorrow. Love you. Leigh* ♥♥ *P.S. I'm back in our room, enjoying coffee and your snickerdoodles! Thanks for leaving them/forgetting them. Yummy!!'* You ate all my snickerdoodles?"

"I did, but you left them behind. I couldn't let them go stale, so I had no choice. There may still be some crumbs in the tin." She laughed at him.

"I cannot believe you ate all my snickerdoodles! I need more pizza before you eat all of it, too." He held out his plate, so she could fill it again.

"Here you are, and I'll refill your glass. Reading out loud is dry work. Should I check on the snickerdoodle crumbs?" She hopped away from his hand as he tried swatting her butt.

"No, but as soon as we have a kitchen, we're baking cookies." He looked as though he was sulking before biting into a piece of pizza. "My first night away, I envisioned you watching TV and eating my snickerdoodles. I couldn't believe I forgot them."

Leigh broke into a fit of laughter. "Edna would have

a good laugh over this tale of forgotten cookies. I can't believe I never told her."

He re-read the last section. "You tried a Gin Buck? We'll stock a quality gin in the house, so we can have them and gin martinis. The hearts at the end are a sentimental touch."

"Oh, my thoughts become downright mushy later," Leigh confessed.

"Then, let's continue. '*P.P.S. Had a fun call with Deb tonight. She'll come for a visit this weekend, so I'll have a host of tales I can write about. Disconcerting observation: I don't have any pictures of you! I'll immediately correct the oversight when you're back. I'm photographing you every day so be prepared! Oh, I have information on the local church and will visit the minister this week. I plan to talk Deb into attending services with me on Sunday before she leaves. Time for bed. I love you! Leigh* ♥♥' Deb was here this weekend? Why didn't she help you with Walker?"

"Something came up, so she couldn't visit as planned. If she'd been here, she would have been all over him and not in a good way." Leigh sighed. "The picture comment is critical. I'm taking pictures of you and us every day from now on."

"Pictures are fine. I'd like one or two to carry with me."

"You've reminded me of something; do you have family pictures?"

"Yeah, family albums are in storage with the furniture. Including a scrapbook Mom made with my grade school papers. I couldn't draw to save my life, but she tucked so many of my so-called art projects in there it's embarrassing."

"I'm anxiously awaiting the delivery of your things. I cannot wait to see how you looked when you were little." She had imagined how a young Garrett looked and wondered how accurate she was.

"Do you have photographs from when you were young?"

"Of course. Mine are in storage. However, if you're anxious to see them, we can visit my parents. Mom has tons of picture albums." The disgust reflected on his face made her laugh.

"No hurry." He drank his pop. "Shall we continue? Looks as though we're at the following day."

"Yes, it's a good day. I'm enjoying your comments on what I wrote."

"Alrighty then. Here it goes. *'Thursday, February 13th. Dearest Garrett, Breakfast featured oatmeal today; I smiled as I brought it up to our room thinking how you would approve of my selection. This morning I'm calling Alex and looking at properties with Nick. I'll tell you about the call and property search later. I plan to call Janet today; I need a pep talk. Dreamed of you last night, we were playing Strip Crazy Eights, and you were losing. How I wish I could win in real life. I miss you so much and fantasize about you throughout the day. Later. Leigh* ♥♥' Oatmeal is a healthy food. I'm shocked you didn't continually eat the Belgian waffles."

"You've had a huge influence over me even when you're not around. I can eat oatmeal provided it's drowning in brown sugar, so it may not be overly healthy the way I eat it."

His robust laughter caused him enough pain he stopped with a wince. "We'll work on a healthier version for you. I missed you, and every day I thought of you, usually at night. I took way too many cold showers."

Leigh blushed at his confession as it brought naughty images into her head. "I'm sorry you suffered through cold showers. You're back with me so only warm or hot showers from now on with many of them taken together."

"Like the sound of that. How did your call with your brother go?"

"Read on and you'll find out."

"'*Continuation, Thursday, February 13th. I took my first pictures since before I met you. Do you realize we met only twelve days ago? Back to the pictures, they're of a radiant red sunset. I wish we could have shared the sunset, but our future will hold so many we can share together, right? Tonight, I used the camera on my phone, but I'll carry my camera with me each day from now on.*' I saw the same sunset and thought of you. I imagined what a gorgeous photograph it'd be and wished we were watching it together. We'll share unlimited sunsets in our future."

"Here are the pictures I took. By carrying my camera with me, I'll never miss a shot." She sat next to him while he viewed the pictures on her phone. "We shared this sunset without either of us realizing it."

"It's our connection. Similar things draw us in, and I wouldn't have it any other way." He caressed her face. When she looked up, he pressed his lips against hers. Ending the kiss, he choked out, "I should read the rest of your journal before we move along any further."

Rather than leave his side, she nestled closer and rested her head on his shoulder. "Read fast."

"Yes, ma'am. '*I had a fabulous call with Alex this morning and told him I was engaged. At first, he thought I was joking. Later, he could hear the truth and love in my voice, so he can't wait to meet you. Best of all, he'll support us, so now the score is two for us and one against us! Mom is outnumbered. Hooray!*' He believed Walker's story of me beating you, so are you certain he'll continue supporting us?"

Doubt rang in his voice, and hearing it pained her.

"Once he meets you, he'll understand you'd never hurt me. I'm surprised he believed David. Alex has never been a fan of his."

"Whatever Walker said must be a convincing story." He sighed. "Whatever. Where'd I leave off?"

She pointed out a spot on the page.

"'*Nick and I drove all over the countryside looking at land for sale, and there were two properties I found captivating. Both are good-sized, and one has a creek running through it. Tomorrow Nick's busy, so I'll visit the church and meet with the minister.*' You chose two ideal properties. Hope we get an affirmative response on our offer."

"The one we selected has so much space. It's exactly what we envisioned. If we have positive thoughts, they'll accept our offer."

"Do positive thoughts work for other things?"

"I recognize the glint in your eyes, Garrett Dane. Positive thoughts work on all types of things." Proving her point, she kissed him.

"Okay, I'm putting a reminder on my calendar for positive thoughts each and every day so be prepared." He returned her kiss before picking up the journal. "'*I had an enjoyable chat with Janet, and tomorrow we're having coffee. She's invited me to their home for supper tomorrow. It's meatloaf night! I promised to bring wine and a dessert. I miss you so much. Thoughts of you torment me, and I dread the night as it is the loneliest time of day for me. I miss cuddling with you. I miss falling asleep in your arms and waking beside you. I miss your kisses. I miss how your touch sends me to heights I never reached before. I seriously miss making love to you. I miss the intensity of our lovemaking. I miss the exquisite sensation I experience when you first enter me. I miss the way your eyes turn a deep warm brown as your passion heightens. I miss your sexy little smile; it shows how ready you are to make love to me. Oh, and I miss your accent! Yes, you have a slight one you must have picked up down South. The drawl is stronger when you seduce me and make love to me. I miss* *kissing you. I miss your scent and your taste. I miss undressing you and running my hands over your <u>exceptionally sexy body</u>. I miss holding your hand. I miss your sense of humor. I even miss playing Strip Crazy Eights!'* You underlined the words you used to describe my body. Do your words truly describe how you see me or are they for your fantasy and your dream Garrett?"

"Yes, I truly see you in that way; you're no fantasy. I find it difficult to believe no other woman has remarked on your physique. I'd drool over you if I wasn't a lady." She laughed at the honest wonderment in his expression. "Why do you suppose women flirt with you even when I'm standing beside you? They can't control themselves."

"Now you're pulling my leg." He gazed at the page he'd read. "I missed many of those same things. We have lots to catch up on. Back to your entry. '*When you return, your office may report us as missing persons because you and I are not surfacing for a terribly long time. I love you so much. You're in my prayers every day, and I ask for your safety and success. Yours always. Leigh* ♥♥♥' You do realize I can't be missing from my office for weeks on end, but we do have two weeks. What was it you said in the hospital, something about bunnies?"

"We'll make love like bunnies. Consider how many rabbits you see. Their reproduction rate alone says they have sex a lot! Keep reading."

"I need a short break because my head is filled with erotic images of bunnies." He received an elbow to his side. "Alright, I'm reading, I'm reading. '*P.S. You called me tonight. My heart sang with happiness when I heard your voice. Now I ache for your arms around me. The bed is cold and empty without you in it. I'm reassured you are safe. You not sleeping well concerns me; you need your rest. How can you be ready for whatever may happen if you're tired? Maybe you should do something strenuous and wear yourself out, so you'll fall asleep. You could try drinking milk in the evening. You need to do something. Crap! Now I'm worrying over your sleeping habits.* ☹' You drew a sad face; I'm sorry for making you sad. Talking with you rejuvenated me. Now I realize I shouldn't have mentioned not sleeping, so you wouldn't have additional worries. One night Karl and I were out until after three in the morning, so I may have gotten a few hours of sleep. We had an early start in the morning, and I required lots of coffee throughout the day. I looked so worn out, Karl wouldn't let me drive. In hindsight, I shouldn't have had any coffee, so I could have slept in the car; he's a maniac when he drives."

"I thought all you law enforcement types were skilled drivers."

"I honestly considered kissing the ground when he parked the car once," Garrett admitted, and his confession amused Leigh. "Continuing on. *'I'm relieved I'll be with Janet tomorrow. I hope she'll have ideas on how I can move beyond this blue funk I exist in without you. I should turn out the lights and get some sleep. I'm checking the church out tomorrow and meeting with the minister, may even attend services on Sunday. I love you, miss you, and I will be here for you when you're done. Leigh XXOO (Those are kisses and hugs for you...you can collect on them when you're back with interest!)'* Hmm, two kisses and two hugs from the thirteenth; since today's the sixteenth you owe me three days of interest. Interest is an additional kiss and hug per day, so adding three of each for interest totals five hugs and five kisses you owe me, right?"

"You're a mathematician, too? I'm impressed."

"Ha. Ha." Garrett turned the page. "I can do lots of things; you have no idea how versatile I am."

Leigh rolled her eyes. "Discovering your many talents is what I live for. Read!"

"Okay. Wait! Weren't there some kisses earlier?" Garrett flipped back a few pages. "Nope, only hearts. There are four hearts on the twelfth and a total of five on your earlier entries on the thirteenth. Too bad I can't collect on the hearts."

"Perhaps we can agree on something the hearts could represent." She laughed as one of his eyebrows raised.

"I'll come up with something; I have an unbounded imagination." Garrett had one thing and one thing only in mind for the hearts. Hearts represented love, so lovemaking seemed the obvious fit, but they'd discuss it later. "I'll track them as hearts, so two plus four days of interest for a total of six on two different entries gives me twelve hearts. Adding the two entries of hearts from the thirteenth plus interest equals eleven, and we have a total of twenty-three hearts."

"Shouldn't we track this on paper?"

"Probably." He smiled at her. "Hand me the pad of paper by the telephone."

"Sure." She watched him annotate his calculations. "Now will you continue reading?"

"As soon as I finish jotting down this heart calculation." He scrawled his notations before continuing. "'*Friday, February 14th. Happy Valentine's Day, Garrett! I'm sad we're separated for our first Valentine's Day, but we'll have others to enjoy together. Note for next year: I love dark chocolate with caramel or toffee centers!*' Oh! There's an envelope in my bag; could you find it for me?"

She nodded as she left the bed to search his bag. After rummaging around, she held up a red envelope. "Is this it? Why is my name on it?"

"Happy belated Valentine's Day, Leigh." He spoke softly, his eyes dancing with anticipation.

"You got me a Valentine's Day card? In the midst of everything going on, you bought me a card?" Overcome with emotion, she couldn't hold back the tears, and they rolled down her cheeks. "I don't have anything for you." She cuddled beside him, brushed her lips against his, and moved a hand around his neck. "Thank you," she whispered in his ear.

"You'd best read the card first, I may not have selected as well as you think I did." The card surprised her as he hoped it would. Their first Valentine's Day as a couple had been spent apart, and his attempt at rectifying it hinged on the verse in the card.

"I'm certain the words will steal my breath away." She opened the envelope.

The quiet tore at his heart. Did the words convey the proper sentiment? He spent over an hour reading each card in the store before finding the one he selected.

"Leigh?"

"You couldn't have picked a better one. I love the card and you for buying it while busy on your assignment." She attacked him with kisses, forgetting his stitches and his broken arm until she heard his stifled groan of agony. "Sorry, I couldn't control myself. I love you so much."

"I'll survive. I couldn't have asked for such a tremendous response, and you can thank me after I finish your journal. Reading again. *'Breakfast brought me a surprise: David Walker is staying in the hotel. Yes, that David. ☹ I sat with him for breakfast to be polite. It wasn't long before I confirmed your superiority over him in all categories. He said he was here for a meeting and to search for a vacation home, but I have doubts regarding his story. He pressed me to join him for dinner tonight, but I told him I couldn't. Thankfully, I have a dinner engagement with the Hendersons. Yes, you're right, I don't need an excuse, so should he ask again, I'll decline.'* You should have kicked him in the nuts or punched him out for having the gall to show his face near you. He didn't impress me."

"I noticed. I appreciated how you handled him the other night, standing up for me and all."

"If he ever comes sniffing around you again, I'm certain unpleasant things will happen."

"Promise me you won't do anything stupid if you ever run into him again. You can't sacrifice everything you have over a confrontation with him; he's not worth it." His growl shocked her, so she tried glaring at him.

"Fine. I promise, but so help me if he pushes, I'm pushing back."

"Seems I should be extra careful what I write in here from now on," she speculated.

"No, you shouldn't. I should be aware of all of this. Enough, let's move on."

Garrett went back to her journal, but Leigh prepared herself for the heated outburst she figured would come up with her later entry on David.

He had a long drink of pop before he continued reading. "'*I had a delightful time with Janet at coffee, and she offered to come with me when I shop for my wedding dress. She and Joe should be on our guest list. OMG! They would be our first guests: not yours and not mine, but "ours." We'll soon have a cluster of "our" friends; it has an encouraging ring to it.*' Yes, we should invite them. I hadn't thought of the 'yours, mine, and ours' aspect of guests. Edna is an 'ours' even though she's not technically a guest."

"You're right she is! Should we send her an invitation? We still have a few weeks before we should finalize our guest list."

"Might as well make her status with us official with one. Continuing on. '*I stopped at the church today and visited with the minister. She is an interim minister as they're searching for a new one. I met the church secretary and a few of the members who were folding programs for Sunday's service. They were so friendly and welcoming; I promised I'd return Sunday. As soon as you're back, we can schedule the marriage class, so we can pay the discounted price for our license. Oh! Almost forgot the most noteworthy tidbit of news; she'll officiate our wedding. She may finish her interim duties before then, but she lives in the area. I believe you would approve of her. We discussed Bible verses for the ceremony. I'm fond of two. The first is from the Song of Solomon 8:6, New Living Translation (NLT). It talks of love and fierce passion. How else would you describe what we have? I jotted it down, so here it is for your consideration: "Set me as a seal upon your heart, as a seal upon your arm, for love is strong as death, passion fierce as the grave. Its flashes are flashes of fire, a raging flame." The second is 1 Corinthians 13:7 NLT. "Love never gives up, never loses faith, is always hopeful, and endures through every circumstance." This is us, too! We have lots to discuss upon your return to include joining the church. I truly look forward to belonging there. We can participate in their many activities.'* You're right, both scriptures fit. Could the ceremony include both?"

"Why not? One is from the Old Testament and the other is from the New Testament, so I would expect we could have both read."

"We're chipping away at the wedding list, aren't we?" At her smile and nod, he returned to the journal. "'*I need to end this for now. I'll write again tonight after this lunch thing with David, bridal shops, and dinner at the Hendersons. Please be aware of the endlessness of my love for you. Some nights you join me in my dreams; those are the best nights. I miss your arms around me and your strength. Love and kisses. Leigh XX* ♥♥' Hot dang, two additional kisses and two more hearts!"

All Leigh could do was shake her head at his enthusiasm.

"Reading onward. '*Continuation, Friday, February 14th. My dearest Garrett, How I miss you! My life truly improved when you fell into it. I'm certain because I now have you to compare David to, and there is no comparison. He falls short in every way, to include sexual prowess. (Thought you'd enjoy reading that!) Lunch with David was horrendous. How did I not realize what manner of man he was? Now my eyes are wide open.'* You were certainly correct with your assumption; it warms my heart knowing I can kick his butt in so many ways. I can't wait until I'm finished reading about your interactions with him. '*He acted so sure of himself as though he expected me to fall into his arms. He wants to have dinner with me tomorrow. Somehow, he knows what room I'm in and plans on picking me up at my room. Maybe I should renege? I haven't decided. He got forceful today and kissed me as I tried to walk past him in the restaurant. The kiss was hard and demanding.'* That son of a bitch! If he ever touches you…"

"Garrett, no! We'll never see him again, please let it go." She instinctively held him down on the bed as he tried springing upright. Her eyes pleaded with him. His eyes sparked ice-cold blue back at her. "You're nearly finished reading the section."

"If you say so," he grumbled, still irritated over Walker's advances on Leigh. "'*I should have slapped him, but he shocked me into a stupor. I refused to ride back to the hotel with him. The funniest thing happened; there was a gentleman who sat in the booth behind us. He heard most of our conversation and chuckled at some of my responses. As he walked away, he gave me a thumbs-up sign. It appeared he approved of my actions. Unfortunately, he left before the kiss; otherwise, I bet he'd have intervened.'* Yes, you should have slapped the crap out of him, and the guy sitting behind you was no gentleman—it was Karl. When I saw you walk into the restaurant with some guy, Karl went in and came out with a name: David. It couldn't have been anyone other than your ex-boyfriend. I'll admit I reacted badly and figured your mom was involved in it all."

"You didn't come charging into the restaurant, so I wouldn't say you reacted badly. You were rather restrained."

"It spurred us into concluding the operation. Karl

made the call, and I'm glad he did. He pushed, and the meth dealers accepted his terms. Otherwise, we might still be out there working."

"Funny how it worked out," Leigh said, deep in thought.

"As I've always said, everything happens for a reason. Okay, I've calmed down some, so I'll continue reading. *'Then Mom called to find out if anything exciting had happened. I didn't mention David or the lunch. I'm convinced she had a hand in David's being here. On the bright side, she said she didn't have time for our scheduled appointment to discuss invitations, so I'm forging ahead without her involvement. Her loss and our gain!'* I was right; she was in on it all along. She downright hates me, doesn't she?"

"As I've said before, I'm the one who counts in this, not her. And you're forgetting the best sentence in the whole section; she's out of the invitations! I've found a possible source in the local area, so we can work with them ourselves. Keep going."

"Ah, where'd I leave off...I've got it. *'I visited a couple of bridal shops today. It will be a challenging decision, and your Christmas tree analogy is accurate. Janet is joining me tomorrow. I'm bringing my notebook for notes and will take pictures, so I'll be prepared for a wise decision. I wonder what the chances are for falling in love at first sight with a wedding dress; can it happen twice in one lifetime—love at first sight? I had a fun time at the Hendersons tonight. Their boys are typical teenagers, and their dogs are adorable. I didn't meet their cat, but Janet says to not underestimate them as family pets. We need a dog or two, especially if we have a lot of property for them to run on. What breed would you want? Are you a hunter? If so, should the dog be a hunting dog? Have you had pets before? We never did, Mom said they were too messy; I think I missed out.'* We did have dogs when I was a kid, and our having pets would be great. I hunted pheasants with my dad, and our dog would retrieve the birds. Since I don't hunt anymore, we can have any breed of dog. A cat might be interesting. We should check with shelters when we're ready; we have plenty of time for deciding on what we'll adopt."

"Wait until you meet their dogs, Butch and Hitch; they are so friendly. I didn't even catch a glimpse of their cat, but next time we might meet Snowball."

"I almost forgot their invitation for dinner on Saturday. We can't forget it."

"We won't; I entered it on my calendar already with a two-hour notification."

"Okay, you're all over it. Continuing with your entry. '*I understand you're doing well and making a difference on your assignment. I'm so proud of you! Because of the late hour, I'm having decaf coffee with the last of your snickerdoodles. LOL! You didn't eat as many of them as you expected; too bad, so sad. I, on the other hand, have enjoyed them. Don't worry. As soon as we have a kitchen, I'll bake you some—I promise. I hope my dreams are of you tonight, and I further hope you're in a playful mood! Yes, I'm talking sex. I'd rather be with you in person, but these days I'll have fun with dream Garrett. I love you with all my heart. Leigh* ♥♥♥' Ah, you promised to bake me snickerdoodles. Believe me; I'll collect in a heartbeat. Tell me; was I in a playful mood?"

"As I recall, dream Garrett was, and I hope you're playful tonight."

"Rest assured I'm here for your pleasure." Garrett waggled his eyebrows at her, making her blush. "You had three hearts, so we're up to thirty-two. And you wrote another entry for this date. '*P.S. I believe my dad has fallen victim to a ploy for reuniting David and me. He called and asked, as a favor to him, for me to have dinner with David tomorrow. He and Mom had dinner with David's parents* tonight. *Of course they didn't inform the Walkers of our engagement. I can understand Dad's reasoning for Mom would have been most critical of you. I will suffer through this for Dad. You cannot come back to me soon enough! Leigh OXOXXX*" I'm ignoring the David conversation, so I can focus on counting the hugs and kisses. I'm making out like a bandit."

"It could be me, who's making out like a bandit." She pursed her lips and blew him a kiss.

"If you continue sending me those, I'll stop reading your journal." Garrett smiled at her with love in his eyes. They were his normal hazel color, signifying his anger over David's actions had passed. "Here we go. '*Saturday, February 15th. Garrett, my love, I learned you may be done with your assignment tonight! I am hopeful it ends successfully and safely for you and your partner. The thought of being with you again has me excited but concerned. Will what we had before you left be gone, extinguished as a lit candle burns down and goes out? Or (my hope) will our love be stronger? Will your sexy smile still make me melt in your arms? Will everything be fresh and vibrant? Will a mere touch send us into a fit of unleashed passion? Will people be concerned when they don't see or hear from us for days on end as we make up for lost time? We shall soon have answers to these speculations and ones I haven't even imagined.*' You thought our love may have petered out? I can't believe you had such thoughts. Oh, wait a minute, I sense Walker's influence in those comments. I'm relieved you noted what your hopes were. Those are our reality. Our love is stronger, made so by adversity. We've overcome the challenges placed upon us, yet our love for one another is still resolute. By the way, I cannot wait for the 'fit of unleashed passion' or did it happen already?" Desire and determination flared in his eyes. His hand roamed over her hip and drifted down, finding the warmth at the junction of her thighs.

"I believe it did, but nothing says our 'fit of passion' should be limited in number, so I'm certain we can have more than one," Leigh suggested with a sigh as she arched her back.

"Is it hot in here? Moving on. '*Janet also disclosed how you saw me with David at lunch. I pray seeing David with me didn't make you doubt my love for you. I now suspect the gentleman I wrote of previously was your partner. I was concerned when she told me. Why? I worried your seeing me with him would be hurtful for you and your concentration would be less than it should be because of it, putting you at risk. Surely you can compartmentalize these things and maintain your focus. OMG! Now realization strikes me…if you never had this type of relationship, then you never had to compartmentalize on an assignment. Now my fear for your safety has increased! You must be safe for I need you. You are my life now, and all I think of throughout the day. Everything I am revolves around you…love is supposed to work this way, right?*' Yes, love works that way; you're my life, Leigh. I'm a better man for your love."

They shared a kiss, and his hand settled on her hip.

He cleared his throat and continued with her journal. "'*Time is ticking away until I have dinner with David. I am not looking forward to this, but I will persevere for Dad. Janet and I have worked out a deal where I can text her 911 and she'll call me with a message, so I can leave. Yes, it's a brilliant plan…thank you.*' You hatched a brilliant plan, and how funny you ended up being the one responding to a 911."

"Not funny at all; I was frantic with worry all the way to the hospital."

"You did well at the hospital, darlin'. I'm proud of how you handled all the excitement. Let's bring this to a conclusion. '*I do hope you'll return tonight, I long to hold you and make love to you all night long. If we get out of* bed on Monday, we can meet with the builders; I think you'll like them as much as I do! We can also look at apartments and move out of the hotel. We should find a place for ordering our invitations. You being back so soon allows for your involvement in all the wedding planning...lucky you! Or is it lucky me?? Gosh! In reviewing my list, it seems as if I've not done much, but I have stayed busy since you left. So, I must have accomplished something. What have I done; you ask? I have laid groundwork, so I/we will have an easier time completing our list!' So, you only accomplished groundwork? Kidding, I'm only kidding." He realized she bristled when he seemed doubtful, so he immediately retreated. His father hadn't raised a fool.

"Reading again. 'Speaking of planning, my wedding dress hunt continues. Janet and I visited two shops. I found a few pretty dresses, but none jumped out at me or as Janet says, they didn't "wow" me. She and I will continue our shopping, and no, you can't be there for this. Why not? Because the groom is not to set eyes on the bride in her wedding dress before the ceremony, it's unlucky. We shouldn't seek out extra trouble! I haven't told Mom and Dad of our wedding plans yet. Guess I hoped you'd be with me for this unseemly task. Whenever you're ready, we'll call them. Well, time for me to change for dinner. Don't worry; I'm wearing the bulkiest sweater I have with me and thick cords. I'm not looking sexy for him; my sexy look is exclusively yours and yours alone. I'll love you forever, Garrett. Yours always, Leigh XXOO ♥♥' Lots of information in this section. First, I have lucky duck status regarding your folks and our wedding plans, freeing me from participation in the call. Second, I appreciate being the one who can claim exclusivity of your sexy look. Third, I count two kisses, two hugs and two hearts." He calculated his additions. "These are adding up fast."

"I'm verifying your math later."

"Feel free, I'm not concerned."

"No?"

"Nope, I have a lifetime of hugs and kisses with you, Leigh." He kissed her forehead. "Only a short entry left. *'Sunday, February 16th. My dearest Garrett, I am thankful you are healthier now than you were this morning. Your condition scared me—I was terrified you might die. Janet didn't hesitate to tell me they would join me at the hospital when I called. She and Joe were supportive and always there for me. I told Joe I'm glad he's your boss, and I truly am. I pray you're resting well and will be bright-eyed and bushy-tailed when I return in the morning. You mean everything to me, and I would be lost without you. Please never leave me. I love you dearly, now and forever. Leigh ♥♥♥'* I'm sorry I scared you. I wasn't careful enough; I should have realized his wife would be there—"

Her fingers on his lips stopped him from going on any further.

"Garrett, you weren't critically injured or killed, so you were careful enough for me. You did your job, and I am so proud of you. Your job is dangerous, and I accept it because you're a package deal." She replaced her fingers with her lips. "Three more hearts, no interest, results in thirty-eight hearts; what do you say we round up and make it an even forty?"

"Thanks for calculating for me, my mind went spinning elsewhere. I'm all for rounding up. Your journal is astounding. I wish I could keep one when I'm gone; I'd love sharing my thoughts and dreams with you. The best I can do is share my love and my life with you when we're together." He closed her journal and set it on the nightstand. "Come here."

They came together with their passion for each other burning hot. It was an evening of tender and loving embraces, gentle and firm caresses, and their bodies joined as one.

Hours later, they lay amid rumpled covers and only a few remaining pillows. Her head rested on his shoulder as he traced calming circles on her skin.

"Leigh, there's something you should be aware of."

"Is it something horrible or something wonderful?"

"Ah, well, I'm not sure."

"This is sounding worse."

"Remember how you thought the guy in the picture looked familiar?"

"Yes."

"And that I thought he looked familiar, too?" Garrett's fingers played with her breast in hopes of distracting her. "I came up with a hunch he could be a relative of Jonas Klein, but nothing is confirmed yet." Her sudden movement took him by surprise.

She batted his hand away and sat, staring into his eyes.

"You're kidding, right?"

"No. I thought of it earlier tonight, so I called Joe. He'll check on it tomorrow."

"You thought of it earlier tonight, but you didn't tell me until now?" Her eyes narrowed, and she glared at him.

"If I told you earlier, our evening would have been spoiled. You need to be kept in the loop, so I'm telling you now."

"Kept in the loop?"

"Well, you wouldn't appreciate finding this out after he'd been identified, would you?" He hadn't expected her ferocity.

"You're right, but you should have told me as soon as you thought of it."

"If I had, would you have enjoyed our evening?" He caught her hand and tugged her closer.

"Probably not." She snuggled against his chest, all anger forgotten. "You may have a point, but I'm still mad at you."

"Can you forgive me?" He kissed the top of her head as his hand roved down her side.

"Eventually." She sighed. "Why now and why here?"

"I wish I could answer those questions for you."

"Haven't we faced enough challenges in our two weeks of knowing each other?"

"Hey! Don't shortchange us; our time together has been two weeks and three days. We can handle this as well as any other challenges thrown at us."

"You think so? Based on what?" She ran her hands over his chest and down his hips.

"Our love is strong and grows every day. As you wrote in your journal…our love burns as a raging flame and will never burn out. Our passion is fierce…so strong and intense it continually builds." He kissed her during each pause as he spoke. "We're formidable together."

"So, demonstrate for me how raging and fierce our love and passion are tonight." The sparkle in her eyes captured his full attention.

Dismissing the stitches across his abdomen and the slight pain accompanying his movements, he rolled her under his body. His hazel eyes radiated a deeper, warmer brown than she'd seen before.

"One demonstration coming right up, darlin'."

His lips tasted her as he positioned himself. They would deal with whatever the future held for them together. During this night their love and passion would forge a fresh beginning for them; one made stronger for challenges conquered.

EPILOGUE

Two days later, their first session of marriage training had been completed. They sat over lunch reviewing their assignment for their next session and the many open items on their wedding to-do list.

"We can mark the training as a third of the way done, can't we?" Leigh pointed at the entry on their list.

"Our list, our rules. We can do whatever we want."

"Any progress is moving forward and deserves an annotation. By Friday or next Monday, we should have our certificate, and you know what comes next?"

"I have no clue." He chuckled at her snort of disgust.

"Once we obtain our marriage license, we cross another item off our list." She struck a line partially across the item in her notebook. "Since we made it through our first training session, we should celebrate!"

"We can celebrate tonight or Saturday with Joe and Janet; your choice." As he took a bite of his hamburger, his phone rang. He pushed it toward Leigh and nodded at her.

"Hi, Joe. Garrett has a mouthful of burger right now. Can I relay a message, or can you hold on?"

"I can tell you. We identified the man in the photograph from Garrett's hospital room. His name is Andrew Klein; he's Jonas Klein's younger brother."

Leigh's eyes went wide. Garrett choked down his burger and grabbed the phone from her now shaking hand.

"I assume this isn't pleasant news." He held her hand. "Leigh's not saying much."

"I can appreciate her reaction. Your mystery visitor is Andrew Klein, Jonas's younger and only brother. Come into the office, and I'll show you everything I found out."

"We'll be there shortly. Thanks, boss." Garrett ended the call. "Eat up; we're joining Joe at the office."

"Klein's brother? Garrett, what'll we do?" Leigh's

voice trembled.

"Survive, Leigh. We'll survive." Garrett's resolve hardened his voice.

THE END

About Elaine M. DeGroot

Originally from Minnesota, I now live in Upstate South Carolina and enjoy retirement. My husband, Mike, is a retired US Air Force Chief Master Sergeant and is loving life with the year-round golfing! We have a pup, Missy, a Belgian Malinois-German Shepherd mix, who keeps us busy and entertained. They are an inspiration, a distraction, and my life.

I served 12 years active duty in the US Air Force. Ultimately, I worked in the federal civil service, beginning with the Department of Veterans Affairs, on to the US Air Force, a fun stint with the US Fish & Wildlife Service, and ending back at the VA. All told, serving thirty years in federal service and loved every minute of it.

I write romance stories...rather steamy ones. Some with a touch of suspense. I've found inspiration in where I've lived, what I've done/experienced, and hobbies I enjoy. In the midst of writing a story, I love it when my characters take hold of the plot and own it!

Social Media

Facebook Page:
https://www.facebook.com/RomanceByDeGroot

Website: https://www.romance-degrootified.net/

Acknowledgments

Again I acknowledge Kathi Sprayberry, Editor in Chief, at Solstice Publishing, for offering me another publishing contract. I appreciate your faith in my writing. To my editor, Brian Cavit, so nice to work with you again. Your skills ensured *Challenged Love* follows in-line with the series starting point and is ready to be embraced by the readers who fell in love with Garrett and Leigh in *Resolute Love*. Thank you.

Next are friends and family who support my writing. From reading drafts of stories and book blurbs to following my Romance DeGrootified Facebook page, you help boost my confidence as an author. Thank you all.

To my four-legged assistant, Missy. I don't dread hours at the desk because you're right there beside me…usually sleeping, but you're there. You deserve the best of treats.

Finally, to the love of my life, Mike. Your support is endless, and your encouragement keeps me going. You are my best friend and keep me grounded when life presents challenges. You have always believed in me. Our love is the best inspiration for any romance.

Other Books by Elaine M. DeGroot

Resolute Love Consequential Love Series #1

Consequential Love is a romantic suspense series of three books. The series features the unlikely meeting of two people in search of a new life, who unexpectantly find love. Introducing Air Force veteran, Garrett Dane, who returns to Minnesota for a career with the Bureau of Criminal Apprehension (BCA), and Leigh Ramsey, who returns to Minnesota, after a four-year self-isolation in Chicago. Past experiences haunt them. After fate brings them together, their determination to help each other and have a life together demonstrates their resolute love for one another, their fortitude to overcome challenges thrown at them, and their strength as a couple to be victorious in the end.

RESOLUTE LOVE - Book #1

Evading an escaped killer from his past, Air Force veteran, Garrett Dane, literally falls into Leigh Ramsey's life. She's been emotionally devastated in the past. Will she open herself to another man's affection? Does love at first sight really happen? Of course, it does! But can love survive a killer, a blizzard, and a disapproving mother?

Theirs is a bold love, a determined love—a Resolute Love.